In Loving Memory

of

Dianne Price

(1933 – 2013)

We'll Meet Again

Dianne Price

**BOOK FIVE OF
THE THISTLE SERIES**

Ashberry Lane

© 2017 Fawn Dianne Price Estate
Ashberry Lane
P.O. Box 665, Gaston, OR 97119
www.ashberrylane.com

Published in association with Terry Burns of Hartline Literary Agency, LLC.

ISBN 9781941720356

Cover design by Miller Media Solutions
Cover images by Ashlee Murr Photography and iStock.com

Use of the Gaelic Biblical Texts by kind permission of the Scottish Bible Society.

Scripture used in this book, whether quoted or paraphrased by the characters, is taken from the English Revised Version of the Bible, Oxford Press, 1885. Used by permission.

Map © 2013 Mary Elizabeth Hall

The Thistle Series
by Dianne Price

Broken Wings, Book One
Wing and a Prayer, Book Two
The Promise of Dawn, Book Three
Never Say Goodbye, Book Four
We'll Meet Again, Book Five

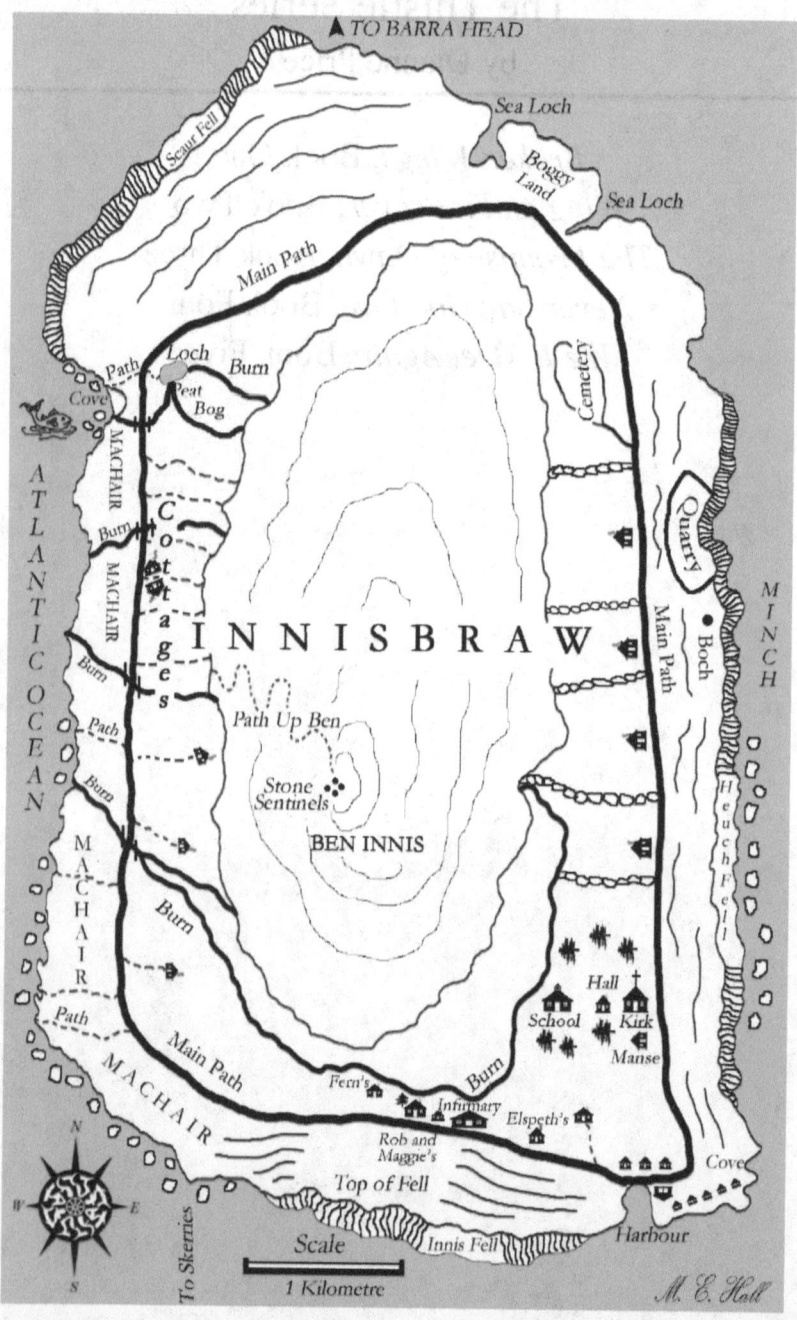

Written with some British spelling, this book also includes a Scottish
Gaelic glossary.

Dedication

For the glory of my Lord, Jesus Christ.
And, as always, for my True, who lived
up to his name in every way.

In Loving Memory

Dianne joined her beloved Savior and
her husband in heaven one week before
her first book released.
She is probably dancing a Scots reel
even as you read this.

Chapter One

Isle of Innisbraw, Outer Hebrides, Scotland
June 1948

Rob Savage tromped through the girse, breathing deeply. *Is it a sin to luve my Maggie so much?*

The raucous caw of a crow mocked Rob Savage's silent question, as though the cannie bird were a mindreader.

Shep, his Australian sheepdog, brushed his leg as though urging him to up his pace.

What a grand gift it was, having a dog who offered such unconditional luve. The thought triggered a forbidden switch in his mind, back to the past. Another Shep—a dynamo of mottled blue fur, puppy breath, and boundless energy, who chewed a lad's toes, nipped at his bare heels, and slept the sleep of the innocent, cuddled tight to his young master's chest. *They'd* given him the puppy, *the couple* who said they wanted him to be their son. He'd never had a dog, never known a furry bundle with a soft tongue could make him laugh aloud and lie in bed at night, marveling at the awakening of a luve so strong it sometimes took his breath. After years of praying, he finally had a family.

Six months later, it was all gone. *They* hustled him into their automobile to return him to the orphanage, offering no explanation to ease the heartbreak, the betrayal. His last sight of the first Shep had haunted him for years: overgrown paws splayed on the living room window, floppy ears cocked forward, blue eyes pleading. Aye, *they* cried, though he couldn't—no' for over twenty years. He vowed never again to trust his heart to another person.

And he hadn't—until he met his Maggie.

It had taken her months to break down the wall he'd built around his heart. But ultimately, how could he resist the safe harbour of her luve?

He slowed his morning run to a trot and raised his face to the sky, its pearly-pink complexion a betraying blush at giving such a public birth to the sun. "'Tis only a sin when I forget to thank You for

1

bringing us together, Heavenly Faither."

A kaleidoscope of mind-pictures tumbled before his eyes: his first sight of Maggie's bonnie face at the Edenoaks officer's club; the fire in her violet-blue eyes when he voiced his fear he would never walk again; the luve in those same eyes melting his heart when they spoke their marriage vows; her exhausted, triumphant smile when she birthed each of their three bairnies; watching her brush her black, wavy hair that spilled down her slim back to below her waist.

He reached the turn in the island path that traced the shore of the mighty Atlantic Ocean.

Waves uttered victorious, deep-throated booms as they crashed upon the rocks lining the shore.

"You've reason to be proud," he muttered to the ocean as his pace increased. "Surely, you're one of our Lord's most magnificent creations."

Is it a sin to contemplate murder? Maggie Savage picked up the sharp surgical scissors and stared at her reflection in the bathing room mirror. Och, thinking like an eejit, she was. How could it be murder if the victim didn't have a beating heart and a mind stored with all those yesterdays, if it didn't bleed?

"I luve the sight of you with your black hair spilling down your back." Rob's voice, permanently etched into the folds of her memory.

But he didn't have to put up with the constant tangles, how long it took to dry, having to pin it high atop her head every time she used the wringer on the washing machine, and those wee ones always pulling at it. 'Twas down to her hips now. Surely trimming off a few centimetres—or mebbe a wee bit more—wouldn't send him into a fash.

The image in the mirror blurred, replaced by Rob's face, the dimples beside his lips deep with a smile, flecks of green dancing a jig in his hazel eyes while he twisted his long fingers in her hair. The vision transformed to the look of awe on his face the first time she released the severe bun she wore to keep her hair off the collar of her RAF nurse's uniform. He'd grasped a lock between two fingers and brushed it across his cheek, lost in a pleasant dream known only to him.

She closed her eyes as a flush of shame set fire to her cheeks.

Murder it would be. No' of her hair, but of Rob's joy. He'd never shared why, but those strands seemed to tether him to his memories of all their yesterdays and his dreams for their future.

2

A loud wail came from the bedroom.

She placed the scissors on the top shelf of the closet and pulled the towel from her shoulders. Beth, it was, demanding her first suckling of the day.

Thank Ye, Faither, for saving Rob from my selfishness.

Half an hour later, Beth suckled and back in her cradle, Maggie raised a corner of the lace curtain and peeked from the kitchen window.

Early summer wildflowers bent 'neath an onshore breeze and tiny whirls of dust tickled the top of the sandy path, mimicking the waves faery-dancing over the harbour below Innis Fell.

Rob suddenly appeared at the crest of the path, long legs making a mockery of the climb, the roll of his trim hips trapping a breath in her throat. Walking, he was, no' running, with Shep fast at his heels. He'd finally heeded her advice about cooling down after running the seventeen-kilometre path around the island.

She checked to make sure she'd turned on the shower-water boiler and put the coffeepot to perk on the hottest part of the peat-burning stove. Tightening the belt of her blue dressing gown, she dashed out onto the entry to greet him.

He leaped the dry-stone dyke and bolted up the stairs. "There's my Maggie."

How she luved that deep-throated purr.

After swiping the sweat from his forehead with a sleeve, he grabbed her up and seated her on the entry railing, drawing her close. She winced inwardly at his groan when he fisted his hands in her hair. Such long, hard hours he worked, building rescue and fishing boats, casting peats, helping the island's crofters when a need arose, and all without a whinge of complaint. An incomer would think he had generations of Innisbraw blood feeding muscle and bone, making him one of this close family of islanders, inuring him to the winter gales, the hardships of living on such an isolated island, the unrelenting labour each day demanded.

How could she have considered depriving him of something that pleasured him so?

His lips brushed hers, soft as a bee seeking pollen, then pressed deeper into the petals of her mouth, speaking luve more eloquently than words.

When he raised his head, she rested her cheek against his damp shirt. "Welcome home, luve. You had a guid run."

"What makes you think that?" he asked, dimples deep.

"We women have our ways ..."

3

He cupped her chin in his large palm and gazed into her eyes. "Are the bairnies still abed? And have you suckled Beth?"

"Aye, the wee piggy." The rapid beat of his heart thrummed in her ear. "She's gone back to sleep and nobody else is stirring."

"Then we'll have some time alone." He picked her up and carried her to his rocker, cradling her on his lap.

Shep plonked down beside the door, flanks heaving, tongue lolling from the side of his mouth.

Maggie squirmed to escape. "Shep needs water and his breakfast, your shower water's hot, and I have to see to the coffee."

"No' till I tell you how much I luve you."

"But that could take hours." He looked so braw, she had to stroke his cheek. "Besides, I already know how much you luve me. 'Tis the same luve I feel for you. Now let me go before your coffee biles all over the top of the stove."

He glanced at his watch and helped her up. "'Tis 0500, so we've an hour before I have to be at the boatshed. I'll meet you oot here on the entry in ten minutes. Pray nobody wakes."

"Ten minutes for a shower and shave? You'll cut your face to pieces with that straight-edged razor."

He was already pulling his shirt over his head when he opened the front door. "On you go. Time me." He raced for the bathing room.

Maggie shook her head. No use trying to slow that one down.

While he showered, she watered and fed Shep, placed the coffeepot at the back of the stove, took a plate of scones from the cupboard, and checked on Beth. Sound asleep the wee lassie was, on her back in her cradle, rosy lips sooking as though she still hungered for one more taste of sweet, warm milk.

Maggie removed her dressing gown and slipped into her underclothes and a light woolen skirt and sweater. Time was slipping away. Hands trembling, mind racing, she ran a brush through her long hair and pulled it off her face with a celluloid barrette. This could be their last peaceful morning for a week. Och, why did Rob's radar expert have to arrive the day?

After stepping into her sandals, she raced into the kitchen and poured a large mug of coffee for Rob and a cup of tea with honey and milk for herself. Mug and cup rattled on the tray while she dashed for the front door and swung it shut awkwardly behind her. She placed the tray on the table between their rockers, seated herself, and fanned her face. Made it.

Seconds later, Rob opened the front door and came out, eyes wide. "You've been busy," he said, tucking his shirt into his denims.

4

"And, as usual, I can't lace this sark." He bent over so she could reach the laces.

"And you never will." Smile teasing, she laced and tied the neck of his Jacobite shirt. "Your fingers are too big for such wee laces."

"I can tie my shoes. Don't see any difference."

"Your chin gets in the way, luve. And speaking of shoes, I don't see any on your feet, nor what you call 'socks,' for that matter."

"Ran oot of time." He sat in his rocker, reached for his coffee mug, took a healthy swallow, and laid his head back, smiling.

She looked over at him. After almost six years of marriage, his dear face still thrilled her. His brown hair shone as the rapidly rising sun struck the entryway. His straight nose, full eyebrows, sensitive lips, and strong chin brought a surge of joy to her heart.

He glanced at her. "Looking for razor nicks? You won't find any." He grabbed a scone and ate half in one bite.

"I was thinking how braw you are." She steeled herself for his usual reaction.

"Maggie Savage, if I've told you once, I've told you a thousand times to stop saying that. I'm too tall, too thin—according to you—and the verra last thing I am is braw."

"Mebbe you're a wee bit thin, though I'm still hoping to put some weight on you this summer." She stifled a sigh. "I know 'tis merely a dream. If only you'd take time to eat when you're launching the new boats."

"Enough blether." He finished the scone and took a long drink of coffee. "On you come, luve. I want to hold you before I have to leave."

She settled onto his lap with a contented sigh. This was the way they belonged, breath to breath, heart to heart.

Cheek resting on the top of her head, he said, "Certain you don't want to meet the ferry with me this mornin?"

"I've reeky laundry piled high ... and I don't know Dale Taylor." She ducked her head to hide a frown. "I'm shamed to admit it, but I'm relieved he'll be biding with Den and Fern, no' us."

"Taylor's Den's friend, no' ours. And we don't have room with Ellie and Richie staying here."

Ah, Ellie. "Has Calum said owt about asking Ellie to marry him?"

A chuckle rumbled in his chest. "You know your brother better than that. Calum's as likely to confide something personal as Flora MacPhee is to no' spread the latest gossip."

"Aye. He's still shy at times, but no' as often as when he was a wee lad." A sudden thought sent her bolting upright. "But Ellie's holiday will end soon and she'll have to return to America."

"Well, we can't let that happen. Ellie and Richie need to be here among those who knew and loved Rich." He groaned. "I never got to say guidbye to Rich, but the Lord's given me a chance to watch his son grow to manhood. We have to convince Ellie to stay."

Would Rob never get over losing his tail gunner in that same bombing mission that almost cost him his own life? She buried her face against his chest. "Och, luve, when I think of all the pain you've suffered … in the war and since." She traced a fingertip over the jagged scar on his forehead.

Soft fingers caressed her shoulder. "Do you …?" Softer lips brushed her forehead. "You seem to be handling the shouts better lately."

"I haven't had that dreadful image of you drowning for months." The truth. But she still feared, especially during in-water rescues. "I've Fern to keep me company, and if she's busy at the infirmary, I call somebody on that list of mothers and wives that Hugh gave me. We pray and share scriptures." Blessed Hugh. Minister, comforter, counsellor, and friend.

"Then it helps them too. Hugh did a grand job bringing family members of the rescue crew together."

She played with the laces on his shirt. "Do you ever think how different our lives would be if you'd taken me to America after the war?"

His sharp breath shrilled in her ear. "Don't even think that. Innisbraw's my home now. I could never live anywhere else."

Och, he was coiled tighter than a wet mooring rope. Was he worried about the new radar arriving the day? *Careful, Maggie Savage, before you ruin your mornin.* "I didn't mean to fash you."

"You scared me is all. All my auld friends are here, anyway. Den, now here for Fern and Katie too. The surprise of Stu and Jill settling here. And Ellie, come all the way from America to make certain the Red Cross hadn't made a mistake in telling her I survived that last crash."

She nestled closer. "Faither's finally retired from his work in Edinburgh and practicing here at his infirmary, and Calum's home too, fishing on a trawler." A laugh burst in her throat. "Don't forget to number in our bairns. Robbie, Annie, and wee Beth bring me more joy than I ever dreamed possible. And there's still five more to go before we have our eight bairns."

His body stiffened. "Are you trying to tell me something?"

"Beth's only six months auld. 'Twill be a while before we add another lad or lass to this family. You did a wonderful turn helping them greet the world."

"I'm no' a doctor, luve. So far, there haven't been any problems, and I thank the Lord for that, but …" He looked at his watch. "Och, I have to give heels to or I'll be late to the shed. I've a heap of work to do before the ferry docks."

She leaped from his lap. "I'll pour you a thermos of coffee and send some butteries. Promise me you'll eat them and no' give them to Graham. Now he's merrit, Rinait can make him a piece to tide him over till dinner."

"I promise, but first my shoes and socks. Den'll be here in a tick."

7

Chapter Two

Rob replaced the telephone receiver and sat at his desk, rubbing his forehead. Exhausted, he was. No' from physical labour, but from spending almost a week with Dale Taylor. Being confined in the trawler's wheelhouse with Den and Dale was like sitting through a vaudeville show featuring half-wit comedians. They fired one-liners as rapidly as a waist gunner knocked a German FW-190 out of the sky.

Den was one thing—they'd been best friends since West Point—and he'd settled down since coming to Innisbraw. But enduring hours of that warped sense of humour from another man made Rob's head ache. Only the superior radar system Taylor had delivered made it bearable.

Now this call from Alec. Rob couldn't work any harder drawing those remodels of existing cottages, no matter the need. Twenty-four hours in a day was one of God's laws even prayer couldn't change.

And there was the basket supper this een.

He broke a pencil and threw the pieces across the room.

"With all Rob eats, a salad and some shortbread isn't enough for me to bring," Maggie said, looking over Fern's list of food for the basket supper. "And there's me, Robbie, Annie, Ellie, Rich—"

"Wheesht." Fern put a finger to her lips. "We'd best keep our voices down. Dale's upstairs packing." She bent over the list.

"We can eat on the sandy strand below the fell," Maggie whispered.

"'Twill be a celebration, though Dale will never guess 'tis because he's leaving." Fern muffled a laugh with her palm. "Calum's bringing twa salmon caught this mornin—he'll cook them over an open fire—Jill promised a basket of Scotch eggs, and I'm making a sticky toffee pudding. Den's request, of course. With your salad and shortbread, that's more than enough."

"With all the sweetenins Rob eats, we always run oot of coupons." Maggie twisted her hair up off her neck and fanned her face. "I can't believe how long rationing's lasted. The war's been over almost three years, and here we are, still fighting to get enough paraffin for our Tilley lamps, and always hoping we'll have enough milled wheat flour for bread."

Fern glanced toward the stairs and lowered her voice. "I'm sorry to have to put you and Rob through another supper with that man, but at least he's no' staying in your house. If I didn't work at the infirmary all day, I'd be a blethering eejit."

"Thank the Lord Katie spends the days at our house."

"As if I'd leave my lass with that man." After stalking into the living room, Fern grabbed the poker and scattered the flaming peat embers across the inside of the hearth, showering sparks into the air. "'Tis too cold in here,'" she growled, mimicking Dale's gravelly voice. "We're about to burn up from Dale adding peats every few minutes and shivering like 'tis winter, no' summer. Our peat pile's shrinking."

"How does Den react to all this? Surely he knew what Dale was like before he asked him to come."

"That's just it," Fern said, voice a hiss. "Den pretends there's nowt wrong with a man who never stops talking or eating or complaining about the cold. Dale acts like this is some fancy hotel with maid service. I'm ready to strangle De—"

The rescue siren wailed outside, ululating through the air like the cry of a banshee.

Maggie scooped Beth up from the hearth rug and pressed Fern's hand. "Come over and monitor the radio with me," she shouted over the noise. "'Tis so much better when we wait and pray together."

Dale Taylor insisted on accompanying them. He changed his mind three times about which sweater to wear, making them miss the conversation between Rob and Control that always clued the women in to the nature of the emergency. He also put the peter on their usual routine. Instead of prayers and reciting Bible verses to calm their fears, they were forced to answer his questions about their radio system, why they called a rescue call a "shout," and why they didn't know more about what was going on.

Thankfully, Katie, though surely worried about her own faither, comforted Annie while Ellie kept Beth entertained, and Robbie and Richie played outside with Shep.

Maggie tuned out the constant drone of Dale's voice and prayed silently. But as the hours passed, her fear turned to panic. She dropped to her knees, pulled Fern down beside her, and they bowed their heads.

A tap on her shoulder interrupted her prayers for Rob and Den's safety.

"I asked how long these shouts usually last."

Dale's raspy voice raised the hair on her arms. She froze. How dare he interrupt at a time like this?

Fern saved Maggie from a rare show of temper. "No' this long. They're having trouble."

"I'll find out." He reached for the radio.

Maggie leaped up and batted his hand away. "I told you. We're no' allowed to broadcast, only recei—"

The radio crackled.

"This is the *Maggie* to Innisbraw Control. Over."

Neil's voice, no' Rob's or Den's.

A sharp pain knifed Maggie's stomach as Fern's nails dug into her arm.

"Innisbraw Control to *Maggie*. Are you ready to come in? Over."

"Aye, Control. We have twa injured crewmen and four near-drowning victims, including another crewman, and six victims with hypothermia. We need John, Fern, and Maggie at the dock, and five cairts. Over."

"Roger that, *Maggie*. When will you make port?"

"Twenty minutes. *Maggie* oot."

"We'll be ready. Control oot."

Maggie and Fern pushed Dale aside and raced into the living room.

"Ellie, can you and Katie watch the bairns?" Maggie asked as she put on a sweater. "When Beth needs to suckle, take her over to the infirmary."

"I'm going with you." Dale's growl.

Maggie shuddered, then started after Fern down the path to the infirmary, followed by Dale, who huffed like a steam engine climbing a ben.

Maggie's father, Doctor John McGrath, was putting supplies into a large medical bag. His salt-and-pepper hair and short beard were mussed, face drawn, but his voice was calm. "I've called Flora and Alice to come and keep watch on the patients here. None are critical."

The women filled a canvas satchel with saline and plasma. John took it from Maggie as they rushed out the door and down to the dock. Maggie and Fern held hands as they waited. Dale sat on a bollard, still panting from the run, face red, forehead dripping sweat.

John ran a hand through his beard as he paced. "After this, they need to broadcast the names of injured crew members. This waiting is no' pleasant."

Minutes later, the *Maggie*'s siren wailed three times as she cleared the harbour mouth.

Extreme emergency.

Maggie fought for breath. *Please, Lord, no' Rob. No' Rob or Den. Please!* One of Jesus's promises echoed in her mind. *Peace I leave with you; my peace I give unto you: not as the world giveth, give I unto you. Let not your heart be troubled, neither let it be fearful.*

The *Maggie* came into her berth too fast and overshot, but Neil quickly backed her into place. Stu Proctor and Graham MacDonald, both Rob's business partners, ran from the boatshed and made the ropes fast while John scaled the railing. Two of the rescue lads raised the hinged railing and pushed the gangplank into place. Maggie, Fern, Graham, and Stu hurried aboard, ignoring Dale's mumbled offer to help.

In the cabin, Rob sat in the commander's seat, head back, eyes closed, face so pale.

Maggie made her way through the crowded cabin and knelt before him. "Rob," she cried, hugging him.

He groaned. "I'm … all right. Help others." His left arm hung at his side.

"Och, luve, you've hurt your shoulder again."

He opened his eyes. Bloodshot, they were, and dark with pain. "It's no' bad, lass. Please help the others."

She heard her name being called.

Fern held a blood-soaked towel to Den's face. "His nob is broken."

Den tried to smile. "Hit a hard elbow. I'm all right. Help James. We came near to losing him oot there."

Maggie looked around for her faither. John was triaging the near-drowning victims. Matthew Campbell, the *Maggie*'s battle-trained medic, had started saline drips on all of them.

Her faither grabbed her arm. "We're ready to transport. How's Rob?"

"'Tis his shoulder again, but I don't think 'tis broken or oot of place."

"Den?"

"A broken nose."

"Then these near-drownings go first. Put James and that lad over there in the first cairt. I'll go with them. The other twa can go in the second cairt." He hurried out as the rescue crew lifted stretchers.

Swallowing her distaste, Maggie said, "Christopher, call that man in from the dock. His name's Dale. He can help Stu carry a stretcher." She and Fern checked the hypothermia victims.

All were shivering and conscious beneath their blankets.

Maggie ran back to Rob's side. He hadn't moved. "I need to know where you hurt, Rob."

"Just strained that … shoulder again."

"Then let me help you to your feet. Can you walk?"

He shook his head and blinked his eyes. "Don't know. I'll try."

"No, you won't." She motioned to two crew members. "Put him on a stretcher."

Rob tried to get up but collapsed with a groan.

Neil, the second coxswainn and Paddy, another member of the rescue crew, helped Rob onto a stretcher. "Take it aisy, Commander," Paddy said in his musical Irish brogue. "We'll soon have you out of here and up the fell."

"Put Rob and Den in the third cairt," Maggie ordered. "Stu and Dale can ride with them. Then get back here to help the rest oot to the path." She shivered. *Be with them, Lord.*

Fern pressed a clean towel to Den's face, nodding at the remaining crew members. "Get oot all the blankets you can find and add to the ones already on the hypothermia victims. Then help them oot to the path. They go in the last twa cairts. Stay and monitor them closely. Graham, you can help them to the path, but stay with Maggie and me till the last victim's gone."

⚓

By the time Fern, Maggie, and Graham made the long climb to the infirmary, Rob was nowhere in sight. Maggie ran to Stu, who was placing a warmed blanket around the shoulders of a hypothermia victim. "Do you know where Rob is?"

"In the third examining room. He's going to be all right, Maggie. He kept telling me to help the others."

"He would," she said as she ran down the hall.

Dale was struggling to remove Rob's wet suit. "This thing's so tight!" he growled when he saw Maggie.

She pushed him aside and soon had Rob stripped and covered with two blankets.

"Everything's going to be all right, lass," Rob said through clenched teeth. "Go help John."

"No' now." She took his blood pressure.

12

Low.

"How's Den?"

"A broken nose, but that's all I know."

"James?"

"They transported him first. He was conscious, but I think he still had water in his stomach. Your blood pressure's too low. Lay you down and rest. Faither needs to look at your shoulder."

Dale touched her arm, eyes averted. "I'll stay with him if they need you."

She bit her lip, then whirled around and opened the door. "Graham," she shouted. "I need you in examining room three."

Graham appeared seconds later.

Maggie squeezed his arm. "Don't leave Rob's side for owt."

In the foyer, Flora and Alice passed out steaming mugs of tea, liberally sweetened with honey, to the hypothermia victims, who still shivered beneath the warmed blankets wrapped around their shoulders.

Maggie, Fern, and the rescue crew worked with John far into the afternoon. When the last near-drowning victim was conscious and breathing easily, the doctor asked to see Rob and Den.

"Den's nob is broken," Fern said, "but he has no other complaints, other than being spent from all that time in the water."

John nodded. "Maggie, I'm going to want a picture of Rob's shoulder. Is he hurt anyplace else?"

"I don't know. Like Den, he's spent."

"Put them in the same room. Fern, go monitor James's vitals. He's oot of danger, but I'll keep him overnight."

Matthew led Den to examining room two.

He could walk, but his legs trembled, and his swollen eyes were already turning colours.

Graham pulled a gurney in from the hall and helped Den lie down, covering him with blankets.

Maggie took Rob's blood pressure again. "A little shocky but no' too bad."

Rob groped for her hand. "I'm all right. I keep telling you, luve."

"I've heard that from you before, Rob Savage." She leaned over him. "Faither wants an X-ray of your shoulder. Can you walk?"

"No' in the scud."

"I'll get you a gown."

"You'll get me a robe, or I'm no' going anywhere."

"Och, you're feeling better. All right, a robe it is. I'll be back in a tick."

His grip tightened on her hand. "Tell me how James is first."

"He's conscious and he's vomited up enough seawater to fill a basin. His vitals are much better."

"And the victims?"

"They should be fine in a day or twa."

"Guid." Rob lay back and closed his eyes.

Rob's X-rays showed no permanent damage.

"You'll have to go back to the sling, of course," John told him.

"I figured as much. Is this going to happen with every rescue, John?"

"How long were you in the water?"

"I disremember. 'Twas a collision between a trawler and a sailboat. Felt like hours."

John's gaze bored into his. "How many people did you pull oot of the sea?"

All these questions. "Three or four, mebbe."

"Well, was it three or four?"

What nevermind did it make? "Aye. After a while 'tis like being on autopilot. Four, I guess."

Gaze unrelenting, arms crossed over his chest, John said, "Then every time you stay in the water that long and rescue that many souls, your shoulder's going to give you trouble."

After Den's swollen nose and black eyes made him the new brunt of Dale's jokes, Den couldn't help but feel relieved when Fern made him stay abed as Dale said goodbye before catching the ferry.

"I saw all those scars on Rob's body," Dale growled, "and the way you two acted like almost dying was nothing to worry about." He poked Den's chest. "You need a full-time nursemaid, not an electronics expert. You look like a raccoon, old buddy. Those are two of the blackest eyes I've ever seen."

Den blinked.

Dale whirled away from the bed, stopped, and turned. "And don't call me for another 'favor.' It'll be a cold day in the Mojave before I spend over thirty hours in cramped airplane seats, and another five hours on a ferry, for the 'privilege' of visiting a piece of freezing rock in the ocean." Then he blew out of the room.

Den had never seen the man away from his home turf. Aye, Dale turned oot a fine product, and he'd always been a joker, but he'd gone way too far this time, ordering Fern around like she was his serving

14

lass and besmirching Innisbraw.

Och, it would take hours—mebbe days—to mend fences after this fiasco.

Chapter Three

Maggie helped at the infirmary until the last victim was released.

Though unhappy with her hours, Rob knew better than to say anything. At least he had a home office, but his own work lasted far into the night. Aye, he'd designed their home after frustrating weeks of pacing and sketching, but he was no architect, so remodeling existing cottages was time-consuming and arduous. "I'm lucky 'tis no' my right arm," he told Maggie late one night. "At least I can write."

"I almost wish it were your right arm," she said. "Then you could take some time off."

"Gunny and Caroline'll be here before we know it."

Her violet-blue eyes turned dark blue, like they did every time he mentioned Gunny's name.

He pressed a finger over her lips. "And don't go nattering about how you'll get along with Gunny. He's easy-going, no' a thing like Dale Taylor."

She chewed her lower lip. "But you've never met Caroline. With as much silver as they have, how can you know what she's like? She most likely wears face paint and prances about in silk dresses with padded shoulders and high, tottery heels she buys in New York City."

Was Maggie jealous? His belly cramped. She'd never complained about how few clothes she had, only that rationing made it difficult to find what she needed for the bairns—and him refusing to wear scratchy tweeds. And doing without face paint was her decision, no' his, though the thought of her with bright-red lips and flaming cheeks threw him into a panic.

Och, Maggie couldn't be jealous. Fearful, more likely.

"Gunny and Rich were the finest lads I ever had on the *Liberty Belle*'s crew. Gunny couldn't be a successful housing contractor if he had a wife who put on airs."

Pray God he was right.

He massaged his temples. "He'll find us the right man to do these remodel plans."

"But can he solve how to build four rescue boats at a time without adding more lads to your building crew?"

16

Her sweet breath addled his thinking. He threw down his pencil and pulled her close, inhaling the scent of heather on her skin and hair. "That's a fankle for another day. 'Tis time for a smoorich with my lass."

Ellie kept delaying her departure. She had a contract to teach kindergarten in New Hampshire starting in September, but she couldn't face the thought of leaving Innisbraw. It didn't help that Calum kept begging her to stay. Unable to make a decision, she went to Maggie with her dilemma.

"Do you luve Calum?" Maggie asked, voice gentle.

"Yes, but that's the problem."

"How can it be a problem?" Maggie's eyebrows arched. "Doesn't he luve you?"

"He says he does."

"You don't believe him?"

Tears blurred Ellie's vision. "I'm *that* afraid. What if he gets tired of me and walks away?"

"Like that lass—Linda—did to Rich?"

"She didn't walk away. She got what she wanted and ran."

Maggie gasped. "Surely she didn't intend to get biggen ootside of marriage!"

Ellie felt her cheeks burn. "Of course not. She wanted to show him she could have him, then discard him like so much … trash."

"Thank the guid Lord you adopted Richie and made him your own. I'm certain that would have pleased your brother."

Ellie had spent sleepless nights wondering the same thing. Would Rich have been happy? Or would he have worried about burdening his younger sister with the result of his rash actions? "I suppose you're right," she said, eyes downcast.

"I know I'm right. That lad of yours has a mither who luves him. All he needs now is a faither he can respect, one who takes care of the both of you. Calum's no' perfect, but he's no' a quitter and he's no' a liar. If he says he luves you, he means it."

"But he's too young to settle down. Suppose he decides he'd rather have his own bairnie someday? What happens to Richie?"

Maggie's embrace warmed her chilled flesh. "The same thing that happened to Robbie. He learns to share his faither and mither with a sister or brither. It happens all the time."

"You really believe that?"

Maggie smiled. "If I didn't, I'd have stopped having bairns when

Robbie was birthed and cheated him oot of a true family. Folk need to learn to share, Ellie, and there's no better time than when they're bairns."

Ellie blew her nose. "You must think I'm an idiot."

"No more than any woman who's afeart of the future. What you need is faith—in God first, then yourself and Calum. Without it you'll cheat yourself and Richie oot of a happy life."

For several days, Ellie mulled over what Maggie had said. What would it be like to go back to the dreary life in New Hampshire? A cramped little apartment over a garage, with slippery, perilous outside stairs to climb when it snowed, daycare for Richie, a run-down car Ellie couldn't rely on—especially in winter—no time to make close friends, no acceptable playmates for Richie.

Making a new life on Innisbraw wouldn't be easy. She'd have to perfect her Scots and learn the Gaelic plus a completely new way of doing things. She'd never plunged butter, didn't know how to spin or weave wool—though she could knit—never had the time to garden or make clothes by hand. And what about her teaching? She'd have to find a way to support herself and Richie. They couldn't stay with Rob and Maggie forever.

But she couldn't imagine leaving Innisbraw. She'd never had friends as close as those she'd made here: Maggie and Rob with their luving acceptance; Fern and Den and their humourous way of dealing with good and bad; and Jill and Stu, practical, down-to-earth, firmly grounded.

And Calum. Tall and strong, with a man's body and a lad's awkwardness and bouts of shyness. His gentle spirit called to hers with a yearning that brought an ache to her heart.

She met Calum's trawler when he returned from four days of fishing.

The setting sun set his black hair afire, and his blue eyes sparkled as his long arms grabbed her into a hug. "My Ellie," he breathed, lips seeking hers.

His kiss spoke of bittersweet longing.

The sparkle left his eyes the moment she wriggled from his grasp. He pulled her toward the bench beside the pier, sat her down, and clasped her hands. "Tell me. I can see from how pale you are you've made your decision."

She nodded, head bowed.

"Look at me. I deserve that much."

She raised her head and studied his face. Like Maggie, his eyes turned dark blue when he was distressed. "I'm staying," she whispered, "but that doesn't mean …"

He pulled her to her feet. "Staying? Och, Ellie luve, you're staying!" He kissed her again, lips demanding, embrace pledging a strong, warm haven from anything life might throw her way.

She melted against him, losing herself in the promises his body spoke.

He kissed her cheeks and forehead. "Marry me, lass!" he cried. "Och, my sweet Ellie, say you'll marry me."

"Are you … certain, Calum?" Och, her halting question sounded like one of her wee pupils begging for reassurance. She needed to be strong for Richie. "Remember, I come with a five-year-old lad."

He picked her up and sat on the bench with her in his lap. "Certain? Ellie, luve, I've never been so certain of owt in my life. If you only knew the hours I've spent imagining a life with you and Richie. I've even been trying to design our cottage, and drawing a straight line never comes easy to a man used to a net in one hand and gutting knife in the other." He tilted her chin with a trembling finger. "What say you, Ellie Florey? Will you become my wife so we—all three of us—can be a family?"

Did it matter that fishing kept him at sea for days? Each time the *Anna* came alongside the dock, their luve would be renewed and strengthened: a fresh chapter with clean, unblemished pages ready to be filled with new wonders, new heights of joy.

Peace settled over her like a blessing sent from heaven, smothering the last ember of doubt. She pressed her face against his throat. "Aye, Calum McGrath, I'll marry you."

Chapter Four

The swelling in Den's nose went down and the rainbow of colours around his eyes faded, but Rob's shoulder continued to bother him. After twa weeks in the sling, he still couldn't move his arm without pain. After enough of Maggie's prodding, he dropped in at the infirmary.

Hair and beard freshly trimmed, white coat riding his shoulders as naturally as foam on a wave, John did a thorough examination and studied the X-rays taken after the shout. "We'll give it another week, then I may have to go in and find the problem."

Rob's belly cramped. Another agonizing shoulder surgery? He'd had both legs, his back, and chest sliced open, but nothing approached the pain of cutting into his shoulder. Forcing the memory from his mind, he shrugged into an old Air Forces shirt with buttons—couldn't raise his arm to slip a Jacobite shirt over his head. "I'm too busy to bother with this."

John helped with the buttons and strapped his arm into the sling. "Are you leaving this on all the time, except for showering and dressing?"

"Every minute of every day."

"Then there's nowt more we can do." The doctor stroked his beard. "Try it another week."

"But Gunny and Caroline Hastings will be here in less than twa weeks."

"You're no' planning on taking him swimming are you, or owt else involving your shoulder?"

"Of course no'. Just hate to have him see me like this." Heat rose in his cheeks. "'Tis embarrassing. And tourists have noticed."

"They're staring at you?"

"And whispering. Why are some people so nosey?"

John chuckled. "No idea. They must wonder what happened to you."

"'Tis none of their business." Rob rubbed the side of his nose. "I'll be glad when the ferry runs end the last of October. Thought I'd get used to having so many strangers around, but it gets worse, no' better."

"I'm thinking 'tis more than that, lad. How long has it been since you took a day off?"

Rob blew out a breath. "There isn't time."

"That could be why your shoulder hasn't healed."

"But I haven't used my arm. I can't with it tied up like some wild-eyed cuddy rearing in the traces."

"Your muscles are tight as a drum. Take a few days off, or that shoulder will never heal, even with surgery."

Rob stared at him for a moment, then sat down on the examining table.

"You ken I'm right, don't you?"

No matter how complicated the surgeries and treatments, John had never steered Rob wrong.

John grabbed a notepad and jotted down a few lines. He tore the paper off and handed it to Rob. "Here's my prescription. Won't cost a farthing, but it will require self-discipline."

Rob read aloud, "'Eat, sleep, sit in your rocker, play with your bairns, blether with Maggie.' That's all?"

Folded arms and a stern look answered Rob's question. "And for at least the next week."

⚜

Rob walked down to the shed, though he could have handled the task with a phone call. But he owed his partners more, and he had to sign checks for his building crew. Why hadn't he listened when Stu asked for his name to be added to the account? After all, as a partner and the boatworks' accountant, he made out most of the checks anyway.

Before Rob left the shed half an hour later, he told Den, Stu, and Graham what John had prescribed.

As always, Den was the most emphatic. "He's right as rain, bucko." He poked Rob's chest. "Remember the time General Wells sent you off to Wales for some R and R after that nasty strike on the sub pens at Saint-Nazaire? Well, that's what you need right now."

When Rob reached the house, he called out Maggie's name. "Where are you, lass?"

No answer.

He searched every room.

Nobody home.

Ah. Maggie, Ellie, and the bairns were at a Women's Aid Society all-day social. What a fankle. He poked around in the food press and refrigerator but didn't find anything appealing. His hand shook when he pulled John's "prescription" from his pocket. *Eat.*

He'd tried that but wasn't really hungry. *Sleep*. Well, why no'? A full night's sleep had been hard to come by lately. He took the sling off, carefully undressed, then strapped it back on and climbed into bed.

He stretched out and closed his eyes.

Maggie stopped at the bedroom door. Rob lay flat on his back in the middle of the bed, fast asleep. She looked down at him, heart bursting with luve.

The worry lines around his eyes and at the sides of his mouth had faded. For the first time in months, he looked completely at peace. Her faither had been right. What Rob needed was one week of doing nowt but relaxing.

Taking care not to disturb him, she pulled up the sheet and turned to go.

"Maggie."

She whirled around.

He smiled up at her, right arm extended.

"I didn't mean to wake you." She hurried to his side.

He cleared his throat. "The meeting ended early?"

"'Tis almost supper time, luve."

His eyebrow shot up. "I slept all day?"

She sat on the bed and took his hand. "Aye, you did that." She laced her fingers through his.

"You're merrit to a lazybones." He arched his back and stretched.

"I'm merrit to a verra, verra tired man. Are you hungry?"

"You're no' asking why I'm in bed." That talented eyebrow rose again. "I'm thinking you've seen your faither."

"I stopped at the infirmary on my way home and met the new nurse Faither hired. Also, I thought you were still at the shed and wanted to hear what he found when he examined you this mornin."

Soft lips brushed her knuckles. "You taste guid."

Och, men and their needs. "I have to start supper, and Beth needs a clean hippen, and—"

His lips sought hers.

She delighted in his taste, in the way his lips moved over hers, in the man-scent of his skin. This was her husband. This was the man who gave his all for others with never a thought for himself. It was his turn for some comfort. She slipped off her sandals and climbed onto the bed. "I'll make time for a wee smoorich."

The bairns were delighted to have Rob home during the day.

He watched the lads play ball, sang silly songs with Annie, played with Beth, and laughed aloud at her unorthodox manner of scooting across the floor. He bundled all the bairns in a hap and lay on the rug in front of the fire with them, telling stories long past their bedtimes.

He also spent hours talking to Maggie, took long baths with her, cradled her in bed, even helped her fold clothes with one hand and kept her company while she cooked. She curtailed her own ootside activities so they could sneak off past the wandering tourists to their private cove for a picnic and a romp on the shore.

The stares of the few tourists they encountered no longer bothered him. John had been right. They probably just wondered what kind of accident had befallen him. He stayed away from the shed, finding himself thinking less and less about how his businesses were faring.

On the Sabbath, he carefully brushed Annie's long curls and lifted the hair from her nape so he could kiss her neck.

She giggled and threw her arms around him. "My faither." She patted his back, planted a kiss on his cheek, and whispered in the Gaelic, "Tha gaol agam ort."

Tears misted his eyes. "And I luve you, my precious lassie."

He held Maggie's hand on the way to kirk. Stu pulled the wagon full of the younger bairns while Katie, Robbie, Richie, and Chris Proctor raced ahead, staying in front of Shep's herding nips.

"Rob looks so much better," he overheard Fern say to Den, "like he used to, young and happy to be alive."

"Aye. This R and R was long overdue."

Eyes turned his way as they approached the kirk. Och, first the tourists, now the island's folk. The gossips must have worn their tongues to a nubbin the past few days.

Their minister's cherubic smile rounded his cheeks into ripe winter apples as he greeted the family on the kirk steps. He squeezed Rob's elbow and leaned closer. "Looks like that rest John prescribed was what you needed. I haven't seen you look so guid in years."

Alec MacDonald removed his dung-soled wellies and carried them through the cottage to the sma' room beside the kitchen where waxed jackets, boots, and Morag's heavy coat competed for room with a basket of eggs, another of neeps, and a large burlap poke of last year's tatties. With the meeting soon to begin, he'd best add peats to the stove, get the teakettle biling, and perk coffee for Hugh.

Guilt weighed on him, heavy as a flagging stone tied 'round his neck. Morag had been redding the cottage all the day. She'd scrubbed the stone-flagged floor, swept the entry, taken a raggit cloth to every creek and corner—even scoured the peat-black from the fireplace surrounds. And after all that, he'd asked her to take their cairt and cuddy and pick up Elspeth from her cottage on Innis Fell.

Her guid-natured smile didn't ease his guilt, nor the fact that he'd been busy with the coos, laying oot piles of hay in their gangs, and mucking the byre for the young heifers. He was the one who'd asked the Island Council to meet in his chaumer this een, adding to the never-ending work Morag tackled every day. How had the guid Lord ever thought him deserving of such a wife?

Voices drew him to the door.

Elspeth NicAllister hobbled up the narrow path to the cottage, probing with her walking stick for each firm flagging stone. The brilliant sunset reflected on the white braids wrapped round her head, colouring them with streaks of red and purple.

Morag and Tormad MacKinnon trailed closely behind, hands at the ready if she faltered. Alan MacCrae and Hugh followed them, slowing their steps to the auld woman's pace. Though always welcome at the council meetings, Hugh seldom attended. Did he have a proposal to put to a vote?

Though 'twas warmer than usual for an August een on Innisbraw, Elspeth wore a shawl pulled close about her thin shoulders and a sweater 'neath that.

Alec's heart jittered in his chest. Nearing a hundred and five, she was. Could she be ill? He threw the door wide, helped her over the threshold, and kissed her lined, tissue-thin cheek. "Thank ye for coming. I wouldn't have called for the meeting if I didn't have a fankle needing discussion. I spoke to Rob the other day, but he had no solution."

"I ken that, Alec." The firmness of her voice and sparkle in her faded blue eyes eased his anxiety.

"I'll put a spunk to the peat. You look chilled."

Elspeth handed Morag her shawl and dropped into the offered chair with a sigh. "Och, no' on my account. We're oot of the blousterin' wind now. 'Tis warm enough."

Alec greeted Tormad, Alan, and Hugh with a handshake and nodded them to their chairs. "I'll help Morag bring in some tea and coffee while we wait for the others."

"Fergus and Alistaire won't be coming," Hugh said, unbuttoning his tweed jacket. "Christiona's taken with a cough, and Fergus is afraid to leave her."

"Seems our Sandy has what he called a 'commission' to carve a large dolphin for a tourist." Tormad's grin stretched his usually sober face wide.

Alan slapped his bunnet on his knee. "Skint as that auld man is, he can't turn down a chance to make silver." A sharp glance from Elspeth erased his smile. "I mean … I didn't mean … och, I know he can't help being poor, and those carvings of his are a marvel, but he's always putting on airs, like speaking only the Gaelic when we all ken he understands Scots as well as any of us."

"And English," Tormad said, his long, thin face dour again. "Anna overheard him talking to a tourist."

Sheila MacNab and Colin Stewart, the last of the Island Council, arrived, interrupting the conversation.

Alec brought a tray from the kitchen and handed out tea and coffee.

Morag seated herself in her rocker. Lamplight cast a glow over her black hair and lit sparks in her blue eyes. "Well, isn't it about time we started? I'm thinking since Fergus and Alistaire aren't here, we can use Scots instead of the Gaelic the een." She nodded at her husband.

Alec stroked his chin and chose his words with care. Only a coo crofter, he was, and Elspeth was chair of the council. "As you've seen, the tourists keep arriving on Innisbraw, eager to see what they call our 'unspoiled' beaches, birdlife, and rare wildflowers." His gaze swept each face. "Morag has told me that every room available on the island is booked through the season, and next year's are already filling up with folk planning to come again."

A buzz of conversation filled the chaumer.

Elspeth thumped her walking stick and nodded at Alec to continue.

"We have to provide more rooms if we want to attract more tourists."

⚓

Elspeth laid her head back and closed her eyes, relieved to finally have an opportunity to voice something that had sent her to her knees in prayer for months. "That's the question, then. How many is no' enough and how many is too many?"

The silence that followed her question throbbed in her ears.

Hugh cleared his throat. "If we're thinking of bringing even more strangers to Innisbraw, you should know that some of our folk have voiced unhappiness over their lack of privacy. At the verra least, we need more signs to remind the strangers no' to trespass on the crofts. Four of Angus's ewes escaped his fauld the other day when someone left the gate in his dyke open."

Elspeth opened her eyes. "Did he get them back?"

"Edert found them on Ben Innis. Poor lad was oot half the night looking for them, using the last of Angus's paraffin in his Tilley lamp."

"Then I agree. We need more signs erected immediately." Elspeth pulled her kerchief from her sleeve cuff and dabbed her lips. Now 'twas time to get to the heart of the problem. "Does anybody ken how many tourists we average with each ferry?"

"Rob told me it stands at above ten," Morag said. "Though most only stay for a week, there are some who bide a fortnight or more."

Elspeth turned to Alec. "Is this why you think we need more accommodations?"

He steepled his hands. "That's what brought it to mind. But after what Hugh said about privacy, I don't know. And you asked a question I hadn't considered. We don't want too many strangers traipsing all over our island." He tapped his fingers together. "Though Rob did warn me he couldn't turn them oot any faster, with the plans for additions to existing cottages he's drawing up, mebbe we'll have enough."

Dear, conscientious Alec. Exactly the answer she'd been seeking. Now her prayers could concentrate on her beloved island folk. "Too many crowds and the verra qualities that draw folk to our shores will be lost." She looked around the room. "Is there any other business?" When no one spoke, she tapped her walking stick again. "Then I have twa items. Calum McGrath has requested a small croft be set aside so he can build a home for his soon-to-be-bride, Ellie. 'Tis to be at the top of Innis Fell by the Savages'. Are there any objections?"

Again, there was silence.

"I'll tell the lad he has our permission." She leaned forward, a sudden spurt of energy making her heart pound. "The last item of business concerns the new academy."

Och, that got everybody's attention.

"Rob's having an architect draw up the plans as we speak. As soon as they're finished and approved by the Board of Education, ground will be broken."

Alec grinned and patted Morag's hand.

For years the folk on Innisbraw had wanted to offer a higher education than the primary grades. Come next fall, they would.

Pray God would allow her long enough on earth to see it. "You men must spread the word. We'll need stonecutters and men to erect the walls, as is the custom. Rob's construction crew will finish the inside."

Suddenly her body weakened and she was so tired.

Och, living to such an auld age could be verra frustrating.

She leaned back in her chair. "If there's no other business, and with Alec and Morag's approval as hosts, this meeting is adjourned."

⚜

The day of Pete "Gunny" and Caroline Hastings' arrival was fast approaching. Rob's shoulder, though sore, no longer caused him shooting pain when he moved it. How could a few days' rest bring about such a change?

"It was basically already healed," John told him. "The muscles needed to relax so they could get the message to the joint."

"Can I quit using the sling?"

"As long as you don't lift anything heavier than one of those coffee mugs of yours until you've had some therapy."

⚜

Ellie insisted on sharing her bedroom with Richie while Pete and Caroline were on the island. Even the argument that Robbie could share his bed didn't sway her. "Richie an' I hae slept thegither afore, sae dinna git in a fash. 'Tis sattled."

Rob tilted his head, grinning.

"I've been practicing all the day, and I still got some words wrong."

He and Maggie laughed.

"Poor Elspeth," Maggie said. "She'll no' be teaching you Scots for verra long."

Ellie frowned. "'Tis the Gaelic that has me afeart."

"Speaking of teaching, have you decided to work at the school this year?" Rob asked. "They really need you."

"I have. My only problem—tickler—is what to do with Richie while I'm teaching."

Maggie's chin rose. "He'll stay here with Robbie, of course. They're already as close as brothers."

"I can't do that to you. You're too busy already."

"It's either that or have a skellum on my hands all winter.

27

Robbie's a handful when he's bored. I insist."

"Then I'll help you around the house in the een and on weekends." Ellie laughed. "To borrow Elspeth's favourite phrase, ''Tis only fitting.'"

Chapter Five

Maggie ducked her head to hide a smile at the dismay on Rob's face. "She only wants you to go faster, luve."

"She's bouncing so hard I'm afeart I'll drop her."

"You know our Beth likes speed. On you go now, put her on your good shoulder. She luves a shoulderie."

He hoisted Beth up.

She squealed with delight and crowed, saliva slicking her chin.

"See? That's all she wanted. She misses the shoulderies you used to give her every een."

"I ken that. Somehow, I've got to cut back on my workload."

Maggie had heard those words for so long she no longer got her hopes up. Rob was at a dead run from sunup to long after sundown. She missed unwinding from a busy day, rocking in front of the fireplace while talking quietly or holding hands as they looked at the brilliant sunsets from their front entry. When would their hectic lives slow down so they could enjoy their eens?

She glanced back at the bairns in the cairtie Ellie was pulling. Robbie and Richie rode with legs dangling over the front, laughing at one another's attempts to whistle. Annie sat on the backseat, dress pulled primly over her knees, the sun glinting off the blonde and red highlights in the light-brown curls tumbling down her back.

How different, their twa lasses. Three-year-auld Annie was quiet and soft-spoken, easily moved to tears. She luved dresses with floral prints and wearing ribbons in her hair. Obedient to a fault, she never deliberately disobeyed an order.

Granted, Beth was only six months auld, but she already showed a rebellious streak. When she wanted something, she wanted it now. She never stopped moving and was already crawling, scooting across the floor at an alarming rate by pulling herself with her arms, squealing and chortling.

"We're almost there," Rob said. "Want me to pull the cairtie, Ellie? 'Tis harder on the pier."

"I'm grand. You've your hands full with wee Beth."

Maggie's heart swelled. How the Lord had blessed them when He brought this loving lass and her lad from America. How could

29

some folk doubt that God performed miracles in this Church Age? Didn't they see a miracle in each bairnie's birth, in lives turned from darkness to eternal light, in the uniting of souls once separated by an ocean to form a family dedicated to His glory?

Rob trailed a finger over her shoulder. "You look fair bonnie, lass."

Och, he was blind. "Wearing an auld cotton dress—and the wind has my hair in tangles." She bumped his hip with hers. "Bonnie indeed."

An arm circled her shoulders. "Your hair looks like a peaty loch shivering in a rare night breeze."

Her cheeks burned. "Quit your blethering. Here comes the ferry."

⚓

Rob pulled the family to a stop on the dock, choosing a place well back to allow room for the gangplank.

A smattering of inquisitive islanders stood nearby, the women gossiping behind raised hands, men puffing on clay cutties, their bairns gazing at the ferry. Several young lads rested against handcairts, scuffing their toes on the rough wood and looking bored, no doubt anxious to offload foodstuffs and other sundries for Anna's General Store.

Rob eyed his bairns, right eyebrow raised, and waited while the ferry's deep-throated whistle announced its arrival, then said sternly, "Kirk manners," using English so Richie would understand. "You three stay in the cairtie and keep your hands to yourselves. 'Tis dangerous here with so many folk offloading." He grimaced at Maggie. "I'm no' sure bringing the bairns to meet Gunny and Caroline was such a guid idea."

"They'll behave. They're kittled up is all."

Rob pulled Beth from his shoulders and cradled her in his arms. "I'd best greet Captain MacNamara."

"On you go," Maggie said. "We'll bide here."

The Andersons and Proctors arrived as the ferry docked. Rob handed Beth to Stu so he could go through the traditional exchanging of salutes with Captain MacNamara.

"I didn't expect to make a habit of it," he told Stu afterward, "but it seems to amuse Colin."

Stu grunted. "It most likely flummoxes the tourists. They must think you have something to do with the ferry."

Suddenly, there was Gunny, an averaged-height, pleasant-looking, sandy-haired man wearing navy-blue trousers and a white polo shirt. A tall, willowy brunette, clad in a green linen dress, grasped his arm.

Och, she wore lip paint.

Rob pushed his way forward as the gangplank was lowered and the passengers filed off. "Gunny!" he called.

Pete Hastings grinned that same grin that sent his grey eyes dancing and his lips turning up like a gibbous moon. They clapped shoulders and hugged, sharing a moment of comradeship still strong.

Rob held him away. "You're looking fit."

Tears welled in Gunny's eyes. "Not as fit as you. You look like a young Samson."

"Maggie just trimmed my hair."

"I mean the muscles. What are you doing, running a gym on the side?"

Rob laughed and extended his hand to Pete's wife. "And you must be Caroline."

Caroline Hastings, dark-brown hair brushing her shoulders and brown eyes warm with humour, grasped his hand and kissed his cheek. "I'm delighted to finally meet the great, and thankfully not late, Colonel Savage. I've heard many a tale of your exploits."

Rob introduced Pete and Caroline to his family, watching Maggie carefully.

She was warm and friendly, showing no reaction to the painted lips and the light, floral scent perfuming the air around Caroline.

"Gunny almost wore out your picture showing it off," Den said, pumping Caroline's hand. "I've seen your bonnie face so many times I feel like I already know you."

Caroline blushed and turned to embrace Ellie. "I've never seen you look better, Ellie. Innisbraw must agree with you."

It was Ellie's turn to blush. "More than you know."

Rob waved a hand toward the shed. "We have one more partner, but he's hard at work on a new boat. You'll have to meet him later."

Gunny looked around. "This is one beautiful place. Why didn't you tell me you lived in paradise?"

"The winters are a bit too wet and windy to call it that, but in summer the wildflowers more than make up for it. Come on, let's collect your baggage."

"It's all at our feet. Caroline took a course in how to pack for an extended trip and fit it all in one bag." Gunny leaned closer. "I think it entails a lot of washing things out at night."

"Oh, Pete." Caroline's smile negated her groan. "It's two large

31

bags, not one."

"On you come, then," Rob said, taking Beth from Stu. "'Tis a bit of a walk, but we have the weather for it."

"So you really don't have any automobiles here?" Gunny asked.

"No' a one. I thought it would be an inconvenience, but now I wouldn't have it any other way."

"Then lead on, Commander."

Rob resolved right then to stop calling Pete "Gunny," his nickname aboard the *Liberty Belle*, where he was a waist gunner. Rob got enough of the "Commander" routine from his rescue crew.

The familiar cadence of Pete's voice, the assurance that their friendship remained strong, and the humourous accounts of delayed baggage, long lines at airports, and cramped seats, relaxed Rob as they walked up the hill.

"The trip wasn't much different than going on a mission," Pete said. "Boring as all get-out until you near your objective."

"But no FW-190s pounding your tail," Rob joked. "And no flak."

"Amen to that."

Pete's practiced eye took in every detail as they were shown around Rob and Maggie's home. "You're in the wrong business," he told Rob. "This is mighty fine craftsmanship."

"And you really made all the furniture, including that gorgeous hutch?" Caroline asked.

"He did," Maggie said. "Even the rockers and cradle."

Caroline ran a hand over the cradle, brown eyes shiny as water-washed pebbles with unshed tears.

Rob remembered Gunny's—Pete's—remark on the telephone about the cobbler with no shoes. Something about Caroline being an adoption counselor and them without bairns. What a shame.

Everyone on the fell gathered together for supper around the Savages' table. Afterward, Maggie ushered the group onto the porch, where they settled back in chairs, eyes raised to the dark-red sky with streaks and whirls of yellow and purple pulled about by high winds.

Maggie took the opportunity to study Caroline. Polished and perfectly groomed, her impeccable manners gave an impression of someone in control. Yet the mournful, fragile spirit in her eyes reached out to Maggie, begging for understanding. What made her so sad?

"I've never seen a sky so beautiful," Caroline whispered.

Rob, Den, and Graham took Pete on a tour of the boatbuilding operation early the next morning.

Pete nodded at the full-size plan drawn on the plank floor. "I had no idea this was how it's done, but it makes sense to me. You can fudge a little when it comes to house plans, but a boat's not nearly as forgiving."

"Exactly," Rob said. "Each plank and beam has to be perfect or you're constantly redoing mistakes."

"How many boats can you turn out at once?"

Rob fought to keep the excitement out of his voice. "We turned out three last year. Two rescue boats and that trawler over there that's almost ready to be launched. We have a contract with the US Coast Guard for four boats a year starting next year. They said they'd settle for three this year, because we already had one under contract, so that's still four boats. The thing that has us chewing nails is how to raise our production to four rescue boats without doubling our crews and running out of room."

Pete snapped his fingers. "Easy."

Rob's breath quickened. "Easy? How?"

"You set up an assembly line. You said you have two crews because you had two rescue boats and a trawler this year. No reason to double your men. Each crew does a task, then moves on to the next boat and repeats that task until you have all four boats at the same stage of development. You keep doing that until your four boats are finished. It saves time because that task is fresh in their minds."

Rob stared at his partners. So simple, yet it had eluded them for weeks.

"Do you have enough room for four rescue boats in here?" Pete asked.

"Aye," Graham said. "We only need one set of lofted plans, and the trawler's about finished. That frees up enough space for the fourth boat."

"Then, voilà, problem solved."

Giddy with relief, Rob slapped Pete's back. "You've earned your first commission as a consultant. Sounds so easy, yet we'd never have dreamed that one up."

"The bigger house contractors use it all the time. Saves time and money."

"And time is money."

"You bet it is."

Price

Rob walked Pete over the island, pointing out the various planned projects. "You can see why I need an expert. I'm working my tail off, and I can't do it anymore. I've a bad shoulder, and it doesn't take kindly to working sunup to midnight six days a week."

Pete stroked his chin. "You need someone who has drafting experience plus building expertise. It won't be easy to bring somebody here, beautiful as it is, without offering him an arm and a leg."

"We can't afford an arm and a leg. These plans are for our local folk. They don't have the silver—the money—to spend."

"How many projects do you have on the boards right now?"

"Counting the academy, which should begin construction anytime, around twenty."

"Twenty?" Pete whistled. "I'd say you're stretched a might slim."

He had no idea how slim. "Right now I'm trying to run the boatworks, command the rescue operation, and head up the construction business. I don't do it alone, but the buck stops here. If I can't produce, it doesn't get done. I need help."

"That's the understatement of the year."

"You have anyone in mind? I know I haven't given you much time, but I'm hoping you've thought of someone who qualifies."

Pete sucked his lower lip. "I have one who might be interested."

"Then give me his name. I'll call him tomorrow."

"Not so fast. What can you offer my man?"

For Rob, that answer didn't require any thought. "A lot of work, for starters. But if he's the right person, he may like living on our island. You called it paradise, remember? I wouldn't go that far, considering the harsh winters we have, but it has a lot to offer the right person."

"Such as?"

No' an easy answer this time, with his all-encompassing, rooted luve for Innisbraw and its folk colouring his judgement. But Pete wasn't expecting a long, complicated reply. Rob took a deep breath. "The finest folk in the entire world—appreciative and giving—a bonnie summer, as you can see, a community that pulls together regardless of the hardships, and no cars or trucks."

"That last one is questionable." Pete's smile faltered. "How about a partnership?"

A partnership? Och, Rob hadn't thought it would come to that.

"If it's the right fit, it's a possibility, as long as he realizes he's never going to get rich. We aren't in it for the money."

"That might narrow the field." Pete turned to gaze at the machair.

Don't lose his interest now, Savage. You need a name. "I realize that. But Den, Graham, Stu, and I agree that all we need is a decent living. There's nothing to spend money on here, anyway. Den and I have a plane, and that's all we want."

Pete whirled around. "You have a plane?"

"A small floatplane. I'll take you up while you're here."

"Well, why didn't you say so? I'd say you found your new partner."

"Who?"

"Me."

Rob couldn't believe what he was hearing. He closed his gaping mouth.

"Say something." Pete laughed. "Is it that bad?"

"Bad? Gunny, are you serious? Ye already hae a business—a verra guid business."

"You must be upset. I can hardly understand you."

"Och I'm no'—not—upset, just gobsmacked. I never imagined you'd consider moving here. Why? Why would you give up all you have to move to a wee island in Scotland? Remember, you can't expect to make a lot of money."

The lowing of a bull tethered nearby broke through the roar of the pounding waves.

Pete brushed off a rock and sat down. "We already have a lot of money, and what's it bought us? A membership in a country club we never use? A beautiful house? It's not as comfortable or as welcoming as yours. Two fancy automobiles, and a travel trailer we never use because there's no time to go anywhere? Huge closets full of clothes we seldom wear?" He slapped his thigh. "I'm telling you, Rob, money can't buy happiness. I swear Caroline and I were happier when we were dead broke and in that little bungalow we lived in before I shipped overseas during the war."

Rob couldn't mislead a friend, especially one he'd cheated death with. "I haven't told you any of the downsides. Our winters are pretty hard to take with the constant wind and rain, and you can't go down to the local store when you're out of bread. We have a General Store, but their space is limited. Unless Caroline's in line outside the store before the ferry docks with what they've ordered, she'll have to bake your bread and plant and tend a garden." He paced in front of Pete.

"And you'll both have to learn Scots and the Gaelic if you ever hope to communicate with most of the folk on the island."

Grabbing Rob's arm, Pete pulled himself to his feet. "Harsh winters are something we put up with every year, only it's snow and rain, and our summers are muggy and hot with rain showers so hard you can't see to drive. As for making bread, Caroline loves to bake and her garden at home is her way of relaxing. I'm not so sure about the Scots and Gaelic. We're a little old to be learning a new language, but we'll try."

This was unbelievable. Only the Holy Spirit could come up with such a perfect solution to so many problems. But had Pete considered the impact such a drastic change of lifestyle would have on his wife? "What about Caroline's job?"

"Like I told you, it's tearing her apart. Every time she places a kid, she wishes it was with us."

"Then why hasn't it been?"

"A lot of the problem's me." Pete threw back his head and exhaled noisily. "I've been too busy to even think about adopting a kid."

"Would you if you could?"

"I suppose so. Anything to make Caroline happy again."

"That's not a good reason."

"I know it. I haven't resolved it in my mind." Pete met Rob's gaze directly. "Let's get back to that partnership."

"On that issue, I'd like nothing better." Rob grinned. "I can't think of another man on earth I'd rather have."

"How about we shake on it and get back to your house? Caroline knows I was going to approach you, and I hate to leave her dangling in the wind."

"So you've already talked about it?"

A grin wide enough to reveal Pete's molars. "You bet we have. She had to talk me out of putting the house on the market that first night I talked to you on the phone."

Chapter Six

Pete was very generous with his buy-in. "It's only money. There're a lot of homes here that need to be upgraded into the twentieth century. I'd like to be a part of that."

The men got to work. Pete drew up a model of a production line for the boatworks. "You'll have to tweak it a little. After all, I'm not a boatbuilder."

Despite Rob's argument that it was too much to put on her shoulders, Pete sent Caroline back to the States to sell their home, cars, and other assets they wouldn't be shipping to Innisbraw. He assured Rob she could handle it.

"What about your company?" Rob asked.

"I have a board of directors. They can run it for now. In the future, I'll probably sell out, but I don't want to take the time that would entail now. You're right at the cusp of it all here, Rob. It has to be done right now or not at all."

Next, Pete applied for a permit to build a home on Innis Fell. "Might as well make it consistent with the others," he said to Rob. "I like your design. It looks perfect on the fell, so I'll just alter the inside a little to fit the way we live, size it down a bit."

Rob felt like he had one foot in heaven. So far this fall, all the shouts had been routine with little danger to his crew. Graham and the boat crews worked out a production line and rearranged the shed. The contract with the United States Coast Guard came in signed and ready to implement, and the trawler was successfully launched, receiving accolades from its new owner. The Board of Education approved the academy plans, so the walls could now be erected.

Perhaps most important of all, Gunny had taken over the remodels for existing homes, and Rob now had time to relax with his family.

He spent his eens playing with the bairns and talking to Maggie. Every night he thanked the Lord for another blessing. Life was finally slowing down enough to enjoy it, and he didn't see how it could get any better.

37

Until the middle of October when Maggie told him they were expecting another bairnie. "Och, Maggie, luve, what grand news. Just think, we're halfway there."

She laughed and swatted his arm. "'Twill be another seven months before that happens. 'Tis a little sooner than we'd planned. Are you sure you're happy about it?"

He held her away and studied her face.

Her smile shone like a full summer's moon, but a wee sliver of hesitation darkened her eyes. The truth was what she needed.

"I couldn't be happier, as long as it's no' too soon for you."

"It could mean twa in hippens at the same time, but with my washing machine, I'll manage."

"You're busy weaving plaids for Ellie and Calum's wedding. I'll help you more around the house and with the bairns. I have the time now."

"Och, Jill's helping with the bairns, so I can weave. I'm no' letting you get busy again. It's been so wonderful having you home for supper every night and no' having you disappear into your office until after the turn o' the night. I'm no' about to keep you busy with my duties."

"I don't have an office here anymore, remember?" He tapped the tip of her nose. "Pete's taken it over."

"We do have a houseful, don't we?"

He nuzzled her cheek. "It won't be long till we're alone again. Ellie and Calum will be merrit during Yule season, and their house should be finished by then. And, weather permitting, they'll break ground for Pete and Caroline's house in about a week."

"Has he heard from her?"

"Aye! Och, lass, with your guid news I disremembered to tell you. She's coming in twa weeks."

"Just in time to catch the last ferry for the year."

Thank the Lord for that. He couldn't bear many more weeks of strangers' stares and whispered asides. "Aye. I think it was right to cut the ferry stops here at the end of October. With no cars, the weather's too bad to get people to their host families' homes without everything getting wet. And we don't have much for tourists to do when the rain's pishing doon."

She nestled into the crook of his arm. "We never seem to have any trouble finding things to do."

A loud sigh escaped his throat. "But we're no' tourists, thank the guid Lord."

✦

Maggie saw Rob and Pete off to the shed and, an hour later, waved guidbye to Ellie and Katie, on their way to school. She hugged herself against the chill wind and turned to go inside.

Fern stopped at the gate.

Exactly what Maggie needed—a mornin blether with her best friend.

Smile bright as a newly minted coin, Fern held out a plate of scones. "'Tis a new receipt I tried. I bought one of those oranges they had at the General Store. It cost more than it should, but these scones taste grand with the orange juice and a wee bit of rind."

Maggie hurried her in and set the teakettle on.

"Where are the bairns?" Fern asked.

"You'll never believe this, but they're still asleep. Rob tired them all out with a game of chase last night. Even Beth suckled early and went right back to sleep."

"It must be a treat having him home at a normal time." Fern got out two plates for the scones and a tin of butter.

"Och, 'tis wonderful." The kettle whistled and Maggie poured the boiling water over the tea leaves. "How does Katie like school so far?"

"She's in heaven. She's first in her class in maths and reading."

"That lass will go far." Maggie brought the teapot to the table and covered it with a cosy.

They sat, smiling at one another.

Maggie reached for Fern's hand. "I'm thinking there's more than the scones brought you over. Tell me. You're smiling so hard your face is about to crack"

"Och, I could never fool you."

"Well?"

Unbelievably, Fern's smile widened. "I'm biggen."

Maggie leaped up and threw her arms around Fern. "Biggen! How far along?"

"Twa months. John confirmed it yesterday afternoon."

"And you're just getting around to telling me?"

"There was a wee something that had to come first—like telling Den."

What a blessing. "Well? What did he say?"

"He turned red as a Yule ribbon, then he burst out laughing. Said Rob wasn't the only real man on Innis Fell."

"He never."

"He did. Then he began to roup like a bairnie. I don't know what startled me more, his laughing or his rouping."

"So he's happy."

"On top o' the world. The last thing he asked me this mornin before he went to work was if it was all right to tell Rob."

"And you said ...?"

"Of course. That's why I rushed right over to tell you."

Maggie choked on a giggle. "I'm thinking Den might be having a bit of a tickler with Rob's reaction to his bragging."

"What do you mean?"

The giggle emerged as a laugh. "Och, Fern, I'm biggen and twa months along too."

Fern's face froze. Then she too laughed. "How Den's going to hate that! He thought he'd finally have one over on Rob." She clasped Maggie's hand. "Just think, we're biggen at the same time."

Chapter Seven

John surprised Rob with a telephone call late one afternoon. "Sorry to interrupt your turn, but I'm thinking you'll be interested that I heard from that anthropologist about those bones found in the Hunter sheep fauld over a year ago."

Rob leaped up from his desk. "Och, let me close the office door, so I can hear you over all the noise." The moment the door was closed, he grabbed up the receiver. "I'm back. So what did the man have to say?"

"About what we expected." John sighed. "The lad was most likely twa years auld and died of a blow to the head, probably from a blunt instrument."

A blunt instrument. So cold sounding, that. Rob sat on a corner of his desk. "Could the man tell how auld the bones were?"

"He said 'twas hard to do. The soil being so peaty should have preserved more of the flesh and any covering over the lad, so 'twas obvious he was verra malnourished and put into the ground naked." Another sigh.

Rob felt sick. "Who … what monster would lay away a bairn like that?"

There was a long silence before John answered. "I don't ken that myself. But the wooden carving of the sheep helped some. He tentatively dated the bones to seventy years in the ground, which would be about right for it to have been Ishbel and Kenneth Hunter's wee lad."

"Who knows what he could have done with his life?"

"Och, he'd never have lived much beyond twa. You've disremembered the lad was grossly malformed."

Rob got to his feet and paced around his desk. "Are they sending the bones back to Innisbraw for a proper burial?"

"That's the main reason he called, lad. The Procurator Fiscal has decided—since 'tis too far in the past to indict anyone for murder—to turn the bones over to the University of Edinburgh Medical School, so students can study them and further their understanding of natal deformities."

"But that's barbar—"

41

"Mebbe to you, but as a doctor, I understand the reasoning. 'Tis a miracle the lad lived as long as he did. A great deal of guid could come from those studies."

Rob took deep breaths, trying to compose himself. "Maggie wanted him to have a real laying away, with everyone on the island there, showing him our luve."

"He's far beyond caring about that now, Rob."

Rob knew he couldn't eat a bite of supper. He called Maggie and told her he would be late that een, that something had come up and she should put the bairns to bed at their usual time. He sent Pete and Den home with an excuse that he had some unfinished tasks to accomplish. Once he cleared his desk of all the paperwork that had accumulated, he sat down, head in hands.

Images of those fragile, twisted bones buried in an auld sheep fauld kept haunting his thoughts. He'd have to tell Den on the mornin. He'd seen the bones too, and was driven to tears at the brutality.

The child had to have been Ishbel and Kenneth Hunter's lad. All the auldtimers on the island said Ishbel had exhibited the same madness that had driven her daughter, Una, to threaten Maggie and try to poison Rob the first time he was on Innisbraw.

He shivered. Such evil was hard to imagine. When he finally arrived home at gone 2200, he found Maggie pacing the floor, near to tears.

"What happened?" She threw herself into his arms. "I knew from your voice something dreadful happened."

Och, when would he learn he couldn't fool her? He pulled her into his arms and sat in his rocker, cradling her on his lap. "'Tis nowt to have you in a such a fash," he soothed before telling her haltingly of his conversation with John.

She laid her head against his chest. "I ken how upset you are, and a part of me is too, but I can see Faither's side. Doctors need training, Rob, and a large part of that is working with ... with the dead."

"I was afraid you'd be upset we can't have a proper burial for the lad." He rubbed his cheek against hers.

"But we can." She looked up at him, eyes shining with unshed tears. "We don't need his bones in a burial box. We can still erect a lairstone and have a going away service. After all, 'tis more for us than for him." Soft fingers caressed his face. "Faither's right, you ken. That wee lad doesn't care what's happening here. He's too busy living in heaven."

⚜

Rob ordered a lairstone from Oban, carefully explaining how he wanted it inscribed:

HERE LIES AN INNISBRAW LAD
KNOWN BY FEW
BUT MOURNED BY ALL

Next summer, when the sun sparkled on the turquoise waters near the shore and a sciffin wind filled the air with the warm-honey scent of heather, there would be a graveside service for the unnamed Innisbraw lad who deserved recognition, if only in the hearts of the folk he had not lived long enough to know and luve.

Chapter Eight

Maggie stirred the porridge and added a bit more milk.

"The rains may be late, but they're making up for it now." Rob turned from the kitchen window and hugged Maggie from behind. "That brose is creamy enough." His breath warmed her ear. "I want a blether with my luve before I leave for the shed."

She laughed and lifted the pot to the warming shelf. "Only a blether?" She turned and snuggled against his chest. "Everybody will soon be up and about. Mebbe a wee bit o' time in your rock—"

His lips devoured hers, stopping her words, her thoughts, time itself, as he carried her to his rocker and cradled her in his lap. She parted the laces of his shirt and buried her cheek in the hollow of his throat. Och, his pulse beat fast as a bodhrán accompanying a jig.

His chuckle tickled her cheek. "You woke in a guid mood. I thought Robbie and Richie would have you in a rare fash with the rain pishing down the past seven days."

She raised her head and smiled at the green flecks dancing in his hazel eyes. "Didn't you see the fine hangars they built on the front entry?"

Those were hangars? "Hangars for what?"

"For their airieplanes, of course." She couldn't resist nipping his freshly shaved chin. "Inside each hangar, you'll find a bomber they Sellotaped together from twigs and bits of cardboard." She giggled. "You should hear them, making growling sounds like engines and swooping down to bomb an enemy target with loud *pow*, *pow* fire raking the entry pavers."

The back of his head hit the rocker. "Och, I never should have answered Robbie's questions about bombing runs. The war's long over."

"But no' his luve of flying. 'Tis innocent play, Rob. You once told me you pretended to fly for years before you ever stepped into a real plane. Besides, the wood scraps you brought home from the shed have kept them oot on the entry all week. The only problem is …"

"Is what?" His gaze bored into hers.

"Is their teasing keeps Annie off the entry." She placed a finger over his lips. "But she's had a grand time playing inside with that doll

I made from one of your socks."

"You're certain they're no' cheating Annie of her time ootside?" Tight fingers gripped her shoulders.

"You ken how she hates the wind and rain."

He rested his chin on her head. "And Beth? Has she had another fit?"

Och, after weeks, this was still a sore subject. At nine months, Beth, no longer content to crawl, had pulled herself up to a stool and pushed it across the floor, leaving scratches. When Rob cut up an old leather belt to cushion the bottoms of the legs, it took more effort to guide the stool over the waxed floor. Beth threw herself down on her belly, kicking and screaming.

Without a word, Rob picked her up and swatted her hippen-padded bottom.

Maggie didn't know who looked more surprised—Beth or Rob. But after he'd soothed away the lass's tears and shown her where to place her fingers for the most momentum, Beth was back to her sunny-natured self. It was too bad Rob couldn't forget so quickly.

"No more fits. And you have to stop feeling guilty for—"

Robbie's bedroom door burst open. He and Richie raced into the living room, hair standing on end, cheeks rosy from sleep. "We're hungry!" Robbie shouted, hands on hips. "We want our brose."

Rob stiffened.

Maggie shook her head and crooked a finger at the lads. "Come you here."

They shuffled to her side, Richie's eyes downcast, Robbie's defiant.

She turned to Richie and gentled her voice. "Why aren't you upstairs in your mither's bed?"

"I ... I ..."

"He had a bad dream," Robbie blurted.

Again, Rob stiffened.

Maggie patted Rob's arm and took hold of Robbie's shoulder. "Was it you I was talking to, lad?"

"But he didn't do anything wrong!" The lad's lower lip jutted out.

"Robert John Savage, haud yer wheesht."

Rob's harsh whisper froze both lads.

Without another word, Rob rose, seated Maggie in his rocker, grabbed his thermos and waxed jacket, and strode out the front door.

Maggie watched him leave, her heart burdened. It wasn't the lads' sleeping together that had Rob fashed, but Robbie's lack of a "guid mornin," his rude demand for brose, and not allowing Richie to finish his reply. What a dreadful start to the day.

🙢🙠

Eyes half-closed against the rain pelting his face, Rob trotted down the path toward the shed. He'd acted the fool—no, worse, like a short-tempered, controlling headmaster of a school for wayward lads. The aulder Robbie got, the less patience Rob had with his son.

Of course the lad wasn't perfect. Who was? But why couldn't Rob take a lesson from Maggie and point out rude behavior without blowing up? *Please help me, Faither. I need guidance.*

Almost to Elspeth's cottage. A glance at his watch assured there was enough time for a blether with his dearest friend—if she was up and about this early.

She sat on her front entry, knitted hap over her shoulders, a magnifying glass and open Bible in her lap. "Guid mornin, lad," she called as he mounted the stairs. "I hoped you'd stop for a few words with a gone auld woman."

"No' gone yet, thank the Lord. You're up early." He kissed her chilled cheek, shook rain from his waxed jacket, and plonked onto the other rocker.

"'Tis your fault, you ken." She grasped his hand and patted it. "Och, don't look so guilty. I'm having you on." Patting his hand again, she said, "I had a most disturbing dream—though I disremember it. I only know it concerned you and it brought me oot here to pray and seek guidance from God's Word."

He pressed a fingertip over the prominent veins mapping the back of her hand. "How do you do it, Elspeth? Always ken when I need help?"

"I don't do owt. 'Tis our Heavenly Faither who plants a need in my heart and mind." She leaned forward and poked his arm. "Now, oot with it. Something has dimmed the light in your eyes."

And put a cramp in his belly. "'Tis Robbie and …" He leaped up and began pacing. "And me. I don't have the patience I need, especially when he's rude to Maggie." He stabbed trembling fingers through his hair. "He runs roughshod over everybody and everything in his way, giving no thought to what he's saying or doing."

She smiled.

He stopped mid-stride. "Did I say something amusing?"

"It isn't what you said now that made me smile, but what I remember you saying to me many years ago."

"And that was?"

She patted his rocker. "You make me dizzy with all that walking. Sit you down, so the mornin breeze doesn't swallow your words."

A shiver of fear drove him to his rocker. Och, she was so involved with island life, so much a part of his heart, he often forgot she was a hundred and five. Or did he push it from his mind, knowing she wouldn't—couldn't—be with them much longer? The cramp sent a knife slicing into his belly. He should never have burdened her with his shortcomings.

His fear intensified when she laid her head back and closed her eyes. What was he thinking, upsetting her like this?

"You once asked me why you had to be so impatient, always wanting everything done now, no' willing to wait for the time to be right." Her eyes opened and pinned him with a stern gaze. "Do you remember what I told you?"

"No." He cleared his clogged throat. "No' exactly."

"I said that this island needed a doer, no' a dreamer. That what you call impatience is a blessing, for it drives you to take action, no' just sit around and think and talk about what needs to be done." That smile again. "I'm thinking your Robbie is much like you. I've seen myself how he runs when others walk, fidgets when others are content to sit, climbs an obstacle instead of going around—and Maggie's oft told me how hard it is for him to wait for anything." The smile turned to a soft laugh. "Sound familiar, Rob Savage?"

It couldn't be true. Robbie had Maggie's black hair and blue eyes. He also had her easy way with words. Shouldn't he have her soft, gentle nature too?

"Has one of the 'wee people' stolen your tongue?"

"I don't want him to be like me."

She poked him again. "We can't order our children the way we do merchandise or machines, for God knew we would soon make a midden of things. They come from the womb already formed, with an auld sin nature, true, but also with that unique combination of mither and faither, auldmither and auldfaither. 'Tis what makes every human different." Her gnarled fingers tapped his knee. "I ken you're so busy 'tis difficult, but spend more time with Robbie. Open your eyes and see your lad as he truly is, no' as you want him to be. Then treat him the way you wanted to be treated when you were growing up—as a valuable, positive gift to the world."

⚜

Elspeth's words resonated in his mind all day. *"See your lad as he truly is, no' as you want him to be."* No' an easy thing, that. But if he

47

heeded her admonition to spend more time with Robbie, it could be a beginning. Rob ignored the papers strewn across his desk and left the shed early, again determined to make up for all the times he'd allowed work to take him from his first, God-mandated priority—his family.

Black clouds, biggen with another cloudburst, settled over the top of Ben Innis, but here by the eastern shore, heavy grey skies laboured in vain to bring forth a single raindrop. Bent stalks of girse released their wet burdens which joined together to form a gushing torrent alongside the path.

Would the lads be inside, driving Maggie and Ellie crazy with their boisterous antics? He'd planned to spend time alone with Robbie. Wishful thinking, that. Richie followed Robbie around like a shadow at the gloaming, dogging his heels, mimicking every gesture.

As Rob released the latch on the gate, Robbie and Richie raced across the entry, arms raised high, hands clutching crude but recognizable airieplanes.

Richie's hand swooped low as he made a loud, explosive noise with his mouth. "Take that, you dirty Krauts!"

Rob winced. Where did that language come from? No' from him. The lads must have another source of information about bombing strikes.

Den, mebbe?

Rob slowed his steps on the stone-flagged walk.

Robbie looped his plane, dove, and climbed, shouting *"Pow, pow, pow.* How do you like the taste of my guns?" Definitely no' from Rob, either.

Sudden silence. A pair of frozen hands and wide eyes greeted Rob's arrival.

"Giving the Jerries a hard time, are you?" Rob smiled.

Maggie was surely right, this was innocent fun. The lads had no way of knowing what a bombing strike was really like—the dense smoke, raging fires, bodies blown into bloody pieces—the smouldering destruction left in its wake.

He ruffled Robbie's hair and took the taped twigs from his hand. "You can't do a loop with a B-17. Too much weight."

"That's no' a bomber," Robbie crowed. "'Tis a P-47 fighter, like you flew—drove—in the war."

Rob took the plane Richie offered and sat down on the steps, signaling the lads to join him. He examined each plane carefully, praising their design and construction. "You've both done a guid turn with these." He nodded to Robbie. "I see yours is sma'er, and you've even widened the nose, like a P-47. But I never told you I drove P-47s."

Robbie's eyes sparked with excitement. "Uncle Den said you were an ace twa times. You shot down twenty Kraut airieplanes."

It was Den, all right. He always called the Germans "Krauts." Rob'd have to talk to his partner about that. These lads were too young to use derogatory labels, too young to understand war. Too naïve to realize that pilots—many only eleven or twelve years aulder than they—went down with each enemy aircraft. He blotted out the mind-picture of a young German pilot dancing like a puppet on strings when Rob's bullets tore apart his Messerschmitt Bf 109.

Richie grabbed Rob's sleeve. "And Robbie said you bombed a million targets."

"A million, is it?"

Robbie smirked and punched Richie's shoulder.

Unwilling to ruin their fun, Rob searched his memory for a sortie he could share. "Sit you still for a bit, and I'll tell you about swooping down on a Jerry munitions train so I could strafe it before it reached a tunnel." He handed the lads their airieplanes. "Then 'tis time for supper."

⚓

Maggie marveled at their fun-filled supper and how relaxed Rob appeared. She'd have to question him the moment the bairns were abed. He supervised the lads' shower, no' once nattering about them using all the hot water in the boiler and even showed them how to use their damp towels to mop up the floor, so they wouldn't dirty clean ones.

Something was afoot. But what?

Her curiosity grew when he bundled all the bairns in a hap on the rug in front of the fireplace. He hadn't told them a story in weeks. Beth always raised such a fuss to be included and interrupted by babbling so loud he'd lost patience.

Tonight, clad in their nightclothes and with eager, freshly scrubbed faces shining in the flickering firelight, all the bairns—including Beth—listened in rapt silence to a new story about the Selkie, her crofter husband, and their bairns. This time, their faither's tale wove a lesson in learning to haud one's wheest before hurting another with a runaway tongue.

The tale involved a fisherman's son who called his own mither "woman" and wouldn't allow anyone to finish a sentence, and though Rob didn't even look at Robbie, the lad's cheeks flushed red.

Message received, and in such a gentle way.

※

"Tell me what happened the day." Maggie pulled Rob into bed beside her and leaned on one elbow, looking into his face.

He stretched out his long legs and burrowed the back of his head deep into his pillow. "Well, I had a long conversation with a supplier about improving his product if he wants to keep our business, shared coffee from my thermos with Stu while he showed me the new tax laws, looked over—"

She swatted his shoulder. "No' about the shed. You went oot of here this mornin like a roaring lion and came back meek as a wedder lamb. Why?"

That maddening eyebrow arched. "I don't roar."

She reached beneath the covers and pinched his thigh. "Och, you think because 'tis only a loud whisper you don't roar?"

No reply, only a lazy smile, with bright green flecks swimming in his hazel eyes.

※

Maggie deserved to know about his visit with Elspeth, but how could he put it into words? To stall for time, he voiced something he'd meant to ask for a long time. "Why don't you sing like you used to?"

"Sing? What makes you ask that?"

"I heard Annie singing in the bath this een. She has an amazing voice for a lass her age. It reminded me how you don't sing aloud as often as you used to, though you're always humming as you work."

"I am? I didn't know."

"Well, don't stop. I luve to hear it."

Minutes passed. S*pit it oot, Savage. She'll no' think less of you.* Mebbe if he eased into it … "Do you think Robbie's like me?"

Her shoulder twitched. "Of course. I've told you often enough."

"I guess I didn't want to believe it."

"What do you mean?"

"I … I stopped in at Elspeth's on my way to the shed this mornin." His hand fisted in her hair. "I was so ashamed at how I handled Robbie's being rude, but I made myself own up to her."

"And?"

He twisted a piece of her hair around his finger. "She said I should spend more time with Robbie. Learn to really know how special he is, to accept him the way God made him, no' try to change him into what I want."

"Bless Elspeth and her wisdom."

50

"'Twill take time, but I want to give my son the faither I never had and always longed for." He traced the arch of her eyebrow with a fingertip. "Will you help me when I falter, Maggie?"

"Anytime, my luve. Though I'm thinking you'll do fine on your own."

Later, Maggie spooned against his back, her silken flesh against his, her soft breath whispering dreams into his ear. He slipped into sleep.

⚜

Rob adjusted his schedule so he could be home at 1730 every een, allowing half an hour to spend with Robbie and Richie before supper. They traversed the burn at the bottom of the brae, the lads open-mouthed at how quickly the fall rains had covered the rocks. They played ball. They explored the strand below the fell, gathering pebbles, shells, and bits of polished glass, laughing when a sneaker wave wet them to the knees.

Best of all were the times they sat on the entry steps, sharing ideas and dreams. All Robbie talked about was reaching the magical age of six when Rob would take him up in the floatplane. Amazing how a lad could remember a promise made when he was only a bairn of three.

Robbie's behavior improved immediately, as though he had been on a frantic search for something—even negative—to attract his faither's attention. Now he had it.

Rob finally realized that, though he had been raised in an orphanage with no faither to set an example, someday—with God's and Maggie's help—he could be the faither his son deserved.

Chapter Nine

Pete paced the dock. A brisk, cold wind blasted his chapped cheeks and penetrated his light jacket, bringing hens-flesh. What was taking that ferry so long to drop the boarding planks? He raised a hand to shade his eyes from a weak sun.

No sign of Caroline on deck.

Where was she?

A queue of tourists waited nearby to board, complaining how rain the past fortnight had forced them to stay indoors and play board or card games or gather at the howff for a pint of ale and a little dancing. What did they expect, taking a vacation—och, holiday—so late in the year?

The tannoy crackled, then blared. "This is your captain. You folk wanting to board, please wait until our passenger has debarked."

The foot-passenger planks dropped into place.

A door opened.

Caroline rushed across the deck and down the planks, gripping the ropes with one hand and dragging a large piece of luggage with the other. Her heavy winter coat billowed in the wind and strands of hair whipped across her face. Och, she looked exhausted.

He rushed forward and wrapped her in his arms, showering her face with kisses. "Welcome home, luve," he said, voice trembling with emotion. Rob had been right. He never should have burdened her with such a journey.

"I'm home, Pete. I'm finally home." She laughed and grabbed the sides of his face, drawing him closer.

Her husky whisper and sparkling eyes weakened his knees. His lips sought and moved over hers, weeks of loneliness cast aside by her sweet, familiar taste. Aye, his Caroline was home. Now he'd something to look forward to after long hours of labour.

She pulled away and stood back, head cocked, index finger stabbing the air. "I'll have you know, Peter Samuel Hastings, that's the last time you'll talk me into selling a house, travel trailer, two automobiles, furniture we can't use here, and a shed full of outdoor lawn—"

The deep bellow of the ferry's whistle interrupted her tirade.

She rested her head on Pete's chest, closing her eyes. "I apologize. My head pounds, my muscles ache, and I feel like I haven't slept for days."

Pete kissed her hair. "It's time to be getting up the fell. You need a guid long rest."

"Guid rest?" Her head popped up. "What's this you're talking?"

"Scots, lass, pure and simple."

She stiffened. "I knew you'd get ahead of me, Pete Hastings."

"Och, luve, I'm sorry. You've such a guid ear, you'll catch up with me in no time."

"I'd better."

Rob joined them on the dock. "He's been dealing with the locals. He has to speak some Scots, or they don't understand him."

A weak smile tilted her lips. Tears misted her eyes. "I know that. I've never been so tired. I felt like grousing."

"'Tis allowed as long as you brought your appetite. Maggie's getting a joint ready for the oven."

"Joint?"

"Roast. A beef roast."

"I wondered where she was." Caroline squeezed Pete's hand. "Let's go. My mouth's watering thinking about Maggie's cooking."

As they walked up the hill, Caroline explained that she had put the furniture in storage until their house neared completion. "It'll take a few weeks to come when we send for the lot, but it seemed like the right solution. A neighbor warned me how strict rationing is here, so I had Sears Roebuck take our refrigerator and washing machine off to be fitted with the proper plugs, but we'll have to replace all of our small appliances."

Pete hugged her, hoping a wee nap would revive her. "Honey, you did it exactly right. I hope you brought some of my work class—clothes. I'm freezing my backside wearing what we packed for summer."

"They're taking several boxes off the ferry now. That nice Captain MacNamara said he'd have his crew take them to the boatshed for me."

"Guid. Did you pack my A-2 jacket in one of those boxes?"

"What do you think?" Caroline tapped Rob's sleeve. "You old Air Forces men are all alike. Can't live without your precious leather bomber jackets."

⚓

Pete and Caroline retired to their bedroom early that een, and Calum, who had returned from a fishing trip, picked Ellie up for an een of dancing at the howff.

At last, with all the bairns tucked in for the night, Maggie fixed coffee and tea and brought them into the living room.

"I'll be back in a tick." Rob kissed her cheek.

"Where are you going?"

"Only oot to the gate."

"Did you leave it open, then?"

"No, I didn't leave it open. I'll be right back." He slipped out the front door and quickly closed it.

Quelling an impulse to peer out the kitchen window, she stood still, worrying her lower lip.

He was back in under a minute, peeking around the door. "Close your eyes."

"What are you up to?"

"Close your eyes. My arm's starting to cramp."

She closed her eyes.

His footsteps kissed the floor, and the door latched. "Don't keek, lass."

"It isn't my birthday. What have you done?"

"You'll see in a minute. Don't keek."

"I feel like an eejit."

"Almost ready."

His hands gripped her arms and a faint, oddly-familiar scratching sound filled the room. "You can have a keek now."

The music startled her as she opened her eyes. The radiogram John had given them during the war stood on the dining room table, a record spinning on its top. "The Nearness of You," played by Glenn Miller and His Orchestra. Beside it sat two tall stacks of records.

Rob kicked off his shoes, and she toed out of hers. She melted into his arms, tears stinging her eyes. He clasped her hand tightly and tucked it beneath his left arm. She rested her cheek against his chest as they danced, the song throbbing around them, transporting her back over seven years to the night they met.

Maggie pictured her Rob as she had first seen him, so very tall and braw in his dark-green uniform and a nervous smile on his lips.

Was he seeing her in her RAF grey-blue wool, black hair pulled off the collar into a bun? If only she'd known the future when they'd met. Perhaps she wouldn't have been so shy.

Tears ran unchecked down her face. When she glanced up, his eyes were so filled with luve, she pressed against him, heart beating wildly.

He buried his face in her hair. "'Tis bonnie you are, lass." The same words he'd whispered so long ago.

She raised her face and stood on tiptoe, his kiss tender as the song ended. "Och, luve. Thank ye."

He picked her up and cradled her close. "I luve you, Maggie. Forever and ever and ever."

⁂

Maggie thumbed through the stack of records early the next morning. Rob had ordered dozens: children's songs and stories, hymns, one new Spike Jones record, some jazz by Stan Kenton Orchestra, and a near-complete collection of Glenn Miller's music. She held up a record. "Let's have a pairty. We'll invite everybody on Innis Fell."

"As long as it isn't too much work for you."

"I'll get all the women to help. You men can move the furniture, and we'll dance all night."

"So a wee bit of American culture rubbed off on you after all." A chuckle deepened his dimples. "The time you spent at Edenoaks is paying off."

"Och, there's only one piece of music I truly luve, but I don't want to share it."

"We won't. That's our song, Maggie, only ours, for when we're alone."

His kiss left her breathless.

⁂

The following Saturday night, Rob turned on all the lights in the house. "Like a lighthouse beaming the way up the fell," he told Maggie. The MacPhee, MacDonald, and Ferguson families kept all the bairns on the fell overnight—except Beth and the Proctors' wee Amy, who were too young. Refreshments were light and simple.

Caroline unpacked two large bags of potato chips from the boxes on the ferry. "I'm a salt maniac," she said with a guilty smile

Since he was one of Rob's partners, Graham was also invited, along with Rinait. She came laden with a basket of her usual crème cookies. Maggie, Fern, and Jill baked several kinds of scones and plates of shortbread. There was tea, coffee, lemon skoosh, and Irn Bru.

They took their refreshments late and listened to the crazy antics of the Spike Jones Orchestra before going back to their favourites. Caroline and Pete gave a demonstration of the boogie-woogie, sending the watchers into spasms of laughter—especially Rob, who wished he'd paid more attention to Den's dance lessons. Den refused to allow Fern to dance to "A String of Pearls" because of her pregnancy, so Rob took it off the stack for another time.

It was almost dawn when the last guest left.

Rob could not remember ever staying up so late for a party. "My legs feel like rubber," he groaned.

Maggie yawned. "We're going to hate ourselves the day."

"I know I am, especially when the bairns want to roughhouse."

She pulled on her nightgown. "Och, what have we done?"

"We've had a daffin time. The lads at the Point would never believe it. They called me '2200 Savage' because I never made it past that time, and I was over fifteen years younger then."

They climbed into bed. "It was daffin." Maggie yawned again. "But I'm still going to hate myself when I have to get up in an hour to suckle Beth."

Chapter Ten

Calum and Ellie's wedding was the talk of the island. The weavers who were not part of the Cottage Weavers had been busy for months weaving tartans to be made into kilts, long skirts, and sashes. Maggie wove the plaid cloth for Ellie's wedding skirt and sash. Having no clan of her own, Ellie chose the red, green, and blue NicAllister plaid in honor of Elspeth.

The womenfolk decorated the kirk sanctuary with greenery, ribbons, and dozens of candles. The fancy altar cloth was taken out of storage, washed, starched, and ironed. The pews were polished and the rugs taken out and beaten. Hugh even arranged for an expert to come from Oban to tune the piano and pump organ.

*

Late on the morning of the wedding, Maggie sent the men outside to play with the bairns while she and Caroline helped Ellie get ready. Thankfully it wasn't raining, so Rob and Pete took the bairns down to the shore to scour for treasures that might have washed in on high tide the night before.

Caroline arranged Ellie's dark-blonde hair into curls cascading to her shoulders from high atop her head. After weaving a crown of shimmering green ribbons through the top curls, Caroline stood back. "There. Go have a keek. If you don't like it, we'll do something else."

Ellie's eyes sparkled with tears when she returned from the bathing room. "I look like a fairy princess. 'Tis perfect."

Maggie helped her dress. "Och, to have a waist so small again would be a dream."

"Your waist's sma'er than mine when you're no' biggen."

"I've disremembered," Maggie said with a rueful smile. "I'm always biggen."

*

The kirk filled rapidly with folk wanting a good seat. Maggie, John, and the bairns sat in the front row, so Rob could easily join them after he finished his part in the ceremony.

"This is a blessed day," John said to Maggie, mopping his eyes with his handkerchief. "I never thought my lad would settle down so

57

young, or choose such a perfect lass."

"They seem made for one another." Maggie wiped her own eyes

Sheila MacNab played the auld hymn "Blest Be the Tie that Binds" on the pump organ. Maggie eyed Beth. She was sat on her auldfaither's lap, playing with his watch chain. Annie gazed around, face rapt, as though mesmerized by all the decorations and the music. Even Robbie and Richie seemed to realize the importance of the occasion, for they sat quietly, hands in laps, grinning impishly at one another.

Calum and Tormad stepped out onto the dais, followed by Hugh.

Maggie fought back tears as she looked at her baby brother. He was a man now, there was no mistaking that. Only a couple of centimetres shorter than Rob, with broad shoulders and muscled arms. His blue eyes glistened with tears, but he didn't appear nervous.

Hugh nodded to Sheila, who moved to the piano to join Neil, who held his violin at the ready. As the music changed, the back door of the sanctuary opened. All the folk stood and turned, waiting for a glimpse of the bride.

Ellie stepped onto the aisle runner, her hand over Rob's arm. The green in her long plaid skirt caught the glitter of the satin ribbons in her hair. Tears shimmered in her grey eyes as they walked slowly down the aisle toward Calum.

Rob's lips curved into a gentle smile.

When they reached the front of the sanctuary, Calum stepped down and offered his arm.

Rob stood quietly as the two young people climbed the steps to the altar. When asked who gave this lass in marriage, his voice trembled with emotion. "My Maggie and I do."

***

Rob battled tumultuous emotions as the ceremony progressed. Visions of Rich flitted through his mind—brief snapshots of a life ended much too soon: the tip of a tongue showing between pursed lips as Rich aimed a dart in the pub; his cocky grin when it hit the bull's-eye. Tears blurred Rob's vision when he pictured their last flight and the thumbs-up Rich gave as he climbed into the *Liberty Belle*. Though a part of Rob wished he'd been able to say guidbye, he thanked God he'd never seen Rich's body. Now he could remember, unencumbered by gut-wrenching, bloody memories, the guid-natured, blond-headed, grey-eyed lad with the runaway cowlick and crooked grin.

Rob brought his attention back to the bride and groom.

Calum slipped a gold band on Ellie's finger. When it was Ellie's turn, she couldn't fit the ring over Calum's knuckle. He pushed it on for her, eyes so filled with luve, Rob fought to control tears.

Hugh's elfin smile was in place as he pronounced the couple husband and wife. "Calum, you may kiss your lass."

Calum took Ellie into his arms as gently as one might handle a wee bairnie. When their long kiss ended, they turned and made their way down the aisle behind their piper, brilliant smiles and tear-filled eyes revealing their luve.

⚜

The ceilidh was a joyous affair, the handsel table piled high with gifts for the new home the newlyweds would occupy for the first time the night. Calum and Ellie danced the Shamit Reel, then Rob whirled Ellie around the floor in an open bob.

"I'm so happy for you," he said, bending over her, "and Rich would be too."

"Aye." Tears shone in her eyes. "I know he'd approve of Calum."

"Welcome to our family." Rob kissed her cheek.

"I can't thank you and Maggie enough for taking me in and treating Richie and me like family from the verra first day."

Though his insides squirmed at the compliment, he smiled broadly and said, "You're verra welcome, lass. It's been our joy and pleasure."

⚜

Rob agreed that Robbie should share his bed with Richie that night, so the newlyweds could have one night alone in their new home. Maggie was afraid the lads would be up most of the night playing and talking, but they were so spent from the festivities they fell asleep almost immediately.

Beth was not so easily satisfied. When they arrived home, she was getting her second wind and wanted attention. Rather than chance waking Annie, Rob took Beth from her cradle and sat in his rocker with her in his lap.

She snuggled down in his arms and jabbered, patting his hand and arm and smiling, drool wetting her chin. He rocked her, savoring the feel of her sturdy, wee body against his until she finally dropped off to sleep. Smile soft, he looked down at his youngest lass with her independent nature.

Maggie stirred and sat up when Rob climbed into bed. "Is she asleep, then?"

59

"All it took was a little rocking."

"Thank ye, luve."

He cuddled close. "Our Beth's going to be different, but she has a bonnie spirit. I can see her becoming a braw woman."

"Aye. She's no' like our Annie, but we can't expect her to be. And she has a tender heart 'neath all that activity. She's like a combination of the both of us."

He muffled a yawn with his palm. "What do you mean?"

"Och, she's no' as brave as she pretends, and she's so impatient."

He kissed the back of her neck. "So you're no' brave? You have me fooled, then. I've watched you birth three bairnies with barely a whimper."

"I notice you didn't mention the impatient part."

He laughed. "Och, we know where she gets that. I plead guilty."

"Rob?"

"Hmm?"

"I've told you so many times, but you never seem to understand how I treasure your impatience."

"Treasure it? 'Tis the bane of my existence."

"It shouldn't be. 'Tis what compels you to get things done. Think of the way Innisbraw was when you first came. It was your impatience that changed it, that and your drive to help folk. I hope our bairns have that same drive. If they do, our family—indeed our entire island—will be blessed by their lives."

"You give me too much credit, lass. Our folk were just looking for a nudge in the right direction."

"Rob."

"Mm?"

"You're impossible."

"I am, am I?"

"You are that."

Chapter Eleven

April 1949

The screech of chair legs being pushed across his office floor set Rob's teeth on edge. He was gleg as a gled, spent, and shameful at missing his pre-supper time with Robbie. Time to get this meeting over with. He tapped the folder on his desk. "This report complete?"

Den slouched deeper into the chair, propped his heels on Rob's desk, and laid his head back, eyes closed. "It's there, isn't it?"

The words could have been construed as argumentative, but the lazy, guid-natured tone in which they were delivered softened the sting.

Den yawned and toyed with his hair.

Rob shook his head, a smile playing with his lips. "What's the matter? No' sleeping well?"

One blue eye opened. "Same as you, I suppose. Or doesn't Maggie get up on her hands and knees to turn over in bed, taking all the bedquilts with her?" Red hair standing up in clownish spikes, Den sat up straight and knuckled his eyes. "I can't wait till our bairnie's birthed. Mebbe then I can catch a full night's sleep."

"A full night's …?" Throwing back his head, Rob let out a snort, then a laugh roared from his belly. How could anybody with even a smitch of common sense expect a full night's sleep with a new bairnie in the same room? He stifled another laugh, wiped tears from his eyes, and surveyed his partner's surprised expression.

Should Rob set him straight?

Och, Den would never believe it. If it involved his life with Fern, when it came to preconceived, idyllic scenarios, Den Anderson was the champion. A perfect bairnie meant just that: no reeky hippens, no frustrated attempts at learning how to suckle, no bouts of lusty rouping.

Let him find out the hard way.

The feet left his desk and clomped onto the floor. "I say something humoursome?" No' a guid-natured remark this time.

If Rob hoped to get home before the turn o' the night, he had to get the conversation back on track. "You got me. Maggie steals the

61

bedquilts every night." He picked up the folder and tapped it on his desktop. "No time to go over it item by item. How'd the *Maggie*'s shouts go the first quarter? Any problems we need to address?"

The glint of suspicion left Den's steady gaze. "Better than expected, what with all the gales this winter. Other than Artair's and Duncan's broken bones during that shout at the southern skerries, the crew fared well—and we'll be back to full strength in another week. With the weather improving, the next quarter should be even better." His gaze dropped to his clenched hands. "Wish I could say the same about my personal life. Fern's no' taking staying home verra well."

So everything wasn't perfect in the Anderson household? "She's biggen. Maggie's emotions go up and down like a heaving sea the farther along she gets."

"Other than worrying about the shouts, 'tisn't her emotions I'm worried about." Den sat up straight. "I'm thinking Fern's jealous of that new nurse John hired to take her place."

"Jealous? That doesn't sound like Fern."

"Och, mebbe I misspoke. No' jealous, more like determined to show she can outwork anybody on the island, biggen or no'. She's even started ironing my socks, for Pete's sake."

"At least she helps at the infirmary when there's a difficult shout. Maggie's fit to be tied about no' being allowed at the infirmary unless 'tis a visit with a sick friend." A sudden grin lit Rob's face. "Fern irons your socks?"

Leaping to his feet, Den reached for his jacket. "We through here? I promised to help Katie with her maths."

They walked silently up the path to the fell, side by side.

Rob glanced at his watch. No' as late as he'd expected. He'd eat, help Maggie redd the kitchen, then spend some time with Robbie— mebbe tell him another story about a P-47 sortie.

Pete kept a tight, disciplined schedule for the building projects. All the island folk made it clear that the work on the academy came first, but he had a small crew of craftsmen working every day on cottage renovations. Despite how difficult it was to find time to do the interior work on his own home, it was finally to the stage of last-minute tweaks, and a guid thing, that. Caroline was becoming impatient.

"We've got to get out of here," she told Pete over and over. "Rob and Maggie deserve to have their home to themselves. With Beth walking now, we're even more in the way."

The Hastings' house was finished the first week of May, and Maggie, Rob, and their bairns had their home to themselves for the first time in over twa years. Maggie's pale, drawn face stopped Rob from suggesting a celebration. Instead, he stopped by the infirmary to see John. "Can you look Maggie over? I've never seen her like this."

"Has she had any contractions?"

"Och, no. With Maggie, the first contraction is the beginning of a rapid birthing."

"Well, her due date is less than a week away. Send her over and I'll have another keek. 'Tis better to err on the side of caution."

Maggie didn't argue with Rob, which frightened him even more as he returned to work.

"This wee one is in a breech position, but there's nowt we can do about it." Her faither patted her shoulder. "I'd like you to stay here until you deliver, but I know you won't."

"I can't, Faither. There's too much to do at home."

"You'll have to let things slide. I'm telling you in no uncertain terms to take it easy. No heavy lifting, no mopping or sweeping, and let Rob bathe the bairns. I don't want you bending over the bathing tub."

"I've never had to be this careful before."

"You've never had a possible breech birth before. I mean it, lass, either you do as I say or I'll have Rob bring your things over here right now and you'll stay until you give birth."

She sighed and lumbered to her feet. "All right, I'll follow your orders."

When Rob came home early that night, she ignored her discomfort and told him exactly what her faither had said.

"You mean the bairnie may no' be born head first?"

"Aye. Unless it turns, it will be a breech birth. Buttocks first."

He grabbed her. "Och, luve, I can't even think of that happening. It would be agonizing for you."

"And dangerous for us both."

"You're scaring me to death." He held her by the shoulders and looked into her eyes. "I want you in the infirmary, with your faither at your side for this birthing."

"But you'll be there with me?"

"Of course. Nobody could keep me away." He held her close. "We'll pray the bairnie turns, luve. It could. There's still time."

Though Rob and Maggie prayed many times a day, the bairnie did not turn.

On Sunday, the eighth of May, Rob insisted Maggie go to the infirmary and stay until she gave birth. While the young, new nurse settled Maggie into her bed, Rob pulled John aside and led him to the admitting desk. "Can we fly in a specialist, John? I don't doubt your ability, but ..."

"But I'm no' an obstetrician. I've already contacted Paul Fergus. He's the head of Obstetrics at the Royal Infirmary, and he's willing to come if we need him."

"Then tell him we need him."

"We're in a fankle here, Rob. Maggie's no' in labour yet. The bairnie could still turn, and we can't expect Doctor Fergus to leave his own patients and come here to wait only God knows how long, especially when there's a chance he won't be needed at all."

Rob paced. "What can we do? I'll no' put my Maggie's life in danger. She could die." He regretted his choice of words the moment he spoke.

John looked stricken.

"I'm sorry. I feel so helpless."

"'Tis all right, lad. This isn't similar to my Elizabeth at all. She bled to death from a detached uterus." John drew a ragged breath and put a hand on Rob's shoulder. "I'll tell Doctor Fergus to stand by for our call. I want both you and Den on hand here. Remember, Fern's due any day too. Can someone else fly that airieplane of yours to pick up Doctor Fergus in Edinburgh?"

"Pete can. He got his floatplane license last month."

"Guid. Then keep him close to a phone. Now, go in and see Maggie. Poor lass, she's no' accustomed to being away from hearth and home."

⁂

Jill and Caroline helped with the bairns during the day, Ellie pitched in at night, and Fern came to visit Maggie several times a day. Rob seldom left Maggie's side and never for more than a few minutes. This time it was he who occupied the second bed every night. He rubbed Maggie's back and kissed and caressed her at every opportunity. They slept as close together as they could, fingers laced. He couldn't remember ever feeling so frightened. Even helping Robbie into the world didn't compare. He called Hugh and Elspeth and requested special prayers.

"Don't fash yourself," Elspeth said. "Our Lord is faithful. It will all turn oot the way He deems fit."

Maggie's water broke early in the morning on the eleventh. As always, her contractions began immediately.

Rob telephoned Pete, who had the floatplane in the air within minutes. Rob also called Elspeth. "Pray. Maggie's in labour and the bairnie's still no' turned."

John moved Maggie into the operating room, where he could monitor both her and the fetus closely. "The bairnie's heartbeat is strong," he told Rob, "but 'tis definitely going to be a breech birth."

Rob held Maggie's hand and kept cold cloths on her forehead.

She moaned and thrashed, grinding her teeth as each contraction racked her body.

He gently rubbed her shoulders and arms, then her scalp, biting back tears at her wet hair. "Hang on, lass," he soothed. "'Tis going to be all right." He could scarcely breathe as he watched her suffer through each agonizing contraction.

After another hour of agony, her skin became so sensitive to touch, he could only grip her hand. Perspiration ran off her face as she strained.

He felt as though he was being torn in two. *Help her, Faither. Please, please help her and our bairnie.*

John monitored her progress carefully. He suddenly straightened and threw the sheet back to her knees. "We can't wait for Fergus. She's fully dilated. The bairnie's on its way."

"Can't you give her something for the pain?"

"I'm afraid to. We don't want to distress the bairnie."

Rob closed his eyes and steeled himself. *Oh, Lord, please, please help my Maggie.* He leaned over her. "Courage, luve, 'tis almost over," he choked.

The cords in Maggie's neck stood out as she strained. Her breath came in short gasps.

The nurse hurried into the operating room. "What do you need?"

"A clamp and suction tube. On that tray."

Maggie groaned.

Rob held her hand and glanced at John.

Sweat beaded his forehead above his mask. The doctor closed his eyes and reached both hands beneath the sheet, lips moving.

Praying, he was.

Och, what was happening?

65

Chapter Twelve

Maggie screamed.

Seconds later, John held up a tiny body. He laid the bairnie near Maggie's belly and suctioned its mouth.

Rob froze. Why wasn't the bairnie rouping?

John pressed his fingers on the centre of the tiny, unmoving chest. Once, twice, three times.

No movement. Still as death, that chest was.

Rob held his own breath. They couldn't lose that precious life now. Not after all Maggie had gone through.

Again, John pressed. Once, twice, three times.

A gurgled gasp. A sudden, loud wail filled the room.

Rob held on to the bed to keep from falling. He grabbed Maggie's hand. "'Tis a lad, luve, like you thought. A braw, braw lad."

John pressed a stethoscope against the heaving chest and listened, face pinched.

Again, Rob held his breath. How could John hear a thing over the bairnie's loud roups? *Please, Lord, let him be all right, please.*

A smile tilted John's beard. "Heartbeat's strong, lungs free of rales." His powerful hand clamped Rob's shoulder. "I'd say our Maggie birthed a fighter this time."

Mind in a fog, caught between gut-wrenching fear and euphoria, Rob watched John clamp off the umbilical cord.

The doctor waited for several minutes—was something else wrong with their laddie?—then nodded at the nurse.

She severed the cord, wrapped the bairnie in a towel, and turned to leave.

"He stays here," John barked.

She stopped and looked at him, mouth agape.

"Give him to Rob," he said, gentling his voice.

Rob held out his arms. He took his lad and cradled him to his chest, body shaking from the effort it took not to sob aloud. *Thank Ye, Lord.*

The bairnie's roups quieted and stopped as quickly as they had come.

Rob took deep, calming breaths and studied the tiny face. Their

66

lad looked like Maggie—long black eyelashes below delicate eyebrows. He held him down to Maggie, so she could see their lad.

Her eyes opened a crack. She tried to smile. "How … is he?" she whispered, voice hoarse.

"He's strong and braw, luve," Rob said, "like our Robbie."

Once the afterbirth came, John changed his rubber gloves and reached for the newborn. "Let's have a keek at this lad," he said, taking the bairnie from Rob's arms.

Rob bent over Maggie's side and dabbed her forehead with a cloth. "'Tis over, lass," he whispered. "You can sleep now."

She opened her eyes. "How is he?"

"He's grand. Your faither's checking him over now. He looks like you, Maggie. His hair's so black and there's so much of it, and his eyebrows are like yo—"

"I … want to hold him."

"You can in a minute," John said from across the room. "He really is a braw lad. Nine pounds, twa ounces. His legs have been up around his head for so long, you'll have to work to get him to keep them down, but a week or twa, they'll be where they belong." John carried the bairnie to Maggie's side. "You can feed the lad after we clean him up."

"Can I bathe him?" Rob asked.

"Of course. Nurse, bring in a basin of warm water. This wee lad needs a bath."

Maggie slept while Rob bathed his son. He saw what John meant about the lad's legs. Once they were released from the restrictive towel, they automatically folded up alongside his head.

John smiled. "I guarantee they'll be down where they belong soon. Just pull them down and massage them whenever you change his hippen." He suddenly straightened and looked at his watch. "It's been hours. Is it too late to reach the airfield in Edinburgh and stop Doctor Fergus?"

"You might catch Pete at the airport," Rob said. "He'll refuel before he returns."

"I'll try, then."

When Rob had his son bathed, he pulled the lad's legs down and wrapped him in the towel the nurse held ready. Then he pinned on a hippen and dressed him in a gown. Those legs really did get in the way. He pulled the lad's legs down again and wrapped him very tightly in a blanket, the way Maggie had taught him with the others.

John came back into the room. "Doctor Fergus must no' have been able to get away from the Royal Infirmary immediately. They radioed Pete taxiing down the runway and called him back for me."

Once Maggie bathed and wore a clean gown, she held out her arms. Rob placed their new laddie in her embrace and tucked the blanket around them both. He leaned over and kissed Maggie's pale cheek. "Thank ye, luve, for another braw lad."

"I'll help the nurse wheel Maggie and your bairnie to her bed." John took Rob's arm. "While they're settling in, meet me in the kitchen. I need some strong tea, and you look like a mug of coffee would go down a treat."

The men soon sat, drinks in hand.

Rob sighed with relief. "'Tis time to tell Hugh to ring the kirk bell."

"First, now the moment is gone, I need to tell you how close we came to losing your lad."

Rob almost dropped his mug. "What?"

"The umbilical cord was wrapped around his neck," John explained. "Doctor Fergus warned me to look for that. It would have strangled him. I was able to uncoil it before the lad's head was born."

Rob collapsed back against the chair.

"That bairnie's a real fighter," John said. "He's a Scot, through and through."

"Half-Scot, John, remember?"

"Och, you have to be Scot yourself, you just don't ken it."

Rob looked down at the wee laddie cradled in Maggie's arms. He ran his fingers lightly over the bairnie's tiny cheek. "I agree with John. He is a fighter, luve. I'm thinking we should give him a strong Scots name. How about William Wallace after the grand Scots warrior? We can still call him Will."

"I like that," she said, looking into their son's sleeping face. "William Wallace Savage. It rings true."

John had a very busy day. Shortly after supper Den brought Fern in. Den had been reluctant all along to entrust her care to Alice Ross, the island's midwife, and it had never entered his head to deliver his own bairnie.

"I've never been so scared," he told Rob later that night in the infirmary's lobby while both Fern and Maggie were sleeping. "I was verra worried something would go wrong."

"So how is the lad?"

"Och, he's braw! And wouldn't you know he has red hair. Fern

68

cried when she saw him. At first I thought it was because she was disappointed, but she insisted it was because she was so happy."

"Can you believe this, Den? I know at least a hundred people who served with us back with the 396th who'd be blown away. Major Anderson and Colonel Savage, both faithers."

Den swiped his sleeve beneath his nose. "I'll tell you right now, I'd repeat all my missions and face the entire German Luftwaffe before I'd live through the last few hours again."

⁂

Maggie stayed at the infirmary for three days, though Fern left after two. John wanted to keep Maggie longer, but she was so restless to get home he realized she would recuperate better in her own bed. Before Fern had left, John wheeled her into Maggie's room on her way out, and the two women compared their sons, smiling.

"What are you naming your lad, then?" Maggie asked.

"Och, I wanted to call him after his faither, but Den wouldn't hear of it. So we compromised and named him Matthew Dennis. Den's always liked the name Matt."

"'Tis a bonnie name. I'm thinking wee Matt and wee Will are going to grow up as close as their faithers are."

Fern's smile had widened. "Since they share a birthday, 'tis only fitting."

⁂

Rob hadn't been to the shed for almost a week, but he wouldn't budge out of the house the first few days Maggie was home. Jill and Caroline were a great help with the other bairns, and every night Ellie took Robbie to her house for supper and his shower, returning him at bedtime.

Rob dedicated himself to helping Maggie. She spent a great deal of time lying down since it was still too painful to sit for any length of time. He bathed Will and changed his hippens, massaging his legs religiously. "I think they're better," he told Maggie. "They don't pop up quite as fast."

"They'll be fine," she said. "In a few weeks, he'll look no different than our other bairnies did."

He sat down on the bed and gathered her into his arms. "I'm sorry this was so hard on you." He kissed her forehead. "I'd have taken the pain for myself in a tick if I could."

Her fond smile and soft fingers stroking his cheek humbled him. "Now you have a wee taste of what I feel when you're suffering. I think 'tis easier to bear it yourself than watch someone you luve go through it."

"It is that. A lot easier." He brushed his lips across her forehead. "Do you have any idea how ... how fine you are to me, lass?" he asked, voice breaking.

She smiled. "Aye, luve. You show it every day in so many ways."

Chapter Thirteen

Pete trotted around a group of tourists snapping pictures from the mids of the path. No wonder Rob was walking so fast in the opposite direction. Pete cut in front of their cameras and upped his pace. "Hoy, Rob! Bide a wee an' I'll walk with ye."

Rob whirled around, frowning, fingers tapping his thighs. "Hurry."

Pete caught up and they walked silently side by side. When they reached the post office, they overtook and passed the last tourists—an older couple out for a slow stroll in the salt-laden breeze.

The wind kicked up swirls of sand on the path leading to the MacPhee croft and sent a profusion of wildflowers into a frantic, colourful dance. In the distance, buds of heather were opening on Ben Innis, creating a carpet of brilliant purple against light-green foliage. Pete breathed in its fragrant scent and looked over at Rob.

Staring at the path ahead he was, no' taking in the island's rare beauty.

"You're going to have to find a way to cope, Rob. The ferry's only been coming in a wee bit over a week and you're already in a fash."

Rob's pace slowed. "Och, we're more ready for them this year. The signs warning them off are posted around each croft, and so far it seems to be working." His frown relaxed into a grin. "Maggie talked me into taking the floatplane up for a spin this mornin."

"I know. Saw you take off when I was having coffee on our entry." Pete tapped Rob's elbow. "Fair warning. 'Tis my turn the morra's mornin."

"Better work it oot with Den. He said something about going to Glasgow to check on those diesel engines we ordered."

"Where is Den? You usually walk home together."

"Over at the school, talking to Katie's teacher. The lass is only ending her first year in primary, and her maths are already fashing him."

They shared a companionable chuckle.

"I've got something I want to talk to you about," said Pete.

"A problem?"

"Och, nowt like that. But before I do, how's Shep taking it—having another bairn to guard?"

Rob's shoulders relaxed. "He's a cannie dog. Knows Will is no' his concern till he starts walking." Rob grunted. "A lot like Robbie, now I think on it. That lad's so busy having a guid time with Richie, I'm no' sure he even kens he has a younger brother." He blew out a sigh. "That'll all change the minute he recognizes he has competition. But what has all that to do with owt?"

"I'm thinking about buying one of Angus's dogs. Raise it from a pup."

"Why?"

Heat crept up Pete's face. "Caroline gets lonely with me working so many hours. It'd give her something to talk to, to care for—you know, feeding him, taking him for walks."

"So would a bairn." Rob's hands shot up, palms out. "I know I'm overstepping here, and I don't mean to be insensitive, but a dog, any dog, will never take the place of a bairn in Caroline's heart."

Och, Rob had changed, all right. He'd always called a spade a spade, just never when it concerned somebody else's personal life. But, hard as it was to swallow, he was exactly right. Pete cleared his throat. "Yep. Buying a dog was a lousy idea."

Rob's slow, easy, grin eased Pete's embarrassment. "Wait till she has her own laddie. Every lad needs a dog."

⁂

Rob cuddled Will in his lap.

Kicking the covers, the wee laddie was, legs straight and strong. Best of all, he looked more like Maggie than Robbie had at that age. Och, he had his faither's straight nose and dimples, but his black hair was already starting to curl, and dusky, blue eyes below arched eyebrows gave promise to their eventual colour. Aye, he favored Maggie.

Reaching for Maggie's hand, Rob grinned. "Our Will's already sleeping well, sometimes enough hours to give you a rest." He squeezed her fingers. "'Tis as though he's trying to make up for all the trouble he caused you at his birth. He's no' nearly as demanding as Robbie was."

Her delicate eyebrows arched. "You've disremembered feeding time. Other than Annie, all the others seem to have inherited your appetite."

He pressed a kiss to her knuckles. "Tell me about the new nurse John hired. Fern should be back to work soon. Why didn't he wait for her return? Or at least keep the first one on loan a little longer?"

Maggie smiled and laced her fingers with his. "He wanted somebody more mature. Mary's from the Hielans and speaks both Scots and the Gaelic, and she's so warm and nurturing, the folk have all taken to her already. With her living with Alice Ross at the bottom of the fell, she's only a few minutes away when Faither needs her."

"John planning on keeping this Mary on after Fern goes back to work, then?"

"I'm thinking he is. With Fern a mither now, and suckling at that, he'll need to give her more time off." She planted a kiss on his cheek. "I want to tell you about my glorious afternoon."

He raised an eyebrow.

"All we women on the fell went down to the school, so the bairns could use the playground equipment while the students were in class. Och, you should have seen Beth and Amy. They even went down the slide."

Her tinkling laugh stirred Rob's heart. "So Amy's as much a— och, I forget the Scots word—what we called a *tomboy* in the States."

"'Tis a *gilpie*. And aye, she is. They're only eighteen months, and already doing almost as much as their aulder brothers and sisters." Maggie's gaze softened. "We women talked and laughed the whole time. I've never had so many close friends. 'Tis almost like we're all sisters."

"So Caroline's fitting in well, then?"

"Aye, she's a dear. I wish Pete wanted a bairn. She yearns to adopt one."

A stab of remorse cramped Rob's belly. "He and I talked about that on the way up the path this een. From what he said, I'm thinking he's afraid he might not luve a bairn that doesn't start out as his own."

"Den seems to luve Katie every bit as much as he does his own wee Matt."

"Aye. She's his pride and joy."

Chapter Fourteen

The shout siren wailed its warning on the eleventh of July.

"Keep erecting these skids," Rob shouted to his building crew. "We need to launch that first rescue boat on the morra." He took off at a run. As the volunteer crew rushed aboard the *Maggie*, Rob grabbed the radio and spoke to Control. "What do we have, Artair?"

"'Tis a distress call from a tour boat out of Oban. They hit the rocks off Innisbraw's southwestern shore. 'Tis bad, Commander. There are three adults aboard and nine bairns."

"Nine bairns? Did I hear you right?"

"Aye, nine bairns under the age of eleven."

Rob's stomach lurched. "How auld's the youngest aboard?"

"Six."

Rob counted the crew. They were all aboard and changing into their wet suits. He fired up the *Maggie*'s engines. "What's the condition of the boat?"

"She's caught fast with the incoming tide tearing her apart."

"At least we're only a few minutes oot. What's their radio frequency?"

Artair gave him the frequency and wished him Godspeed.

Rob prayed as they left the harbour and passed Innis Fell. Once there, he turned the helm over to Neil MacLean, his second coxswain, and alerted the crew to the gravity of this rescue as he changed into his wet suit. Then he radioed the floundering boat's skipper and gave him strict instructions not to abandon ship unless his vessel was in danger of sinking. "Do all the bairns have life vests on?"

"Aye, since they boarded. They're taking this well, though some of the younger ones are carrying on a bit. Over."

"We'll be there verra shortly. Get on deck and keep things under control. *Maggie*, oot."

"I'll try. Out."

Rob studied the southern shore of Innisbraw. The early morning breeze was starting to calm, and the incoming tide had already covered most of the large rocks standing off from the shore. He thought he knew which rock the vessel had hit—verra large with jagged points that hid underwater shortly after the tide turned. The skipper must have cut the corner too sharply as he rounded the southwestern-most tip of Innisbraw. At low tide, the shore was littered with the old bones of fishing vessels whose skippers had made the same mistake.

Guide my thoughts and hands, Lord. With all those hidden rocks, 'twill be a dangerous rescue for crew and victims alike.

He sent three of his lads out to ready the transfer sling. "We'll need someone to ride the sling with each bairn. We can't chance bringing them over alone." The rest of the crew, he ordered to the fantail. "Tie your lifelines now and stand by. Don't wait for the *Maggie*'s siren."

Den's usually florid face was pale. Probably from imagining what it would be like if young Katie was caught in a similar situation.

Rob blocked out mind-pictures of his own bairns and strained to see through the windscreen.

The *Maggie* was at full throttle. They'd almost overshot their objective when Rob pulled the siren rope and signaled Neil. The water sprayed over the rescue boat's prow as the second coxswain cut power.

"Get close enough for the transfer, but keep the engines idling, and be ready to reverse power," Rob told him. "The tide will try to pull us in." His heart sank as he ran out of the cabin.

The floundering boat was small and in poor condition. As auld as she was, her planking would not hold up to the relentless pounding of the surf for long.

As soon as they were close enough to be heard, he got on the bullhorn. "We're sending over a sling. Get ready to receive."

A man waved his arms in acknowledgment and cleared the railing of passengers.

Rob gave Christopher MacLean the signal to shoot the line.

When it was aboard the boat, the skipper tied it fast.

Den prodded Rob's arm. "Pray the railing holds. That boat's seen better days."

Alex MacIntosh, the lightest of the crew members, climbed into the sling and clipped on his line.

"Youngest bairns first, Alex!" Rob shouted as the lad went over the side.

Five minutes later a small, sobbing lass was unclipped from the sling and hurried into the cabin by Matthew, the *Maggie*'s chief medic. Alex immediately readied himself for another transfer.

They made five more successful transfers within the next twenty minutes.

Price

"She's no' going to last much longer!" Den shouted over the roar of the surf. "Listen to her timbers scream!"

Rob wiped the sweat off his forehead. "I know. Pray God we get the last three bairns before she goes down."

Chapter Fifteen

Rob ordered the skipper to abandon ship after two more transfers. "Tie the last bairn to an adult!" he shouted through the bullhorn. "Jump as far away from your boat as you can!" He and Den raced to the fantail, where five crewmen stood ready.

Rob and Den slipped into their flippers, pulled up their hoods, and tied their lifelines to the taffrail. "Alex, you, Matthew, and Christopher stay here to pull in our lines," Rob yelled into the wind. "Paddy, you and Stephen take those twa adults in the water by the prow." He tapped Den's arm. "Stay close to me. We'll go for the bairn."

Den nodded.

Rob jumped into and swam through the roiling surf, dodging submerged rocks and fighting to remain on the surface when conflicting waves tried to pull him under, several times looking over his shoulder to see Den's location. Ten minutes later Den was only a few strokes behind him when he reached a woman and the bairn, who were roped together.

Rob grabbed the lad, who struggled to keep his face out of the water. "I'm a rescue swimmer!" he shouted in English. "Put your arms around my neck!"

The bairn reached out. A strong right arm clasped Rob's neck. A shaking left arm, twisted and shorter than the right, tried to follow, failed, and fell limply to his side.

Och, why wasn't he transferred first? Rob raised his hand to signal Den. "Take the woman!" he shouted as he untied the rope holding her and the lad together. "I'll get the lad!"

Den took hold of the woman's life jacket and pulled her to his side.

"Ride my back and keep your right arm around my neck," Rob told the lad. "Hang on. We're going for a swim."

The lad's teeth chittered together as he slid around to Rob's back, his hand clutching the neck of Rob's wet suit.

Rob gave his lifeline three jerks, the signal he was ready to be pulled in, then swam along to lessen the time his victim was exposed to the icy water. Time and again, the incoming waves washed over their heads. *Hope that lad has enough sense to hold his breath.*

When they reached the *Maggie*'s fantail, Matthew waited at the top of the ladder.

Rob lifted the lad off his back and pushed him up as high as he could.

The medic grasped the lad by his life vest and hauled him onto the deck.

Rob clung to the bottom of the ladder, rested his forehead on his hand, and took deep breaths, muscles quivering.

Den appeared at his side, towing the woman.

"Get her aboard fast," Rob panted.

They boosted her up the ladder and into Christopher's waiting arms.

Stephen Ross was soon pulled in with another woman, then Paddy McDonald with the skipper. All of the victims were helped aboard before Rob motioned the crew to proceed him.

Only three rungs on the ladder, but they felt kilometres apart.

When Rob reached the main deck, he hurried into the cabin. "Get us out of here," he called to Neil. He looked around and did a quick triage. The crew were stripping the victims who had been in the water and covering their trembling bodies with blankets. Those bairns who had been transferred earlier cuddled together on the floor. Den, right eyelid twitching, wrapped blankets around each child, hugging the lasses and patting the lads on a shoulder.

Rob tore down his hood, toed off his flippers, and hurried over to Matthew. "How's the lad?" he asked as the engines growled and the *Maggie* moved.

"He swallowed a bit of water, but I couldn't hear any in his lungs—and he's cold—but he will make it."

Rob looked down at the shivering lad.

His lips were blue, face pinched.

"You're verra brave," Rob said with a smile. "I'm proud of ye."

The lad pulled the blankets up over his face.

Rob helped insert saline lines in each of the last four victims. They all shivered uncontrollably but were conscious and coherent.

The aulder woman Den had pulled in stared at the ceiling, face waxen, lips moving. Was she praying?

"We'll need at least six cairts," Rob told Neil. "Be sure to tell Control the crew is all fine, and have John meet us at the dock."

"Aye, Commander."

When the *Maggie* entered the harbour, Rob was dismayed to see the ferry at her dock. Och, he'd forgotten it was Monday mornin. He grabbed the radio. "Colin, this is the *Maggie*. Do you read me?"

"I read you, Rob. Control already alerted me. I've ordered all passengers to remain on our deck until you've transported your victims."

"Bless you. We have twelve souls. We'll need time to transport them."

"Take all the time you need. MacNamara, Oot."

"Thank ye. Oot."

John appeared in the cabin only seconds after they docked. He went immediately to the lad Rob had rescued, gave him a cursory examination, and pronounced him fit to transport.

The lad and the woman Den had rescued were carried out on stretchers to the first cairt, followed by the other woman and the skipper.

Jack Ferguson, Paddy's bartender, and Graham appeared in the doorway. "How can we help?" Jack asked.

"Each of you carry one of the bairns," Rob said. "Though they weren't in the water, they're still fair terrified."

Alex and the other crew members who hadn't been involved in the in-water rescue each carried a child out to a waiting cairt, and Rob radioed Artair at the boatshed, asking him to call in three lads from the skids to help carry the rest of the children.

When the last child had been transported, Den and Rob changed into their clothes. "I want to check on that lad," Rob said. "He's a brave wee soul."

"I noticed he had trouble hanging on to you."

"He's only got one guid arm. There's something wrong with his left." Rob tied his shoes. "Coming?"

"I'll catch you right up."

Rob stopped in the doorway. "I'd best call MacNamara first and tell him he can let his passengers debark."

"I'll do that," Neil said.

"Thank ye. And thank him again for me."

* * *

Rob and Den walked slowly down the pier to the path, muscles still twitching. A sudden tide of tourists pressed against them, and they stood aside as the visitors filed past, talking in raised voices about what they had witnessed.

"On we go, then," Rob said after a few minutes.

The crowds of tourists along the path made the going slow, and it took them over a handful of minutes to reach the infirmary at the top of Innis Fell. When they finally got inside, several island women were holding and comforting children or offering cups of sweetened tea and plates of jelly pieces. Rob spotted Jill and Caroline in the crowd.

They made their way back to the examining rooms. Rob spied the new nurse, Mary MacGruder, taking the pulse of one of the women victims, and waited until she was finished. "Mary, do you know where the young lad is—the one who was in the water?"

"John has him in the second examining room. He's a strange one, that lad."

"What do you mean?"

"He's so shy he won't show his face."

"Mebbe he's afeart."

"He doesn't act it. But he is timid."

"Suppose it's all right if I go in?"

"I don't see why no'. John should be aboot finished by now."

Den caught his arm. "I'm going to check on the woman I pulled oot of the water. She was a little auld to go through something like that. Catch you up later."

"Aye, later." Rob pushed open the door.

John sat on the examining table beside the lad. "Well, here's one of the men from the rescue boat. Maybe you remember seeing him."

One brown eye peered around the corner of a blanket.

Rob reached over and ruffled the lad's hair. "I see you've met Doctor John. How are you feeling, then?"

The eye blinked rapidly. There was no reply.

Rob looked at John. "This is one brave lad. He did exactly what I asked while I was pulling him through the water. Made my job a lot easier."

"So you're the one who saved him. Might have known."

"He really saved himself," Rob said, grinning. "He latched right on for the ride."

"How's the shoulder, Rob?"

The grin evaporated. "Fine, no' a twinge."

"Let me have a keek."

"I mean it, John. See?" Rob flexed his shoulder and extended his left arm. Och, it trembled like a sapling in a blousterin' wind.

"No' a twinge, eh?"

Rob extended the other arm. Guid, it also trembled. "I'm a bit tired. Muscles don't like swimming against an incoming tide."

"If you have any trouble with that arm, I want to know about it immediately."

80

"So you can put it back in that sling?"

"So I can catch it before it gets worse."

Rob glanced at the lad.

Two brown eyes peeked above the blanket.

"See, I'm the one in trouble here. I've got a bad left arm, but if I take care of it, I can do almost everything I want."

The lad blinked and lowered the blanket a little. Was that a hint of a smile?

"What say I get us both something to drink? If your mouth is as dry as mine, you're spitting cotton wadding."

A wee nod?

"I'll have somebody bring it in," John said, getting to his feet. "You stay here."

Rob took John's place on the examining table and extended his hand. "I'm Rob. What's your name?"

The lad's eyes widened.

Rob kept his hand extended. "After all we've been through together, it'll sound a bit daft for me to have to call you 'hey, you,' won't it?"

A real smile.

"Well?"

The lad cleared his throat. "Malcolm." He reached a hand out from beneath the blanket.

Rob had to force himself not to react as they shook hands.

Malcolm. An image of skipper Malcolm MacNeill, lying dead on the cabin deck in front of him, flashed before his eyes. That the skipper had died of a massive heart attack before his trawler was struck by the ferry had not lessened Rob's grief. He'd been a guid friend.

Rob blinked the tears away. "That's a fine name. One of my best friends was named Malcolm."

"Was he a cripple too?"

"Cripple? What do you mean?"

"The other lads call me a cripple."

"Because of your arm?" Rob leaned closer. "I have a bad shoulder and arm too, but I'm no' a cripple."

"It looks the same as your other arm."

Rob smoothed a shock of brown hair back from the lad's forehead. "With clothes on, mebbe, but it's a mess of scars and all torn up on the inside. That's what Doctor John was talking about. I'm no' supposed to do some things."

"Like what?"

81

"Like what ...? Och, like climbing trees, or throwing a ball with my left hand, or even lifting something heavy ... things like that."

"I can't do that, either."

"But there are still a lot of things you can do. Like run, play marbles ..."

The door opened and Caroline Hastings came in, carrying a tray with glasses of water, a mug of milky tea, and one of coffee.

Before the lad could escape beneath his blanket again, Rob took his hand and squeezed it gently. "This is Caroline. She's a friend of mine. Caroline, I'd like you to meet Malcolm. We've been for a swim in the sea."

"Well then, I'm thinking you're both thirsty," Caroline said with a smile. "Swimming's hard work."

Malcolm relaxed. "It was cold too," he whispered.

"It must have been. Would you like some hot sweet tea?"

He nodded, forelock bouncing on his forehead.

Rob caught Caroline's eye and winked. "We two lads are having a bit of a problem with our left arms. Why don't you leave it on that counter over there?"

"So you hurt it again."

"No' really. It's tired from the swim."

"I hope that's all. You've had enough trouble with that shoulder." She put the tray down. "It was nice meeting you, Malcolm," she said before leaving.

They both drank the water down in thirsty gulps, then sat sipping the hot drinks. "So," Rob said, "my left arm's been bothering me about six years now. How about yours?"

Malcolm grimaced. "I don't know. It's always been this way."

"Mine was hurt in an airieplane crash."

The lad's eyes widened. "You know how to fly?"

"I do. Flew in the war."

"My father was a pilot. He was in the R.A.F. He was in a crash." Before Rob could react, the lad went on. "Did the Germans shoot you down too?"

"Aye, I guess you could say they did."

Malcolm looked confused. "But you didn't die like my father."

Another family torn apart. Rob felt so much compassion it was all he could do to keep control of his emotions. "No, but I almost did. My arm's never been the same."

"Then you're a hero." A quiet statement, but an emphatic one.

Rob knew he was treading on shaky ground. "Some folk say I am."

"You are. My mother told me if you get shot down by the Germans you're a hero."

"She was right. Your faither was a hero."

"Yes, she said that right before she … she died …"

"Died?" He was an orphan?

"She was very sick."

"I'm sorry, lad."

"That's all right. She went to heaven a long time ago." Malcolm's face brightened again. "Want to see her picture?"

Rob's stomach cramped. He nodded.

Malcolm opened a locket that hung around his neck.

Rob looked at the smiling picture of young, sweet-faced lass. Luckily, the picture was behind glass and didn't appear damaged by the seawater.

"That's her," Malcolm said, pride ringing in his voice.

"She's verra, verra bonnie," Rob said.

"I know. Her name's Julie."

Rob closed the locket and tucked it beneath the blanket. "She must have luved you very much."

"She did. Before she went to heaven, she said I had to be very brave, that God had a special family already picked out for me. But it's been a long time." Malcolm ducked his head. "I guess she was wrong."

"Och, you don't ken—know—that. I'll bet your mither was right. Somewhere, there's a very special family waiting for a lad like you."

"A cripple?"

"You're no' a cripple unless you decide you are. I'm no' a cripple and neither are you. We'll show the world—right?"

This time Malcolm's smile sparkled in his eyes. "Right."

Rob stayed with Malcolm long after they transferred him to a room. "I'd like to keep the lad till mornin, at least," John told him. "Want to make sure he doesn't have any water in his lungs."

Shortly after the turn o' the night, Rob opened the front door, and Maggie rushed across the living room.

"Thank ye for having Neil tell Control the crew was uninjured. You'll never know how guid it was to hear that over the radio."

He gathered her into his arms, savoring her softness, her sweet scent. "Sorry I'm so late. I've been with a bairn we rescued."

"I know, Caroline called and told me. Poor lad, there's

83

something wrong with his left arm. Did he break it?"

"'Tis a birth defect, I'd imagine. Poor wee lad. He's an orphan."

"Och, Rob, all the bairns you rescued were from an orphanage in Oban." She led him into the bedroom and removed her robe. "One of the benefactors gave them silver to rent a boat to take some of the bairns for a sail."

"Too bad they didn't choose a newer boat." He undressed quickly, crawled into bed, and pulled her close. "This lad has an added problem. The other lads call him a cripple."

"Bairns can be cruel. We both ken that."

"Aye. But it really hits home when you can see what it does to someone like Malcolm."

"Malcolm?"

"Aye, that's his name. I had a hard time controlling myself when he said it."

"I can see why." Her voice trembled.

Rob laced a hand in her hair and ran his lips over her cheek.

She hid her face in the hollow of his throat. "Caroline says he has enormous brown eyes crying out for luve."

So it wasn't only the lad's name that upset her.

"Caroline should ken, for 'tis her training, being an adoption counselor for so long. I couldn't leave him, lass. He has such a needy heart."

She cuddled close. "Thank ye, luve, for being there when he needed you."

Chapter Sixteen

Rob paused on the infirmary flags, the taste of sea salt sharp on his tongue, an early morning breeze kissing the back of his neck. To the east, a summer sun thrust higher into the sky, flaunting its promise of a rare, perfect day. He should be at the shed, adding his back to the crew manhandling the first US Coast Guard rescue boat from cradle to skids. But first he had to see how Malcolm fared the night.

The chairs in the foyer stood empty, patiently awaiting the island folk seeking treatment for a myriad of complaints—some minor, others serious.

Rob skirted the empty admitting desk and headed down the far hall.

Mary MacGruder hailed Rob from ootside Malcolm's door, her arms laden with two trays bearing empty teacups, a plate littered with toast crumbs and bits of uneaten egg, an empty honey pot, and a bowl, rim crusted with drying brose.

He hurried forward. "Let me help."

She blew a strand of greying hair from her cheek and nodded at the kitchen door. "Open that for me. If I let go now, I'll have a midden to clean up." After setting the trays on the bunker, she turned, blue eyes dancing. "He's still a wee bit shy, but that lad can do a breakfast proud."

"He ate all that? Twa trays of food?"

With a hearty laugh, she scraped the plate and slipped it into the jawbox full of soapy water. "Och, of course no'. That nice Missus Hastings spent the night with him."

"Caroline was here all night?"

With the cups and utensils ready to wash, she tackled the bowl. "Aye, and a guid thing too. She said he drank almost twa pitchers of water, then had her hopping, fetching the bed pot."

Rob turned on his heel. "I'd best give her a break, then," he said over his shoulder. He keeked in the open door.

Caroline scrubbed the lad's chin with a face flannel. "You're sticky." She laughed. "I warned you not to use so much honey."

They both looked up when Rob walked in.

"Rob, what a nice surprise." Caroline gave one last swipe with the flannel. "We've been getting acquainted, haven't we, Malcolm?"

Rob leaned over the bed. "So how are you feeling after our swim?"

"Fine. But I'm thirsty all the time."

"So am I. It must be all that salt water we swallowed."

"That's what Caroline said, isn't it?" The lad looked up at Caroline.

"That's what I said."

Rob pulled over another chair. "Why don't you give heels to, Caroline? I'll stay a bit."

She straightened the bed cover and smoothed Malcom's pillow. "After a while. This room's a mess, and he's oot of water. Be back in a tick—minute."

"Know what I have to do this mornin?" he asked Malcolm.

"What?"

"I have to launch another rescue boat like the one that saved us."

"Is it red and black?"

No' much got by this lad. "No, this one's grey. It's for the United States of America. Know where that is?"

Malcolm's forehead creased. "They helped us fight the Germans."

"You're right, they did."

"So you have to go," a hoarse whisper.

Rob's breath caught at the look of disappointment on the lad's face. "No' right now. I can stay a while."

"But you should go." No doubt, only resignation.

Caroline placed a pitcher on the bedside table and signaled to Rob that she would stay.

He shook his head. "I can stay for as long as you want me." Rob took the lad's hand. Limp, it was, as though all hope of finding an anchor to cling to was lost.

"I know men have their work to do. My mother told me so." Malcolm's lower lip trembled. A tear trailed down his cheek. "She said what men do is important, that we can't … can't …" He ducked his head. Sobs shook his body.

Deep sadness swept over Rob. He'd known rejection. Adults so overwhelmed by "duties" they had no time to meet emotional needs. Potential parents turning away from a lad too quiet, too shy, to pretend he fit into their idea of a happy family. He couldn't allow another poor, wee soul to retreat into a secret hiding place deep within himself. He pulled Malcolm into his arms. No work Rob had was that important. "I'm here, lad. I'll no' leave you."

The lad burrowed closer, weeping.

Rob rubbed his back, whispering, "I'll no' leave you," over and over again. This poor, brave lad had given up more than most in that dirty, stinking war.

Even when Malcolm's tears were spent and he fell asleep, Rob continued to hold him.

"You can go if you have to," Caroline whispered.

"Den can handle getting the boat to the water. Nowt's more important than this."

Her eyes welled with tears. "I wish Pete felt that way about bairns."

"He's never even met the lad. He's a guid man. Give him a chance, Caroline."

⚓

"I can't leave him." Rob lowered his voice to a whisper. "He's been deserted by too many folk too many times."

John stroked his beard. "But they've sent a boat for all the survivors. 'Tis standing by to load."

Rob looked down at the sleeping lad. His lips were parted, and he occasionally twitched, as though caught in the throes of a bad dream. "He can't go yet, John. Surely you can come up with a medical reason. Please."

"Well, it could be a bit soon." The doctor squeezed Rob's shoulder. "Perhaps I should keep him here for at least twa more days to make sure he doesn't develop pneumonia. After all, he's the only bairn who was in the water."

"Thank ye."

Rob closed his eyes and rested his cheek against Malcolm's head. *Please, Heavenly Faither, please help John say the right words. I feel so akin to this poor lad.*

When John walked quietly back into the room, sadness showed in John's eyes. It disappeared almost instantly, replaced by a look of detached interest. Most likely steeling his heart against emotions no doctor could allow himself to feel. How hard that would be, always having to cover heartbreak.

"What did they say?" Rob whispered, indicating the sleeping lad with a jerk of his chin.

"I delivered my opinion, and Caroline talked to them too." John rocked on his heels. "It seems the lad's a bit of a misfit, and they don't know how to handle him. They said he could stay for another week, as long as 'tis no imposition."

"Imposition!"

"Calm down. That's a verra large orphanage. They take in all the orphans in the Hielans and do the best they can, but they're understaffed."

Orphanage. How familiar that sounded. Babies in the nursery crying for attention, helpers running around, up and down stairs, out into the yard, looking overworked and overwhelmed. Cooks trying to fill empty bellies from a pantry sparsely stocked with tins of tuna, burlap sacks filled with sprouting potatoes, tubs of peanut butter, a few loaves of coarse, brown bread. "I know all about how that works. Thank ye, John, from the bottom of my heart. I'll repay you someday."

"I can't imagine what you expect to accomplish in so little time."

"I don't know. I hate to have the lad go back to a place where they consider him a cripple. He isn't, John. He's a lad who has a problem with his left arm. That's all."

✦

"Want another sip of water?"

Malcolm settled back on his pillow, rubbing his eyes and yawning. "Maybe later." He looked up as Caroline opened the door, a sleepy smile tilting his lips.

She kissed his forehead.

"You smell like flowers."

She blushed. "I've been sent to fetch Rob, laddie. He's needed at the dock."

Rob glanced at his watch. Och, that late already? He got to his feet and stretched stiff muscles. "I have to launch a boat, lad. I'll let you watch us launch the next one." Why no reaction? Had Malcolm suffered so many disappointments he no longer dared hope? "You'll be fit enough to be up and ootside by then."

"That's all right. I understand."

Rob sat on the bed. "Look at me." When the lad finally met his gaze, Rob smiled. "I don't lie, lad, or say things to make you feel better. We launch the final boat in three days. You'll be there." So far to go to gain the lad's trust. And so little time.

✦

Malcolm hopped from foot to foot, giggling and pointing toward the crowd on the shore. Rob had been concerned the lad would be afraid after his last experience on a boat, yet here he was, acting like any normal lad given an opportunity to be aboard a boat about to be launched.

88

"Now, watch," Rob said. "When I lower my right arm, they'll cut the ropes holding us, and we'll slide backward into the water. There'll be a big splash, and then we'll float like we're supposed to."

Axes descended.

The new boat lurched and slid backward.

A cascade of water inundated the stern.

Within seconds, the boat floated back into deeper water.

A loud roar erupted from the watching crowd. Would they never tire of watching a launch?

"That was a big splash!" Malcolm laughed. "It got me wet!"

"Och, what's a little water when you've been swimming in the sea?" Rob mussed the lad's hair. "Come on, I need you to sound the siren, then help me start the engines. 'Tis time to get this boat to her berth."

⚓

Caroline phoned Rob at the shed, asking to see him after work. He went directly to her home after leaving for the day.

She greeted him at the door and asked him in.

Knowing the answer, but stalling for time, he asked, "Pete's no' home yet?"

"He's at a meeting with his building crew."

He looked around the room, hoping for a diversion. Vibrant red and yellow pillows decorated a pale yellow-striped sofa and chair. Vases filled with wildflowers graced two side tables, and slick-covered magazines were stacked on a low table. His eyes were drawn to several photographs above an ornate aumrie. "Nice pictures."

Caroline's eyebrows rose. "Only a man could call pictures of homes Pete has built *nice*." Her smile looked strained—and tired.

"Can't stay long. I promised to take Robbie and Richie down to the strand before supper."

"This won't take long." Her lips trembled. "I'm certain you already know why I called you."

"I have an idea."

"Well, what do you think?"

"Pete's the one you should be talking to, no' me."

"But I want to adopt Malcolm." The pleading in her eyes pained him.

"I'm sure you do. Has Pete even met the lad?"

She bowed her head. "He's been too busy."

"That's no' a reason and you know it. That lad needs twa parents who both want him, no' only one."

Price

Tears filled her dark-brown eyes. "I know it. Och, how I know it."

"Have you talked to Pete about it?"

"I've been afeart to." A whisper.

Rob sighed and went to look out the window. "I'm no' the one to bring it up to Pete, if that's what you're thinking. And I'm no' even certain the government will allow you to adopt the lad."

"They will, I checked. As long as this is our permanent home now and we wait six months before it becomes final, we can adopt him."

He should have known she'd talk to the authorities before mentioning it. "I'm still no' the one to talk to Pete." He turned and faced her. "If this is something you really want, then it's worth fighting for. But Pete will have to agree, or it won't work."

"I know that!" she cried. "I'm so afeart he won't want him because ... because ..."

"Because of his arm?"

Her face crumpled. "Aye."

"If Pete doesn't want him, it won't be because of his arm. 'Twill be because he isn't cut out to adopt a child. No' everyone is, you ken."

"I don't think I can bear it if he says *no* again." She pulled a handkerchief from her apron pocket and dabbed at her eyes.

Why me, Lord? My Maggie's the only one I can talk to. "Let Pete meet the lad. It's no' fair to second-guess what he will or won't do. The lad's at my house right now." He thought for a moment, then spoke his mind before he lost courage. "Why don't you bring Pete over after supper?"

She smiled through her tears. "I'm skeered to death, but I'll do it. You're right, it isn't fair to think the lad's arm will matter."

Maggie wiped her wet hands and went into Rob's arms after he told her about his conversation with Caroline. "No' every story has a happy ending, luve," she said, hugging him.

"And no' every orphan gets adopted."

She closed her eyes at his bleak tone. Rob, of all people, knew how true that was. "That's right," she said softly. "As much as it hurts to even think it, 'tis true."

When Caroline and Pete arrived, Pete didn't even raise an eyebrow to find Malcolm there.

Maggie asked Caroline to help make more tea and coffee. "Why don't you take the bairns ootside to play," she said to Rob, "while 'tis still warm enough."

Cannie lass. Rob herded the bairns ootside, plucking Will from his cradle on the way. He and Pete settled themselves in the rockers on the entry while the bairns played in the yard, the boys throwing a ball to Shep.

"That Malcolm's got a nice right arm," Pete said. "That was a guid throw."

Rob glanced at him, brow raised.

Pete was grinning. "Don't think I know what this is all about? Caroline's all but slubbering. She wants that lad so badly she can't see up from down."

Rob couldn't think of a thing to say.

Pete's grin faded. "I know my lass. This isn't the first time she's set her sights on a bairn for us, though he is a lot aulder than the others."

Will whimpered and Rob cradled him in his lap, offering the bairnie a knuckle to sook on.

"That's the difference between us." Pete nodded. "You know exactly what to do. Me? I'm clueless."

"I was clueless with Robbie, and skeered. I didn't have the slightest idea what it meant to be a faither."

"Come on. Some have it and some don't."

"And you think you don't have it."

"That's about the size of it."

Rob was about to do the very thing he'd told Caroline he wouldn't do, but he couldn't stop himself. "How did you feel when you started Gunnery School during the war?"

"Like an eejit who couldn't hit the broadside of a barn. I'd never fired a gun."

"How did you feel five weeks later?"

"Come on, Rob, there's no comparison."

"Och, isn't there?"

"We're talking about a human life, here, no' shooting down some German FW-190 trying to blast us oot of the sky."

Rob quelled a groan. "There was no human life involved in that? How about a crew of ten?"

"You ken what I mean." A husky tremor in Pete's voice betrayed his discomfort.

Rob leaned closer. "But do you ken what I mean? You were a green lad when you started, but a short handful of weeks later the

Army Air Forces declared you fit enough to help defend ten crew members against enemy attack. Did you think they were wrong?"

"Of course no'. Like all of us, I was skeered spitless about going to war, but I knew I was ready." A hint of pride in that firm statement.

"But what difference could six weeks make? Och, you had some training, to be sure, but what made you *ken* you were ready?"

Pete jumped to his feet and paced. "I knew I was ready because I had confidence in my ability."

"And what gave you that confidence, Gunny?"

An abrupt stop, hands on hips. "All right, I'll say it if I have to. Experience, pure and simple."

"That's what made me a pilot. Experience. The first time I climbed into a cockpit, I was shaking so hard I could barely sit still, and it wasn't all because I was kittled up."

Pete looked out at the harbour, the bairns' chatter and laughter filling the air. "I'm that afeart. What if I'm a lousy faither?"

"Is there any reason you should be?"

Grey eyes dark with worry. "I don't ken. I do ken there are some really bad ones oot there."

"And some really guid ones. You don't hear about the successes." A sudden thought electrified Rob. "How about *your* faither?"

Pete ducked his head and toed the stone flags. "Dad was a contractor, like me. He ... he was too busy putting food on the table to spend time tossing a baseball—or the likes." He raised his head and gazed oot at the Minch. "No' much of an example to follow, if you ken what I mean."

"But it was an example. Now you ken what no' to do."

A quick toss of Pete's head toward the yard. "He's got a lot of baggage, that lad has."

"No more than most. His happens to be more obvious."

"Och, I don't mean his arm. I mean losing his parents and living in an orphanage. It must have damaged him. 'Tis a lot for anybody to overcome, especially such a young lad."

For the first time, Rob was not reluctant to share his background, though only those closest to him knew he had been raised in an orphanage. When he finished telling about his rearing, Pete stared at him, open-mouthed. "You're no' putting me on, are you?"

"'Tis the truth. Every word."

"I didn't know. Never would have guessed it in a million years."

A slight smile tickled Rob's lips. "Why should you? I don't think I'm so different I stand out in a crowd."

Plonking into his rocker, Pete shook his head. "Och, you do, but for all the right reasons. What I'm talking about is your self-confidence, what you've made of your life. And you never were adopted?"

This was treading on a very sore spot, but Pete deserved the truth. "As I said, I was taken there as a wee bairnie when my parents were killed in an accident. When I was five, a couple did take me home with them, but before I turned six, they took me back to the orphanage without even telling me why. I was at the orphanage from then till I graduated from high school and went off to West Point."

Pete suddenly leaped out of his rocker and rushed to the railing. "Nice throw, Malcolm! Way to go!" He turned to Rob, face creased in a sheepish grin. "What can I say? It really was a guid throw."

"This laddie Will needs his mither." Rob got to his feet. "He's about suckled my knuckle to the bone."

The wave of a hand dismissed him. "On you go," Pete said, returning his gaze to the bairns. "I'll stay oot here for a while. Those lads need some pointers. Did you know I was a pitcher at university?"

Chapter Seventeen

Malcom's departure was put on hold again while John did a complete examination, took X-rays of the boy's left arm, and came up with a surgery that would straighten it considerably. "It still won't have the strength of the other arm, but by cutting the tissue holding it in a bent position, he should be able to extend it."

Cutting. Rob winced. "Is it as painful as shoulder surgery?"

"No' at all. All we're doing is excising some extra tissue the lad was born with. He'll need physical therapy, of course, but it's no' verra painful. I couldn't believe those X-rays. The lad's bones are normal size."

"Why is his arm so short, then?"

"I couldn't find anything wrong with the bones. I'm thinking there's tissue that's drawing it up, making it look shorter."

"Can you lean on the orphanage to get their approval right away?" Pete asked. "Or are they like the usual government bureaucracy—hurry up and wait?"

"I have a guid friend who happens to sit on the board," John said with a sly smile. "They meet the night to study and vote on the issue."

Caroline clasped her hands and offered a tremulous smile. "We can't thank ye enough."

"Malcolm's a brave lad. All he needs is a little improvement in how that arm looks and functions. He should overcome much of his shyness verra quickly."

Pete poked Rob's chest. "If we can get him to handle a mitt, that lad will make a fine pitcher someday."

"Och, Pete." Rob groaned. "They don't play American baseball in Scotland."

"No' yet, they don't. Give me time, Commander, give me time."

❧❦❧

John's reputation as one of the world's foremost orthopaedists, and the added incentive of his donated services, gained the orphanage board's unanimous approval.

To cover unforeseen complications, John contacted a neurosurgeon at the Royal Infirmary who agreed to assist in the surgery. He also arranged for an anaesthesiologist and OR nurse to come from Edinburgh.

⚜

Fern wasn't about to take such news without a protest. She cornered John in the infirmary hallway. "There's no reason I can't be your OR nurse. Wee Matt's almost twa months auld. I'm more than ready."

"Den left me verra strict instructions." John's beard twitched. "You're no' to work for at least another four months."

"But that's ridiculous!"

John backed away, hands raised. "'Tis a bit on the cautious side, I agree, but I did promise."

⚜

The Hastings asked Rob to talk to Malcolm about the surgery.

Caught unawares, his breath stuttered. "That's a big responsibility. I'm no' sure I'm the right one to do it."

"He trusts you, Rob," Caroline said.

"But the lad's staying at your house now. Surely one of you—"

"You've had several surgeries on your shoulder." Pete pinned him with a stare. "You can relate to what he'll be going through."

Caroline's brown eyes filled with tears. "And John said he's reluctant to operate on a lad skeered oot of his mind. Please say *aye*."

How could he refuse? And how did he get himself into such fankles?

⚜

A bright morning sun gifted the island with a rare show of warmth. Bees—most likely from Angus's skeps—swarmed over Maggie's garden, and buzzed off, heavy with pollen. Rob yawned as he turned toward the Hastings' house. Sleep had come reluctantly. He'd prayed and racked his brain most of the night for a way to put the lad at ease before explaining what John wanted to do. Pray God he'd come up with the right solution.

Resting his hands on Pete and Caroline's dyke, he bowed his head. "Give me Your words, Faither, and open his heart to the changes this could bring to his life."

He found the three sitting at the kitchen table. Two plates of congealed eggs and minced sausages sat in front of Pete and Caroline.

Malcolm forked in pancakes as honey dripped down his chin. "This is good," he said after a hasty swallow. "I never had pancakes and honey before." He gulped down half a glass of milk before attacking the pancakes again.

95

Pete nodded at an empty mug on the bunker. "Pour a cup of coffee and join us."

His hopeful gaze and Caroline's weak attempt at a smile added to Rob's discomfort. He filled the mug, took a swig, and settled onto an empty chair. *Your words, Faither.* He voiced his rehearsed proposal. "'Tis sunny with only a sciffin breeze. I'm thinking this might be a guid day to take this lad flying. I promised him I would."

The surprise on Pete and Caroline's faces might have tickled Rob's funny bone under any other circumstances.

Pete closed his gaping mouth. "Sounds guid! What do you think, Malcolm? You ready to make like a bird?"

The lad shoveled in another mouthful, pushed away his plate, and leaped to his feet. "In a real plane? Am I ever!"

Caroline grabbed Malcolm's sleeve and dragged him over to the jawbox. "Not until we wash that sticky face."

"So you think you might want to be a pilot someday?" Rob asked the lad as they were walking up the pier.

"Can I be a pitcher and a pilot?"

"I don't see why not. I'm a boatbuilder and a pilot."

"And a commander."

Rob laughed. "Aye, and a commander." He helped the lad down the ladder to the lower dock.

The look of awe on Malcolm's face when he saw the floatplane brought a lump to Rob's throat. It wasn't a spitfire like the lad's faither most likely flew, but it had wings and a propeller and could transport an active imagination into a sky filled with every promise imaginable.

Malcolm hunkered down, fingers reaching for the pontoon. He looked to Rob for permission, smiled at the nod, and caressed the smooth surface like he was touching a treasure of immeasurable value.

Eyes bright with interest, Malcolm watched Rob carefully as he did his pre-flight inspection, asking questions and—Rob was certain—memorizing the answers. When they climbed in and he had Malcolm strapped in tightly, Rob deliberately used his left hand to test the lad's belt. "This is verra important. Seeing to the safety of your passengers is one of the most critical things you do."

As he hoped, the lad didn't miss the object lesson. "But I can't reach with my left arm. Could I use my right?"

"Aye, but there are times when you need to use your left arm if you're going to fly."

Malcolm's smile faded. "Then, I guess I'll just be a pitcher."

Rob allowed the seaplane to drift away from the dock, hoping the pause would add strength to his words. "What if something could be done so you could straighten your arm?"

"Like what?"

Engaging the engine, Rob adjusted the rpms. "Och, surgery, say, and then lots of exercises to make your arm strong."

"Surgery—you mean cutting?"

Steady, Savage. Don't ruin it now. "Aye, that's what surgery is. Cutting. Of course, you're asleep, so you don't feel anything." The plane skimmed across the water on its pontoons until Rob eased back on the yoke, and suddenly they were airborne.

Malcolm's smile bloomed to a toothy grin.

Rob headed the plane north toward the cliffs of the southern Outer Hebrides, where all the birdlife should interest the lad—but he wouldn't go as close to the cliffs as he had before. This time of year there might still be some birds with new hatchlings, and it wouldn't be right to disturb them.

The lad was so excited he bounced in his seat, pointing to birds, seals, and anything else that caught his eye. Every few minutes, he closed his eyes, lips moving. Was he telling his mither in heaven what he was seeing? Or his faither, *"Look, I'm flying, just like you"*? Before his raging emotions took hold, Rob spotted a trawler and put the airieplane into a steep bank.

For the first time since he had come to the island, as far as Rob knew, Malcolm laughed aloud.

They buzzed the trawler and Rob waggled the wings.

A real, belly-whomping laugh.

"That was Calum's boat," Rob said, grinning. "You remember Calum—he's my Maggie's brother?"

"He smelled like fish."

They flew over Innisbraw. Rob buzzed Innis Fell, knowing he was going to catch it from Maggie and Fern if he woke up the napping bairnies, but wanting to thrill the lad again. When they landed and taxied up to the dock, Rob cut the engine and reached over, once again with his left hand, to unclip Malcolm's seat belt.

The lad watched him intently. "Did they cut you?" he asked suddenly. "Your arm?"

"They cut my shoulder, because that's what was making my arm weak."

"Did it hurt?"

More than any pain I've ever felt. But another truth needed voicing. "Aye, but I wanted to use my arm so badly I didn't care. And it dinna hurt forever." Rob helped Malcolm out of the plane, elicited his help in the tie-down, and pushed him up the ladder.

The lad seemed preoccupied as they walked up the hill, but when they reached the Hastings' house, he launched into an excited narration of everything he'd seen.

Caroline looked at Rob, eyebrows raised.

Not knowing the answer, he shrugged his shoulders.

Malcolm tugged at Pete's elbow. "Did you see us go over the house? We were real low. We even made some sheep run!"

"I saw you. You were low, all right."

Was that a look of pride on Pete's face, or was Rob only imagining it?

"Rob said I can be a pilot and a pitcher."

"You can, that. I'm a pilot and a builder."

"But I got to get cut first to make my arm straight."

Caroline's hand flew to her mouth.

Pete's smile froze. "Is that so?"

"Yes. It'll hurt a little bit, but it'll be worth it. Then I can make sure my passengers are safe."

Pete looked at Rob.

"I guess you've forgotten. Sometimes we have to use our left hands to check the seat belt."

"Och, I did forget," Pete said with a soppy grin.

Caroline seemed to have a sudden need to rearrange things on her kitchen bunker.

⚓

Rob flew the floatplane to Edinburgh and picked up the surgical team from the Royal Infirmary on Thursday afternoon, because Malcolm's surgery was scheduled for early Friday morning.

He felt like a fifth wheel, but Rob made certain to be there before the surgery started.

The lad was stoic after John explained what was going to be done. "Rob said it'll hurt a little after you cut me, but it'll be worth it. I'll try not to cry."

John's usual crisp bedside manner softened. "I don't think it'll hurt that much, lad. We'll give you some medicine to take the hurt away."

"I'm going to be a pilot and a pitcher," Malcolm said solemnly.

"I see no reason why you can't be both."

Caroline held Malcolm's hand while they wheeled him into surgery. She bent over and kissed his forehead.

"You still smell like flowers." A sleepy whisper.

Tears shone in her eyes when she and Pete and Rob went to the foyer for prayer.

⁂

The surgery took longer than John had warned them to expect, but he was smiling when he joined them in the foyer. "We had a bit of a surprise when we got in. There was a large hole in the main muscle running down his forearm where it didn't come together properly in utero. We sewed it up, as well as excising a great deal of tissue keeping him from straightening his arm." He patted Caroline's shoulder. "I'm thinking over time that arm may be more usable than I anticipated."

"Can we see him?" she asked.

"The lad's still asleep. Give him an hour to wake up until you go in. He'll be back in his room by then."

Pete laid a hand on John's arm. "What about his hand?"

"'Tis going to take months of physical therapy, but his hand should strengthen along with his arm."

The Hastings went home with Rob to wait. Maggie made tea and coffee, then suckled Will while the four sat out on the entry, watching the bairns play with Shep.

"Where's Malcolm going to stay while he has physical therapy?" Maggie asked.

Pete's face flushed. "With us, of course. I have a surprise for him when he comes home. Found some old baseball pennants from the major leagues, and we're putting them up in his room."

"It's been half an hour." Caroline held up her watch. "I think we should go over to the infirmary and wait. He may awake early, and I don't want him afeart and alone."

Rob rose and stretched. "On you go. I've some phone calls to make. Catch you up later."

⁂

Remembering how exhausting surgery could be, it was after supper before Rob joined Pete and Caroline to visit Malcolm.

Eyelids drooping, Malcolm smiled. "It only hurts a little bit, and look at my cast."

An unusual cast it was, almost straight, with only a slight bend at the elbow. Rob whistled. "Will you look at that. I've never seen your arm so straight."

99

"It's heavy."

"It looks heavy."

The lad dozed, so Rob sat quietly for a while, then bent over him. "I'm going to let you sleep now. I remember how sleeperie I was after surgery. I'll be back tomorrow."

"Promise?"

"I promise."

Chapter Eighteen

Sea trials for all three United States Coast Guard rescue boats they had built that year kept Rob and Den busy every day. Commander Zeke Evans of the US Coast Guard came to the island on the twenty-ninth of the month for the capsizing trials. With all the rooms at the manse booked by tourists, he stayed in one of Rob and Maggie's upstairs bedrooms.

"You don't have to fix anything special for me to eat," he told Maggie. "I'm an old sea dog. I'll eat anything that isn't nailed down."

"You sound like Rob. He likes everything but mutton."

"I've never had any, but if it can be chewed and swallowed, I'd probably like it."

Rob grimaced. "No' if you tasted it first."

"I can't risk a capsizing trial without Elspeth's prayers." Rob held Maggie close, rubbing his cheek on her hair. "I'll run down to her cottage while Zeke's shaving. Den'll be here in a tick."

She hugged him, then wriggled away. "Only if you promise to take some scones. You didn't eat breakfast."

That pert smile made his blood race. He sat on the edge of his rocker and pulled her onto his lap. He was busy, but no' too busy for a proper kiss. His lips moved over hers, nipping, tasting, savouring. So sweet, those lips, so soft and filled with luve.

She kissed his chin. "Give heels to Elspeth's before Zeke finishes shaving. I'll give Den a cup of coffee if he gets here before you."

He groaned and set her on her feet. "Wrap those scones in a napkin. Be back in a tick."

Though short, the run down to Elspeth's cottage always invigorated him. The sun played a game of chase with high, grey clouds, sending shadows flitting across the Minch and harbour. A guid day, no' too windy, the temperature perfect for shirtsleeves.

He opened Elspeth's gate, gaze raking her garden.

No' there.

His heart juddered. She always spent the cool mornin hours

tending her flowers. He bounded up her stairs and hesitated before the door.

Nobody on the island knocked—just walked in—but he'd never thought it proper to invade the privacy of a woman's cottage before being asked in.

He rapped on the door, heartbeats thudding in his ears loud as his knuckles.

"'Tis open, lad." Her voice so thin and reedy, like the call of an injured nestling.

Och, the door wasn't even on its latch. He pushed it open and stepped inside, blinking to adjust his vision from daylight to semi-darkness. Suffocating heat washed over him like hot shower water.

Elspeth knelt before her rocker, flaming peats in the fireplace casting red and yellow flickers across her lined face.

He dashed to her side and went to his knees, quelling the urge to take her pulse. Instead, he sat back on his heels and clasped her hand. Cold, it was, despite the heat already bringing sweat to his brow. "Did you fall?"

She brushed aside his hand, struggled to her feet, then settled into her rocker with a *humph*. "Fall? I was on my knees in prayer, where an auld, gone woman like me belongs."

Weak with relief, he pulled up a chair beside her and plonked down, feeling foolish. Of course she was in prayer. Wasn't she always? He looked at the sheet pinned over the front window. No wonder it was so dark and hot in here—a fireplace stoked high with burning peats and no window glass to let in a little morning coolness. He placed a hand on her arm, relieved when she didn't brush it away. "Why do you have it so hot in here? Are you suffering the chills?"

Her stern gaze softened as she patted his hand. "When you're auld as me, you won't be asking such a question. Makes more sense to cover the window and keep peats burning than wearing my winter coat in the mids of summer." She smiled, newborn stars twinkling in her eyes. "I'm already praying about your capsizing trials, lad."

"How did you know?"

That throaty laugh that so delighted him. "You're the one who talked me into getting one of those telephones. How do you think?"

Och, he should have known. Nowt on this island got past Elspeth. He fought panic. This mornin's fright was only a precursor of worse to come. How could he survive when God called her home? Where could he go for common sense and direction when his impatience left him floundering? Maggie gave him luve and comfort and so much more, but Elspeth was the one who had taught him to know and trust his Saviour. And all the other folk on the island? She held each and every one of them up before the Lord, by name, every day. What would they do without—?

"Our Faither isn't calling my name yet, my precious Rob." Her gnarled hand patted his knee. "Rest easy in His perfect will."

So easy to say. So hard to do. He swallowed the lump in his throat. "Hugh says we don't have to be on our knees to pray. Why don't you sit in your rocker, where you won't raise bruises?"

Again, that delightful laugh. "Och, I ken that, lad. I pray all the time, working in my garden, redding up this cottage, even in the night when the Lord awakens me with a need." She placed her hand on his. "But there are times when I must place myself where 'tis only fitting—kneeling at His feet." She struggled to stand and reached for her walking stick. "Let me walk you oot to the entry." A sly smile. "That, too, is only fitting."

"You'll get a chill."

"I'm going to let those peats burn down to embers, have a cup of hot, strong tea, and take down that sheet. I only suffer from the cold when I leave my bed of a mornin."

Rob gripped her elbow and walked her out to the entry.

She hobbled to the railing and gazed silently out at the harbour and the Minch, eyes unfocused, as though watching something take place behind a veil his gaze could not pierce. A sudden *knowing* flooded Rob's mind, bringing understanding and awe. He'd always wondered how Elspeth knew his needs, often before he did. The answer was so perfect in its simplicity. She had dedicated her life to accomplishing God's will—spent every waking moment in His presence. The Holy Spirit allowed her to use His omniscient knowledge to divine one's innermost secrets and desires.

He left her on the entry and walked slowly up the path, tears wetting his face. *Thank Ye for allowing me to see Your truth, Faither. Elspeth's body bides on earth, aye, but her soul already worships at Your feet.*

⚓

All three boats capsized and returned upright within ten or eleven seconds. Though Rob wasn't surprised, when God smiled, he felt humbled. Who was he to be so blessed?

Zeke shot his arm into the air. "Yahoo! I don't have any idea how you do it, but keep 'em coming!"

"We'll have four boats for you next summer. I haven't accepted any orders but yours."

"So you had to turn some down?"

"Aye, twa—two. But you were first."

"Yeah, thank God. We'll be bringing in crews to sail these babies home. They should be here on the Monday ferry." Zeke grinned. "My stomach's growling. What say we have lunch—oops—dinner at the howff, Uncle Sam's treat?"

"You're on."

Zeke's United States Coast Guard uniform generated a buzz of talk among the tourists in the howff dining room, but he appeared oblivious to it all. The special that day was tattie bree, which he said was his favourite. He ate twa bowls and wiped up the last traces of bree with his fourth piece of bannock.

It pleasured Rob to find someone who luved to eat as much as he did. He pushed the empty bowl aside and sipped his coffee. "So how're Carol and Zeke Junior?"

"He's growing like a weed. For a preemie, it sure didn't take him long to catch up." Zeke looked up from beneath dark brows, the sun wrinkles around his eyes deep. "Carol's pregnant again."

"Och, that's guid news! Be sure to keep us informed about how she's doing."

"Are you kidding? Of course we will. She's talking about coming with me next year. She wants to see this remarkable island I keep raving about."

Rob clapped Zeke's shoulder. "That would be grand. I know Maggie would luve it."

⸎

Rob chuckled at the tourists' reaction to the three United States Coast Guard commanders, eighteen lesser officers, and seamen lining the ferry's deck when it docked Monday morning. New visitors aboard the ferry bandied questions back and forth—why was the US Coast Guard here? Why were three Coast Guard boats tied up at the dock of a tiny island in Scotland? Nobody had any answers.

Tourists queuing up to leave the island looked smug as they snapped photos. Most likely, their host families had bragged about the three rescue boats built right here on Innisbraw.

Rob swallowed a smile as he went through his saluting ritual with Captain MacNamara. Cameras clicked, faithers hoisted children onto their shoulders for a better view, women clapped, and teenagers hooted.

With Zeke, Rob escorted the "Coasties" to the shed, where the Innis Fell women had laid out a large early dinner. The men dug in with gusto. They drank gallons of coffee, ate two huge pots of tattie bree and dozens of Scotch eggs, plus piled their plates high with scones and shortbread.

When they finished eating, Zeke returned to the Savage home to pack. After the trials, he'd be hitching a ride on one of the new boats into Oban, where he'd catch a train to London.

Rob took the Coasties on a tour of their boats. Each boat had already been painted with its USCG identification number, sent a month earlier, and the men quickly unfurled American flags and ran them up the flagpoles, along with signal pennants.

The young American seamen looked to be having a grand time. Many of the tourists still on the island stood about the dock, taking pictures, joined by celebrating islanders. A few of the local halflin lasses flirted with the young, braw Yanks in uniforms so white 'twas hard to look at them.

Rob ushered the commanders into his office. "Dennis Anderson, who's another of the *Maggie*'s commanders and one of my partners, and Neil MacLean, my second coxswain, and I will accompany you while you become acquainted with your new boats. We'll be there in an advisory capacity only and to answer questions. Put the boats through their paces. They're yours now."

Rob chose to accompany the most sententious commander, a short, burly officer with a greying crewcut and piercing brown eyes.

After the crew came aboard, the order was given to cast off. This commander was a no-nonsense man. He followed harbour protocol to the letter, warning two fishing trawlers of his approach well in advance and waiting until they were far into the Minch before asking for full speed. The only indication that he seemed pleased was a slight deepening of the dimples in his cheeks.

The man spent six hours testing the systems aboard the boat. He used the radio and the radar, put the engines through all their speeds, tested going from full speed to full stop and examined every cupboard and every stretcher rack. He crawled all over the boat and looked from the fantail emergency deck to the clamps on the top of the cabin holding the inflatable rescue craft in place. He examined each railing, each cleat, and even the abrasive paint on the deck.

Amused, Rob sat in the second coxswain's chair and watched. The commander had asked only one question pertaining to the radar equipment. This was no affable Zeke Evans. This man knew what he wanted, and he expected to get it.

When they tied back up at the dock, he called Rob over. "Well done, Commander." He snapped a salute and left the boat.

105

Price

✤

The three rescue boats sailed late that een. They would pick up all their gear and provisions in Oban, a town on the western coast of Scotland, before sailing for America the following day.

Rob shook Zeke's hand before Zeke boarded the last boat. "I expect Carol to be with you next year."

"It all depends on how this pregnancy goes." Zeke punched Rob's shoulder. "Watch yourself, Rob. I'm counting on four new boats when I come back."

✤

The Innisbraw Boatworks' partners held a short meeting in the shed long after quitting time.

"Well, 'tis over," Rob said. "Any comments?"

"The check's in the mail," Stu said. "I heard it directly from the cuddy's mouth."

They all grinned.

"You get any complaints, Den?"

"Only one. They weren't here long enough to check out the local lasses."

A roll of laughter.

"So overall, the commanders seemed pleased?"

Den raised a finger. "My commander certainly was, and Neil said his was gobsmacked."

"Then that makes all three." Rob looked around at the men. "I'd say we had a guid year. The rescue boat for Ayr was delivered early, and we made it in under the wire for the US Coast Guard. Stu, make sure the lads get their bonuses; the checks are in my top desk drawer. On the morra's morn, we start cleaning up for next year's production."

Pete held up his hand. "Now might be a guid time to let you know we have fifteen new cottages on the drafting table, with no end in sight. These young lads and lasses are getting merrit at an alarming rate. I understand it has something to do with the peat in the water."

He was hooted down.

"That's what makes bairnies, Pete, no' getting merrit." Den slapped his knee and laughed.

Pete was unfazed. "Either bairnies result in marriage or marriage results in bairnies. 'Tis the same difference."

The meeting went downhill from there. Giddy with exhaustion and relief, the partners relived how well the rescue boats had performed. A year of hard labour and long hours had paid off.

106

Still flying high when he got home, Rob picked Maggie up and twirled her around.

"Och, I'm getting deezie. What has you so kittled up? Did they like their boats?"

He planted a kiss on the tip of her nose. "They did. They sailed about an hour ago. Thanks to Pete's advice and our Lord's blessing, we did it. Four boats in one year."

She hugged him, laughter tinkling like a burn dancing over rocks. "That's wonderful, luve. Now you can fauld yer fit for a while."

He threw back his head and laughed. When he could control himself, he kissed her rosy lips and patted her bottom. "Och, Maggie, lass, the morra's the beginning of a new business year."

Her face crumpled.

The moment he spoke, he had wanted to take the words back.

She studied the floor.

"Though now I think on it, I suppose I could get by with a five-hour day on the morra. The machinery has to be cleaned and recalibrated, and they don't need me for that. How about a picnic at our cove on the morra's afternoon?"

A wee smile. "All afternoon?"

"Aye, all afternoon."

Chapter Nineteen

Maggie, Will in her arms, waited with the rest of the bairns on the entry, faces bright with anticipation. Rob's conscience tweaked. Why had he waited so long to bring them pleasure? Robbie and Annie both wanted to walk, so Rob loaded their basket dinner, towels, a blanket, hippens, and gowns into the wooden cairtie with Beth, and they took off down the hill.

Rob concentrated on his family, ignoring the gazes of tourists on the path.

Maggie ducked her head and pulled a light blanket over Will's face when a camera clicked. One man, belly bulging over plaid shorts, crowded so close, Shep growled, showing his fangs.

"Guid dog," Rob said under his breath.

Maggie squeezed his fingers.

Odd, but no locals on the path the day. Most likely staying in their cottages, grateful for a respite from strangers.

Shep apparently forgot his herding instinct the instant they turned off the main path and skirted the fishermen's cottages. He bounded ahead, nose twitching, tail high. Robbie tried to keep up with the dog, his tanned legs pumping hard as he ran. Annie, ever hesitant, stayed with her parents.

Rob looked down the track.

No tourists in sight.

He motioned Maggie to go ahead, and they both turned onto a narrow rut between the marram grasses. "Don't touch the marram," he warned Beth. "It might cut your fingers."

She jerked her hand back. Probably remembering the last time she'd disobeyed and suffered a nasty scraped knee from a fall off the entry railing.

Away from the crowds at last, Rob pulled Maggie to his side and slowed his steps, enjoying the soft breeze cooling the sun's brilliant rays.

Overhead, a golden eagle rode a thermal, dark wings outlined against a cerulean sky. Before them, patches of sea pink and yellow mallow dotted the rocky girse, and pewlie and herring gulls' strident calls pierced the air as they searched the gently sooking surf for morsels of food.

When they reached the large rock they used as a shelter and backrest, Rob whistled in Robbie and Shep, unloaded the wagon, and spread the blanket on the sandy ground. Sneaking a kiss on his luve's cheek, he helped Maggie settle into her favourite spot, with Will on his back beside her.

He held up the basket. "Is everybody hungry?"

The bairns all danced about, exclaiming they were gleg as a gled, so he opened the containers of food and handed the meal out. Shep lay down nearby, his head between his paws, while Rob poured tea and coffee from the thermoses and handed each bairn a bottle of lemon skoosh. "Don't throw the bottles into the girse," he cautioned. "We'll take them home."

Maggie unwrapped a Scotch egg and fed it to Rob.

"Mmm, guid." He took a swig of coffee and settled his back against the rock, smiling down at Maggie. "Every time we come here I wonder why it's been so long."

"'Tis hard to find an entire afternoon."

A nibble on her earlobe sweetened his tongue. "Remember our first time here?"

"Of course." She smiled, bonnie face soft with memories. "'Twas just the twa of us."

"I couldn't keep my hands off you."

"I didn't want you to."

He reared up. "Now you tell me. You kept nattering on about somebody seeing us."

"Well, they could have."

He laughed and reached for a roast-beef-and-cheese sandwich.

"Faither!" Robbie called. "Beth spilled her skoosh!"

Rob jumped up.

Beth knelt nearby, skirt wet, eyes wetter.

"Now, don't roup," he said as he picked her up. "Come you on, Faither'll get you all washed off."

"Shep did it."

He stopped. Poor dog, always taking the blame for any mishap. "And what were you doing that Shep spilled your skoosh?"

She squirmed in his arms. "Doon, Daddy."

Och, that lass. She'd started calling him that when she had heard Amy refer to Stu that way, and no amount of coaxing by Maggie could get her to call him by the Scots *faither*.

He laughed and threw her over his shoulder. "No' till we wash you off." He carried her to a tidal pool and rinsed her hands and legs.

"You're all sticky." He nuzzled her cheek.

She giggled and hugged his neck.

Robbie raced by, a stick in his hands and Shep at his heels.

"Don't go in the water till I get there!"

Beth kicked to get down.

The moment Rob set her on her feet, she grabbed his pants leg and pulled him toward the shore.

"Och, you want to plouter in the water, do you?"

She grinned up at him, eyes flashing.

"On you come, Annie!" he called.

He took his lasses down to the water's edge, pulled off his shoes and socks, and cuffed his pants. "Annie, Beth, hold tight to my hands." He waded into the water.

The lasses squealed when Robbie splashed by, laughing and waving the stick, Shep nipping his heels, barks shrill.

The water sucked around their ankles. Beth stopped and squatted to pick up an empty cockle shell, holding it out to Rob.

He admired it, turning it this way and that. He gave it back to her, but when she reached up and tried to slip it into his pocket, he put it in for her and smiled when she scooped up a handful of sand, squishing it between her fingers.

Annie was not so adventuresome. She held tightly to Rob's hand, squealing every time a tiny wave washed over her ankles.

He gazed down at his two lasses who looked so much alike yet were so different. A pang of regret stirred his heart. Was his own mither a gilpie like Beth or as feminine as Annie? It grieved him that he would never know.

The tide turned, washing waves farther onto the shore.

Rob picked up his shoes and socks, tucked a lass under each arm, and trotted back to Maggie.

Robbie was sat beside her, eating a shortbread and showing his mither an unusual rock he'd found. Shep lazed nearby, tongue lolling from the side of his mouth, flanks heaving.

Maggie wrinkled her nose and held out a towel. "Was it fun?"

Beth nodded and reached for Rob's pocket.

He took out the shell and handed it to her, then dried off Annie's slim feet.

Admiring the shell, Maggie said, "Verra nice. We'll have to start a memory kist for you."

Nose wrinkling like her mither's, Beth asked, "What's that?"

"A wee box for all the treasures you want to keep."

Rob snagged the shell and slipped it into his pocket.

Annie held out her hand. "For you, Mither."

Maggie fingered the smooth piece of blue glass Annie had found. "'Tis bonnie. I'll add it to my collection."

Chapter Twenty

It was like having four sisters. Maggie said a quick, silent prayer of gratitude as she sneaked a keek at the women in her kitchen. Fern, her dearest friend, sharing prayers and support each time the shout siren sounded. Jill, the perfect foil for her serious husband, warm, lighthearted, yet steadfast when a friend needed help. Ellie, blooming into the full potential of a woman living the dream she'd had since childhood. Caroline, lavishing her luve on the lad she'd always wanted, though vacillating between hope and the dread he might be taken away.

Maggie dropped the last handful of snapped beans into boiling water. At least the bairns were occupied and no' under foot.

Katie played dolls with Annie, and Jill and Stu's fourteen-year-auld lass, Brenna, kept the lads and Beth and Amy busy playing keepaway.

Heaving a sigh of fatigue, Maggie returned to the bunker and helped peel, dice, and blanch the rest of the vegetables before stuffing the bounty into sterile jars and placing them into water canners. She lifted the heavy spill of hair from her sticky neck. Even with all the windows open, the radiated heat felt like a midsummer sun. A glance at her watch brought a shock.

The women gathered on the front entry. Caroline, Jill, and Ellie perched on the entry railing, faces turned to the onshore breeze that blew errant strands of hair around. Fern and Maggie took the rockers and suckled their bairnies.

Maggie smiled when Katie and Annie plonked down on the girse, joining the circle of bairns around Brenna.

No' a one fidgeted. Most likely listening to a story.

Jill heaved an exaggerated sigh. "What am I going to fix for dinner? After a whole afternoon in the kitchen, I'm fresh out of ideas."

"Why don't we throw together some sandwiches?" Caroline winked. "If we have to suffer through this heat to can vegetables for our men, they can do with a light supper."

"I like that idea." Maggie patted Will's back. "I have part of a roasted joint we can slice."

Fern tried to snap her fingers, winced, and said, "I have half a loaf of that guid cheese Morag makes."

"I'll hard-boil some eggs," Jill said. "Every single hen has been laying one a day. I need to use them before they spoil."

Caroline and Ellie looked at one another.

Ellie smiled. "I have shortbread I baked last een."

"And I have plenty of bread, and Pete laid in several cases of ale." Caroline laughed so hard she slipped from the railing. "After some ale, our husbands won't notice they're getting a cold supper."

✥

"I wouldn't mention the cold supper," Rob whispered to Den as they set up two large pieces of plywood on sawhorses.

"And get my lug skited?" Den plucked two ales from the bucket Calum set on the table. "I saw all those jars cooling on your bunker." He waited until Rob had his ale uncapped, and they tapped bottles. "To our amazing wives!"

Rob raised an eyebrow. "Any reason you shouted that loud enough to carry to the harbour?"

"I only hope it carried to Fern's ears in your kitchen." Den smirked. "I'm collecting points."

Maggie appeared at Rob's side. "Whistle the bairns in, luve." She gave him a pert smile. "'Tis time to eat."

Half an hour later, John trudged across the girse. "Sorry to be so late, but I brought a peace offering." He placed a box on the table. "A colleague sent chocolates from Switzerland." He sat and reached for a sandwich. "I'm gleg as a gled."

Rob pulled a chocolate from the box, popped it into his mouth, and sat back, quelling a moan. The morsel melted on his tongue and slipped down his throat, satisfying a desire he'd long disremembered.

The aulder bairns raced about the yard playing chase, their strident screams startling a flock of ravens from the tree at the back of Rob and Maggie's croft. For a time, the adults watched Malcolm play with the younger bairns.

What surprised Rob was how normal the lad's arm looked, though he still used it sparingly. "How's his therapy coming?" he asked John.

"Verra well. That lad has a goal. You, Den, and Pete had best find a way to see that Malcolm has flying lessons someday. He has a dream and he's working hard toward it." John emptied his bottle of ale and wiped his mouth.

"How's his hand coming, then?" Den asked.

113

"He can keep a mitt on it, that lad can," Pete said, his face filled with obvious pride. "Won't be long afore he's doing more."

John leaned across the table for the salad bowl. "His small-muscle skills are improving. He can pick up light objects already. I agree with Pete. He'll be picking up a ball with that hand in no time."

"He's got a big heart, that lad has." Rob slipped another chocolate into his mouth.

"There's nothing the matter with *your* small-muscle skills." Den elbowed Rob. "That's your third chocolate."

The picnic broke up at 2200 hours, right after sunset. The workday started early and there were bairns to be bathed and settled into bed.

Early on Saturday, Rob and Den slipped away from the boatshed, carrying a heavy burden wrapped in a blanket. They eased it into Alec's cairt and climbed onto the bench.

"Have a spot picked oot?" Alec asked Rob. He slapped the reins on his cuddy's back.

Rob blew out a sigh. "No' yet. We'll have a keek when we get to the cemetery."

Den grabbed the bench as the cairt jerked, then rumbled west on the path. "I've only been there once—to Malcolm's laying away. Don't ken where we're going to find room for over twa hundred folk to stand." He tapped Alec's arm. "Has the word gone oot about the lairstone being here?"

"It has." Alec chuckled. "I'm thinking those poor lasses in the telephone exchange are earning their silver the mornin."

"The cairts lined up to take those too feeble to walk?" Rob asked.

A tired frown creased the crofter's broad face. "Everybody with a cairt has been called and asked to bring any neighbours too auld or infirm to walk to the cemetery. And those with bairnies or wee bairns, of course."

Den straightened. "But what about the tourists? Won't they follow our folk, asking questions and taking pictures?"

"No' if they ken what's guid for them." Rob tapped his fingers on his thighs, anxious to put the peter to the blether. He needed time to prepare for a most important turn. "Hugh called each host family and told them to warn their guests that this was a private island affair—no outsiders welcome—and if they do show up, they'll be escorted back to the path."

Den snorted. "That'll go over a treat. Especially when they find Paddy's only serving sandwiches, Irn Bru, and skoosh at the howff—no' that I blame him, being alone and all. Hope there isn't a riot."

⁂

At 1400 hours, the kirk bell pealed, filling the air. The islanders, men and lads clad in kilts, women and lasses in long plaid skirts, slowly trod the path from the kirk to the graveyard. A procession of cairts preceded those on foot. Elspeth and Auntie Mairet sat on Alec's benchseat, the Savage and Anderson families crowded into the back. Dolly MacSween, Catriona Douglas, and other auld widows rode with Angus.

Maggie looked off in the distance. Burns, hidden behind low-wood, enticed the eye with glimpses of dancing water. Thatched roofs and peat piles laid claim to each cottage's place between drystane dykes and emerald-green girse. Overhead, a rare skylark bubbled its song as it flitted high into the clear, blue sky, and on the horizon, the Minch rolled toward shore in undulating waves. She smiled up at Rob. "You chose the perfect place, on this high mound overlooking the crofts and sea, and apart from the other stones."

He hugged her shoulder. "Is that the stone you wanted, then? I tried to remember what you said, but it was last year."

She read the inscription aloud, smiling. "'Here lies an Innisbraw lad, known by few but mourned by all.' 'Tis perfect, luve."

Families filed by to see the lairstone, prayed for a moment, then moved far back, so others could have the same opportunity. The aulder bairns gazed in wonder at the tall, light-grey stone.

Maggie squeezed Rob's hand. "What a blessing. Fergus has brought Christiona."

Fergus MacCrae, clad in a wrinkled, stained kilt, yellowing shirt, and patched wellies, led twa brawny lads carrying his crippled sister in the chair he had made to fit her twisted back. He stopped in front of the stone.

Christiona struggled to place a bent finger on the word *lad*. She smiled, nodding. "Tha gaol agam ort," she said, voice ringing clear. *I luve you.*

Rob's heart swelled with luve. This precious auld woman, crippled since a young lass, outwardly lived a life of pain and solitude, yet inwardly she dwelt in a place of grace and joy.

Elspeth hobbled to Christiona's side and kissed her cheek. Twa auld souls united in luve for their Lord.

Rob's gaze took in the auld, lichen-covered stones, a few

decorated with fresh flowers, others so ancient their inscriptions were indecipherable. Folk wandered around, nodding and pointing at names, most likely explaining to their bairns that these stones marked their family plot. A mess of dark-purple heather sprawled between winding paths, its sweet scent perfuming the air.

This was his island, these were his folk, his family, and their luve and respect for those biding with them now and those who had passed filled him with unspeakable joy.

Hugh raised his hands, and the soft talk was borne away on the breeze. "My beloved folk," he said in the Gaelic. "We are gathered here to symbolically lay away a wee lad. We grieve his untimely death, but I want to remind ye no' to dwell in sorrow. Our lives on this earth are but the blink of the eye in the face of eternity. Don't waste time looking back. Look forward to what our Heavenly Faither has in store for us." He opened his Gaelic Bible. "These are our Saviour's own words of victory: 'I am the resurrection, and the life: he that believeth on me, though he die, yet shall he live, and whosoever liveth and believeth on me shall never die.' Let us pray."

Beth wrapped her arms around Rob's leg, and he patted her head.

"Our Heavenly Faither, we thank Ye for this promise of immeasurable worth. We ken from Your Word that this laddie we gather together to remember now lives in a straight body, with strong legs able to kneel in worship, and fully developed lungs capable of singing Your praises. Give us guidance through another of Your lessons: 'Whoso shall receive one such child in My name receiveth Me.' We offer this prayer in the name of Your Son, our Saviour, Jesus Christ. Amen."

Graham Stewart, the island's piper, readied his instrument.

Hugh held up a hand. "In a minute, lad. I've one last thought to share." His gaze swept over the crowd. "The Lord has placed a burden on my heart. Every week, from June through October, tourists flock to our shores. Many of you have opened your homes and see to the tourists' comfort, while others consider their presence an imposition, a bother to be borne with typical Scots stoicism."

Rob swallowed hard.

"How many of you have looked upon these strangers as children eager to hear the Word? How many have offered smiles of welcome or ignored loutish behavior? You do a grand job of welcoming incomers who move to our island. Now is the time to offer that same welcome to those who only visit for a week or twa." He grinned his elfin smile. "That last was for the benefit of this minister, who must

116

now present his lesson in the Gaelic and English." He nodded to the piper.

The haunting melody of "All Things Bright and Beautiful" echoed off Ben Innis' braes and rose to her rocky peak, skirling around the ancient monoliths before traveling from the Minch to the Atlantic. Girse and rock caught the notes and flung them upward again, where they whirled and danced on their journey to heaven.

Rob's eyes filled with tears when several bairns, including Annie, sang the words to the familiar hymn.

"'All things bright and beautiful, all creatures great and small, all things wise and wonderful, the Lord God made them all. He gave us eyes to see them, and lips that we might tell, how great is God Almighty, Who has made all things well.'"

He bowed his head and swallowed the bitter taste of guilt. He was one of those who resented the tourists, who railed against their nosiness, their rudeness, their seeming lack of civility. How could he have been so selfish? He could never consider himself capable of giving a salvation message, but he could learn to smile more.

One morning in late August, Elspeth hailed Rob from her entry. "Will you give me a minute, lad? I'm in a bit of a fankle."

Taking the steps in one leap, he stooped to kiss her cheek. "A fankle? You?"

Her deep sigh alarmed him. "Aye. I need your help and you're no' going to like what I'm about to ask of you."

"What can I do for you?" He eyed her apprehensively.

"Well, for starters, you can stop looming over me like yon ben and sit down. 'Twill only take a minute oot of your busy day. I've a cup of coffee already poured."

He helped her into her rocker and plonked down beside her, taking a sip of coffee, pulse pounding like a runaway cuddy. If Elspeth had a problem asking him to do something, it must be a task he truly hated. "So ... what is it you want me to do?"

A hand fluttered at her throat. "I need you to attend the ceilidh this Saturday een."

His heart sank like a boat caught in a giant wave. The last thing he wanted to do was make a public spectacle of himself again. "And how is this going to solve your fankle?"

She placed her hand over his. "I ken how ill at ease you are at ceilidhs, but if our local folk don't start going, we'll have to cancel them."

That was startling news. "Why?"

"Because there's no one there to teach our visitors how to dance, for one thing. And for another, the brochure we printed up and had put in the ferry terminals say the tourists can get a taste of real Scots culture. All they're getting now is a glimpse of some of our done auld folk, like me, lining the walls on chairs."

Dark dread washed over Rob. The memory of that ceilidh made him shudder. He couldn't bear the thought of having to parade about in his kilt while women tourists flirted outrageously and their husbands glowered. Why had he ever carried through with the idea of bringing in the ferry, anyway? He'd put himself in a trap, pure and simple.

Elspeth pressed his hand. "You've nowt to say?"

He drained his coffee cup, stalling for time. What if he laid it all on the line? After all, Elspeth was his dearest friend. If she didn't understand, who would? He looked down at the harbour, unable to meet her steady gaze. "It makes me feel like a monkey in a cage. I canna stand the women staring at me like I'm someone from another planet. I luve my Maggie, and it turns my stomach, pretending to have a guid time dancing with a stranger. Can't you find someone else? I don't think I can go through that again."

Her smile looked pensive. "The young women there aren't looking for luve. They're looking for a man who fulfills their dream of what every Scotsman should look like, and for one dance with that man."

"But I'm no' Scots."

"They don't ken that, nor should they. And you're only partly right. You may have been born in America, but your heart and soul belong to Scotland. I'm right, am I no'?"

He bowed his head. Once again, she'd outfoxed him. "I can't go every Saturday night, Elspeth. My first allegiance is to the rescue boats. I don't have the energy to do both."

"I'm no' asking you to. The Island Council is going to ask each of the young men on the island to go to one ceilidh a month. If they agree, we can continue to hold them. If they don't, we'll have to discontinue them at the end of October."

"Then it isn't only me?"

"Of course 'tisn't. I agreed to talk to you, because I consider you verra special."

He sat back with a grim smile. "And because you knew I couldn't refuse you."

She laughed into her palm. "Aye, that too."

Maggie knew what a busy month he'd had. Rob was grumpy. No man who worked such long hours wanted to spend time entertaining strangers. For the first time in her memory, she resented their having to do something for Elspeth.

He pushed away from the supper table. "Please say you'll go with me, Maggie. I have to dance with you too, or I canna go through with this."

"Of course I'm going, but we're no' taking all the bairns. Ellie is keeping Robbie all the night, and Brenna's coming over to watch Annie and Beth. We're taking wee Will only because he canna go that long between feedings."

He sighed and gathered her into his arms. "I hate having you watch me dancing with other women, especially the young ones Elspeth expects me to dance with."

"'Tis only for show, luve." She pressed closer, molding her body to his. "I ken where your heart is."

"My heart, soul, and mind." He groaned. "Only my body will be dancing—and hating every minute of it."

"On you go. Put your kilt on." She kissed his chin. "'Tis getting late."

Chapter Twenty-One

The moment they arrived at the ceilidh, Rob understood Elspeth's concern. A few islanders milled together beside the door, women sober, men looking like they had sooked a lemon. Only the younger lads, a few from Rob's building crew, eagerly eyed the tourist lasses, most likely scouting out the bonniest to ask for a dance.

He guided Maggie through the crowd of noisy, celebrating tourists, trying to ignore their frank stares, repeating over and over one thought: *You will smile, you will smile.*

The back wall of the kirk hall was lined with the island's elderly folk, all out for an een away from their humdrum, oft lonely lives.

Elspeth raised a hand and beckoned them over. "Let me hold Will. I haven't spent enough time with this laddie." She settled the bairnie on her lap, twisted fingers sifting through his black curls. "Dance with your lass, Rob. 'Tis a lively reel. 'Twill get your juices running."

"Those juices would like to run right oot of here," he said under his breath as he led Maggie out to the dance floor.

Those young, unmarried lads from the shop grinned at him. Easy for them to have a guid time.

He kissed Maggie's cheek.

Her smile shone bright as the mornin star. Soft fingers laced through his, relaxing his taut muscles. She understood.

They danced the reel before he led her toward the refreshment table. "One cup of coffee," he said, wiping the sweat from his forehead. "Then 'tis off to the slaughter."

She squeezed his arm. "'Tis only for a few hours, Rob. And 'tis for a guid cause. The tourist money has brought so many improvements to the island."

Morag handed him a cup of coffee. "Courage, Rob. Ye look like a coo on its way to the killing hoose."

"'Tis how I feel." He took a healthy swallow. Just what he needed.

She reached across the table and tapped his hand. "I've an eye on someone you should ask to dance. See that blonde lass over there, in the white sundress? The one with the blue ribbon in her hair?"

He took a quick keek. At least she wasn't staring at him. "Why her?"

"She's a verra nice lass from a guid family. They're staying at the manse. She and her sister came in on yesterday's ferry, but their parents have been here for twa weeks."

"Twa weeks?"

"Aye. Say they luve it here. On you go, Rob, before one of the younger lads gets to her first. She's a bonnie one."

"There'll always be later."

"On you go!" Morag took his coffee cup. "Her name is Trish."

"Trish? What kind of name is that?"

Maggie squeezed his arm. "Ask her to dance. She looks nice."

Rob escorted Maggie back to where Elspeth was sitting.

Paddy and his lads launched into an open bob as Rob made his way through the crowd toward the blonde. There were so many stares his skin itched.

One woman even tried to grab his arm as he passed.

He took a deep breath and forced himself to smile before stopping in front of the blonde. Well, as Maggie oft said, in for a penny, in for a pound. "Would you care to dance?"

If first impressions meant owt, her's was surprisingly favorable. Startling blue eyes, only a touch of light-pink lip paint—and she was verra tall. After a slight hesitation, her smile radiated warmth. "At last, a man I don't tower over." She took the arm he offered. "Lead on, Rob Roy. You've rescued a damsel in distress."

"They're playing a bob," he said, as he led her to the dance floor. "That means we can dance any way we want."

"As long as it's Scots, I don't care. I've been dying to learn some new steps."

He showed her some movements.

She learned them quickly and was very light on her feet.

He began to relax. "Why did you call me 'Rob Roy'?"

She laughed—a warm, throaty sound. "Because it was the only Scots hero's name I could come up with. I wasn't a Lit. major. Why? Did I make a huge social faux pas?"

"No' at all. I was curious, since my first name really is Rob."

Her eyes widened. "No kidding! Well, I'm Trish, short for Patricia." A slow smile teased her lips. "I saw you on the dock yesterday morning when you and the captain saluted each other. What was that all about? Are you in the Scottish Navy or something?"

"'Tis a kind of joke the captain started. I go along with it, because he's a guid man and I like him."

"No navy, then?"

"No navy."

"But why?"

"Because I command the Innisbraw Coastal Rescue Boat."

"Sorry for being so nosey. There were at least ten different reasons the others on deck were arguing about."

"I think that's why Captain MacNamara does it, to create a bit of a stushie—commotion."

"Your English is really very good."

At last, an American woman who could carry on a conversation without batting her lashes and pouting her lips. "Thank ye. It should be better, but we don't speak it much here."

"What do you speak?"

Her voice had lost its bantering tone. Could she really be interested? "Scots and the Gaelic."

"What most people consider two very obscure languages."

"And you don't?"

"I don't think there's such a thing as an obscure language. Some just have fewer people speaking them."

Rob was surprised when the music ended. That hadn't been bad at all. In fact, he'd enjoyed their conversation. "Would you like something to drink?"

Her eyes sparkled. "I would, as long as it's coffee."

Morag had left the refreshment table, so he poured them both a cup.

Over the background hum of conversation, Paddy announced a simple reel.

"Now that looks Scots! If you teach me to dance to that, you're off the hook for the rest of the evening."

He spent the next few minutes showing her the rudiments of this particular reel.

"It really is easy," she exclaimed.

"Only if you're a guid dancer to begin with."

They continued their conversation whenever they were paired together. "Tell me, Rob, is that beautiful little woman with the long black hair your wife?"

"Aye, her name is Maggie."

"The name that's on your boat."

"You're verra observant."

"That's one thing my father taught me. 'Details, Trish,' he always says. 'Never overlook the details.'"

"Sounds like me. I'm a detail man myself."

A change of partners separated them anew.

When they joined hands again, Trish asked, "So what do you do besides command a rescue boat?"

"I build rescue boats."

"Is that your boatworks down by the dock?"

"Aye, it is."

"How on earth did you come up with that profession?"

"There was a need for them."

The music ended with a loud fanfare, and Paddy McDonald stepped forward to the microphone. "Ladies and gentlemen, you're in for a real treat tonight. Elspeth NicAllister, our Island Elder, is goin' to tell us a story in the Gaelic. I see Rob's here tonight. Rob, could you do the translatin' into English?"

Trish patted his arm. "Thank you, Rob Roy. I enjoyed it immensely." She moved off before Rob could reply.

Paddy came across the room and helped Elspeth to her feet, moved her chair into the centre of the floor, and gave her his hand as she seated herself.

Rob made his way to her side.

Her faded blue eyes held a mischievous glint, and a smile creased the myriad of wrinkles on her cheeks.

Paddy took his position on the raised stage. "This is a story told to our young lads and lasses from the cradle on. Elspeth?"

Elspeth began the story, her voice stronger than Rob had heard it in a long time.

He translated. "There once was a verra beautiful seal who lived in the deep sea." Tears pricked his eyelids. "She felt a strong yearning in her breast to journey far, far away." He continued to translate the story, though he could have told it himself, word for word. Even the ending was the same, with the Selkie marrying her crofter lover and staying on their wee green island in the sea forever and ever and ever.

This was the story Maggie had told him time and time again when he was so badly injured in both B-17 crashes. Only her soft voice had kept him from giving in to the looming darkness.

The applause was loud and lasted a long time.

Rob bent down and kissed Elspeth's cheek.

Her smile shone soft with memories. "I always did prefer a happy ending."

He kissed her cheek again. "Thank ye. 'Tis my favourite story."

"Of course. 'Twas your Maggie's favourite too."

The musicians took a break, and Rob helped Elspeth back to her place against the wall.

"Your laddie needs his faither." Maggie placed Will in his arms.

He brushed his cheek against his son's soft black curls, inhaling the sweet scent of milky innocence and heather soap.

Smoothing the wrinkles from her skirt, Maggie said, "The lass you were dancing with seemed to be verra nice."

"She was—surprisingly so. Not the usual tourist type."

"I'm glad. I was so afeart Morag was mistaken."

"So was I. If there are more like Trish, mebbe my faith in mankind might be restored."

She bumped him with her hip. "You mean womankind, Rob."

He smiled down at her.

"I'm thirsty. Would you bring me a skoosh?"

"Of course. Be right back." He walked off quickly before she could take Will. Surely no tourist woman would accost him with a bairnie in his arms. He carried the laddie over his shoulder to the refreshment table.

Trish was after another cup of coffee. She caught his eye. "Rob, I'd like you to meet my family."

She introduced him to her parents and then to her younger sister. The women exclaimed over Will and his beautiful black hair and long, slim fingers. Trish's faither, Bill, had her same startling blue eyes, but his were lined with creases as if he had spent a great deal of time out in the sun. Her mither, Paula, was also blonde and very young-looking to have daughters in their twenties. Trish's younger sister, Mel, looked like her mither, with dark-blonde hair and hazel eyes.

"Trish tells me you're a rescue boat builder," Bill said. "Funny. You bear a striking resemblance to someone I once knew, but he would know nothing about boats."

Rob looked closely at the man. The face—especially those blue eyes—seemed familiar. "Perhaps we'll meet again," Rob said, still searching his memory. "I hope you enjoy your holiday here."

Rob danced the next dance, a slow ballad, with Maggie before she went off to nurse Will.

He looked around the hall, panic blooming again. Who could he ask this time? Och, there was Mel, standing alone. Why no'? If she was half as pleasant as her sister, he'd be satisfied. He hurried up to Mel. "Would you care to dance?"

"Rob, hello again. I'd love to."

Mel was not as good a dancer as her sister, but she was every bit as easy to be with. "My dad keeps going on and on about you looking like a pilot he knew. He's always thinking he sees a buddy from the war. So far he's batted a big fat zero."

"He was a pilot?"

"Only a wannabe, though he is one now. He was a navigator on a B-17."

A mind-picture formed before Rob's eyes—a brown-haired fellow with a pleasant smile and startling blue eyes. A navigator. Bill. Bill Townsend. He'd been at Edenoaks when Rob first took command of the base. B Squadron, the … the *Gentle Jeanie*.

A tap on his shoulder brought him back to the present. "Hello up there. Did I say something wrong?" Mel stared up at him. "I lost you."

"Och, sorry. Gathering wool. Your faither's right this time."

"Excuse me?"

"I mean I remember him now. We served on the same airbase in England."

She looked confused. "But the Rob he was talking about was an American."

"So am I."

She stopped dancing. "What's this whole thing, anyway, some rich developer's way to get even richer by putting one over on the tourists?"

What a fankle. "No' at all. I was born in America, but I live here now. I have since nineteen and forty-three."

"But you speak the language. Or was that also a sham?"

"No sham. I learned to speak Scots and the Gaelic, because there was no other way I could communicate with the folk here. Where's your faither? I owe him an explanation."

Her hands went to her hips. "Then why the heavy burr while we're speaking right now?"

"Because I hardly ever speak English. I even dream in Scots. It's replaced my native tongue."

"You sound like my sister."

"I beg your pardon?"

"Trish teaches foreign languages at a college in our hometown."

Rob scanned the crowd. When he spotted the rest of the Townsend family, he took Mel's elbow and guided her toward them.

Och, no. They were talking to Elspeth.

Feeling foolish, he stood quietly until there was a break in the conversation.

Elspeth looked up at him. "I believe you already ken this young lady," she said with a nod toward Trish. "These are her parents."

"We've met."

"Rob, here you are again," Bill Townsend said. "We were telling Miss NicAllister how much we enjoyed her story. Gaelic is a beautiful language."

Rob didn't know where to start. "You were at Edenoaks Airbase in forty-twa, weren't you? Your surname is Townsend and you were a navigator for Walt Josephs on the *Gentle Jeanie*."

Townsend's eyes narrowed, then he smiled. His smile quickly turned into a laugh. "I knew it," he crowed, pumping Rob's hand. "You are him." He turned to his wife. "Honey, this is the commander I told you about—Colonel Rob Savage. He took over command of the 396th six weeks before I finished my full twenty-five."

Rob smiled until Bill turned on him.

"But what's with the Scots get-up and the accent? You didn't have that burr when you briefed us."

"I dinna have it then."

Townsend still looked confused.

"On you come," Rob said. "I'll get you a cup of coffee and fill you in."

Once Rob had told Bill enough to take care of the misunderstanding, they spent the next half-hour catching up. Bill was now a pilot for American Airlines, and he and his family lived in a small college town outside of Chicago. "It's a bear of a commute but worth every minute," he said. "Not that you'd know about that, living on an island that doesn't have a single automobile."

"True. We have a floatplane for long trips, and you'd be amazed how enjoyable it is to walk to work every day. No exhaust fumes or cars trying to run you off the path."

Bill grinned. "You make a good point. That's why we live in a small town, to escape those very things."

While the two men enjoyed a second cup of coffee, Elspeth finished telling her second story of the night, but this one was true and had a hero named Rob.

The three Townsend women sat quietly, tears darkening their lashes.

Elspeth turned to Maggie, who had quietly taken the seat beside her halfway through the narration. "Now, I'd like you to meet Maggie, Rob's wife."

The women shook hands.

"It seems that Rob and Bill Townsend, Paula's husband and these lasses' faither, were both based at Edenoaks," Elspeth told

Maggie. "Before you served there, I believe."

Maggie wiped a bubble of milk from Will's lips. "I wondered why you were telling them about Rob's crashes."

Elspeth patted her hand. "I was explaining to them how an American pilot showed up at a ceilidh on Innisbraw wearing a kilt and speaking English like a Scotsman."

⚓

Rob danced once with Paula Townsend before he felt his obligation to Elspeth had been fulfilled. As the ceilidh ended and they were all gathering at the door to leave, he told Bill Townsend they would definitely get together in the near future. "If I can find time, I'll take you up in the floatplane and give you a keek—look—at the Hebrides from the air. And there are twa other Americans from the 396th living here. We'll all have to get together and talk about auld times."

Townsend gripped his hand. "I always thought there was a nice guy beneath that hard-nosed exterior. Good to know I was right."

On their long walk home, Rob had so many emotions battering his body he couldn't speak. Thank the Lord Maggie understood and didn't expect him to make conversation. Talking to Townsend had brought back memories he'd tried so long to bury. Though he'd shared some details of his bombing missions with Maggie over the years, he'd told her only the rare, humorous incidents.

Most he could never share with anyone. They were still locked up in his mind, bits and pieces of horror and mind-numbing grief that only escaped occasionally into the nightmares that sent him clawing out from 'neath the covers, body bathed in sweat, heart pounding out of his chest.

He pictured the faces of other navigators, engineers, gunners, radiomen, bombardiers, and copilots, so many dead and gone forever—yet tonight, they all came alive in his mind. It was so difficult to think about those awful, adrenalin-filled days.

As they neared the house, one thought made it all worthwhile. He might be a boatbuilder on a small island off the coast of Scotland, but his life would forever be enriched by the incredibly brave young men he had served with in the 396th Heavy Bomber Group.

127

Chapter Twenty-Two

Bill accompanied Rob on a tour of the boatworks, where the crews were busy working on the keels for the four new rescue boats. Power saws whined, sanders whirred, and men's shouts reverberated through the large shed. Since it was too noisy for conversation, Bill waited until they were having coffee at the howff to ask Rob the one question foremost in his mind. "You mean you dreamed up the design for a boat that will right herself when you'd never done any sailing?"

Rob rubbed the side of his nose. "Only after weeks of pouring over every boatbuilding book I could lay my hands on. 'Tisn't aerodynamics, but 'tis similar, and I had a lot of help from local skip—"

A young man, shoulders and black hair sprinkled with sawdust, rushed up to their table. "Sorra to interrupt, but you've got to see this, Rob."

"Now, Graham?"

"Aye. 'Tis aboot that air baffle in the mids—the one by the engine room."

Rob pushed his chair back. "This shouldn't take long, Bill. Have some more coffee."

Bill poured another mug of coffee from the pot on the table and sat back, tapping his fingers. Rob's answer about designing a boat that could right herself after capsizing seemed anticlimactic—like he was leaving out the most vital part. No man could design a boat like that without years of training. And yet …

His thoughts tumbled back to his last weeks with the 396th Heavy Bomber Group. After a succession of desk-flying, by-the-book commanders, some lasting only a few weeks, morale was so low the gutter would feel like an improvement.

Bill was near the tail end of a crowd of yawning, shuffling flyboys filing into the briefing hut at oh-dark-thirty. Another new CO. Why hurry? Just another frustrating briefing with an empty pep talk about "stopping Hitler in his tracks." Sounded good on paper. Reality was another story.

A fellow navigator had bumped his shoulder. "Lookie that. No route map or chairs. What's up?"

"Got me." Bill pushed his way to a place at the side of the room and looked around. Almost two hundred men crammed shoulder to shoulder: pilots, copilots, navigators, bombardiers, engineers, and— radiomen and gunners? What were they doing here?

"Ten-hut!"

Muttered complaints stopped instantly. Chins tucked. Spines stiffened.

An unbelievably tall officer with long legs bypassed the stairs and stepped easily onto the raised platform. When he turned and faced the front, a soft hiss of surprise broke the uneasy silence.

His young, gaunt face spoke of past horrors and the grinding fatigue only war can bring. Three rows of ribbons below pilot's wings decorated his chest and the silver eagles of a full-bird colonel rode his broad shoulders. He offered no greeting. Only a gruff, "At ease," in a voice so low, it scraped bottom. "I'm Colonel Savage."

A shiver of anticipation shot through Bill's body. This was no desk jockey.

The colonel unrolled a large photo, propped it on an easel, and slapped it with his pointer. "This is your last strike. Can anybody tell me what percentage of your bombs hit the rail yard?" He studied the men, face grim.

"Zero percent ... sir?"

A few laughs died as Savage's gaze settled in on the joker. "What's your name, son?" Little above a whisper, but it sliced through the silent room like a sharp axe through kindling.

"Uh, First Lieutenant Steven Hobbs ... sir."

"Bombardier?"

"Yes, sir."

The new CO tapped the photo. "You're only a tad on the low side, Lieutenant Hobbs, though you may be right about *your* bombs." His eyes narrowed, focused on the hapless bombardier. "Twelve percent of the bombs dropped by the 396th were on target. Full service to the rail yard was restored within hours." His gaze shifted, traveling from face to face. "Confirmed destroyed: an orchard, a deserted winery, a flock of hens, and two cows."

Bill held his breath.

Savage raked the photo onto the floor and squared his shoulders, eyes strafing the room. "This is not a walk in the park. This. Is. A. *War*. Gentlemen!" He waited for a moment, then stepped to the front of the platform. "Listen up. The changes on this base are as follows: No leave or passes will be issued until strike photos improve; downtime will be spent bombing mockup targets; navigators, you will be expected to *find* those targets; gunners will practice firing from the back of a moving truck—yes, the way you did it in Gunnery School; at the end of a month, every crew member will be evaluated and reassigned if he can't—or won't—cut the mustard." The colonel rocked back on his heels. "Major Hirsch, my aide, will hand out your assignments at the door." A pause as he once again scanned the room. "Dismissed!"

Bill would never forget the elation he felt at that moment. The time spent honing skills meant a longer wait until he reached his twenty-five, but for the first time since being assigned to the 396th, he had felt proud.

A hand on his shoulder startled him back to the present.

Rob stood beside him, grinning. "You want more coffee, or are you ready to have a look at the *Maggie*?"

He scrambled to his feet. "Ready, sir—Rob."

Maggie and the Townsend women visited the Weaving Shop. The Americans expressed amazement at how quickly the young lasses worked, and appeared amused by the gay, girlish chatter.

"This doesn't look like one of those 'sweat shops' I've read about in the paper," Mel said. "They look like they're enjoying themselves."

"'Tis a pleasant way to pass the day. Some of my happiest times are spent at my loom."

"You weave too?" Trish asked.

"Och, every lass on the island learns spinning and weaving at a verra early age. I'm already teaching our auldest lass, Annie, the basics—carding the wool and twisting it into tight, smooth strands for spinning. 'Tis how we get cloth for clothes and household needs."

Paula frowned. "But it takes so long to get enough cloth for, say, a skirt. That's a lot of work for an article of clothing that won't last more than a season or two."

Maggie ran a hand down the light woolen plaid skirt she was wearing. "I've had this skirt over ten years. The colours are still as bright as they were the day I took the wool out of the dye bath."

Trish fingered the material. "Amazing. How do these new ones hold up?"

"Every bit as well. Dark colours don't fade and the cloth never wears oot."

Paula Townsend shook her head. "I've had brand-new skirts and dresses that didn't look good for a year. What's the difference between what I'm buying and your clothing?"

"We use only local wool, and we always use natural dyes from herbs and plants, plus alum to set the color. We've learned to take verra special care when we wash our woolens. There's no dry cleaner on Innisbraw."

The women wandered over to the General Store, which had little on the shelves.

"Most of us grow and can our own vegetables," Maggie said. "And our crofters raise sheep for mutton and Hielan coos for beef. A few have swine, most of us have chickens, and there's always seafood."

Mel poked a bruised apple. "What do you do for fruit? All I see are a few overpriced oranges and some apples—oh, and jars of 'bramble jelly.'"

Apparently, Americans had no idea that strict rationing still dogged those in the UK. "That's one place you have an advantage. The guid weather doesn't last long enough, especially for fruit trees, but we gather wild berries for bramble jelly, and have to do with tinned fruit when it's available."

Anna MacKinnon cornered Maggie as they were leaving. "Maggie, I've already received a shipment of canned pumpkin for your Thanksgiving pies, and I've ordered some more of those extra-large California pitted olives."

"You're a dear." Maggie hugged her. "Jill's mither wrote that we can make the pies ahead and freeze them unbaked. Think of all the time we'll save the day before Thanksgiving."

"You mean you celebrate Thanksgiving here too?" Paula asked. "I thought that was only an American holiday."

"It really is, but Rob wanted our bairns to celebrate one American holiday on Innis Fell, so he chose Thanksgiving."

Mel pointed back at the meat display. "Do they bring in turkeys?"

"No turkey. They don't have that here, so we substitute other meats, but Rob and the others from America say that, other than the turkey, our meal is verra similar."

"Well, where there's a will, there's a way." Trish winked at Mel and Paula.

❧

Rob and Maggie invited the Townsends to their home for supper the following Friday een. They also asked Den and Pete and their families, so the men could have some time to talk about their experiences at the 396th. Since it was unseasonably warm, Maggie fixed partan bree, fresh bannock, and a large salad with greens from her garden.

Rob eyed two clootie dumplings on the warming shelf above the stove and kissed Maggie's flushed cheek. "You've outdone yourself, lass. We haven't had clootie dumplings or partan bree for months."

"'Tis a taste of Scotland, luve. I was tempted to fix haggis, but I wasn't sure they'd like it. Partan bree seemed a better choice."

Den entertained everyone with exaggerated tales of the bomber crew's escapades in the village of Edenoaks. "Of course, the commander didn't take part in the brawling. He'd have had to confine himself to the base, and then who would have led the strikes?"

"The commander didn't *want* to take part in the brawling." Rob shot Den a stern look. "I was having enough trouble with the Jerries. No reason to take on the pub owners too."

"Bill said you were one of the first commanders to take an active part in the bombing missions," Paula said. "Why is that?"

"Well, up to that time, the entire focus was on tactics. The commanders planned the strikes by the book, and the crews carried them out. Unlike the fighter groups, where the commanders took an active role." He leaned forward in his chair and twisted his napkin. "Remember, this kind of air war was all new. Before this, there was no teamwork. It was every man for himself, a lot like it was in WWI. But if you wanted to run the bombing war like you would a business, you had to have teamwork. It seemed to me the commander who planned the strike should lead it, a lot like how the president of a company or captain of a football team take an active role." He dropped the napkin, face burning. "Sorry for the lecture."

"You left out one very important element," Bill said. "Morale. It's a lot harder to respect the commander who flies a desk than it is the commander who leads the dirty missions."

"It sure is." Pete stabbed his finger for emphasis. "I know for a fact there wasn't a man on base who wouldn't have flown through a solid brick wall for Rob, myself included."

⁂

Maggie could see Rob's growing distress. "Why don't you men carry some more chairs out to the entry? We'll have our sweetenins out there, so the bairns can play in the yard."

The women cleared the table while the men carried out the chairs. Fern washed Beth's face and hands. Seconds after rubbing her cheeks dry with her palms, the lass disappeared into Robbie's bedroom and came out carrying a ball in each hand. Most of the bairns chased her out the door and into the yard, Shep at their heels.

"I don't see how you can handle four small children," Paula said as she rinsed bowls and dishes and stacked them on the bunker. "I thought two was a handful."

If only Paula knew. "They are, as you say, a handful, but for the most part,they entertain each other."

Annie shambled from her bedroom, carrying her sock doll. "Mither, I can't find my bairnie's blanket."

"'Tis on the shelf in your closet. I washed it."

"It looks like Annie would rather play 'mama' than toss a ball," Trish said, smiling.

"She's no' one to run about ootside verra much. I'm surprised Katie didn't stay inside to play with her. She usually does."

Fern picked young Matt up from the hearth rug and felt his hippen. "Katie's got a new project. She's determined to help with Malcolm's rehabilitation. She even said she's going to play ball with him every day when school starts next week."

"Rehabilitation?" Paula asked. "Oh, you must mean his arm. I noticed he seems to favor it." She turned to Caroline. "Did he injure it?"

"It was a birth defect. Doctor John, Maggie's faither, operated on it weeks ago to straighten it. He has therapy every day."

"It's a wonder what medicine can do these days," Trish said. "I understand a lot of new techniques came out of treating the wounded during the war."

"Aye, they did." Maggie nodded. "Otherwise, Rob might not be alive today."

"Malcolm's an adorable boy." Paula wiped her hands. "He certainly favors you, Caroline, with that brown hair and those large brown eyes."

Maggie held her breath.

Caroline's face paled. "Malcolm's not our lad." Her voice trembled. "He's living with us while he has his therapy."

"Oh, for heaven's sake," Paula said, "I'm sorry. I couldn't help noticing how your husband dotes on the boy and assumed ..."

"He's become verra fond of Malcolm," Maggie put in quickly. "We all have."

Maggie left the bairns with Fern and Jill the next day, so she and Rob could see the Townsend family off on the ferry.

When Rob and Captain MacNamara went through their saluting

ritual, Trish laughed. "Now we'll have to listen to all the conjecture on our way to Barra and back to Oban."

He bumped her arm. "No' a word, young lass, or Rob Roy will haunt you."

Bill hugged Maggie. "Our reservations are already taken care of, so look for us next year." He clasped Rob's hand. "Thanks for everything. You'll never know how great it was seeing you again, Commander."

"And you. Have a safe journey."

"Godspeed," Maggie called as the Townsends boarded the ferry.

Chapter Twenty-Three

School started the following week, with the Elspeth NicAllister Academy opening its doors for the first time.

Hugh rang the hand bell and the entire student body walked single-file to the kirk for opening chapel. His heart swelled with gratitude as he opened the service with silent prayer.

No longer would the halflins have to board on the isles of Harris, where they were ridiculed for their language and naïveté. And for a fraction of the cost of Harris Academy, no' to mention the high cost of room and board, the Innisbraw students could remain at home where they belonged and still receive an accredited education. He thanked the Lord for Rob and his partners and their generous donation. Without it, none of this would have been possible.

During the third week of September, the *Maggie*'s crew was shouted out in the mids o' the night. One of the large trawlers out of Oban had run aground on the skerries and was being torn apart on the rocks. The sea ran high, and darkness made the sling transfer treacherous.

Rob ran the transfer crew from the deck, with Den assisting. There was no margin for error the night. They had successfully transported five of the trawler's crew, lights turned toward the lines, when the trawler's skipper hailed the *Maggie*. "We're abandoning ship!"

"Stay aboard for another transfer!" Rob shouted into the bullhorn. "Do no' abandon ship!"

Four men jumped from the aft deck of the listing boat, another from amidship.

Why had the skipper ignored his order? Rob grabbed Den's arm. "Get Christopher back here now. Either that skipper's an eejit, or there's a problem we canna see." He ran to the ladder, slid down to the fantail, and tied his lifeline to the railing. "Paddy, Ewan, Alex, take the four who jumped toward the aft. James and Stephen, stand by our lines and be ready to pull us in. The minute Den has Christopher aboard, get them both down here to help you." He pulled up his hood, slipped into his flippers, climbed onto the railing, and signaled his men to jump.

Maggie's bright emergency lights reflected off the waves, nearly blinding Rob as he struck out toward the trawler. He bumped into Ewan, who floundered in the glare. "That way!" Rob pointed and pushed Ewan to the left. Rob's long strokes quickly outdistanced the lad.

A wave caught him and spun him round.

He shook his head to clear the water from his face. *Show me the way, Faither God.*

Farther from the *Maggie*'s lights, the glare was gone, but the waves were so high, night so dark, he was almost blind again. He thought he spotted a man a few metres ahead, being carried about like a piece of flotsam by the surging sea.

Rob's leg hit something solid. A rock! He put his head down and dove beneath the next wave, backtracking.

Och, he'd lost sight of the man.

Rob struggled to keep from being thrown into the rock again.

The water around him suddenly lit up. Somebody aboard the Maggie was using the portable spotlight.

Another wave crashed over his head. He swam hard, spitting out seawater, muscles screaming, heart pounding.

Where was the victim?

He lost momentum. The pounding waves and roiling currents tumbled him backward.

His leg hit the rock again.

Rob gasped in pain.

Swallowed more water.

Something inside him snapped. Hot anger propelled him through the spume crashing high above the rocks.

The spotlight lit on his victim, who was slammed against the splintered hull of the trawler.

Rob ignored the pain in his leg and grabbed a sleeve.

A white, panic-filled face stared up at him. Och, only a lad.

"I'm a rescue swimmer. Put your arms around my neck!" Battling the pounding waves, it took Rob the better part of a minute to take the slack out of his lifeline. He jerked it three times.

The rope tightened around his waist.

The lad's hands slipped.

Rob took hold of the lad's life jacket and used the momentum of a wave to flip the lad over onto his back. "Don't fight me!"

The journey back to the *Maggie* lasted an eternity. Rob's leg burned and pulsed with each heartbeat. The hand gripping the lad's life jacket turned numb with cold.

When they finally reached the fantail, Christopher jumped into the water and boosted the victim up, and James pulled him onto the fantail deck.

Rob treaded water with one leg, gritting his teeth against the pain in the other.

Christopher helped him position his hands on the ropes, then pushed him up, rung by rung.

When Rob reached the deck, he collapsed onto his knees, yelped with pain, and retched.

Hands gripped his arms and lifted him up.

He tried to stand but his right leg buckled.

Den's face swam into view. "We're going to carry you, Rob. Try to relax."

He wanted to help but didn't have the strength. After they got him to the main deck, they carried him into the cabin and laid him on a stretcher.

⚓

Den fought his panic. He should have been with Rob, not safe on the *Maggie.* "'Tis his right leg," he said to Matthew, "and he's swallowed a lot of water."

Rob tried to sit up. "The others!" he gasped, then retched again.

Den held Rob's head to one side, so he wouldn't choke. "They're all back. Get us oot of here, Neil!" He took off Rob's hood and flippers and peeled off his wet suit.

Christopher shoved blankets into Matthew's waiting hands.

The medic covered Rob and bent close to examine his leg. "A deep laceration on his calf, and his knee's swelling."

Rob tried to sit up.

Again, Den pushed him back. "Stay put. You banged your leg up pretty bad."

"I'm all right. Want to check the victims." Only a croak, that voice.

"They're being seen to. That's what your crew's for."

"The lad I pulled oot?"

Den glanced across the cabin. "Looks like he's conscious, but he swallowed a gallon of seawater."

Rob lay back, panting, turned his head and retched yet again.

"That's the way, bucko, get it all up."

Twenty minutes out of Innisbraw, Rob's vitals had improved enough for Den to leave his side. He stepped around four other

137

stretchers and five blanket-clad fishermen sitting on the deck. Grabbing the radio from Neil, he said to Control, "We'll need four cairts and ask John to be at the dock. We've five in-water victims and five transferred by sling." He didn't mention Rob's leg. No need to send Maggie into a panic.

Seconds after the *Maggie* bumped against the dock, John rushed in, gaze sweeping the cabin. When he saw Rob on a stretcher, he looked shaken.

Den took his arm. "I don't think 'tis serious. He's gotten rid of most of the seawater he swallowed, but he did bang his leg up a bit."

John threw back the blanket and removed the bloody gauze from Rob's calf. "More than a bit from the size of this cut. He'll need stitches." He pressed his fingers lightly into Rob's knee.

Rob yelped. "Take it easy, John," he rasped. "That hurts."

"I'm sure it did. You've a massive hematoma there." He looked at Den. "The other victims?"

"All conscious and alert. Twa swallowed a lot of water but got most of it up. Vitals are stable."

John straightened. "Put Rob in the first cairt. That leg needs attention. One more can ride with him, and the other three can go in the next cairt. On you go."

⚓

As Maggie ran down the hall, John stepped out of the x-ray room and stopped her. "Rob's all right," he said, gripping her shoulders. "He cut his leg and bruised his knee, but none of it is serious."

"His left leg again?"

"His right this time. He'll have to use crutches for a while, but his patella's no' broken."

She clenched her trembling hands. Why hadn't they called her to meet the *Maggie*? "I have to see him. Where is he?"

"Still in the x-ray room."

She pulled away.

He drew her back. "He's hoarse from retching. Don't let him talk too much."

She opened the door, ran across the room, and threw herself over Rob.

Warm fingers stroked her cheek. "'Tis all right, luve."

All right? How many times had she heard him say those words? She clung to him, shaking. "You were almost killed again. When will this end?"

"It wasn't that bad, lass. I promise."

138

Another empty promise? She pressed her cheek to his chest—his warm, *living* chest—the thrumming of his heart bringing no solace. So fragile, the timing of those beats, so easy to interrupt. To stop. The thought pierced her heart, bringing a gasp. "You canna keep tempting fate. Someday you … you won't come home."

His arms tightened. "What's this about fate?" He pushed her away and held her face between his palms, staring into her eyes. "Our Lord has His eye on me and His hand holding me up. Fate has nowt to do with it." A deep, hoarse cough burst from his throat, then another and another.

No matter the many times she'd promised herself it wouldn't happen, she'd done it again. She'd allowed her worst fears control of her thoughts, her tongue. "I'm sorry." She moaned. "I ken you're right. I get so afeart. Den came to the house and pulled Fern ootside to talk. The minute I saw her, I knew from her look you'd been injured again … or worse."

"Och, Maggie, I'm so sorry."

"When am I going to start trusting the Lord?" Exhausted, she pulled down the sheet and rested her head on his bare chest. *My faith has faltered again, Faither. Please help me rest in Your promises.*

Rob went home on crutches the night. He wanted to curse at having to use the metal contraptions again, but he'd been fortunate. The rescue could have ended verra differently if all the men had jumped from amidship.

He took the next day off from work, relearning how to maneuver on crutches. Sitting at the kitchen table while folding hippens for Maggie, he had a sudden thought and laughed.

She tossed a hippen on the pile at her elbow. "What has you cackling like a broodie hen?"

"'Tis a wee bit drastic, but I finally found a way to keep from going to the next ceilidh." He wiggled a crutch.

Her lips thinned, cheeks flushed. "Och, 'tis indeed too drastic, and no' only a wee bit."

"But I've been saved, lass. No more having to dance with tourists until next year. I feel like a condemned man who got a last-minute reprieve."

Though Rob did not have to dance at the last ceilidh of the year, Elspeth did ask him to attend and translate her Gaelic story into English. "Nobody can do it but you, Rob, and it's been a month since we did it last, so 'twill be the Selkie story again. Besides, I'm thinking you'll cut a fine figure in your kilt. Everyone will wonder how you hurt your leg."

"And I suppose you'll tell them."

"A little publicity for the Innisbraw Rescue Boat Foundation surely would no' be remiss. Remember, you need donations to keep operating."

"No' that badly. Besides, no tourist is going to donate money to our fund."

How could eyes that had seen so much over the years look so guileless? "I wouldn't be so sure of that. 'Tis all part of a Scotland experience, giving to continue the heroic rescue of hapless victims of the sea."

He shook his head and chuckled. "Och, Elspeth, you should have gone on the stage. You could convince an audience up is doon and in is oot."

"Then you'll do it?"

"Have you left me a choice? But I warn you, the first tourist who mentions the word 'hero' is getting an earful."

She patted his hand. "Of course, dear lad, of course."

Chapter Twenty-Four

If it wasn't for having to go to the ceilidh, Rob would have enjoyed the ride to the kirk hall in Angus's cairt. Cold licked his ears and the back of his neck—typical for an een in late October—but the louring clouds promised no rain and the wind was light, bending spikes of girse like long green fingers waving at their passing. Thank the Lord he didn't have to dance or make inane conversation with some simpering female. He could do this.

He changed his mind when Paddy introduced him to the crowd. "And Rob will be doin' the translatin' for our Elspeth. He's the *Maggie*'s brave commander, who was injured during a daring night rescue a few days ago."

"I'm about to take that lad off the rescue crew," Rob whispered to Maggie.

"Don't blame Paddy, luve. I'm thinking Elspeth put him up to it."

Indeed, Elspeth's smile was radiant as she launched into the Selkie story.

Rob was so embarrassed at the tourists' stares he almost faltered over the words, but his pride wouldn't allow that to happen. Let them all stare. When the last words of the story left his mouth, the audience erupted into thunderous applause. If he wasn't on these awkward crutches, he'd walk out right now.

Morag appeared at his elbow with a cup of coffee. "Your voice was even deeper than usual. I'm thinking you need a sip of something hot."

He accepted the coffee with a grateful nod. "Thank ye, Morag. I'm still a bit hoarse is all."

"The seawater will do it every time."

Maggie laced her fingers through his. "It was wunnerfae, luve. You made the story come alive."

"No' as much as you always did for me." He leaned down and kissed her cheek.

Angus wove his way through the crowd toward them, eyes downcast, ruddy cheeks flaming. So the tourists made Angus uncomfortable too. Rob said his guidbyes to Elspeth, hoping she

141

wouldn't say something about their early departure, but she only smiled and thanked him for coming.

⁂

"Elspeth looked spent the een," Maggie said after Angus dropped them at their gate.

"I didn't notice."

"Och, Rob, haud yer wheesht. Elspeth wants the ceilidhs to be a success. Don't dismiss her, no' after the friend she's been to you all these years."

The truth in her words cramped his belly. Elspeth had been his staunchest supporter since he first came to Innisbraw. Now that he thought about it, she had looked spent, and her voice was no' as strong as the last time she told the story—and that only a month ago. He embraced Maggie's shoulder and led her up the entry steps. "You're right. I'll stop acting the fool. She's my closest friend, and I luve her dearly."

⁂

When the rescue crew held their meeting to discuss the month's rescues, Rob found out from Christopher why the skipper had given the order to abandon ship.

"There was a muckle hole in the hull 'neath the fish holds. The sea was rushing in so fast it popped both hatches, and fish and water were half a metre deep on the deck. Only hanging onto the railing kept me from sliding over the side."

Rob nodded. "I'm glad to know there was a guid reason. Now I've a question. Who used the handheld spotlight?"

Den's hand shot up. "Guilty as charged."

"We'll have to do that more often during night rescues." Rob grinned at his friend. "It concentrates the light so you can orient yourself. Thank ye, Den."

Returning the grin, Den drawled, "Any time, Commander."

⁂

Rob tucked the bedquilt cover over Robbie's shoulders and sat on the side of the bed, looking down at his sleeping lad.

Hair a mop of loose, tousled curls, long black lashes kissing ruddy cheeks, arms flung above his head, knobby wrists peeking out of nightclothes already outgrown. Five years auld, a month past. His lad was growing up.

He kissed Robbie's cheek and wandered around the bedroom, amazed at how orderly it was. No' a ball in sight—must be tucked

142

into drawers below the shelves filled with toys, oddly shaped rocks, shells, and books. He touched a fingertip to the tin airieplane, safe on the highest shelf, that Auld Malcolm had gifted the lad on his first birthday.

A deep, familiar ache twisted his belly. How he missed the gruff, kind skipper.

Chapter Twenty-Five

The weather changed overnight. By mornin, the cool, dry, late fall weather changed to gusting winds and drenching rain. A dark, roiling cloud obscured the top of Ben Innis. Angus, cairt covered with a waxed-cotton tarp to keep his passengers dry, showed up early to ferry the residents of Innis Fell to the kirk.

In the sanctuary, the aisle runners, soaked by wet wellies and dripping waxed jackets, reeked with the musty smell of damp wool, which overpowered the redolence of beeswax candles.

Hugh took his place at the lectern. "The weather this mornin reminds us once again how important it is to pray for our fishermen and our rescue crew," he said in the Gaelic. "The work they do is necessary, or they would all remain safe in their cottages when the wind howls and the rain comes doon in torrents. Hold them up every day, by name, before our Lord. It is our duty to do so. All of these men belong to our family and are beloved. Never forget that we canna ken when their lives may depend upon our prayers. Let us pray silently and fervently." He bowed his head.

⚓

After the lesson, a continuation of Hugh's study on intercessory prayer, Rob gathered his rescue crew and told them to be especially alert. "If you fall sick or cannot answer the shout siren for any reason, let me know so I can schedule someone to fill your place without waiting until you don't show up aboard the *Maggie*. In weather like this, every tick counts."

⚓

The siren on Innis Fell wailed its strident warning as Angus was taking the Savage and Anderson families home. Without being asked, he turned Feona around and headed back down the hill.

"Drop Den at the pier, then take me to the shed!" Rob shouted to Angus. Rob leaned closer to Den. "Take a crew of nine, including yourself. I'll man the Control radio to free up Alex. Don't take chances without someone to cover your six. Godspeed."

"Will do, bucko." Den kissed Fern and his bairns, pulled aside a corner of the tarp, and jumped from the back of the cairt.

144

At the boatshed, Rob grabbed his crutches and climbed down from the cairt. "Pray!" he called.

The crutches sank into wet sand, slowing his steps to the door.

After brushing the rain from his hair, he hobbled toward his office and the control room at its side. Making certain he could read Alex's notes on the call, Rob sent him to the *Maggie*, then sat down at the radio.

The distress call had come from a large trawler that had lost engine power in the southern Minch. No way could the *Maggie* tow a trawler that size in the mids of a storm.

Rob radioed the Barra rescue service and asked for an assist.

Twa rescue boats should have power to do the job, but such an endeavor was still fraught with danger.

He radioed the trawler and told the skipper that help was on the way. "Can you keep your boat headed into the sea? Over."

"We're trying. We have two men at the helm. Over."

"How many souls aboard?"

"Nine. Repeat, nine."

"Are your men vested up with lifelines tied?"

"We've taken every precaution we can, but our holds are full. We were on our way in when our engines quit, so we're low in the water."

"Roger that. I'll give your frequency to the *Maggie*, so stand by to receive. Oot."

"Thank you, Innisbraw. Oot."

Rob radioed Den and gave him the trawler's location and frequency, Barra Rescue's frequency, and told him of the assist. "If you think you can't wait that long, or the tow won't work for any reason, try the sling. I know you'll make the right decision."

No question, Den could handle the call, but it didn't mean Rob had to like being left on land.

Keying the mike to Receive, he sat back to wait. The hands on the wall clock ticked away the minutes. The radio remained silent. He prayed for each member of his crew by name, then for the souls on the stricken trawler and those aboard the Barra rescue boat.

Violent wind gusts shook the shed. The large timbered doors groaned and rattled against their overhead tracks.

"Innisbraw Control, this is the *Maggie*. Do you read me? Over."

Rob grabbed the mike. "Den, this is Rob. I read you loud and clear. Over."

"We're still at least ten minutes oot. Sea's running so fast and high our deck's awash."

"How's the trawler? Are they still keeping her headed into the waves?"

"Aye. Skipper says he has a seasoned crew. Will transmit the minute we see them. *Maggie* oot."

"Roger, Den. Control oot." Unwilling to rely on the wall clock, Rob checked his watch and blew on his hands, flexing his fingers. Why was it so hard for him to sit and wait?

He had a sudden vision of Maggie huddled over the radio every time he went on a shout. No wonder she was afeart. The waiting alone was enough to unnerve anyone.

Nine and a half minutes later he received another message from the *Maggie*. The trawler had been sighted, and the *Maggie* was attempting to get as close as possible.

"Take it easy," Rob ordered. "Don't try to get too close now. The Barra boat must still be a long way oot."

"Roger. They just notified us they're at least twenty minutes from our coordinates. But the trawler looks guid. We'll stand by and see what develops. *Maggie* oot."

Rob poured himself a cup of mashed tea from Alex's thermos. Tepid and bitter, but it gave him something to do. He sipped it, fingertips tapping on the desk. He fidgeted another ten minutes, then keyed his mike to broadcast. "Innisbraw Control to *Maggie*. Over."

"Nothing much to report, Rob. Barra radioed us they should be on-site within ten or eleven minutes. Wind's dying a bit, but the sea's still running high and heavy."

"If you can, let me know when they arrive. Oot."

"Will do, Commander. Oot."

Rob chafed at being still, wanted to get up and pace. Shivering, he blew on his hands again. It was cold in the shed without the heaters going. He checked his watch one more time.

The second hand ticked forward, yet time seemed to stand still.

He started to get up but sat back down. It would be his luck to be halfway across the room on his crutches when he received a message.

Why hadn't he gone on the shout, crutches or no crutches? But keeping one's feet was hard enough atop a heaving deck. He closed his eyes and prayed again.

A few minutes later, Den's voice came through. "Innisbraw Control, this is the *Maggie*. Over."

"Is Barra there? Over."

"They're here, Rob, but there's a problem. With the seas running this high, and almost zero visibility, even using our radar, there's no way we can attempt a tow, and Barra agrees. We're both going to try

146

our slings."

"Did you say both?"

"We'll stay on the portside, and they'll take the starboard. Too rough oot there for our inflatables. Over."

It would be a bear shooting sling lines in this storm. But what other option did they have? Pray God those at the helms of all three boats kept tight control. "Then go for it. Put another man on the helm to help Neil keep the *Maggie* steady if you need to, and check those lifelines twice when you go on deck. Oot."

"That's what we're doing. Catch you up later. Oot."

It was back to the waiting. But this time, Rob did get up. He used his crutches to pace into his office and back again, envisioning what was going on aboard the *Maggie*. Surely Den was running the sling operation. Shooting the sling line to the trawler in the wind and rain would be difficult, but the actual transfers would be even more dangerous. Rob's heart pounded.

If the helmsmen couldn't keep the boats steady, the sling lines could snap, dropping the lads being transferred into the icy, unforgiving sea.

He paced until his knee throbbed. The pain helped, kept his mind off all the grim possibilities. When even the pain could no longer distract him, he checked his watch again. Twenty minutes had passed.

His mind raced. Had something gone wrong? There were only nine souls to transport. With two boats each using a sling, they should have been finished by now. He knuckled his forehead. Under ideal conditions it took four or five minutes for each transfer. In the mids of a storm, the time could be double that—or longer.

He resumed pacing but kept his right foot off the floor. No reason to add more time to his recovery—more shouts where he would be manning the radio instead of in command of his boat.

Another fifteen minutes passed, and he sat down, propping the crutches on the side of the control desk.

"Innisbraw Control, this is the *Maggie*. Over."

He grabbed the mike. "How did it go? Over."

"It was hairy, Rob. When we were bringing James back over after all the transfers, the line fouled. We worked a long time but finally had to cut it and dump him into the water. Christopher and Paddy jumped in, and for a while it looked like we might lose all three. They swallowed a lot of water, but they're getting it up. We've started back in. Have John at the dock. We'll need three cairts. The Barra boat's coming in with us. We'll be chasing the sea, so we should be back in about thirty minutes. *Maggie* oot."

147

"Thank God. Control oot." Rob left the radio on Receive, in case there were any more broadcasts, and telephoned Elsepth for the cairts and John at the infirmary. His heart lurched even as tears of relief filled his eyes.

Den was safe. His crew was safe. All victims alive.

"Thank Ye, Lord. Only Your hand on those helms, and Your calm instructions whispered into the hearts of those lads involved, brought about another successful rescue."

Chapter Twenty-Six

Rob thumbed through his daily calendar, excitement growing. Only two days till the fourth Sunday in November, the date chosen to celebrate Thanksgiving on the fell. Propping his feet on the desk, he leaned back and relived memories of two years ago's celebration.

His thoughts slid past the food heaped high on three tables: roasted beef joints, leg of lamb—the first he had ever tasted—candied yams, mashed tatties and gravy. But it wasn't memories of food that warmed him. It was the fellowship, the unity of spirit, the prayers of gratitude for all the Lord had provided.

He made a mental list of what he had to be thankful for this year: another healthy laddie in their family, an island growing toward prosperity, he was finally off the crutches and back to work—

The phone rang, interrupting his thoughts.

He swung his legs from the desk and grabbed the telephone receiver. "Innisbraw Boatworks. Savage here."

"This is Oban Air Freight. We have a package for you. It's frozen, so you'll need to pick it up as soon as possible."

Frozen? A package for the boatworks? "How large is it?"

"It weighs two stone, one pound."

"We can fly over. Is it at the airstrip?"

"Aye. It's addressed to Commander Rob Savage, in care of Innisbraw Boatworks. If someone else is going to pick it up, they'll need written authorization."

"I'll be there in about an hour." Rob listened for the dial tone, then jiggled the receiver to call Maggie. He might be late for dinner.

❧

A weak, lemon-yellow sun glittered off whitecaps as the floatplane went airborne. Rob adjusted the heading and airspeed and trimmed the plane. Thank God the rain and cold wind they'd endured for weeks had moved south. He snorted. More likely holding its breath for a full-blown gale on Thanksgiving.

When he arrived at the freight counter, his confusion grew. The return address belonged to the Townsends. What could they send him that had to be frozen? He loaded the box into the plane, refueled, and

149

took off.

When he reached Innisbraw, he carried the package to the shed and put it on his desk. He didn't look forward to lugging it all the way up the fell. No' a problem normally, but he'd only been off crutches a few days, and the added weight could tax his knee. No way was he going to delay getting back in the commander's seat.

Graham knocked and leaned around the open door. "Rinait came by for a wee blether. Want a ride up the fell for dinner?"

Rob swallowed a laugh. Elspeth must have been praying overtime. He waved Graham in. "Would you grab that box and carry it oot to the cairt?"

"Hoot, aye!"

What was up with Graham? His cheeks were splotched with red, and his grin was wide enough to swallow a cat. Once they got outside, he gave Rinait, who was in the cairt, a long, hearty kiss.

They couldn't have been apart more than a few minutes. Rob had never seen the lad act that way in public.

He took up the reins and slapped Feona's rump.

The ride up the hill was filled with more puzzlements. The lass giggled, turning on the bench to wave at everyone they passed, jiggling her legs, twisting her handkerchief.

Maggie stood on the entry when they arrived.

Rob retrieved the package from the back of the cairt.

"What is it, Rob?"

"Don't know. 'Tis from the Townsends." In a few long strides, he reached his Maggie.

Her lips softened and moved beneath his.

If Graham could do it … "Open the door for me. I'll take it in the kitchen, and we'll have a keek."

Rinait dogged their heels. No' unusual, that. She'd always been a curious lass.

Rob grabbed a knife and cut the string at the top of the box. He pulled a large white package from the heavy box.

Maggie and Rinait gasped.

"Och, for …" Rob laughed. A turkey!

"What is it?" Maggie asked. "Some kind of joke?"

"'Tis no joke, lass. 'Tis a turkey!" He read the label. "A twenty-five pound, nine-ounce tom turkey."

Maggie clapped her hands. "A turkey!" Her laughter joined his. "For our Thanksgiving dinner."

Rob read the care instructions and made room in the refrigerator, so the bird would thaw gradually, then sat down to a bowl of bree, while Rinait and Maggie sipped their tea.

"'Twill be a verra festive dinner with a turkey," Rinait said. "I canna wait to taste it."

"Turkey's guid," Rob said. "Even better than chicken."

Rinait tossed her heavy red braid over a shoulder and giggled again.

Maggie pushed a plateful of scones toward the red-faced lass. "Try one of these. They're made with orange juice and rind."

Rob steeled himself. If she giggled again ...

"I don't think I'd better. My stomach's a bit uggit lately."

A smile warmed Maggie's eyes. "Why would a lass young as you have an uggit stomach?"

Rinait grabbed Maggie's hand. "Och, Maggie, Mither's visiting the sick today, and I have to tell someone or I'll burst. I'm biggen!"

Smiling, Rob shook his head. Such a simple answer to his wondering. "Congratulations. So that's why you came to see Graham the day?"

"Aye. Doctor John just told me it was certain. I couldn't wait."

Maggie hugged her. "We're so happy for you, lass. Another wee bairnie on the way. Innisbraw's growing, and that's a fact."

Maggie said a prayer of thanks when all the women on the fell pitched in to prepare dinner. One turkey, even such a large tom, would never feed twenty adults, twa halflins, and seven bairns, so Jill roasted a beef joint, and Caroline, a leg of lamb. Tatties were boiled and mashed, cabbage shredded for slaw, candied yams prepared, gravy thickened with corn starch, dozens of rolls baked, canned peas heated, and olives, sweet pickles, bramble jelly, and heather honey placed in small bowls. Pumpkin pies, clootie dumplings, and a sticky toffee pudding lined Maggie's bunker, and three pots of tea joined two of coffee on the warming shelf. By the time the last guests arrived, three tables placed end to end groaned under the weight of the food.

Everybody liked the turkey, especially Elspeth. "If I'd known what I was missing all these years, I'd have been biling. It has a fine, rich taste."

Word about the couple was already all over the island in the last few days, and everyone congratulated Rinait and Graham on their expected bairnie.

Calum leaped up to propose a toast.

Where was the quiet Calum they all knew and luved?

151

"To all those with new bairnies on the way, especially my bonnie wife, Ellie. Slainte mhath!"

A new round of congratulations followed, with more toasts. Maggie smiled and wiped a tear away. Ellie was biggen. What blessed news. Maggie and Calum's mither would have luved to have been at the table with the family the night.

The loss was never truly gone.

Maggie stole a glance at Caroline. She looked to be bearing up well, smiling and whispering something to Pete.

He nodded and pushed back from the table. "Well, we auld folk can't compete with these two young couples when it comes to such news, but I'd still like to propose a toast to Malcolm, who has worked verra, verra hard for several months. Come you here, Malcolm."

The lad pushed back his chair and stood beside Pete, studying the floor but smiling.

"Show them, lad."

Using his left hand, Malcolm took the full glass of milk Pete was offering. He brought it to his mouth, drank several sips, then handed the glass back. Not a drop spilled.

Pete hugged him and raised his coffee mug. "To Malcolm, who's shown us aulder folk a thing or twa about courage. Slainte mhath!"

The adults leaped to their feet and raised their cups and mugs. "Slainte mhath!" they shouted.

Maggie caught Rob's gaze and nodded. She was certain there wasn't a person present who doubted what kind of future lay ahead for the once shy lad with the malformed arm who had come such a long way. Pitcher or pilot, or anything else he chose, it didn't matter. He would excel. If only Pete and Caroline would be able to claim him as a son.

Chapter Twenty-Seven

March 1950

John received an unexpected, early afternoon visit from Pete and Caroline. Pete's pale, taut face and Caroline's haunted eyes were a clear indication this involved Malcolm. He led them to his office, pulled two chairs in front of his desk, and eased himself down onto his.

Pete clasped his chair's arms, knuckles blanching. "Caroline received a phone call from the Oban orphanage this mornin'." He leaned forward, gaze pinning John. "They want a medical update on Malcolm."

"Why would they contact you and no' me?"

"I don't know, but he's still having therapy," Caroline said. "Surely he isn't ready to go back yet."

John had been expecting something like this for weeks, but the orphanage had no business contacting the Hastings.

It was obvious Caroline wanted to adopt Malcolm. Pete took the lad flying, played ball with him by the hour, yet hadn't voiced his commitment.

John leaned back in his chair and steepled his fingers. "We could delay it for another twa or three months, but no longer than that. He's almost reached the maximum use he'll ever have from that arm and hand."

Pete's cheeks flushed. "But won't his control improve even more as he grows older?"

"His hand may some, but his left arm will always be a wee bit weaker than the right—though, unless he decides to be a stonemason or the like, it shouldn't impede his ability to find a profession." John sighed. "'Tis much like Rob's arm. There'll always be things he shouldn't do."

Pete snorted and leaped up, pacing. "I don't notice it slowing Rob down."

"It doesn't, but it should. Some day that lad's going to pay the piper, but I can't run his life for him. He does what he thinks he must and the de'il with the consequences."

"You're saying sometime in June at the latest?"

Though Caroline's soft question tore at John's heart, prolonging her agony would be cruel. "Aye. That's the truth of it."

Tears sparkled on her lashes as her gaze followed Pete's steps to the window overlooking the ben.

"You were right, you know," Pete said, turning to face John. "The lad's shyness has all but disappeared, but he's still struggling at school. I'm not sure I'm skilled enough to help with what he needs. He didn't receive much of an education at the orphanage. He's small for his age, but I suppose he always will be."

The doctor stroked his beard. "That particular orphanage has an excellent school, and they have received many commendations. And I don't find the lad small for his age. Quite the contrary. What problem are you talking about?"

Pete looked at Caroline.

"He doesn't read as well as the other ten-year-olds," she said, "and he—"

"Ten-year-olds!" John exclaimed. "What makes you think he's ten?"

"Den and Rob both said he was the last in line to be transferred to the *Maggie*," Pete answered for his wife. "That means he was one of the aulder lads in their rosters."

John got up and removed a file from his cabinet. "That doesn't agree with his skeletal development at all. And his front incisors just came in. That lad canna be over eight. We need to get this cleared up right now." He thumbed through his Rolodex and picked up the telephone.

⚓

Pulling her handkerchief from her pocket, Caroline dabbed at her eyes. Was it possible? Was Malcolm younger than they thought? She twisted the cloth between shaking fingers. Would this change Pete's mind? *Help me, Lord. Settle this once and for all. I can't go on hoping like this.*

John hung up the phone. "Malcolm Peter MacEnroe is eight years and one month old. He was born on February fifteenth, nineteen forty-twa."

Caroline met Pete's stunned stare, eyes swelling with tears again. Malcolm Peter MacEnroe. Even his name ... surely this meant he was destined to be their son.

"I can't believe it," Pete said. "And all this time we thought he was a little slow."

"If he's been able to remain in that class at school, I'd say the lad's extremely bright," John said.

"Malcolm *Peter*," Caroline whispered. She looked at Pete, eyes imploring him to make a decision—the right decision. "He's only a bairn."

Pete ran his hand over his face. "Could we be alone for a few minutes, John?"

"Of course. I have patients to see." The doctor quit the room, closing the door behind him.

Pete pulled Caroline up into his arms. Ashamed, he was. He wasn't like his father, who put work ahead of family, who missed every baseball game, who never took time to help with homework or attend a birthday pairty. Even if the lad had some challenges, Pete would be there to help. "I guess I've been a coward long enough. That young bairn has shown more grit in the past few months than I have in my entire life." He pressed his face against her hair. "I'm ashamed, honey, and humbled. If that brave lad still wants me for a faither, I'd be an eejit to turn him doon."

She buried her face against his shoulder and sobbed.

Pete took Caroline over to tell Maggie the good news, then went on to the shed. He found Rob wrapping up his monthly meeting with the rescue crew. "I want to talk to you about Malcolm's rescue."

Rob raised an eyebrow. "What about it? That was months ago."

Pete paced the office. "Why was one of the younger lads the last to transfer to the *Maggie*?"

"There were six- and seven-year-olds on that boat. I guess they put that above Malcolm's arm."

"But Malcolm wasn't even seven and a half. Why was he pushed to the back of the line?"

Rob stood. "Stay here." He left the office and returned several minutes later with Alex, the crew member who had supervised the loading of the sling aboard the doomed boat. "I want you to think back to the rescue that involved the orphans," Rob told Alex.

"All right, but it's been a fair while."

"I told you before you transferred over to the boat that I wanted the youngest bairns brought over first. Remember?"

Alex nodded.

"It seems that Malcolm, who was left to last should have been transported among that first group. What happened?"

155

Alex's face paled. "The adults there were the ones what put the bairns in line, no' me. I told them youngest first—took them as they handed them over."

"But why?" Pete asked, shaking. "Why did they do it? How could they do it? Malcolm could have drowned. With his bad arm, he should have been transferred first, no' last."

"I don't know why."

Rob turned to Alex. "None of this was your fault. You couldn't have known his age, or even that he had a bad arm."

"They kept shoving bairns at me, and I clipped them into the sling with me. I'm sorry, Pete, I truly am."

Pete slumped against the desk. "Rob's right, it wasn't your fault."

"You can go now, Alex," Rob said. "'Tis the orphanage that has some explaining to do, no' you. Thanks for setting us straight."

Alex touched his forelock. "Aye, Commander." He quit the office, eyes troubled.

"Come on, Pete," Rob said. "I'll walk you home.

Rob leaned against the kitchen bunker, smiling at the folk crowded into the living room. Bless Maggie for knowing those on the fell would want to celebrate Pete and Caroline's application to adopt Malcolm.

Other than flushed cheeks, the lad appeared to take it in stride better than the adults. Only his reference to his new parents as "Faither" and "Mither" and his calling the other adults "Uncle" and "Aunt" revealed a permanent change in the lad's status.

Caroline no longer hovered over the lad, but sat smiling, content to watch him from afar. And why no'? She had plenty of time now.

The pride in Pete's eyes warmed Rob. It had taken the Lord years to answer Caroline's prayers, but His timing was always perfect. Malcolm now had a faither who wanted him for all the right reasons.

Elspeth winked at Rob from Maggie's rocker. Though in front of a glowing peat fire, she huddled beneath a heavy hap. Two Sabbaths in a row she had missed kirk, because she was too tired to attend, and he'd had to carry her from Angus's cairt to the house this verra een. The joy he'd been feeling faded. He couldn't deny it any longer. His dear friend was failing.

Chapter Twenty-Eight

After the rainiest winter Rob could remember, the first sunny days of spring were greeted with sighs of relief. Every time he took a mornin run, he saw bedding being aired, rugs to be beaten hung from clotheslines, and cottages being cleaned from top to bottom. With the lambing season over, ploughing and planting began. Pete's builders took several weeks out of their busy schedule to make repairs to roofs.

Rob decided it was time to teach his bairns English. He sat them down on the hearth rug before story time every een to practice. Beth amazed him by how quickly she grasped a new word and used it correctly. She was only two and a half years old, yet her pronunciation of the English words was often superior to that of her aulder siblings. And she still insisted upon calling him Daddy. This youngest lass of his seemed fascinated with anything American.

The first ferry came into the harbour on the second day of June. Rob had his usual mixed feelings about the start of the tourist season. Aye, the added revenue for the island had brought many changes for the better, but dread for the summer influx of strangers filled him.

The ceilidhs.

He broke out in a cold sweat thinking about having to parade around in his kilt while strangers stared at him.

Elspeth couldn't be the storyteller this year. It had always taken a great deal out of her, and she was becoming frailer with each passing week. The women on Innis Fell now kept her garden weeded and pruned while she watched from her rocker on the entry. Rob began stopping each day on his way home from work to sit a spell and bring her up to date on all that was happening.

She still did the primary telephoning for the rescue service, but she turned over the chairmanship of the Island Council to Alec MacDonald. This woman, who took second place in his heart only to Maggie and his bairns, would no' be with them much longer. The thought of losing her tortured him.

One een in early June, they sat in their rockers on her entry, gazing out at the harbour and the sea beyond. Her eyes had a dreamy, unfocused appearance. What was she truly seeing?

Elspeth turned and smiled at him. "I've a proposition to put to you."

He took her tiny hand in his. Blue veins stood out against the paleness of her thin, wrinkled skin. "What's that?" he teased. "Another favour I'll hate doing but canna refuse?"

For a moment, her eyes sparked with youth. "You've a saucy tongue on you, Rob Savage." Her fingers tightened. "I don't think you'll hate what I have in mind."

"Then let me have it. What's your proposition?"

"You young folk are all alike, so impatient. You have no tolerance for the fine art of conversation."

He chuckled. "The longer you stall, the worse I think it's going to be, Elspeth. Oot with it."

"Och, all right. Here 'tis." She leaned forward in her rocker. "I ken how you hate dancing with strangers at the ceilidhs, so I'm thinking of having you released from this once-a-month duty."

"And ..."

"And in exchange for this most generous reprieve, I'd like you to translate the stories from the Gaelic into English every Saturday night." She leaned back, hand at her breast. "There. What say you?"

His eyebrow rose. "Let me get this straight. Instead of dressing in my kilt and suffering the stares of strangers only once a month, I now get to do it every Saturday night?"

"But you don't have to dance."

He was beginning to enjoy this conversation. "What if I want to dance with my Maggie?"

"Then you should. 'Tis only fitting to take your lass for a few turns round the floor."

"But I don't have to dance with the tourists, no' even once."

Gnarled fingers tapped his arm. "That's what I said. Is there something wrong with your hearing, lad?"

"Can I leave the ceilidh early?"

"Of course. You're an adult. Take your leave when you're ready." She sat back and closed her eyes.

Rob knelt in front of her. "What is it? Are you feeling ill?" He took her cold hand and clasped it between his palms.

"No." She stroked his cheek. "'Tis just that I won't be telling the tales this season, and Auntie Mairet has a tendency to ramble. I'm counting on you to keep the story going, even if you have to embellish on what she's saying a wee bit, or even change the story completely if she gets so badly off track she doesn't make sense. You're the only one I trust to do this, lad."

A lump formed in his throat. Another activity she could no longer keep up with. He rose and leaned down to kiss her cheek. "'Tis a generous offer. I'll do it gladly."

Her tears mirrored his. Both knew time was running out, and quickly.

⚜

Rinait delivered a healthy, eight-pound lad on the seventh of June. Graham was delighted that the bairnie was a redhead like his mither. They named him James Angus MacDonald.

Ellie, after a difficult delivery, presented Calum with a lass on the tenth of June. Wee Julia Anne had curly black hair like her faither and was so tiny Calum and Richie were afraid to hold her.

The folk on Innisbraw were becoming accustomed to the steeple bell ringing out the news of another birth. The young lads and lasses who had married in the past two years were producing bairns at an ever-increasing rate. The general store could no' keep enough hippens in stock. Fern started up her wellness clinic again and had a steady stream of young bairns receiving their smallpox shots, and new bairnies their first inoculations against childhood diseases.

Innisbraw was truly growing.

Chapter Twenty-Nine

On June 19, Rob and Pete were returning to the shed from checking out a problem on a cottage renovation on the western side of the island when Den ran down the boatworks' pier to meet him.

"You aren't going to believe this!" he shouted, waving a yellow paper. "The telegraph office called your home number, and when nobody answered, they sent a boat from Oban. You got greetings from Uncle Sam."

Rob grabbed the paper. "Greetings? What are you talking about?" He hastily scanned the body of the telegram, steps slowing to a stop. "This has to be a mistake. They can't do this."

"If you didn't check off that wee square on your discharge papers saying you didn't want to be recalled, they can. Otherwise they can call you up again anytime there's a war, or rumors of one." Den groaned, his face red as a rowan berry. "Don't tell me you checked the wrong square."

Rob grabbed Den's shoulder and hustled him through the shed doorway and into the office. "I got a medical discharge, remember? There were no wee squares."

"Do you have it—your medical discharge, I mean? This is serious."

Rob threw the telegram on his desk and pulled open the bottom drawer of his file cabinet, rifling through old folders, breathing heavy. He pulled up a paper and waved it. "Here 'tis. Don't know why I kept it, but I did." He scanned the document quickly and passed it to Den. "See? No boxes to check. And it's signed by Major General Harlan Fielding, Wing Command, and a Lieutenant General Peterson of the Eighth Army Air Forces Bomber Command."

Den wiped the sweat from his forehead and sat on the edge of Rob's desk. "Then it's a mistake, plain and simple. You need to get on the phone and take care of this, bucko."

Rob picked up the telegram and read aloud. "'Colonel Robert J. Savage, USAAF: You are hereby ordered to return to active duty. Stop. Report, in uniform, to the Adjutant Officer in charge of USAF. Recall at the Pentagon in Washington, D.C., no later than July 1, 1950, where you will be required to take a physical. Stop. If you do

160

not report by that date, you will be considered AWOL and subject to arrest and Court Martial. Stop. Major General Thomas H. Wells.'"

The Wing Commander who had given him so much grief when Rob was assigned as Commander of the 396th Heay Bomber Group at Edenoaks, England.

"General Wells," he said softly. "That pompous jerk. So he finally wants his pound of flesh for all the arguments I gave him at Wing Command. The conflict brewing in Korea is the perfect opportunity." Rob threw himself into his chair and stared at the telephone. "A phone call isn't going to unsnarl this fankle." He looked at his desk calendar. "I have less than two weeks before they start out for me with their handcuffs. Knowing Wells, he already has MPs in Glasgow or Oban, waiting for his go-ahead."

The two men stared at one another for a long moment.

"Then what are you going to do?" Den asked. "And don't tell me you're going to re-up again so you can get a chance to fly one of those B-29 bombers they'll use in Korea. You know Wells will stick you behind a desk at the Pentagon and sneer in your face every time he passes you in the hall."

"I'm no' about to leave Innisbraw now. This is my home. There isn't a plane built that I would rather fly than be a husband to my Maggie and a faither to my bairns. Besides that, I won't fly a desk for anyone, anytime, anywhere, and I'll flatten any man who tries to make me." Rob leaped to his feet and grabbed the telegram, folded it, and stuffed it into his back pocket. "I'm going to see John. Phone Hugh and have him meet me at John's office."

"Gotcha."

"And call Heathrow and try to get me a seat on a plane leaving for Washington, D.C., or anyplace close, on the morrow's morn—any seat." Rob opened another file drawer and drew out his contracts with the United States Coast Guard for the rescue boats, including those under construction. He rummaged through the files until he found another file he wanted and slammed the drawer. "At least I gain a few hours flying to the States. I'll call Pete this een and give him a heads-up about flying me to Heathrow. That'll leave you free if there's a shout."

Den nodded and picked up the phone.

Rob darted out of the office, gripping his medical discharge and the files so tightly his knuckles whitened. His heart thudded painfully as he raced up the path, dodging tourists and locals alike, barely seeing them.

What was he going to tell Maggie? She was going to be skeered to death.

He passed Elspeth's cottage. She was nowhere in sight, but he knew exactly what she would advise him to do: confess his sins afore he asked for help.

He voiced his anger with Wells and his fear as he ran, and then he asked the Lord for guidance. "Please, Lord," he panted under his breath, "I don't ken what to do. I'll have to leave it in Your hands. Please guide me, Faither." He took the infirmary steps two at a time. Dashing inside, he turned into the far hall.

Mary, a load of dirty laundry in one arm, loomed in front of him. He skidded to a stop.

She gasped and fanned her face.

"Sorry. Where's John? I have to see him right now."

"In his office. Is someone hurt?"

"Business," he called over his shoulder. He didn't bother to knock but opened the door and stepped inside, running a sleeve over his sweaty forehead.

"Rob!" John dropped a chart on his desk and got to his feet. "What's wrong? Is someone injured?"

Rob took several deep breaths, shaking his head. "No, but I need your help." He plomped into a chair opposite the desk and dropped his head back. "I got this telegram." He handed it across the desk.

John scanned the telegram quickly, then sat down and read it again. "This has to be a mistake. This General Wells must no' know you were given a medical discharge."

"He has to know. If he ordered me recalled, he had to read my records. A copy of that discharge should be the final page in the file, or they'd have arrested me for desertion years ago."

John tugged at his beard. "He can't get away with this. General Fielding and I corresponded regularly from the time you arrived back here on Innisbraw in a deep coma to just before he sent you your medical discharge." He got up and went to his file cabinet, nodded, and pulled out a thick folder. "Here are your medical records, from the first surgery I did on your back at the Royal Infirmary in forty-twa to your last injury aboard the *Maggie*. General Fielding's letters are in here, along with a copy of the letter I sent him regarding the long-time prognosis for your left shoulder and ankle."

"Before my medical discharge."

John put the file on the desk and sat down again. "I don't know what sort of physical they give, but I can't see you passing it, what with your shoulder being so prone to injury and that pin in your left ankle." He paused and scanned the last sheet in the file. "And there's the last injury you suffered to your right leg. How's the knee? And don't give me any blether."

"'Tis fine unless I sit too long, or turn it when I run."

The doctor tapped his fingers on the file. "Then there has to be more to this than what's on the surface. I know you told me General Wells didn't like you, but surely no man in his position would go to such lengths to get even for a few disagreements."

Rob exhaled noisily. "You don't know Wells. I've never met a more ignorant, conceited, vindictive officer in my life, and after all the time I spent in the military, that's saying something. His by-the-book orders cost me hundreds of good men and a lot of B-17s we couldn't afford to lose. The only reason he signed off on my single-plane mission over Metz in forty-twa was because he was sure some FW-190 would blast us out of the sky and he'd finally be shut o' me." He brushed impatiently at the lock of hair falling over his forehead. "I don't know how he's earned another star on his shoulder, but I can guarantee you it isn't from doing a guid turn—unless you consider kissing behoochies a turn."

John leaned back, nodding. "What are you going to do?"

"I'm going to report to the Pentagon on or before the first of July. Then I'll use owt I can to shoot Wells down once and for all. He's a disgrace to the uniform too many guid men have died for."

There was a tap on the door, and Hugh came in, his smile fading when saw the look on Rob's face. "Has something happened?"

John pulled a chair from the corner and asked Hugh to sit next to Rob. "I hope you're prepared for a real fankle," he told the minister. "It looks like Rob's in for another test, and 'tis going to take every bit of help from us to solve it."

Rob filled Hugh in with the background, showed him the telegram, and waited for him to gather his thoughts.

Hugh placed the telegram back on the desk. "It appears the de'il has been up to a bit of mischief. If there's anything he hates, 'tis having faithful Christians succeed in the Lord's work." He paused for a moment before turning to Rob. "The confusion between USAAF and the USAF? Could this all be a mistake?"

"I don't think so. The US Army Air Forces was renamed the US Air Force when it became a separate branch of the military in forty-seven. They're even talking about building their own Air Force Academy instead of using West Point, which is run by the Army."

A smile played on Hugh's lips. "So they finally realize how effective airieplanes can be in winning a war." He patted Rob's shoulder. "Now 'tis time to go to our Heavenly Faither for guidance.

163

After all, this is His plan, no' ours, so it will be Him who solves this fankle."

They bowed their heads.

"Dear Faither," Hugh prayed, "it is with a fearful heart that Rob faces what could be his hardest fight to keep Your plan in operation. Give him Your thoughts and the confidence that what You have begun on this wee island will be worked out according to Your perfect will. Comfort Maggie and his bairns with the same assurance. We ask this in the name of Your Son, Jesus Christ. Amen."

The three men huddled around the desk for over an hour while they discussed strategies. John and Hugh agreed that Rob had to make an appearance at the Pentagon. If arrested for being AWOL, his allegiance to America could be called into question.

Rob's gaze traveled from John to Hugh. "Do either of you have access to a pair of handcuffs and a small leather case with a handle?"

John's brow furled. "I have a leather case I carry my notes in when I travel. But why handcuffs? What are you thinking now?"

"I don't have any handcuffs personally," Hugh said, "but the Island Council has a pair somewhere—though they've only used them once, to arrest that Brit soldier who went AWOL in forty-one and hid out here on Innisbraw." He snapped his fingers. "Now that I think on it, I believe Alec has them."

Exactly what Rob wanted to hear. "Call and have him drop them off here at the infirmary. I'm going to handcuff John's case to my wrist. I'll put everything in it—all the files and whatever else you can gather up. That way I'll make sure nowt suddenly disappears into the wrong hands."

"All they have to do is take the key from you and open it, lad," John said.

"No' if they can't find the key."

"But where could you hide such a thing?" Hugh asked. After a second's thought, his face flushed red.

"Nothing so drastic," Rob said with his first grin since they sat down. "I'll be wearing my auld dress boots, but I'll no' implicate you by telling you more. I don't want to be separated from those files till I can present them to Wells' superior in person."

"And if that doesn't work?" John asked.

"I'm no' going to sign one thing, and I'm thinking that with a medical discharge, my first enlistment signature won't hold water. The muckle problem is that physical. If I pass it, I'm in a real fankle, but I'll no' sin my soul by holding back on what I can do." He rubbed the side of his nose. "If I find myself backed into a corner, I'm trusting the Lord to deliver me, like He did Daniel from the lion's den." He stood and gripped their shoulders. "We all know what we have to do. I'll leave these files on your desk and pick them up, along with that leather case and handcuffs and owt else you can come up with, on my way to the floatplane on the mornin. I'd appreciate your prayers while I tell Maggie what's happened."

"Godspeed," they called when he quit the room.

Chapter Thirty

Maggie tied her apron strings. She'd have to hurry to have supper ready on time.

The front door opened.

It had to be Rob. She ran to him and hugged his waist, smiling. "I just got home from a Women's Aid Society meeting. I didn't expect you home this early." Her smile faded when he held her tightly and his body trembled. "What is it? What's happened?"

He scooped her up into his arms and walked to his rocker by the fire, sitting down with her in his lap. "Where are the bairns?" Voice so soft, almost sad.

"Over at Caroline's croft, playing, and Will's down for a late nap." She pulled back and looked up at him. So pale, that face, and his hazel eyes so dark. "Please tell me what's happened." She wiped at the tears gathering in her eyes. "It has to be terrible to have you in such a fash."

He pressed her face against his chest and rested his cheek against the top of her head. "I … I got a telegram from America. I think you should read it afore we talk." He dug into his pocket and pulled out the rumpled telegram while she fidgeted. "Here."

Rob watched the changing expressions on her face: first surprise, then fear, and lastly anger.

"'Tis a mistake!" She refolded the telegram. "Whoever sent this either doesn't know you got a medical discharge so long ago or thinks your injuries were minor—and how dare they threaten you with arrest and a court-martial! You're no' in the American Air Force. You need to call them immediately."

He took the telegram and returned it to his pocket. "It isn't that simple, luve. That was signed by General Wells, and he's wanted my hide since I took command of the 396th."

"But that was eight years ago. And he might be a general, but he isn't *your* superior now." She shook her head and sighed. "I don't understand any of this."

"He hates me, lass. He knows all about my medical discharge, but even that hasn't stopped him. For some reason, he's counting on me passing that physical."

"You … you aren't even going to fight this? You're going to go away to war and leave me and your bairns here to wait and wonder and go half-crazy with fear?" She bit her lower lip as the tears spilled down her pale cheeks.

He pulled her against his chest again, tangling his fingers in her hair. "Of course I'm going to fight. But I can't do it on the phone. I need to face him down, luve, in person, like I always did. Your faither's making sure my medical records are up to date, and Hugh's praying. I'm going to face Wells with enough paper to choke him, and if that doesn't work, I'll go over his head. I only have a little over three days to the deadline. I … I leave for America on the morrow's mornin, and I need all of the prayers you can offer to see me through this."

"I'm going with you." Though her voice was muffled against his chest, there was no mistaking the firm tone.

He rubbed his cheek against her hair. "You have to stay here, Maggie. I need to picture you and our bairns here, on Innisbraw, where you belong, waiting for me to come home—where I belong."

It took a long time to convince Maggie she couldn't go with him, and even longer to explain to his older bairns that he had to take a trip but would be home in a few days. Though Maggie tried to help, her red-rimmed eyes and forced smile didn't fool Robbie or Annie or even Beth. No one ate much supper and even a new Selkie story could not comfort his bairns.

After prayers were said and the bairns abed, Rob rummaged in the back of the closet and put together his uniform. Maggie pressed the blouse and two uniform shirts, while Rob spit-polished his dress boots. Then he pinned the decoration ribbons onto his blouse. He had considered going in mufti, but showing up in the dark-green uniform of the American Army Air Forces after the United States Air Force had changed to blue uniforms would be a statement in itself.

When they crawled into bed, they were emotionally exhausted. Rob stroked Maggie's shoulders and back, storing memories of her silken skin and heather fragrance. He was in such a turmoil, he would have been satisfied with a good smoorich, but Maggie needed more. It broke his heart to think he had not convinced her he would be returning in a few days.

"I always seem to say the same things over and over," he

whispered as they lay spooned together later. "If only I could find the words that are in my heart to tell you how much I luve you."

"I don't need more words. You show your luve in so many other ways. Hold me as close as you can. Please, hold me."

168

Chapter Thirty-One

Pete had the floatplane checked and ready to go when Rob and Maggie arrived at the dock at dawn.

"Be sure to call Elspeth and explain why I didn't visit her before I left," Rob reminded Maggie. "Hugh called her last een, so she could pray about this, but I didn't want to wake her this early with her feeling so weak." He didn't share his main reason for not seeing Elspeth. How could he bear saying guidbye when it might be the last time he saw her on earth?

"I'll drop in to visit her later the mornin." Maggie hugged him. "I need the comfort her words always bring."

"Then spend as much time with her as you can, luve. I'll call you the minute I know anything, but I might not have any real news until the day after the morra." He clasped her tightly, hoping to imprint the feel of her body on his flesh, muscles, and sinew. Their kiss was long and fervent. "You're my life, Maggie," he whispered. "You and our bairns are what I live for. Please remember that."

"How could I forget? Godspeed, my precious Rob. Tha gaol agam ort." *I luve you.*

"Tha gaol agam orsht-fhein." *I luve you too.*

Pete tapped him on the shoulder and pointed at his watch. "Better get going, Rob. We have to top off the fuel tank in Oban, and we're going to have to hustle to make it to Heathrow in time."

Maggie stepped back and watched Rob climb down the ladder to the lower dock, the slim leather case already manacled to his left wrist. She blew him a kiss as he climbed into the right seat.

He caught it and placed it over his heart.

Pete untied the tether, settled into the left seat, and closed the door.

So final, the click of that door. She stood on the dock as the floatplane drifted away, turned, skimmed across the water, then rose on her pontoons before lifting into the sky. No reason to hold back the tears now. They poured down her face, wetting the front of her sweater. "Och, Faither," she sobbed, "bring him back. Please bring

169

my Rob back home soon."

Later that afternoon, Rob stared out the round window of the British Overseas Airways Corporation's Boeing 377 Stratocruiser at the clouds enveloping the plane in a shroud of white. Pete had been unnaturally quiet on the flight to Heathrow, giving Rob time to think, and the few times he had spoken, he had not called Rob "Colonel" or "Commander." Pete must have recognized that the uniform Rob wore was a costume only—a statement of rebellion from a private citizen.

He sat with his legs stretched out, grateful Den had been able to get him an aisle seat, even if it was just a reclining seat and not one that made into a berth. Even with long legs, climbing over a seat companion could be awkward. Rob kneaded his right knee, which was already aching from sitting so long.

The passenger next to him, an aulder man with heavy, bottle-bottom glasses and thin lips that turned down at the corners in a perpetual sneer, stopped sneaking glances and snapped open a newspaper, holding it close to his face.

Rob settled the leather case beside his lap and picked up the cup of coffee from the tray in front of him. Aye, it made him uncomfortable, but he'd known the case shackled to his left wrist was bound to attract attention. The other passengers most likely assumed he was some sort of courier traveling with top secret papers from London to America.

Too bad there was no direct flight to Washington, D.C., but Den had reserved a seat on a connecting flight from Idlewild to Washington National, leaving only an hour after he landed in New York. Should be enough time to clear customs.

He finished his coffee and ran a hand through his hair, grateful he still wore it in a military cut. Maggie had been busy enough without giving him a haircut this mornin.

Maggie. He closed his eyes as he remembered the grief on her face when she threw him that kiss. Why did he cause her pain when she brought him nowt but joy? *Heavenly Faither, please be with my Maggie. I don't know why You've allowed this to happen, but I know You'll settle it according to Your perfect will, so don't let me get in Your way. And help me with my anger every time I think of General Wells. It isn't what You want eating away at my heart.*

He prayed for his bairns, his partners and their families, his crews, John, Hugh, and the rest of the folk close to him on Innisbraw. Especially Elspeth.

After four hours of sitting, his knee throbbed. He got up and, trying not to limp, made his way down the wide aisle to the circular staircase leading to the lounge below. He hadn't been able to eat any dinner, so he propped the case on the counter, ordered another cup of coffee, and stood nursing it, ignoring more stares as passengers, drinks in hand, settled into the comfortable seats by the windows.

Why did people always stare at him? Didn't they have anything better to do with their time? Out of patience, he sighed, left most of the coffee, and made his way back upstairs.

He reclined his seat and closed his eyes. Why did the Lord allow this to happen? He recalled his disbelief, then grief at receiving that medical discharge. He remembered thinking that they couldn't just throw him away after all the years he had spent in the Air Forces—especially not with a war still waging on two fronts. He'd fought so hard to do his best, from his four years at West Point, through all of his flight training, then the years he'd spent at Randolph Field training new cadets.

When the United States joined in the fight against the Third Reich and he was sent to England to fly P-47s, his dedication to duty became stronger with every sortie he flew and every command he gave. Even being bumped up to full-bird Colonel and put in charge of the 396th Heavy Bomber Group at Edenoaks hadn't diluted his resolve to give every day, every strike, every long mission-planning meeting at Wing Headquarters his very best.

Then he met Maggie, the bonnie Scots lass with the soft burr and luving heart. He ground a thumb into the corner of his eye. Their courtship had been difficult, but it had also been filled with more luve than he had ever experienced. *Surely You know I don't want to take my Maggie away from Innisbraw, Faither. It's my home as much as it is hers. I don't want to return to the Air Force. Surely You didn't help me with designing and building and commanding the rescue boat only to take it away when we've barely started. And the construction business—our auld folk are getting their cottages updated, so they don't have to go outside to the watterie and will be warm in beds instead of sleeping on a straw pallet on the floor. Please quiet my heart, Faither. If I ever needed Your peace, 'tis now.*

He lost himself in the monotonous drone of the engines and fell into a troubled sleep, not awakening until the stewardess tapped his shoulder and asked him if he wanted a moist serviette so he could wash his hands for supper.

He took the napkin but declined the supper.

"Colonel, you haven't eaten a bite since we boarded," she said,

171

her voice soothing with its familiar Scots burr. "We have a fine beef fillet with mashed tatties and green beans. We cook it right here onboard. Or I could bring you something else …"

A sudden hunger for a taste of home spurred him to ask, "Do ye have any scones?"

Surprise registered in her eyes—most likely because of the heavy Scots burr used by an American colonel. She covered it with a warm smile. "Aye, we do," she whispered. "And we've clotted cream and heather honey to go with."

He winked at her. "Ye jist made me a verra happy man. And anither carafe of coffee, if ye please."

Much later that night, after a twelve-hour flight into New York, and another two-hour connecting flight, Rob tossed his duffle on the hotel bed. Den had struck out on a good hotel room close to the Pentagon, but Rob did have a room reserved, even if it was not in one of the better places.

He eyed the room with surprise. If this was a second-rate hotel, what was first-rate like? The floor was carpeted, there was a double bed with two pillows and a thick comforter. Even a separate bathroom with a large tub-shower combination. He took off his crush cap and hung his blouse on a hanger, then reset his watch before telephoning to ask for an 0600 wake-up call. The operator must have been accustomed to hearing military time, because she didn't ask for a clarification. He dug the key to the handcuffs from its hiding place, undid the lock, and slid the case beneath his bed, sighing with relief as he massaged his wrist.

After showering, he threw back the comforter, turned off the heat to the room, and lay beneath the sheet. Exhausted and heartsick, he did not fall deeply asleep until long after the turn o' night.

It was already warm and getting muggy when the taxi dropped him off at the main entrance to the Pentagon at 0900. Even though he had caught a glimpse of the huge structure as the plane circled for a landing at Washington National, he looked in amazement at the façade. Columns marched five stories into the sky, and the front of the building seemed to go on forever in both directions. How would he ever find the office he wanted in such an enormous building?

A young MP stopped him outside the door.

From his pocket, Rob pulled a sheet of hotel stationery with the

to this door? "Thank ye, Lieutenant," Rob said with smile, "and ye have a grand day."

The major sitting at his desk in the reception room did not smile as he pushed a button on his intercom. "Colonel Savage is here," he said in a throaty growl. He stared belligerently at Rob, got up from his chair, walked stiffly to the closed door at the side of the room, and threw it open.

The battle is the Lord's. Rob stepped through the doorway and stood at ease in front of a large walnut desk. He glimpsed another officer in the room, standing against the far wall, arms folded, face impassive. Rob did not salute or speak, but fastened his gaze on the shiny, balding head of Major General Thomas H. Wells, who sat behind the desk. *Help me say only what You want said, Faither.*

The general's gaze swept scornfully up and down Rob's uniform before lighting on the leather case manacled to his wrist. "So you made it on time after all."

Rob had forgotten the general's high, reedy, irritating voice, and quelled a shiver of distaste. He deliberately lapsed into the Scots. "Ye're supreesed, then? Didna ye ken I cud mak it fra a wee isle a hunert-saventeen kilometres fra the coast o' Scotland?"

Wells shot to his feet and leaned over the desk, finger pointing at Rob's chest. "I don't know what kind of games you think you're playing with that gibberish, Colonel. You will sign this!" He grabbed a paper from his desktop and waved it in front of Rob's face.

"Nae, General, I willna sign onie paper," Rob said very quietly. He swallowed a smile.

Wells stared at him, face flushing with rage. "Speak English, Savage. Your little charade won't work here!" His eyes went to the leather case.

Wells grabbed for it, but Rob planted his feet firmly.

"What is this?" the general asked, voice dripping with scorn. "Another game you want to play?" His hand moved to the telephone. "Well, I'll show you what happens to insubordinate officers." He dialed the phone. "Send two MPs to room—"

The officer who had been standing quietly by reached out and took the receiver. "This is General Frazier. Disregard this call."

Rob looked at the three stars on the general's shoulders and let out the breath he'd been holding. He might have a chance to pull this off if Lieutenant General Frazier had authority over Wells.

"Sir, I object," Wells sputtered. "No officer in the United States Air Force should be allowed such insolence."

"I am a private citizen," Rob said, no longer using the Scots, but broadening his burr. "I am no longer an officer in the Army Air Forces, as you well know, sir."

The red creeping up from Wells's tight collar over his chin and cheeks was a familiar sight to Rob. But there was an odd, almost wild look in the general's eyes. Wells pounded on the desk. "See? See? He *can* speak English. This is another of those harebrained schemes like he pulled at Edenoaks." He swiped spittle from his lower lip and looked at General Frazier with a triumphant smile.

Frazier's eyes met Rob's. Was that a glint of humour in the general's steady gaze? "Take a walk, Thomas," Frazier said. "A long walk. And I suggest you take your pipe. It always helps you calm down."

"But, sir, this is my case. I've worked on it for years. I'm the one who brought Savage to your attention. I deserve the credit. I—"

"Now, General!" Frazier barked, gaze icy.

Wells cast one more imploring look at his superior officer before grabbing his pipe from his desk and storming from the office.

Frazier closed the office door and pushed a chair over for Rob. "Take a load off, Colonel—or perhaps I should say, Mister Savage." He sat behind the desk as Rob took the chair.

"It is Mister Savage, General," Rob said in his best English, "and I have the proof." He lifted the case and set it on the desk as he studied Frazier.

The general looked to be in his mid-fifties, with close-cropped grey hair, piercing blue eyes, broad shoulders, and a chest full of campaign ribbons. This was no armchair general. He'd seen action—a lot of it.

Frazier smiled and leaned back in the chair. "Ah, yes, the secret courier routine. Very ingenious."

"But necessary, General."

Frazier tapped the case with one broad forefinger. "And what secrets have you brought us all the way from Scotland? You are living in Scotland now, I understand."

"'Tis my home."

"And the home of my mother and father. They came from what they called the Hielans just before WWI, dead broke and nearly starving to death from trying make a living crofting."

Thank Ye, Faither. "'Tis a hard life, crofting, even on the Isle of Innisbraw, where I make my home."

"Innisbraw?" Frazier leaned forward, a grin creasing his weathered face. "I've been there. I snuck in a side trip to some of the Outer Hebrides when I was asked to check out the RAF bases on

Tyree and Benbecula in thirty-nine." His grin faded as he leaned back, eyes softening. "Wasn't much there, if I remember correctly. Bonnie island, as my folks would have said, but one old woman who spoke some English seemed concerned about losing their population to places with industry—more job opportunities."

"That was Elspeth NicAllister, our Island Elder." Rob smiled at the seeming coincidence. "And Innisbraw was like that when I first got there too, but you wouldn't recognize the island now. We're growing every day. We even have the ferry stopping with tourists, and we've jobs to offer, with guid pay."

The general appeared surprised but glanced at his watch and frowned. "Well, I could talk about Scotland forever, but it seems we have what my folks used to call a 'fankle' to solve. I've heard enough to be sure you're familiar with the Scots language, Mister Savage?"

"Verra familiar. 'Tis all we speak except the Gaelic."

"You speak the Gaelic?"

"Tha, math."

"Yes, well." He grunted. "I actually understood, though it's been years since I even heard the language." Frazier leaned forward again. "Now, back to our fankle ..."

"If you'll allow me, I'll remove my boot and get the key to the case."

"By all means."

Frazier grinned again as Rob removed his boot and took a pen from the desk to pry a small key from the inside back of the heel.

Rob put his boot back on and unlocked the handcuffs from the case and his wrist. He opened the case and pulled out a thick file, sliding it across the desk. "My medical records."

The general eyed the file. "Medical records? Not necessary. You'll have to take and pass a physical to be recalled to duty."

Rob opened the file and handed him the first page. "The file backs up this piece of paper, General. Knowing Wells, I doubt he mentioned to you I was given a medical discharge in the fall of forty-three for injuries I received in a crash landing after a bombing strike on the rail yards at Mannheim."

Frazier studied the document, gaze narrowing. "You're wrong about that. General Wells told me about your medical discharge, but he hinted at some sort of collusion between you and General Harlan Fielding, the Wing Commander who took Wells's place when he was recalled to the States—though I didn't buy that. I've known Hal Fielding for years, and he's the last man to pull a stunt like that."

"Indeed, he is."

Frazier leaned forward, his gaze intent. "But General Wells also mentioned that your activities since your recovery prove you're fit and able to return to duty."

"And what are those activities he mentioned?"

"Something about running a sea rescue service, which, he informed me, involves a lot of swimming."

So Wells had done some snooping. "I'm the commander of the *Maggie*, Innisbraw's Coastal Rescue Boat. I designed the boat and helped build her." Rob pointed to the thick medical file. "And while it's true I can swim, I'm prone to injury and there are things I can no longer do. However, I'm willing to have that physical. I'm sure your Air Force doctors will want to substantiate what's in that medical file."

Frazier rose and pushed the file into the leather case. "Then that's the first thing we need to get out of the way. I'll have a driver take you to Andrews Air Force Base, across the Potomac, for your physical. In the meantime, I'd like to peruse everything you have in here." He tapped the case. "If you trust me, that is."

Rob stood quickly. "Of course I trust you, General, as long as it doesn't end up in Wells's hands."

"I'll personally carry it back to my office."

⚓

Three hours later, Rob was once again escorted to the fifth floor. But this office was on the outer ring of the Pentagon with a brass sign on the door: "Lieutenant General Gordon S. Frazier."

His heart pounded. The flight surgeon who had conducted the physical had refused to give him the results. "I'll phone General Frazier himself with my decision," he said, gaze adamant. "Those were the general's orders."

Rob was sure his physical limitations, especially his weaker left shoulder and arm, would wash him out of pilot status. But there was always the possibility of being forced to fly a desk. *Och, Faither, I need one of Your miracles,* he prayed silently as he stood before a major sitting at the desk in the anteroom.

"Colonel Savage, the general is expecting you," the major said.

Rob couldn't read a thing from the man's practiced, blank expression. He took a deep breath as he followed the aide across the room to a closed door. So much depended upon the following minutes—his entire future with Maggie and his bairns and that of the Innisbraw Coastal Rescue Service hung in the balance. He steeled himself as he was ushered into a large office with a window

178

overlooking a huge parking lot.

General Frazier sat at his desk with Rob's folder arranged in front of him. He nodded at a chair. "Pull up a seat. We've got some serious talking to do."

He and Rob spent a long time going over everything. General Frazier was very businesslike as he thumbed through the medical records, contracts for rescue boats for the United States Coast Guard, sheets listing the homes and schools Rob and his company had built, and a letter Hugh had procured from the Innisbraw Island Council outlining Rob's successful efforts to save their dying island, signed by every member. He paused over the last paper in the file, and looked up at Rob. "So you have four children—*bairns* I remember them being called. Did you marry a local Innisbraw lass?"

"Aye. She was the nurse who wouldn't let me give up until I could walk after I caught some flak in my back over Metz in forty-twa. Her name is Maggie."

"I remember seeing her name in your medical records." Frazier sat back, tapping his knuckles together. "I know you're anxious about the results of your physical, so I won't leave you hanging any longer." He cleared his throat. "According to Major Rivers, who conducted your physical, there is no doubt in his mind that you cannot qualify for flight status. Apparently, your shoulder injury in particular makes that conclusion absolute."

Rob's heart thudded painfully, and he had to force himself to speak. "But ...?"

"But there is no reason you can't perform desk duty, as long as you walk around once in a while to alleviate the pain in your right knee."

The breath left Rob's lungs. Despite his foolish, emotional vow never to fly a desk, the Lord had taken the decision out of his hands. A picture of Maggie filled his vision, tears spilling down her cheeks. He closed his eyes, swallowing the bitter dregs of defeat.

Chapter Thirty-Two

"Before we talk more, I'd like to clear something up. What's caused this bad blood between you and Wells? And don't worry, it won't go any further than this room."

Rob tried to concentrate on the general's question.

First, he had to quit imagining what his life would be like without Maggie and his bairns. The three months he and Maggie had been separated during WWII had been the hardest he'd ever had to endure. How could he live through another war, possibly a long one, without his family?

He cleared his throat and fought for the words to explain his relationship with Wells without using profanity. "I ... I suppose it started when I suggested ways to make a mission safer for my crews—no' changing the objective, for I knew that was out of General Wells's control—just ideas for some way to give my men a better chance approaching the IP and returning to base after we dropped our loads."

"He objected?"

"To put it mildly. But there were a few times when I wore him down."

"Did he say why he objected?"

"Because it wasn't 'by the book.'" Rob shook his head. "I might have understood if they hadn't pulled me from the fighter base I was commanding with the idea of having a bomber group commander with flight and combat experience. That's what I was giving the general—the results of my experience. The P-47s my men and I flew only carried two wing bombs, but planning our sorties carefully and using evasive techniques became second nature. If applied to bombing strikes, they could have saved some of the B-17s—and crews—we lost."

Frazier nodded. "I can recall a few conversations my group commanders had with me when I took over Wing Command in Italy—served with the 12th Army Air Forces there. I often signed off on their suggestions, because they were the ones who had the most to lose."

Rob lowered his eyes and shook his head. "The luck of the draw,

180

I guess, or I should say, the bad luck of my draw."

"I'm sure you know General Wells has never had any combat experience."

"That was obvious, General."

"What you may not know is that he washed out of pilot training—for your ears only, of course."

No' even a pilot. Now Rob knew why Wells was so antagonistic. "I wished I'd known that during my arguments with the General at Edenoaks Hall. I could have couched them so they didn't heap coals of fire on a previous humiliation."

Frazier glanced at his watch. "Our little talk has been very informative. Too bad I didn't know all of this before the committee I headed reviewed almost fifty military files and chose unanimously to recall you."

Rob prayed silently. Had years at the Pentagon turned this WWII military hero into another milksoppy politician?

Frazier pulled a piece of paper from his desk drawer and shook his head as he scanned it. He tapped a file on the desk. "These contracts for US Coast Guard rescue boats clear up a perplexing message I found on my desk when I came in this morning. It was from Rear Admiral Whidbey of the Coast Guard Station in Long Beach, California, chewing out my hide for interfering in Coast Guard affairs by hijacking the designer and builder of his only source of rescue boats capable of righting themselves after they capsize. I'll have to call him when we're finished here and soothe some ruffled feathers. Don't want the Coast Guard on our backs."

Rob didn't reply. It was all in the Lord's hands now. Nothing he could say would make any difference.

General Frazier met Rob's steady gaze and sighed. "We sure could use you. With your planning our strikes from inside Korea and interfacing directly with the infantry troop commanders instead of sitting at a distant base in Japan, we hoped to win this one quickly."

Rob almost nodded. Just the sort of technique he would have used, had he been in charge.

"So I suppose you can see why we want you, Savage," Frazier continued, gaze boring into Rob's. "Even without General Wells's lack of cooperation, you have the Eighth Army Air Forces Bomber Command's finest record for bringing your planes and men home."

The next few minutes would define how Rob lived his life— either apart from his Maggie and their bairns or a continuation of the Lord's mandate. If he was recalled to duty, even when the conflict in Korea eventually ended, everything on Innisbraw would be changed.

Price

He didn't fear for his life, though serving on a remote base in war-torn Korea—North or South—was not danger-free. Living without Maggie was the one thing he wasn't certain he could survive. She was such a part of his soul he didn't think he could live even one month without her, let alone the years this war could last.

But General Frazier was not a man to take defeat easily.

Rob steeled himself for the worst. *This is it, Lord. The lion has me pinned down and is opening his jaws. 'Tis up to You now, and I'll do Your perfect will somehow.*

182

Chapter Thirty-Three

Frazier broke eye contact and returned the file to the case, closed it, and placed the manacles on top. "I noticed the last page in your medical file mentions you were injured on one of your rescues not long ago. How is it you can swim but it's hard for you to sit for long periods of time?"

This was a sharp opponent, and he deserved the truth. "Swimming in salty seawater is actually guid for my shoulder and legs, but sitting makes my knees and other joints stiff, because of all the scar tissue I've built up."

"I noticed you're limping some."

"A bit. Sitting on that plane ride over the pond wasn't verra comfortable."

"Well, since you're already helping our Coast Guard in a vital role, and unless you've gone off the deep end and want to volunteer for the job, I'm afraid your days as an officer in the United States Air Force ended in forty-three." He snapped the case closed. "There are other qualified candidates for the job, and I'd say you've done more than your share for your country." He took the reenlistment paper from a corner of his desk and tore it in two before he stood and saluted Rob. "Thank you for your sacrifice, Colonel."

Rob couldn't believe it. He had been delivered! He leaped to his feet, stiffening his trembling legs as he returned the salute. "Thank you, General—for everything."

They shook hands warmly, sharing the unique kinship of two men who had stared into the face of the enemy—and not blinked.

General Frazier generously provided a car and driver to take Rob back to his hotel. "It's the least we can do, since we made a big hole in your wallet with those plane tickets and lodging," he said.

As Rob was leaving the office, Frazier held up a hand.

"I don't expect this to go any further, but I feel you deserve to know that General Wells has been turned down two times for another star. He won't be around much longer."

Rob put General Frazier's parting words out of his mind while he returned to his hotel, called the BOAC, and changed his open return reservation to late that afternoon. In mufti, he threw his Dopp kit and soiled clothing into his duffle bag, paid his hotel bill, and dove into the backseat of the General's car. He laid his head back and took a deep breath, closing his eyes.

There are no words to thank You enough, Faither, for what You've done. He prayed as the staff car careened down the road toward Washington National Airport. *As always, I'm stunned by the way You delivered me from the hands of my enemy.*

His thoughts eventually turned to General Wells. For the first time since Rob had met the stiff, uncompromising brigadier general at Edenoaks, he felt a twinge of pity. Scuttlebutt around the 396th had been that Wells was the only son of a much-decorated WWI flying ace and the last hope of a family involved in the military for generations. The humiliation he suffered when he washed out of pilot training must have broken him. But instead of giving up and resigning his commission or applying his talents to another area, he had emerged from a dark cocoon of dashed hopes with anger and retribution the driving forces in his life.

The sergeant steering the car pulled up to the curb in front of the American Airlines terminal, tires screeching. "I'm to carry your bags, wait until you've checked in, and stay with you at the concourse until you board, sir." He took the duffle bag and leather case from Rob.

"Thank ye, Sergeant," Rob said. It had been a long time since he had been afforded such amenities, and he had to admit it was a pleasure. He was already exhausted, and he had to sit at least another fifteen hours before he reached London.

After he checked in, he glanced at his watch and saw there was time to call Maggie. He looked around and spotted several telephones nearby. As he made the collect call, it occurred to him that it was five hours later at home—Maggie was most likely putting the bairns to bed and hearing prayers. He tapped his fingers as the phone rang and rang. When he heard her breathless "Hello," he fought back a sob.

After the overseas operator had ensured the charge would be accepted, Rob choked oot, "'Tis me, luve. I'll be home on the morra's afternoon. Have Pete meet me at Heathrow at 1500."

"Rob? Och, Rob is it really you? And you're coming home?" She wept.

He swallowed the tears filling his throat. "I'm coming home to stay, lass, and unless you're with me, I'll never leave Innisbraw again."

❧

The sun was low in the sky when Pete set the floatplane down at the entrance to Innisbraw harbour. Rob looked out the windscreen at Ben Innis, its sides blushing pink as the bell heather came into bloom. The turquoise water near the shore was darkening, and there were already several trawlers and creelers tied up at the dock. His eyes smarted as he looked at the island he luved so much. He was stiff, back and knee aching from sitting so long, and he was starving, but he'd never felt better. He was home.

As Pete pulled the seaplane up to its dock, Rob gazed at the pier and shore, thronged with waving folk. Pete opened the door with a wide grin. The kirk bell was ringing, filling the air with its joyous music. The tears Rob had been fighting for hours gathered in his eyes and rolled down his cheeks as he scrambled up the ladder and tossed his duffle bag and John's case onto the dock. He flung his crush cap across the harbour water before he pulled a sobbing Maggie—*his* Maggie—into his arms.

Chapter Thirty-Four

Rob was still hoarse twa mornins later from explaining to so many of the folk how the Lord had performed yet another miracle. He gathered Maggie closer in his lap as they rocked on the entry, inhaling the familiar warm-honey scent of heather on her hair and skin. "I'm thinking you're going to need a nap with Will the day," he said as he caressed her shoulder. "You didn't get much sleep."

She nestled her cheek against his chest. "What pot is calling the kettle black?" She raised her smiling face.

He kissed her tenderly, savouring the memories of the time they had spent renewing their vows of luve the night before.

She poked his shoulder. "I know you have work at the shed the day, but first you're going to have a guid, filling breakfast."

He chuckled. "With all I ate last een, I should be full, but I'm starving again."

"Then, this morn 'tis sliced sausage, eggs, tinned beans, and fried bread for my starving man."

꧁ꕤ꧂

At the ceilidh that een, and every Saturday from then on, Rob kept to the bargain he had made with Elspeth. Though it had never occurred to him that the American Air Force might recall him to duty, the close call had shaken him, and he resolved to do anything he could for the island that had captured his heart. He often changed the stories Auntie Mairet was telling, especially when they wandered off in a strange new direction, and whenever she told the Selkie story, he never followed her words, but instead told the tale Elspeth had originated, with the happy ending. The island folk who spoke English never said a word about it.

There was always someone present to watch Will, so Rob and Maggie could have a dance or two. Rob no longer resented the whispers of the tourists, especially those who talked about his four "adorable" children and his "beautiful wife." After coming so close to losing his family for a long time, he realized the tourists' comments were not rude, but complimentary—and true. For the first time since the ferry began arriving at Innisbraw, he greeted visitors with a hesitant, but genuine, smile.

The four rescue boats for the United States Coast Guard were launched in mid-July, with sea trials starting immediately afterward. Rob's right leg was back to its full strength, and he tackled his busiest season of the year eagerly, stealing time for an occasional run or a quick flight in the floatplane. Innisbraw was thriving and so was his family. The only disappointment was a call from the Townsends. Bill's schedule had been changed, so they had to cancel their reservations. Other than that, life had never been better.

Zeke Evans arrived on the island for the capsizing trials the second week in August. He didn't bring Carol, their son, Zeke Junior, or their six-month-old baby girl. "Maybe next year," he told Rob. "It's too hard to travel so far with such a young kid."

Rob grinned. "I'm disappointed but understand completely. The baggage alone would be overwhelming."

Zeke questioned Rob at length about his trip to the Pentagon. "I'll tell you, the admiral was spitting mad when I passed along Den's message. I'm sure his call to General Frazier melted the phone wires, even if he wasn't in his office to receive it."

Once again, the capsizing trials went well, as did the Coast Guard crew's introduction to their new rescue boats. Another year for the boatworks had drawn to a successful conclusion. A few days of cleanup in the shed and machine maintenance, and next year's production would begin.

The een before Zeke was scheduled to leave, the siren on Innis Fell sounded as they were finishing an early supper. Rob asked Zeke if he would like to come along on the rescue.

"Would I!" Zeke exclaimed. "Lead the way."

Rob kissed Maggie and each of the bairns and was walking out the door with Zeke when Den, Fern, and their bairns arrived.

The three men took off at a dead run down the hill. When they reached the *Maggie*, Rob ordered Zeke into a wet suit. "You never know what'll happen," he said as he reached for the radio.

The rescue didn't sound dangerous. A small sailboat with four souls aboard was taking on water off the northern coast of Innisbraw. "We're all right as long as it isn't too close to Heuch Fell," Rob told his crew as he changed into his wet suit.

187

Price

They reached the stricken vessel in only ten minutes and found the situation much worse than it sounded on the radio. The small craft was almost on its side, and the waves washed it closer and closer to the rocks off the fell.

Den spotted three victims already in the water.

Rob pulled Zeke aside. "Stay at the helm with Neil. Needs be, you can take the *Maggie* into the channel, but watch those rocks."

"I know how dangerous they are. I'll be careful."

Rob prayed as he and Den raced to the fantail with the rest of the crew. "Paddy, Ewan, and Den, tie your lines," he ordered as he tied his own lifeline and pulled on his flippers. "Christopher, Alex, and Matthew, stand by to pull in the lines. Neil's going to take the *Maggie* in as close as he can, and if he has to, Zeke will steer her into the channel. If he does, hang on tight!"

The crew tied their lines to the taffrail.

Rob pulled on his hood and looked them each in the eye. "On my signal." He raised his hand.

When he dropped it, they all jumped.

Rob reached a female victim first. Fighting the waves, he pulled the slack out of his line, then gave three pulls. Within moments they were at the *Maggie*'s fantail.

Matthew pulled the woman aboard.

Rob climbed up behind her. "Get her into the cabin, and then come back down here," he ordered Alex. "We'll need you on the lines." He scanned the waves.

Paddy and Ewan and their two victims were being pulled in on their lines.

Where were Den and the fourth victim?

Rob's stomach knotted.

Two men were soon brought aboard, followed by Paddy and Ewan. Rob pulled Christopher close. "Get up there and tell Zeke to take us into the channel. I can't see Den." He ordered Matthew topside to take care of the victims. "The rest of you stand by and hold on tight. We'll capsize when we get into that trough."

The *Maggie* inched forward between the rocks. Rob kept looking for Den's red wet suit.

No sign of him. They eased by the sailboat, which was impaled on a rock.

Rob pulled on Den's lifeline.

No resistance—it must be severed.

His muscles tensed. He wanted to jump in and swim to Den's rescue, but where should he head? He caught a glimpse of red far off

188

the starboard. The *Maggie* bucked violently in the waves. He readied himself to jump.

The rescue boat tilted to port.

She was capsizing.

He held onto the railing until the right moment, then jumped clear. Demanding the utmost from his body, he struck out with all his strength. The waves washed over his head, and he prayed for strength and wisdom.

As he was thrown from side to side, the roar of the surf drowned out all other sounds.

He swallowed water, gagged, then struck out again, feeling a surge of energy. Another wave washed over him. When he surfaced, he shook his head and looked around. Where was Den? Rob's mind seemed detached from his body. He prayed and swam, prayed and swam, gaining ground only to lose it as another wave inundated him.

The rope tightened around his waist.

He pulled on it, taking care not to jerk it three times. *Don't pull me in,* his mind screamed. *I have to find Den!*

His lifeline still held him back. Had to be caught. He jerked and jerked again and again until it suddenly relaxed. Must have tangled around a jagged rock and snapped.

He didn't care.

He fought the waves, frantic to find Den before it was too late. One wave washed over his head and before he could grab a breath, another. As he surfaced, still another wave hit him, sending him tumbling end over end. He was sure he would never breathe again, until he finally felt fresh air on his face. He sucked in one breath, then another, before he was once again caught in a maelstrom of currents that sucked him below the surface.

It became harder and harder to fight, but he had to fight for Den. *Help me, Lord, please help me!* He kicked his legs as hard as he could and pulled with his arms until his face broke the surface. He struck out with his right arm. His hand hit something and he grabbed hold, looking up.

It was Den, caught in conflicting currents, drifting around and around.

Rob grabbed him and held on. He shouted Den's name, but all that came out of his mouth was seawater. He struggled and flipped Den over onto his back.

His face was ashen-gray, muscles flaccid.

Rob tipped Den's head back and tried to breathe into his mouth, but he didn't seem to have enough air in his lungs. He reached for his lifeline.

Och, it had snapped.

Another wave washed over him, and he swallowed more seawater as he struggled to keep himself and Den afloat.

A loud buzzing droned in his ears.

Bright lights flickered in front of his eyes.

The sky darkened and disappeared.

Chapter Thirty-Five

Rob regained consciousness with a start. He gagged and retched.

"That's the way. Get it all up."

He opened his eyes. He recognized Zeke's voice but all he could see was the deck boards.

"Keep it coming, Rob," Zeke said. "There's a lot more in there."

"Den," Rob choked. More seawater poured from his mouth.

"They're working on him. He's got a pulse."

Rob couldn't stop the tears once they started. He sobbed and retched for several minutes as Zeke continued to press on his back.

"We're on our way in," Zeke said. "The *Maggie* did great. She righted herself in a little over ten seconds."

Had to get up—see Den.

Hands pressed him down. "Not so fast. You're not out of the woods yet. Are you cold?"

Rob tried to answer but his mind wouldn't function. His stomach convulsed again. He retched until he gasped for air.

The *Maggie*'s siren blasted three times—extreme emergency.

Everything went black again.

❧

When he regained consciousness the second time, Maggie was bent over him, sobbing. He tried to speak her name aloud, but no sound came out. He attempted to sit up.

She fell across him, pinning his body.

"I'm … I'm all right," he was finally able to whisper.

She raised her head and looked at him. The pain in her eyes was almost more than he could bear.

He clasped a handful of her hair. "Don't cry, lass."

She grabbed his hand and covered it with kisses. "Och, Rob, Rob. I thought I'd lost you."

"Den," he choked. "How's Den?"

She smoothed his forelock back. "He had a pulse when they brought him in. They're working on him now."

❧

Fern knelt in front of Den, monitoring his pulse. Her body felt numb,

191

only the light fluttering beneath her fingertips having meaning. *Breathe, Den.*

A gurgle broke from Den's throat, and he retched, spewing water in an arc across the floor. He gasped for breath, then retched again and again. His muscles spasmed, back arched. He coughed, took in a short, ragged breath. Coughed again.

"Stop AR," John said to Matthew. "It's spasmodic, but he's breathing. Heartbeat's stronger."

Every nerve in Fern's body came to life—knees burned, hips ached, head pounded. She wept silently, her mind filled with praises. *Thank Ye, Faither!*

When the retching stopped, Den's face lost its pallor and his breathing and pulse steadied.

She scooted aside as John and Matthew turned Den over and lifted him onto a gurney, propping his head up before covering him with blankets. Fern struggled to her feet and replaced the almost-empty IV bottle with a new one, then administered a large dose of penicillin. Pneumonia could strike a near-drowning victim at any time. Plus, she had to keep busy, had to keep from thinking how close he had been to—och, not Den, her precious luve, with his wild sense of humour, loyalty that knew no bounds, and tender, needy heart.

John inflated the blood pressure cuff and took a reading. "He's stabilizing, lass. The worst is over." He patted her shoulder. "You stay with him. I'm going to check on Rob. I'll be right back."

John stepped into the hall, running his hands over his face. He took a deep breath and entered the next examining room.

Maggie was taking Rob's pulse.

"How is he?" John asked. "Has he brought up more?"

She nodded. "He's been asleep for half an hour. How's Den?"

"He'll make it, though I wouldn't have thought it possible when they brought him in. That's the closest I've ever come with a near-drowning victim without losing him."

She went into her faither's arms. "What makes them do it, Faither?" she cried. "Time and time again they risk their lives. Why?"

He held her close, heart aching. Why indeed? "I don't know, Maggie. They're special lads, is all I can say. God's given them a mission few would embrace. They're verra special lads."

John kept Rob flat on his back for twenty-four hours before allowing him up.

192

He slept for almost twelve of those hours. His diaphragm muscles were sore and his throat raspy, but after lying in bed with nothing to do, he was ready to go home. As soon as he visited Den.

Fern sat at Den's bedside, holding his hand. "Well, look who's here," she said brightly. "How are you feeling, Rob?"

He cleared his throat. "Grand. How's the patient?"

Den snorted and coughed.

"Stop making those impossible sounds and you'll no' cough," Fern scolded.

Rob waited until his friend quieted before he approached the bed. "Don't give your nurse a bad time," he said with a grin. "She'll make you pay through the nose later."

Den raised a hand.

Rob grabbed it and held on.

They looked at one another for a long time, tears gathering in their eyes.

"You had to one-up me, didn't you, bucko?" Den whispered. "Here we were, all nicely tied one to one, and you had to go and ruin it all by saving my life again."

"I don't ken who saved whose life," Rob said. He cleared his throat a second time. "But it doesn't matter. We both made it."

"They ever find the lass I was going after?"

"No."

Den closed his eyes. "I'm sorry, Rob. Lost my lifeline when I tangled with a rock. I tried to hold on to her, but she was fighting me, and the waves were too wild."

"It happens. We try, but we can't save them all."

Den lay back, eyes closed.

"But the *Maggie* capsized and righted herself in a little over ten seconds. That's as guid as it gets. And if Zeke hadn't followed my orders to take her into the channel, we'd both be feeding the fish right now." Rob regretted his rash words at the stricken look on Fern's face. "Anyway, they got to us in time and pulled us both aboard."

"What'd Zeke think about it all?"

"He said it was one of the hairiest rescues he's ever been on. He went back to the States a verra happy man." Rob got to his feet. "I'll let you rest now before your efficient nurse runs me off. Take care. Catch you up later."

"Ciao, bucko. And thanks."

Rob was back at work in two days and Den in five. Though they paced themselves, they still tired more easily than usual. Both dreaded the official inquest into the fatality aboard the sailboat and were relieved to hear that their presence was not required. A ruling of "Accidental Death" was made on the testimony of the three survivors.

But Maggie was unusually quiet and seldom smiled. When Rob tried to talk to her about it, she put him off with one excuse or another. The final straw came when she decided not to accompany him to the Saturday night ceilidh. She gave no reason, nor even an excuse. She simply refused to go.

"Then I'm no' going, either." He threw down his black jacket so hard the metal buttons clacked as they hit the floor.

"You have to. There's no one else to do the translating for Auntie Mairet. And you promised Elspeth you'd do it."

"They'll have to forget the story tonight. I'm no' going without you."

"Stop acting like a bairn, Rob. They need you."

He stared at her. The words were bad enough, but it was her cold tone that shocked him. He sat down on the bed and reached for her hand.

She pulled away.

"What is it, Maggie? What have I done that makes you draw away every time I try to touch you?"

She didn't answer but turned her back and began putting the clean laundry away in the closet.

He didn't know what to do, what to say. He couldn't force her to talk if she didn't want to. He picked up his jacket and put it on. "I'm off, then," he said stiffly as he quit the room. He ran all the way to the kirk hall. He didn't go in immediately but stood outside, looking up at the brilliant sunset spread across the sky. The bright colours mocked his black mood. The supper he had eaten that een lay like a lump in his belly. He felt sick.

Why was Maggie treating him like an unwelcome guest? He racked his brains.

That last dangerous rescue.

Maggie had been aloof since he came home from the infirmary. His warm, funny, tender lass had been replaced by an indifferent, distant stranger.

Well, that was going to change. She was going to talk to him, start treating him like her husband again.

He heard the music end. When it didn't resume for several minutes, he went into the hall and made his way to Auntie Mairet's side. Why couldn't it be Elspeth? Being with her for only a few moments would relieve his anxiety.

Auntie looked up at him. "Ye're late, Rob. Are ye feeling poorly?" she asked in the Gaelic, her only language.

"No, sorry. I got held up."

A smile deepened the wrinkles around her blue eyes. "No' problems at home, I pray."

"Nowt that canna be solved," he said, almost choking on the words. "Are you ready?"

"Whenever you are."

He translated her story, which happened to be a particularly gory account of the Battle of Culloden. The words matched his mood, so he translated them verbatim, taking on the persona of a stern, chisel-faced warrior from the past, visage grim, deep voice harsh, as though relating a battle he had lived through. His frustration lessened as he raised an imaginary, heavy claymore sword in both hands and brought it down with a shout of victory.

When the story ended, there was a hushed silence, but once the applause began, it seemed to go on forever.

He pressed Auntie Mairet's shoulder and strode from the hall.

He didn't go directly home. Instead, he skirted both schools and climbed the slopes of Ben Innis, legs moving automatically as he leaped over heather and girse. The brave thoughts he'd had before he entered the hall mocked him now. This was no trifling matter.

After all this time and countless hours of prayer, Maggie was still terrified that he was going to die during a rescue. And perhaps she was right. Only God the Faither knew the moment Rob Savage would enter heaven.

He reached the top of Ben Innis and sat down, back against one of the tall stones, arms around his knees. He gazed out through the lingering gloaming at the harbour and the Minch beyond.

Aye, Maggie could be right. Someday the sea could claim his life, but only if God deemed it time. She had a strong faith. He saw evidence of that every day. Maybe all the hours she had spent in front of the radio had worn her down.

So why was he sitting here when he should be at home with her?

He scrambled to his feet and ran down the ben.

The bedroom door was closed. Maggie must be abed. He flipped on the shower heater and went out to the entry to wait, so filled with grief he could scarcely breathe. He'd hurt Maggie time and time again, and she had finally broken. He sat on the railing and looked out at the gently undulating sea, calm and yet capable of such unspeakable destruction.

He could make a promise and easily solve this rift. He could still command the *Maggie* if he promised no' to take part in the in-water rescues. But that went against all he believed in. How could he sleep at night, or ever look in a mirror again, if he asked his men to take risks he was no longer willing to take? That's what rescue was all about, pitting one's own life against one's skills to save others' lives. No, he would give up his command altogether before he would do that.

But if he gave up his command, what could he do?

Graham ran the shop efficiently, and Pete was the experienced contractor. Rob was no accountant like Stu.

And Den—how could he face Den every day? Was it only pride holding Rob back from such a drastic step?

"I don't know what to do, Faither. I've hurt my Maggie so many times, but this is who I am. Please answer my prayer the een and somehow convince Maggie my fate rests in Your hands, no' hers or mine." He stepped back inside to check on the shower water.

The phone rang.

He hurried into the office to answer it before it woke the bairns.

Hugh's voice. "Rob, you and Maggie come to Elspeth's right away. She's had a heart attack."

196

Chapter Thirty-Six

Rob held on to the desk to keep from going to his knees. "Did you call John?"

"He's with her now."

"We're on our way." His hand shook as he jiggled the receiver and asked for Den's number.

Den answered and Rob told him quickly what had happened.

"Fern'll be right over to stay with the bairns."

Rob stumbled into the bedroom.

Maggie sat up in bed, looking wide-eyed at him.

"It's Elspeth," he said, holding out Maggie's robe. "She's had a ... a heart attack."

She ignored the robe, slipped out of her nightgown, wrigged into a skirt, and pulled a sweater over her head. She stepped into her shoes and grabbed his hand. "I'm ready."

They were leaving the bedroom when Fern burst in the front door while trying to button her robe. "Go. Hurry!"

Rob measured his steps to Maggie's—she was running as fast as she could. He was so frightened each breath choked his throat. No' Elspeth. No' his Elspeth.

They raced through the gate, up the steps, and in the front door.

John stood in the chaumer, talking to Hugh. He held them back when they tried to enter Elspeth's bedroom. "I want to talk to you first, and you need to catch your breath. The last thing she needs now is any sort of commotion."

Maggie collapsed onto Elspeth's rocker, gasping for breath, tears streaming a burn down her face.

Rob stood beside her, chest heaving. "How is she?"

"She's resting right now."

"She's really had a ... a ... heart attack?" Rob didn't want to speak the words, didn't want them to gain validity by voicing them aloud.

"Aye. A massive one, I'm afeart." John knuckled his eyes.

Rob grabbed his arm. "I'll help you carry her to the infirmary."

John sighed and shook his head. "She doesn't want that. She wants to stay here in her own cottage, and I agree. 'Twould do no guid to move her."

The meaning behind John's words washed over Rob like a towering wave, threatening to carry him to the bottom of a sea of grief.

Maggie leaped up and came into Rob's arms.

He clasped her to his chest, his tears mingling with hers. "When can we see her?"

Hugh embraced them. "She's asked to see you together. But no' before you stop rouping."

John wiped his own face before handing Maggie his hand-kerchief.

She fought to control herself, but it was so hard. This woman had been her mither since Maggie was eight, the one who kissed her bruised knees and told her stories and explained why stars twinkle and wept proudly when she graduated from nursing school. This was the woman who had given her hope that Rob would live when it seemed impossible.

Rob remembered the soft caress of Elspeth's hands. Remembered even a few words she spoke to him when he was in a coma after his last B-17 crash.

"You're no' a quitter," she had said. "God holds you in the palm of His hand, lad."

Those words had sustained him through pain so excruciating he couldn't even acknowledge it. Later, she'd spent countless hours teaching him Scots and the Gaelic and encouraged him when he doubted the *Maggie* would float when she was launched. She'd always believed in him and what he was attempting to do.

He couldn't face a future without her. It was unthinkable. He wiped his face on his sleeve.

Maggie dabbed at her cheeks with the handkerchief. When their eyes met, she nodded. "We're ready."

Hugh held up a hand. "A word of prayer first. We must think of our Elspeth and her well-being."

They linked arms and bowed their heads.

"Our Heavenly Faither, we ask that You guide our thoughts and words as we face this most difficult of tasks—that of saying guidbye. We know You are bringing comfort to Elspeth right now. Don't allow us to say or do anything that will fash her. In Jesus's name we pray, amen." Hugh opened the bedroom door.

198

Rob and Maggie tiptoed in.

Elspeth lay propped up on pillows, white hair released from its braid surrounding her head. A candle flickered on her bedside table, illuminating her pale face and the thin blue veins crisscrossing her closed eyelids. She opened her eyes and raised one tiny hand, beckoning them closer.

Maggie sat on the edge of the bed and rested her head on Elspeth's chest.

Rob knelt beside the bed. He took Elspeth's hand in his and brought it to his lips, fighting to control his raging emotions.

"Dear ones," she said, voice so weak they leaned closer to hear. "I'm happy you came to see me off on my journey."

Rob reached his free hand for Maggie's.

Her short nails dug into his palm.

"I know there will be tears. 'Tis human to weep at loss, but remember the guid times. 'Tis only fitting." Her trembling fingers stroked Maggie's cheek. "I held you when you were only a few minutes auld. I knew then we were going to be verra close, and you haven't disappointed me. You've been the daughter I never had. You've a gentle spirit, lass, but you canna give up."

Maggie nodded.

Elspeth rested a moment before continuing. "'Tis a hard road our Lord has chosen for you, but you are up to it. Don't give in to fear. It defeats God's purpose for your life and Rob's." Her smile radiated luve as she looked into Maggie's face. "If you haven't told him yet, do it soon."

Rob's breath caught. Had Maggie phoned and told Elspeth she'd forgiven him for putting his life in danger again? For almost dying?

After another moment's rest, she beckoned Rob closer, her fingers tight around his. "I couldn't luve you more if you were my own. You're a special lad, Rob, a verra special lad. I remember the first time I saw you lying on that stretcher on the dock. Something turned over in my heart, and I knew you were destined for a purpose God had in mind just for you. You must stay strong and keep focused, my precious lad, for that purpose has only begun."

But how could he carry on with that purpose without Elspeth's prayers and wise counsel—her luve?

Closing her eyes, she took several shallow breaths. When she looked at them again, her eyes were clear, voice stronger. "I had a dream but it wasn't for me. It was for the both of you."

The candle flared, illuminating her soft smile.

"It was a bonnie day, filled with sun and a sciffin breeze. You were sitting in rockers on your entry, and there were bairns all around you, playing at your feet and running about. You were holding hands and smiling at one another. My heart swelled at the luve on your faces."

Rob choked back a sob.

Elspeth stopped and caught her breath. "I knew it was a dream, because you both had white hair. You were verra auld but you were surrounded by your grandbairns and happy to still be together and in luve. I woke up feeling such peace."

Her words bathed his soul, peace fighting grief.

Her eyes closed. "Keep my dream in your hearts when you grow afeart, for our Lord is faithful. He will no' allow you to be parted too soon, no' until you're verra, verra auld, and even that parting will be verra short before you are reunited in heaven." Breath steady, she drifted off to sleep.

Hugh came in and touched their shoulders.

Rob kissed Elspeth's hand and laid it on the bed. "I luve you, Elspeth," he whispered. He pushed himself to his feet and took Maggie into his arms as she rose from the bed. He held her silently as the echo of Elspeth's parting words washed over him. *Our Lord is faithful. He will no' allow you to be parted too soon.*

They quit the room and John joined Hugh in Elspeth's room.

Rob sat in Elspeth's rocker and pulled Maggie onto his lap. Tears scalded his cheeks as they stared wordlessly at one another. He read Maggie's thoughts as clearly as his own. Elspeth had given them a precious parting gift: her vision that they would grow auld together. How could they doubt it?

Maggie smiled through her tears. "She knew, luve. I haven't told anybody yet, no' even you, but our Elspeth knew I'm biggen."

Rob clasped her to him, rubbing his cheek against hers. "Och, Maggie, you couldn't have said anything else that would bring me joy at such a moment." He kissed her tenderly and rocked as they waited.

Only minutes later, Hugh and John came out of the bedroom, weeping and smiling.

"Our Elspeth is in heaven," Hugh said, tears on his cheeks. "Imagine the rejoicing going on there—the songs of praise, the greetings from friends and loved ones. One of God's most faithful has returned from a verra, verra long journey here on earth."

Chapter Thirty-Seven

The kirk bell tolled the death knell early the next morning. Within moments, everyone on Innisbraw knew that Elspeth NicAllister had passed. Work ceased, businesses sat empty, deserted trawlers and creelers crowded the dock, and paths emptied, as families clutched each other and wept. Only the howff opened for dinner—the tourists had to be fed.

Most tourists respected the islanders' grief, but some became weary of their hosts' long faces and the lack of vendors selling their handmade wares.

"Wouldn't it just be our luck," one man complained to Paddy. "Who was this woman, anyway, some modern-day Scottish saint?"

Fisting his hands, Paddy pasted a false smile on his face. "Why, o' course," he said in his thickest Irish brogue. "The likes o' Elspeth NicAllister's the thing legends are made of. 'Tis said only those who mourn her properly will make it past Saint Peter at the pearly gates."

The tourists who arrived by ferry on the day of the funeral were delighted to find every local dressed in their clan plaids. Their delight soon turned to dismay when their host families fed them a cold dinner of sandwiches and crisps before disappearing. A few visitors, drawn by the intrigue of witnessing some sort of Scottish gathering, followed their hosts to the kirk. When told it was a funeral, they returned to their cottages to unpack and take a nap until the whole dreary affair was over.

Hugh stepped to the front of the dais and laid a hand on the plain wooden kist on its bier beside him. *This part of the service should no' be as hard, Faither, but please be with me later.* He looked out at grief-stricken faces. "Before we begin the service, I want to share our Elspeth's verra specific wishes with you." He pulled a paper from his jacket pocket and adjusted his eyeglasses. "They will reveal just a wee bit of the humble saint we were blessed to call our own."

Only a few muffled sniffles broke the silence.

He cleared his tear-clogged throat. "'It would pleasure me if Rob and Graham made the kist to hold these done auld bones. No decorations, lads. My earthly body, though a gift from God, fails me so often of late.'"

Hugh's breath caught when Rob glanced at Graham across the aisle and blinked back tears. What a difficult turn it had been for twa lads who luved Elspeth, auld bones and all.

"'Angus's unadorned cairt is to be used to carry my kist to the kirk and then on to the laying away grounds. I don't want any fuss and bother, and The Lift is too long a walk for our lads carrying a heavy burden. I've journeyed all over the island in that cairt. If it was guid enough for me in life, it will be guid enough in death.'"

Hugh nearly smiled when Angus sat a wee bit taller.

"'Rob and his rescue-crew lads will carry my kist into the kirk, out to the cairt, and to my burying place. Those brave lads face death every day. I trust them to treat these auld bones gently.'"

Hugh raised his glasses and wiped his eyes.

"'The service will be conducted in the Gaelic. It will be a private affair. No strangers need be privy to our family secrets. One song only, and that played by a single piper. 'Amazing Grace' will never grow auld, and it tells what is in my heart much better than I ever could. There will be no eulogies. We're a sma' family here on Innisbraw. If we need reminding of the guid someone's done, let it be around the supper table where 'tis most fitting.'"

Sobs broke the silence as Hugh folded the paper and returned it to his pocket. "Let us bow our heads for silent prayer."

✦

Rob pulled his gaze from the kist he and Graham had fashioned from the clearest, finest-grained decking boards in the shed. So plain, it looked, but that was what Elspeth wanted.

Every pew was filled and many of the younger lads stood along the back wall of the sanctuary. Rob held Beth, and Maggie cuddled Will, so the Anderson family, John, and Ellie and Calum and all their bairns could share the pew.

Maggie looked drawn and tired, her face wet with tears.

He squeezed her hand. *Thank You for the time You gave me with Elspeth, Lord. And if You approve, let her know I'm looking forward to the time we'll meet again.*

He felt hollow inside, tears long spent. It was as though Elspeth secretly inhabited his body while she was alive, giving him purpose, direction, and strength. Pray God he had enough doctrine to take directions from the Holy Spirit without depending on Elspeth's words of wisdom to intercede.

Maggie gripped Rob's hand, drawing strength from his warm flesh. *Thank Ye for bringing Elspeth into my life, Faither. I'll miss her so.* She wiped her cheeks with a sodden handkerchief.

Would the tears never cease?

Please don't allow me to give in to selfish thoughts. Ye've blessed me beyond my every dream. Give me the strength to be the wife, mither, and friend You desire me to be. But I so wanted Elspeth to hold all my bairns before she ... went home.

She took the handkerchief Rob offered and bowed her head, sobs racking her ribs, sore from prolonged weeping.

"Amen." Hugh's gaze swept over the folk. *No eulogies, Elspeth, just as you so wisely decreed.*

Every person there, from the oldest to the youngest, could have told a story about how Elspeth had touched their hearts and changed their lives.

He raised his arms. "Listen to the comforting words of our Heavenly Faither, all chosen by Elspeth."

No need to read them from his Bible. They filled his mind and heart and overflowed.

"Matthew 5:4. 'Blessed are they that mourn; for they shall be comforted.' Isaiah 43:2. 'When thou passest through the waters, I will be with thee; and through the rivers, they shall not overflow thee: when thou walkest through fire, thou shalt not be burned; neither shall the flame kindle upon thee.'" He paused and wiped his cheeks.

He would miss Elspeth's wise counsel and the prayer support she always offered, no matter how difficult the situation. But most of all, like everyone on their wee island, he would miss her unconditional luve.

Clearing his throat, he fingered the smooth wooden kist. Only her body, weak and auld, but so treasured.

"Our final scripture is the uplifting words of I Corinthians: 15:55. 'O death, where is thy victory? O death, where is thy sting?'" He nodded to Graham Stewart, who stood at the door to the narthex, redding his pipes.

The haunting notes of "Amazing Grace" skirled through the sanctuary, caressed the stained-glass window of the Risen Christ, wrapped around the bowed heads of the folk, fluttered the candle flames that scented the air with the sweet smell of honey. Though no voices raised in song, Hugh was certain each mind repeated the words, claiming them for their own.

Maggie clung to Rob's hand. Aye, this was Elspeth's song. At this verra moment, she could be adding a youthful voice to the heavenly choir, praising her Lord for the grace which allowed her to minister on earth so long. *Thank Ye for these words of comfort, Faither. Remind me of their truth when I miss her dreadfully.*

The graveside service was very brief, as per Elspeth's wishes.

Her words echoed in Hugh's mind.

"If I pass in the winter, the poor folk will have to bear the rain plomping doon, and if 'tis in spring, summer, or fall, there are far better things to do with their time. I may no' have merrit and had a family of bairns, but I did have my own special luves. 'Twill be for them I request this, no' me."

Over two dozen people lined up to take a flower from the bouquet that came from Elspeth's garden. Among them were John; Calum and Ellie and their bairns; the Proctors; the Sims; Morag and Alec; Graham and Rinait; the Andersons; and the Savage family, including wee Will. Each dropped their flower onto the top of the casket, the bairns' eyes wide. Maggie, who was last, went to her knees and placed a sprig of heather on the kist. No' only was it tradition, it was fitting.

The graveside service over, Rob knelt beside Shep, who'd followed them from the house.

The dog lay near the foot of the burying place, head on paws, eyes anxious, as he watched members of the Island Council shovel dirt over the kist. He trembled when Rob rubbed his neck.

"Guid lad," Rob said. "Don't worry. She'll never be in danger again."

A soft tongue licked his hand.

Head lowered, Rob helped the bairns into the wagon, and the family began the long trek back home to the other side of Ben Innis.

An onshore breeze ruffled the lace curtains at the bedroom window, casting dancing, intricate patterns across moonlit walls.

"You answered the bairns' questions well, luve." Maggie ran her fingers across Rob's bare shoulder, a smile trembling on her lips.

"How can we live withoot her, Maggie?" He buried his face 'neath her hair, his tears wetting her neck. "No matter the problem, her words always showed me the way."

A tear-clogged breath caught in her throat. What could she say to him when the same question resonated in her mind?

Help me, Faither. Give me Your words.

She opened her mouth and words spilled out without thought. "We live one day at a time, placing our trust in our Saviour, Who promises we'll meet Elspeth in heaven when our own journeys on earth are over." She pushed the forelock back from his forehead. "One day at a time, luve, with joy and gratitude that our Faither's allowed us another day to serve Him."

205

Chapter Thirty-Eight

Robbie hopped from foot to foot, toothpaste dribbling down his chin.

"Settle yourself." Maggie pressed his face into the bathing room basin. "Spit and rinse. I'll see to your hair next."

He palmed water into his mouth and spat, then made a face in the mirror. "My tooth's loose but it still hasn't come oot. I want to spit across the room like Richie." He wriggled a tooth. "Where's Faither? He promised to be here."

"You talk fast as a tinker peddling dented pots." Maggie rummaged in the closet. "Your tooth will come oot when 'tis ready and no' afore, and if you spit, it won't be in the house but oot on the girse. As for your faither, he's on his way." *Och, Lord, don't let Rob forget.* Maggie held out a towel. "Dry your face and turn around, so I can comb those tangles from your hair. You don't want to go to school looking like a blousterin' wind caught you up." Maggie's pulse quickened.

Her auldest bairn's first day of school. How quickly time passed. Just yesterday, he was a wee laddie in hippens, toddling about the house, clutching his cloth rabbit, slubbers wetting his chin.

Fighting tears, she ran a comb under water and worked on his stubborn forelock. Just like his faither's, it was, with a mind of its own.

"Where's my sark? And my piece-box?"

She slipped a shirt over his head and laced it, jerking him back when he fidgeted. "Your piece-box is on the kitchen bunker. Let me see your feet."

"They're clean. Faither scrubbed them last een till my toes burned." His head shot up. "I hear Faither." Robbie dashed out the door.

⚜

"Let's be having you." Rob grinned and gathered Robbie up in a hug. "Look at you, all ready for school."

The lad wriggled and slid to the floor, dimples dancing. "Mither said I don't have to wear shoes till the rains come. And these are my new shorts."

A chuckle tickled Rob's chest. If ever there was a typical lad. A plaster rode one skinned knee, tincture of Merthiolate the other. His sark laces were in a jumble, and a dab of dry toothpaste rested at the corner of his mouth. "You look grand. When you get home, we'll walk across the fell, and you can tell me all about your first day." He patted Robbie's bottom. "You'd best hurry. Malcolm, Richie, and Katie are almost to the gate."

Robbie grinned and wriggled his tooth again, then dashed for the bathing room, most likely to check the incisor's progress in the mirror.

Rob swallowed around a lump in his throat. This was a big change in their auldest bairn's life. He'd never be that rosy-cheeked, chubby lad again. The day, he took his first giant step toward becoming a man.

How perfect it was, Maggie being biggen again. Fast as his bairns were growing, Rob ached for a wee one to cradle close.

Maggie patted Rob's arm and handed Robbie his shiny, new piece-box, newly arrived from Sears, Roebuck & Co. "A guidbye to your sisters and brother, a kiss for Faither and me, then on you go."

After a perfunctory wave to his siblings and a quick kiss to his parents' cheeks, the lad tore out to the entry, shouting at Malcolm and Richie to "gie heels tae," so they wouldn't be late.

Rob and Maggie stood in the doorway as Robbie raced down the flagged walk with the other lads, Shep barking at their heels, Katie skipping after. The only lass, she appeared content to be alone.

Robbie's tanned legs flashed in the sunlight, bringing a smile to Rob's face. "I'm thinking I'll soon have company on my runs." He picked Maggie up and settled her onto his lap in a rocker, then thumbed a tear from her cheek. Man and woman—God made them so different. Maggie, ever the mither hen, grieving to see her first chick leave the nest, and he celebrating the beginning of his lad's journey into adulthood.

She rested her forehead against his chest. "Why walk when you can run—isn't that what you always say?"

"Only makes sense." He rocked for a while, fighting indecision. All the way up the fell the morn, he'd been battling with himself. Should he ask her now, or would it open the still-raw wound of Elspeth's passing? He took a deep breath, blew it out. He couldn't answer the next shout fearing her reaction.

Maggie's warm-honey scent sweetened his tongue, reminding him of the times she'd spooned close, gently asking him to share his fears.

He gathered his courage. "I hate to ask this, but will you still worry when the shout siren sounds?"

Maggie reared back. "I'd thought that settled." She cradled his face between her palms. "I ken you can be injured or a near-drowning victim again, but I also ken, deep inside, you'll never be lost to the sea." She smiled, blue eyes bathed in violet. "You'll always come home."

Thank Ye, Heavenly Faither. Praise Ye for Your grace, Your—

"I want to go to school too."

Annie's wee, soft voice tangled Rob's thoughts. He pulled her close to his side, fingering the curls spilling over her nightdress. "Och, my precious lassie, it won't be long and you'll be going to school."

She smiled up at him, eyes so filled with trust and luve his heart ached.

Maggie sat up in bed, her hand groping for Rob. A cold, empty pillowbere met her palm. She switched on the lamp and shaded her eyes, squinting at the bedside clock. Only 0300. What was Rob doing up so early? Shivering, she rolled out of bed, stepped into her baffies, and slipped into her dressing gown, hens-flesh peppering her arms and legs. Summer, it was, and the nighttime temperature seldom fell below ten degrees. Why was she so cold? *Because your man crept oot of bed, taking his warmth with him.*

No light on in the living room, just a pale glow of peat embers outlining Rob, hunched forward in his rocker, head in his hands. A pang of fear quickened her breath. Was he no' well? She flipped on the light and hurried to his side, throwing her arms around his bare shoulders. "Och, you're cold as a burn in winter. Why are you sitting here with no sark?"

His head fell back. "Maggie? Did I wake you, then?" Voice a husky whisper.

Sliding onto his lap, she buried her cheek against his icy chest. "You didn't wake me. What's the matter, luve? Are you no' feeling well?"

He pulled her closer, resting his cheek on her head. "I'm no' sick. Just thinking about Elspeth and how empty the island feels since she passed. Folk seldom stop for a blether, and only the bairns and halflins laugh or look like they're enjoying life."

Fighting tears, she nodded. "'Tis only been a few weeks. 'Twill take time for the grief to fade." A tear escaped her lashes. "She was the one constant light that shone on Innisbraw, always showing the way to God's grace and luve." *And keeping me on the right path when my emotions led me astray. Och, how I miss her.*

He sighed, deep and long. "She was the auldmither I always wanted, and now I feel I'm failing her."

She sat up, gazing into his eyes. "Failing her? How?"

Another sigh. "You know how practical she was. How she hated folk moping around and no' getting the starch back in their spines after something mischancie happened." A sma' smile deepened one dimple. "If she was here, she'd be telling me to start living each day again. That the time for tears is over. That I need to show you and our bairns the joy that comes from trusting in God, through bad times as well as guid."

Did Rob realize how much he'd grown spiritually? He'd come to Innisbraw with no knowledge in his soul, just a bairnie-like faith in Christ. In the past years, he'd absorbed scripture like a dry sea sponge thirsting to be filled.

Birthed and raised on the isle, she'd listened to Elspeth's wisdom—and Hugh's lessons from the Word—most of her life, and yet she'd allowed grief to smother her 'neath a blinding fog. "Then I've failed her too. What can we do about it?"

His eyebrow rose. "You're asking me? That's like the sun begging shining lessons from the moon."

"Och, you're impossible." She tapped a forefinger on his chin. "Cold as you are, you've been oot here for hours, praying and thinking. How does Colonel Savage plan to approach this target? And wipe it oot?"

Long arms pulled her close. Chilled lips trailed over her forehead, her cheeks. "You're too cannie by half, lass. I do have an idea, but it could put you in a fash."

A fash? A niggle of worry quickened her breath. Did it involve putting himself in danger? Or another turn that would leave him with less time to spend with his family? Or—enough of borrowing trouble. Only shouts put him in peril, and he'd promised no' to take on any new turns. "Tell me, Rob. Now."

A hand fisted in her hair. "I can't do much to raise the folk's spirits—except mebbe lead by example. Robbie's a birthday next week. I'm thinking it's time to give him his first flight in the floatplane. With the weather about to turn, I don't want to wait much longer. I haven't flown since Elspeth's death, and 'twould be a step in the right direction."

Was that all? Rob had often promised to take Robbie up in the floatplane when he turned six. "Robbie has school the day, luve."

"Early Saturday mornin. If the weather holds." He waited, body taut as a wet mooring rope.

She couldn't keep him on tenterhooks any longer. "That sounds grand."

He gathered her close and leaped up, carrying her to their bedroom.

She hugged his neck, buried her face in the hollow of his throat. He must like her answer.

Maggie poured another cup of tea, listening to Rob whistle snatches of the same off-key melody over and over as he shaved. What a shame he was tone-deaf. He enjoyed music so. Aw weel, he'd wakened in a guid mood, and no wonder. The day, Robbie took his first flight. She glanced at their lad, spooning brose into his mouth so fast his cheeks bulged like a red squirrel hoarding pine nuts. She poured Rob a mug of coffee and carried it into the bathing room.

He pushed the door closed and took her into his arms, inhaling deeply as he kissed the back of her neck. "The scent of heather needs to mix with the scent of Maggie to be at its verra best." He ran his lips over her forehead, across her cheeks, and down her throat.

She laced his shirt collar and handed him his comb. "If you take much longer, you'll have a lad with an uggit stomach, he's that excited."

"That makes twa." He ran a comb through his hair, opened the door, and grabbed his coffee mug.

Moments later, Robbie perched on the entry railing while Rob laid down ground rules for flight safety. "Never, ever touch the yoke or rudders without permission. If I tell you to haud yer wheesht, swallow the next word." Rob stabbed a finger. "Once I get you buckled in, don't touch your harness. And you'll get your turn at the yoke when I say 'tis time, so I don't want to hear any nattering." He stared into the lad's eyes. "Got all that?"

Was that a spark of resentment in his lad's eyes? Had he been too strident, taken the joy oot of the mornin? What had he been thinking? He wasn't lecturing a green Air Corp's cadet about to take his first flight in a PT-17 trainer.

He ruffled his son's hair and softened his voice. "Understand, lad?"

Robbie jumped down and hugged his faither's leg. "Aye,

Faither."

"Guid. Let's go in and kiss your mither guidbye. We're wastin' a perfect mornin."

Chapter Thirty-Nine

Robbie skipped ahead on the path, an early mornin wind smearing his black forelock across his forehead, blue eyes bright as rain-washed stars.

Rob shook his head. Had he ever had so much energy? A smile died unborn. It wasn't energy but impatience. Nowt ever happened quickly enough—for himself or his lad.

The harbour water ebbed and swelled 'neath a blinding sun, tips of foam icing the wind-kicked waves. A perfect day for flying.

Gulls wheeled and nattered overhead as Rob explained each step of his pre-flight check. Once completed, he showed Robbie how to untether the mooring rope, then boosted him into the passenger seat. "Sit on your knees, so you can see oot the windscreen. I'll buckle you in." Rob glanced up at the windsock.

Streaming to the northwest, it was, perfect for a takeoff into the wind.

He secured the door and buckled them both in. Explaining each action to Robbie, he stroked the primer, set the mixture level to Rich, and flipped on the master and starter switches.

The engine coughed and started with a belch of black smoke.

Only half a tank of fuel?

It was more than enough, but somebody, probably Pete, since Den knew better, needed a reminder to top off the tank after every flight.

Using his rudders to steer, Rob taxied away from the dock and raised the rpm to take-off speed.

Robbie clasped his hands, staring out the side windscreen as the floatplane rose on her steps and plowed through vulnerable waves.

Moments later, they went airborne.

"We're flying!" Robbie shouted. "We're flying, Faither!"

"Aye, we are, that." Rob grinned, caught up in his lad's excitement. Robbie's smile was so radiant Rob's eyes teared. He could remember his own first flight. Och, aye, each minute was etched into his memory. "I'll let you take the controls and fly a while."

"When? When can I fly?"

Rob patted the lad's bare leg. "In a few minutes, after we gain some altitude."

Though he'd planned to overfly the islands to the north and show Robbie the same sights that had thrilled Malcolm, he decided to take Robbie as far over Scotland as Glasgow, then head inland a bit to see Ben Lomond towering around 3,200 feet into the air. He turned the plane southeast.

The moment they had enough altitude, Rob trimmed the plane to level flight and showed Robbie where to place his hands on the yoke. "No fast moves or jerking. It doesn't take much to make this airieplane respond."

Robbie's smile faded. The tip of his tongue peeked out from between his lips.

"Now, look at the symbol of the wee airieplane on the instrument panel. Keep those wings level and you won't have to make any large corrections."

Robbie's face turned red.

Rob hid a smile. "You can breathe, lad, you're doing grand. You're flying the airieplane, see? My hands are in my lap."

The lad glanced at his faither's hands, then looked immediately out the windscreen again, shoulders pressing up against the harness to see over the yoke. His gaze darted from windscreen to instrument panel as he made small corrections while Rob controlled the foot pedals.

"Want to try a bank?"

"Aye!"

"All right. This first time we'll both have our hands on the yoke. Rest your hands lightly. Let me do the turning while you feel how the airieplane responds."

Rob put the plane into a left bank.

Robbie let out a triumphant shout.

Recovering from the bank, Rob took the plane higher to regain lost altitude. "Now I'll rest my hands on the yoke. See if you can bank the way I did."

Wide blue eyes pinned Rob. "What if I do it wrong? Will we crash?"

"I'll just correct. Ready?"

A tentative nod.

Robbie turned the yoke to the left but was too timid.

Rob exerted a bit more pressure and tromped on a rudder.

The plane dipped steeply into a smooth left bank.

"Guid. Straighten her oot."

Robbie shot his father an exultant grin.

"Verra guid. Now 'tis Faither's turn again. You just kneel there and look oot while I show you what Scotland looks like from the air."

Leaving the Minch far behind, they flew over lochs, braes, and hillocks, some green with girse, others spilling purple heather down their slopes. Farther inland, small freshwater lochs competed with craggy scaurs and sun-dappled glens. A large eagle appeared briefly off to their right.

Robbie turned in his seat and watched it.

Rob took the floatplane lower.

"Faither!" Robbie suddenly exclaimed. "Bottlenose dolphins! Look at them."

"They're in the Firth of Clyde, lad, outside of Glasgow. 'Tis time to change our heading to north, so you can see Loch and Ben Lomond."

An eager nod.

A sudden bit of turbulence jolted the plane.

Rob scanned the skies.

A few clouds were building to the west.

The airplane bucked again.

Rob smiled at Robbie. "We're in for a few bumps. Put your hands back on the yoke, but lightly. I want you to feel what I'm doing." He pulled back on the yoke and climbed to 5,000 feet.

The look of those darkening clouds was troubling, and the turbulence was becoming worse with each passing moment. Where had this front come from? No word of an impending storm when he'd called Scotland Weather this mornin.

Och, he should have refueled at Glasgow, but he hadn't wanted to throw Maggie into a fash by being late. If he were alone, he'd welcome an opportunity to liven a routine flight, but why subject his lad to a bumpy first ride?

He tapped Robbie's leg. "Unbuckle your harness, sit on your behoochie, and buckle up again. Pull the belt as tight as it will go. Don't touch the yoke."

Robbie's mouth popped open, eyes widened. "Did I do something bad?"

"Of course no', but we're in for a bumpy ride. Do it now, airman. That's an order."

The lad unbuckled his belt and sat, fumbling with the harness as the plane lurched from side to side.

Once he got the buckle done, Rob reached over and tightened the belt. "'Tis going to get verra rough soon, and dark. Understand?"

The lad nodded.

Rob grinned at him. "There's the spirit. Now hang on tight. Faither's going to be too busy to explain things. There's nowt to be afraid of, as long as you don't touch the yoke."

The clouds turned from grey to black. Spates of rain lashed the plane, thundering on the metal overhead. It bucked, bounced, and juddered, buffeted by conflicting air currents.

Rob concentrated on the instruments, but the constant jouncing made it difficult to get accurate readings.

A bright flash of light pierced the darkness ahead of their right wing.

Rob flinched. Lightning.

Though the chance of it hitting the floatplane was small, lightning always posed a threat. He checked his altitude. As long as he maintained 5,000 feet, he had plenty of clearance for Ben Lomond. But there was always the chance of a downdraft plunging them lower—and lower.

"How are you doing?" Rob shouted.

"All right, Commander."

Was there a bit of a tremor in the lad's voice? "We're going to be fine, lad. Bow your head and we'll say a prayer." Though his eyes remained open, Rob's words were no less fervent. "Heavenly Faither, You hold us up with the wings of Your angels. Guide my thoughts and hands. In Jesus's name, amen."

There, straight ahead. A clearing in the clouds. A bright ray of sunshine shone its alluring beam through the darkness and rain.

"Och, no you don't," Rob muttered. It was what pilots called a "sucker hole," a brief parting of the clouds. If he followed it down, it could close up at any time, leaving him at a lower altitude and still caught in darkness. The perfect scenario for crashing into a ben or scaur.

He checked his fuel gauge. Getting low. Fighting these winds took time and used precious fuel. Why had he chosen the day for Robbie's first flight?

Would this ruin his enthusiasm for flying—make him fearful?

Rob prayed no'.

The airplane buffeted violently from side to side and up and down as the storm cell intensified.

He kept his eyes riveted on the instrument panel, knowing better than to trust his own judgment. Too easy to become disoriented, to no longer know if the plane was climbing, flying level, or diving.

By his reckoning, they should be near Oban. If they overshot land and ended up over water, he could always set the floatplane down and radio Den for a tow. *If the sea's no' running too high for a safe landing.*

His gaze darted to the fuel gauge again, and his stomach cramped.

No' much fuel left.

They had to descend.

Chapter Forty

Certain he was near Oban and well away from any of the higher scaurs, Rob contacted the airstrip by radio. He breathed a sigh of relief when he wasn't asked to circle and hold—no other aircraft in the vicinity needed to land. As he began his descent, the turbulence gradually lessened to little more than a bumpy ride, and the clouds thinned, improving visibility. At five hundred feet, they broke into sunshine, and the girse landing strip appeared below his left wing. *Thank Ye, Lord.* He lowered the wheels.

He set the floatplane down just as the fuel gauge hovered on empty.

Too close by half.

After taxiing over to the fuel station, he shut off the engine and sat for a moment, working the cramps out of his fingers. "We're at Oban, lad."

"Where Calum unloads his fish?"

"The same."

"But it's no' pishing rain." No tremor in his lad's voice this time.

Rob unbuckled his seat harness, then Robbie's. "I think a wee prayer of thanks is in order, don't you agree?"

A solemn nod.

Rob bowed his head. "We thank You, Heavenly Faither, for once again protecting us. Thank You for Your guidance and faithfulness. In Jesus's name, amen." He held out a hand. "On you come. I'm thinking a candy bar and a lemon skoosh for you and a coffee for me. Sound guid?"

"Grand."

Rob lifted Robbie down, holding him a little longer than necessary.

Though it took the lad a while to regain his equilibrium, by the time all three fuel tanks had been topped off, his candy bar and lemon skoosh were only a memory, and he was running around the strip, inspecting the planes tethered in the girse.

Only a cursory walk-around check was necessary after a refueling, but Rob went over every inch of the floatplane. Rain alone shouldn't do any damage, but fierce winds could loosen rivets or wires, causing something to shake loose or peel back at airspeed. Satisfied with the check, he whistled Robbie over and lifted him onto the seat. "Onto your knees again, lad."

Robbie clutched his faither's arm. "You mean I can—you'll let me—I can fly again?"

"Once we're oot of the Sound of Mull and over the Minch."

Robbie scrambled into his seat, settled onto his knees, and ducked into the harness. Despite trembling hands, he pulled it tight, shooting his faither a satisfied smile.

Thank the Lord the lad still wanted to fly. When the time came for Robbie to execute a steep bank, Rob would make it to the right, so his lad would have a view off the edge of his leading wing.

Rob did a quick cabin and instrument check, started the engine, and taxied out to the end of the strip, foot on the brake, revving the rpms into take-off range. "Listen up, lad. I have to get clearance before I take off."

"Clearance? What's that?"

"Like asking for permission." Rob keyed on the radio. "Oban Control, this is Whisky Alfa Lima November zero niner zero, requesting clearance for departure."

"Whisky Alfa Lima November, no other traffic reported in area. You are cleared for departure."

Robbie's fingers tapped a tattoo on his thighs. "You didn't do that when we took off from Innisbraw."

Smart lad. "You're only required to get clearance if there might be other airieplanes in the area, like around an airstrip or airport."

"Oh." The lad's smile widened as they sped down the girse runway and lifted off.

Nose up, airspeed high, the plane climbed to altitude. Rob retracted the wheels, trimmed the plane, and set a new heading. Toward home.

He pointed out the Lismore Lighthouse and other landmarks as they followed Mull Sound. Sunlight glittered off rocks and tumbling burns. Inlets foamed with an incoming tide, small boats rocked at rickety, auld piers, and an occasional cottage appeared, a wisp of peat smoke trailing from a stone chimney, sheep grazing between the door flags. A ship plowed through the sound below.

Rob pointed at the ship. "Look down, lad. There's a sight you won't often see."

"That's a muckle boat," Robbie shouted. "'Tis even bigger than the one that brings your lumber from America."

"'Tis a cargo ship, no' a boat. See those wooden containers

stacked on deck? They're full of all sorts of things being shipped to a port someplace in Ireland—or Norway, if they're bound for the North Sea."

"Wait till I tell Richie. He'll ne'er believe what I've seen the day." Robbie's face scrunched into a calculating smile.

"Telling him what you've seen is fine, lad, but don't blaw your own horn. You'll hurt Richie's feelings."

Robbie continued to look out the side windscreen, jaw moving, tongue most likely probing the empty space between his front teeth. "Why would it hurt his feelings? Uncle Calum took him oot in his trawler, and he even caught some fish. It didn't fash me, even when he said he didn't get an uggit stomach."

Rob had thought himself beyond it, but these "why" questions still put him in a quandary. Sometimes a simple sentence could set things straight, but other "whys" required a lengthy explanation. He blurted out the first thing that came to mind. "Do you want to go oot on a trawler and catch fish?"

"Ugh. Richie says the boat's reeky and the fish are slippery and bloody when you cut them open."

"Does Richie want to fly someday?"

"Aye, but—" Robbie leaned his forehead against the side windscreen.

Careful, Savage. He's so young. "But what? His faither's a fisherman, no' a pilot, so he doesn't think he'll ever have a chance to fly?"

Robbie turned around, studied his laced fingers, frowning. "All Uncle Calum talks about is Richie growing up and joining his crew." His eyebrows lowered into a scowl. "He never listens when Richie talks about wanting to fly."

It would be easy to make Calum the problem, say he couldn't understand because all he'd ever wanted was to crew a trawler. But what guid would that do? Or, Rob could say that Richie could be both a fisherman and pilot. That had satisfied Malcolm, but Pete encouraged the lad to be both pilot and pitcher. To six-year-olds, every day felt like an eternity. This fankle needed an instant solution. "As long as the guid weather holds, we could take him flying with us."

Amazing how a few words could transform a full-blown gale into blinding sunshine. Robbie rocked on his knees, eyes sparkling, grinning like the Cheshire cat. "We're going flying again? You'll take Richie with us?"

"Why no'? You've made a guid start the day, but this is only a taste of all you need to learn." Rob returned Robbie's grin. "As for Richie, I'll have a talk with Calum. Don't mention it till I have something worked oot."

"Aye. I'll haud my wheesht."

He should add that having Richie along would mean less yoke time for Robbie, that his lad needed to give his friend a turn without resenting it, but, och, Rob was already tired. No reason to expose himself to another round of "whys." "You ready for some more hands-on? We're over the Minch."

"I'm ready."

Robbie executed several more banks, gaining confidence each time. The last was so smooth, the recovery so perfect, Rob sent the lad two thumbs-up. What a grand outcome to the day. His son was one of those rare breeds—a natural pilot. What had been a faither's dream was now a given: there would be another pilot in the Savage family. *Thank Ye, Faither. Thank Ye for answering my prayers.*

Rob took the controls as they approached the harbour at Innisbraw.

Though still eager, Robbie's legs trembled. It couldn't be easy, sitting on one's knees so long.

Rob landed and taxied up to the dock, cut the engine, and shut down all systems.

Robbie unhooked his harness and scrambled out after Rob, racing to tie the floatplane to its mooring line.

"There's a guid lad. Up you go now." Rob boosted him up the ladder, followed, and grabbed hold of Robbie's hand. This was his lad. Rob was so proud he wished the whole island could ken how well Robbie had done the mornin.

On the way up the path, Rob disregarded the impulse to soft-pedal the experience when he told Maggie about the storm. Lies of omission were still lies. The truth could put her in a fash, but she knew flying had its risks, just like sailing a boat or, for that matter, driving a car.

※

Maggie dashed from the entry and threw herself into Rob' arms. "You're so late!" She reveled in his kiss, his strong, familiar embrace.

Robbie hugged her hips, blue eyes sparkling like sun-glimmers on the Minch. Och, when had he grown so tall? She laughed. Such a silly, worrisome goose she'd been. They were both home safe.

The lad pulled on her apron. "I flew the floatplane, Mither. Faither's hands were in his lap. I flew it all alone."

Maggie cupped his chin. "You never."

"I did, and we had a storm with rain and wind and lightning, and I did some right and left banks and pulled up, and I kept the wings level the way Faither showed me, and—"

"Slow down, lad," Rob said. "Don't try to tell it all at once. Catch your breath."

"A storm?" Maggie's breath caught. "How bad a storm, Rob?"

"Bumpy as all get-oot, but there was never any real danger. And he didn't get airsick. He's a born pilot, Maggie."

A born pilot. She stepped back and stared into Rob's eyes. "We'll talk about this later." After pulling Robbie up the flags, she planted a kiss on his head. "I'm proud of you. So you liked flying, did you?"

Beth inched down the entry steps, eyes wary.

"'Twas better than anything in the world. I'm going to be a pilot. I'm going to be the best pilot ever."

Maggie pulled him to a stop, a tease tickling her tongue. "Better than your faither?"

His grin faded, then blossomed again. "I'll be just as guid. There can be twa best pilots." He grabbed Rob's hand. "Faither and me."

Beth pushed between Robbie and her mither. She stamped her foot. "No! I'm going to be the best pilot too!"

Rob rubbed the side of his nose. "I'm thinking I started something here."

Maggie swatted at him. "Och, I'm thinking you did."

Robbie ignored Beth. "It got real dark and the rain was pishing doon real hard, and the wind was sooching something fierce."

"Where was this, Rob?" Maggie asked, waving a hand. "There isn't a cloud in the sky."

"Before we reached Oban. It was one of those isolated storm cells we sometimes get in summer, especially over tall bens that create their own weather." He kissed her cheek. "Our lad didn't blether, so I could concentrate on flying. I tell you, he'll make a fine pilot someday."

She held her oldest bairn tightly. "I'm so grateful you're home safe," she said, brushing tears from her eyes. "Now inside and wash for dinner. Annie and Will are already at the table."

Beth tore up the stairs, sticking her tongue out at Robbie when she beat him to the door.

Maggie's thoughts churned as she stared up at Rob. "I'm thinking things were much more serious than you're letting on. Why didn't you turn back? Or fly around the storm?"

221

He took her arm and guided her up the entry steps. "I didn't have enough fuel to do either, lass. It wasn't a large storm, just a verra windy one. I'm sorry he had to go through it on his first flight, but he handled it well."

She shivered. "You could have crashed again." Vivid pictures leaped into her mind: red flares bursting behind crippled Forts, rousing ambulance crews to race to hardstands, stretchers and plasma at the ready; black smoke pouring from a Spitfire lying crumpled beside the landing strip; pinched faces of surviving RAF and AAF crews, attempting to absorb the loss of mates and friends; Rob, still as death, being carried onto a transport plane. *Help me, Faither! Don't let the de'il's lies make me afeart. Everybody says Rob's the best pilot they've ever seen, and the war's over.*

Warm lips brushed her cheek. "Maggie, we were never anywhere near crashing. I'm telling you the truth, luve. It was fearsome for Robbie, but I've been in many, many storms worse than that one." He held her away and looked into her face. "Don't spoil his joy. He's proud of himself, and rightly so."

That again. How could she win an argument when he used his ultimate weapon—logic? "Och, I had to marry a pilot."

His body stiffened, eyes darkened. "You're sorry you did, then?"

She'd gone too far—attacked the very thing that made him who he was. "Of course I'm no' sorry. I luve you, you know that. It just seems that everything you do is dangerous, and no' one but twa of our bairns want to be pilots too."

He sat down in a rocker and pulled her onto his lap, cradling her head against his chest. "Everything in life can be dangerous, Maggie. Folk are killed in accidents all the time. 'Tis the same auld question of faith, and knowing all our days on earth are numbered. Only God Himself knows when He'll call us home, so we live every day to the fullest, being grateful."

"Your faith seems so much stronger than mine." A ragged whisper, but all she could manage.

"That's no' true. 'Tis just that you're the one who has to wait at home. 'Tis much easier for me. I'm so busy doing I don't have time to worry about the outcome." He rested his cheek against her hair. "I didn't know Beth was interested in flying."

"Then you must be blind and deaf." She softened her impetuous words with a nip on his chin. "She listens to every conversation about flying, her eyes wide and full of dreams. Even Fern's noticed it."

"Next you're going to tell me Wee Annie wants to be a pilot."

"Annie?" She giggled. "All our Annie's cared about for the

longest time is taking care of her doll and singing it to sleep with lullabies." She leaned into his embrace. "But just this mornin she told me she wants to learn to cook, so she can have supper ready when you daft pilots come home tired and hungry."

"'Daft pilots.'" He sighed. "I suppose that's me and Robbie. If he's anything like me, he'll be remembering the feel of the yoke beneath his fingers and reliving the thrill of that perfect left bank, dreaming of the time when he's tall enough to reach the rudders, so he can bambase everybody—especially me—with how well he can fly."

The yearning in his voice touched her heart. "You've given him a wondersome gift, Rob. Only yesterday, flying was all in his imagination. Now, unlike you growing up, he knows what it looks like, how it feels. You told me that when you were a lad at the orphanage, you lived in a dreamworld where the skies were always blue and the airieplane responded perfectly, just like the Jennys you watched perform." She kissed the hollow of his throat. "You've planted the seeds in fertile soil. Given time, they'll sprout and mature."

"And you, luve? Do you still want to learn to fly?"

"Mmm, of course. After our last bairnie's birthed and weaned, you can take me up into the sky." She smiled and raised her face to the sun. "And then mebbe I'll understand what it means to fly where only angels dare, to climb until the golden radiance from God's face blinds me with its glory."

Chapter Forty-One

A telephone call from Bill Townsend the last Monday in September offered another distraction from their grief at Elspeth's passing. "I've got a break in my schedule. How'd you feel about four visitors bumming rooms at your house for a few days starting the sixth of October? I know it's short notice, but the manse has only one room available."

Their impending visit was just what Maggie needed. She prepared the spare bedrooms with fresh linens and placed canning jars filled with asters and dried berries on the bedside tables. Small rugs were taken out to the clothesline and beaten, the entry flags scoured, fresh butter plunged, and dozens of scones stored in the freezer. The night before the Townsends' arrival, she fell into bed exhausted but satisfied the house had never looked cleaner, the floors shinier.

Rob pinned Maggie with a stare. "But I planned on the family meeting the ferry, no' just me."

"Beth needs to bathe after helping Shep dig a rabbit oot of a hole 'neath the entry." Maggie propped her hands on her hips. "And don't go raising that eyebrow. The rabbit got away through the gate Robbie left agape when he left for school this mornin. Besides, I've a grand Scots breakfast to prepare, with Will hanging on my apron begging to suckle, and him weaned well over a month."

All true, but disappointment dogged Rob's walk down the path.

The ferry pulled in at the dock, her deep-throated horn boasting another on-time arrival. After Rob and Captain MacNamara put on their usual show of saluting, the captain smiled and pointed to his right. There stood the Townsend family, backs ramrod straight, chins tucked, hands raised in salute.

Rob returned their salute and burst into laughter. He raced up the gangplank, ducked beneath the rope, and greeted them with handshakes and hugs.

"How was that, Rob Roy?" Trish smiled, raking a strand of windblown hair from her cheek. "Dad already had it down pat, but we gals have been practicing for hours."

"The graduating classes at West Point couldn't do better."

Tourists crowded close, eyeing the tall Scotsman the captain had saluted. Certain he was receiving enough stares to last a lifetime, Rob looked at Trish and recognized the humour in her eyes. Smile broad, he touched fingers to his forelock—and bowed.

Mel and Trish hugged one another, laughing.

"Our handsome Scots hero is loosening up," Trish crowed.

Maggie carried platters laden with a late breakfast to the table: sliced sausage, gammon, eggs, tinned beans, fried bread, and black buns. Her body tingled with joy. Conversation, laughter, and gentle teasing tasted like a breath of warm summer air on a dreich day. What fine friends, the Townsends. If only they lived closer.

"Elspeth went to heaven." Annie's soft voice cut through the chatter at the table louder than a shout.

Cups and utensils clicked on china, throats were cleared, eyes lowered.

"Haud yer wheesht," Beth hissed.

"She gets to talk to Jesus." Annie smiled, dimples deep beside her lips. "And He talks to her."

Maggie squeezed Annie's hand. "You talk to Him every een, when you say your prayers."

The lass shook her head, curls bouncing across her back. "But He doesn't answer."

"He always answers, lass." Rob's soft, rumbling voice broke the beginning silence. "Sometimes you have to listen with your heart, no' your ears, for He whispers deep inside you, reminding you to smile when you're sad, to luve when you're angry, to wait when you're impatient. And most important of all, to remember you're His bairn and He luves you."

"Elspeth told me you can hear God's voice when the birds sing." Beth cast her faither a sideways glance, as though daring him to disagree.

"That's right, lass."

"I hear His voice in the purr of well-tuned engines when I'm cruising at thirty angels." Bill "flew" his hand across the table.

Trish raised her hand, wriggling her fingers. "How about in the questions students ask, showing you they've been listening?"

"Or in the honk of a horn when you step off the curb without looking?"

Everyone laughed.

Paula ducked her head. "I can't help it if I'm a little absent-minded."

Mel tapped her teacup with a spoon. "I've got one. A stranger saying hello when you're having a bad day."

Will pounded a spoon on his highchair tray and squealed, arching his back.

Maggie handed him a piece of fried bread.

He bit off a bite, melted butter and slubbers dripping down his chin.

Beth's hand shot up. "Your belly growling when you're hungry."

After the laughter died, everyone attacked their food. Maggie smiled at Rob. *The blethering of guid friends who understand your sadness and want to lift your spirits.*

The platters of food quickly emptied as Bill had a second helping, and Rob a third.

Humming under her breath, Maggie left the table to fetch more coffee.

The rescue siren wailed.

Maggie returned the coffeepot to the stove, eyes on Rob. Och, that dreadful siren. Why did it interrupt so many joyous times?

Rob swigged down the last of his coffee and leaped to his feet. "Sorry, folks. That's me off." He ruffled Will's hair, then hugged and kissed Annie and Beth. "Help your mither redd the kitchen." Ignoring Beth's grimace at being told to do a lass's work, he pulled Maggie into his arms. "Remember Elspeth's dream," he whispered into her ear.

She rubbed her cheek against his chest. "Of course. But I'll still be praying."

"I'm counting on it."

His long kiss spoke of luve and the sorrow of having to leave.

The Townsends all raised a hand as he hurried to the door.

"We'll be praying," Bill shouted. "Keep safe."

With a thumbs-up, Rob darted across the entry and down the flagged walk, leaping the stone dyke as the siren wheezed its dying breath.

Maggie watched until he disappeared 'neath the brow of the path. "I have to turn on the radio in Rob's office. I'll be back in a tick."

⋙✦⋘

Maggie tightened plugs, flipped switches on the radio, and turned a dial.

Only a slight hissing sound came from the speaker.

She straightened a stack of papers on Rob's desk, then returned a pencil to others crammed into a chipped mug.

"Rob's going to be fine. He's young and strong and experienced."

Maggie whirled around. "Och, Trish, I didn't know you were there." A smile warmed her face.

Trish pulled out a chair. "Sit and share your worries. Then we'll pray about them."

"I've turned the radio loud as it will go. I should redd the kitchen and then—"

"Sit down." Trish drew up another chair. "Mel and Annie are clearing the table, and Mom's rocking Will. Dad's gone out to the porch to pray in private."

"And Beth? Is she hiding in her bedroom?" Maggie sat with a sigh.

"The last I saw, she was rocking beside Mom, listening to her sing Will a lullaby." Trish giggled. "I have to admit, that's the first time I've ever seen Beth sit so still. She even wriggles at the table."

Tears wet Maggie's lashes. "Rob and I made a terrible mistake, no' sharing Elspeth's dream with the bairns before now. 'Twould bring them peace, like it has me."

The radio crackled.

Maggie leaped up and turned a dial.

"Control, this is the *Maggie*. What's the word on the shout, Paddy?" Rob's deep voice.

"'Tis a strange one, Commander. Maritime Emergency took a 'suspicious' call about ten minutes ago. The voice on the radio sounded verra young, and there was laughin' in the background. The caller said they had collided with a sailboat that sank like a stone, and their trawler was takin' on water."

"So there's folk in the water?"

"No mention of it."

"Then why did Maritime Emergency pass it on to us?"

"Why do you think, Rob? 'Tis called 'covering your bum' in Ireland."

"Any coordinates, or do they expect us to search all o' the Atlantic and the Minch?"

"The caller gave the following coordinates: 55 degrees north by 5.90 degrees west."

"Got it. Say a prayer. I'm thinking we're about to go on what the Yanks call 'a wild-goose chase.' But what if I'm wrong?"

227

Maggie sat back, worrying her lip.

"Do they have many calls like that?" Trish reached for Maggie's hand.

"This is the first I've heard, though Den did mention what he called a 'false alarm' a few years ago."

"Then isn't this a time to celebrate? Tell the others there's little to worry about?"

Maggie jerked her hand from Trish's, then smiled an apology. "When our lads answer a shout, we never take it lightly. Even a tow or a medical emergency can turn bad in an eye-blink." She looked at the patterns of lace flickering sunlight and shadows across the wall. "And if a sailboat really did sink, Rob, Den, and the other lads will go into the water, searching for survivors and pulling them to safety." A smile defeated her frown. "But with Elspeth's dream in my mind and heart, I no longer have to worry about my Rob being lost to the sea."

Trish tucked a strand of hair behind an ear. "This dream of Elspeth's ... care to share with a nosy friend?"

Maggie spent the next fifteen minutes relating Elspeth's dream and what it meant to her and Rob—especially her. "I've been fearful of losing my Rob to the sea since he began building the *Maggie*. Horrible mind-pictures of him sinking below the waves haunted me day and night, making me resent him answering a shout. I'm shamed to say I even begged him to hand one call off to another lifeboat, even though Innisbraw was closer. But Elspeth's dream took all that away. This is his first shout since she passed, and the peace I feel is such a relief, and so complete I cannot give it voice." Her throat tightened for a moment. "Rob could still be injured or near-drowned, but I know we'll grow auld together."

Trish nodded. "Then it's time we prayed. For Rob, for Den, for the rest of the *Maggie*'s crew, and any people who might be in danger. Like Rob said, what if it's not a wild-goose chase?"

Chapter Forty-Two

Rob slapped the console with his palm. "We've circled the coordinates three times in ever-widening loops without sighting one piece of debris." He looked at Den. "Any ideas?"

"Plenty, but they all end with me wringing some lad's neck for sending a bogus Mayday."

"I like your thinking." Rob sat back, hands clenched in his lap. "We'll follow the sea-flow in till it reaches Mingulay. If we don't see anything by then, we head for home."

"Artair and Stephen? They've been oot there spotting a long time."

"We'll replace them with the both of us." Rob grinned at Den's frown. "Come on, aren't you the one who's always saying nobody can spot as well as pilots?"

"The wind's rising. It's cold oot there."

Rob shot out of his seat. "Your helm, Neil. New heading, dead west. Go as far as Mingulay." He grabbed Den's elbow. "Put your jacket over your wet suit and grab your binoculars. Let's go show them how it's done in the Air Forces."

Half an hour later, Rob rubbed his smarting eyes and blew on icy fingers. He returned the binoculars to his face and swept them over the sea, squinting against the shards of sunlight piercing his eyes. His belly cramped. He should be at home, having a blether with guid friends, watching his Maggie laugh and charm their guests in her gentle, unassuming way. Instead he—

What was that?

He raced to the cabin door. "Neil! Cut the engines!"

Den joined him at the railing. "See something?"

"Aye. I'm no' sure what. There! Bits of planking, a wooden bucket, and what looks like a life jacket. Those coordinates must be wrong. This has to be the collision site." He raised the binoculars again, sweeping them from side to side. No sign of large debris or victims in the water. "Tell Neil to maintain course slowly, then get back oot here and help me spot. If there are survivors, the sea'll pull them toward Mingulay."

The *Maggie* crawled through the waves, engines burbling.

No sign of survivors, only the Isle of Mingulay, a purple smear growing larger by the minute.

Rob ran a shaking hand over his face. Had they all perished?

"Rob! Something in the water! Two o'clock, low."

Den's shout sent a burst of adrenaline coursing through Rob's body. He raced to the bow. "I see it. Looks like a piece of planking or door, and mebbe something else."

His glasses zeroed in on a long, dark object.

Several smaller objects bobbed beside it.

He dropped the binoculars and ran inside. "Neil, stop engines and hold against the waves. Lads, we've spotted victims. Rope up and hie ye to the taffrail!" Rob scooped two ropes off their cleats and tossed one to Den, tying the other around his own waist, then he slid down the ladder.

"I counted four," Den shouted.

"So did I. Listen up, lads. Matthew and Ewan, stand by to pull in the ropes. The rest of you, into the water as fast as you can."

Rob and Den tied off their ropes, scaled the railing, and jumped together.

As always, Rob's long strokes outpaced Den's. *Be with us, Faither. And give those poor souls the strength to hang on for a few more minutes.*

A wave curled over his head, and he swallowed water. Och, they were so close to the shores of Mingulay that the waves came one after the other, gathering strength against the shallower seabed. He caught another wave, swallowed more water. He raised his head.

Almost there.

Arms slicing, feet kicking, he reached out and finally touched a life jacket. Reaching below the jacket, he grabbed a handful of clothing and pulled.

A woman stared up at him, gaze frozen, expression blank.

No. She couldn't be dead.

He tried to pull her closer.

She didn't move.

His hand groped at her clothing. Found a rope.

Och, tied to a door, she was.

Den grasped his shoulder. "I'll untie her. The man beside her had no jacket. He's dead."

Rob wrapped his arms around her waist and squeezed. He squeezed again and again as Den struggled to untie the rope.

Water trickled from her slack mouth.

"Got it!" Den shouted. "Get her back to the *Maggie*. I'll help

Stephen and Patrick untie the others."

Rob yanked his rope three times and flipped onto his back, pulling the woman to his chest. He could keep squeezing the water oot if she rode his body all the way to the *Maggie*.

Maggie and Trish were on their knees, praying, when Robbie burst into the office. Eyes wild, gasping for breath, he launched himself into Maggie's arms.

"Faither! How's faither?"

Maggie pulled herself up and sat, hugging him. "Why aren't you in school? Did you run all the way home?"

He leaned back, cast Trish a shy glance, then gazed into his mither's eyes. "Aunt Ellie—och, Missus McGrath—let me come home early. Said the shout siren put her in a swither too. Is Faither on the *Maggie*? Shep's sitting oot at the gate, so he must be." He tugged on her sweater, glancing at the silent radio. "Faither. What say you about Faither?"

Trish slipped out the door.

Maggie sighed. She drew him into her arms. "Aye, he's aboard the *Maggie*, but Maritime Emergency thinks it was all a joke—some lads thinking it was fun to put one over on everybody."

He fisted his hands and scowled. "I'd like to punch them in the nobs."

"I'd like to punch some nobs."

Rob ignored Den's muttered comment and swiped a sleeve over his sweaty forehead before resuming AR. "Pulse getting stronger?"

"Aye, but she's no' come around yet."

"At least she's breathing. I thought she was dead."

"Dead is what the lads who did this will be when I catch them."

"You'll have to stand in line. There isn't a lad aboard who hasn't had the same thought."

"What do you expect after listening to that victim raving about the rusty auld trawler appearing oot of nowhere and plowing into them, then motoring off, laughing while their sailboat sank?" Den's voice rose. "They're murdering yobs, is what they are. One dead, three near dead, and even if they make it, they'll have nightmares for the rest of their lives. And that's not counting the loss of a new sailboat."

"Wheesht," Rob hissed. "She's moving her legs."

The lass moaned and tried to raise her head.

Rob looked over his shoulder.

His crew sat on the floor, backs against the wall, eyes unfocused, as though examining each action they'd taken the day, wondering if they could have done better.

The dead man lay against the far wall, wrapped in a blanket covering his face. The other man, who had recovered first, slept on a stretcher, blankets piled high. A lass lay next to him, eyes closed, breathing laboured.

Matthew bent over her, replacing a spent saline bottle.

"Den, fetch a stretcher. This lass needs another saline too."

Rob and Den rolled her onto a stretcher, lumbered to their feet, and carried it across the cabin, clipping it into its holder.

Matthew grabbed his stethoscope and moved the diaphragm over her chest, then her belly. "Some water in her lungs, but her stomach's empty." He covered her with blankets and pulled a new saline bottle from the medicament cabinet.

Rob studied her fluttering lashes, the sprinkle of freckles across her nose and cheeks. Like Jill's and Brenna's. Young, she was, most likely in her mid-twenties. She needed John's doctoring—and fast.

"How long to Innisbraw, Neil?"

"We're off Barra Head now. Should dock in about fifteen minutes."

The engines beat a steady thrum beneath Rob's feet. At full speed, they were. He collapsed into his first coxswain's seat and rubbed his stinging eyes.

It would have been so easy to give up at the first coordinates, to assume the call had been a hoax. Or to leave the collision site, certain no victims could have survived such a lengthy exposure to the cold sea. *Thank Ye, Faither, for giving me the right decisions and for helping Den spot the victims.* He tapped Neil's knee. "Did you tell Control we need John and Fern at the dock, along with a few cairts? And to notify the Coast Guard to be on the lookout for a rusty auld trawler with damage to the prow?"

"Aye, and I also told him all crew members are safe, with no injuries."

※

Rob eased the front door closed, picked up Maggie, and settled onto his rocker on the entry. He'd been looking forward to this for hours. The hush of the gloaming, stars spread across the sky like raindrops frozen and sprinkled by the hand of God, his Maggie's fragrant hair and skin filling his mouth with the sweet taste of warm honey.

She kissed his cheek and nestled against his chest. "The Townsends and our bairns are all settled in to sleep. You should be abed, luve. It's been a long and tiresome day."

She'd never ken how much he needed her soft voice soothing the din of voices in his head, voices clamouring for answers he didn't have. "I've so much going through my mind. I need you to help me sort it oot."

"About the shout, you mean?"

"What caused the shout." He sighed, pressed his cheek against her hair. "I'll never understand the evil in this world, the need to harm others to satisfy some dark desire in a heart blacker than a peat bog." A humourless laugh escaped his lips. "I'd never make a polisman."

"Fern telephoned while you were in the shower. The polis arrived from Oban. They're interviewing the survivors, and Den left the infirmary in a rare fash."

He sat up. "Fern's still on duty?"

"Aye. I offered to take her place, but she said the lass you rescued needed to talk, especially after hearing all the questions from the polis. She's from a sma' village north of Stornoway on Lewis, she is, and all the other victims, as well." Maggie raised her head.

Rob stared out at the Minch, his face bleak.

"Her name is Marsaili. She speaks verra poor English, so Fern had to translate her Gaelic for the polis."

Rob clenched his hands. "And the lad who died? Were they a pair?"

Maggie straightened one tight hand and laced her fingers through his. "No' the way you mean, luve. They were all dear friends, had been neighbours since birth, sharing the poverty affecting so many sma' villages—the empty bellies, the lost hopes."

So close Innisbraw had come to a similar fate. It had lost some of its young to the war and experienced a lack of opportunity at home. Only Rob's dream of a boatworks had kept a spark of hope alive.

She returned her cheek to his chest. "The other lad, Breannan, once crewed a trawler, until he suffered a fall and was let go because he limped. He designed the wee sailboat for Rory, the lad who died. Breannan's sister, Brighde, and Marsaili joined the lads in building the sailboat, saving every pence earned at odd turns to buy what Rory needed. All four aboard that boat spent years labouring to fulfill a dream—to escape to a place that offered warmer weather and a future no' found in crofting or fishing—only to lose it all less than a day's sail from home."

"They'll have to go back to Lewis. Back to no' enough to eat, to

233

threadbare clothes and skin red and rough from labouring ootside. To a future withoot hope." Rob kneaded his forehead with his free hand. "The polis have to catch the criminals who did this."

"They will, Rob. If we pray long enough and hard enough, surely they will."

Chapter Forty-Three

A snell wind from the north drove the sea high onto Innis Fell, the loud boom of each wave making conversation impossible. Rob pulled Maggie close to his side, shielding her from the icy blasts. She shouldn't have been called in to help at the infirmary, but Fern, exhausted from spending two days and nights on duty, couldn't handle her regular patients and take care of the two women survivors.

Maggie said something.

He leaned down. "I can't hear you, lass."

She pulled him to a stop in front of the infirmary. "I said you shouldn't have come," she shouted, gathering her coat around her shivering body. "Fern says the lasses won't want to see you."

"Then I'll talk to the lad."

"About what?"

His stomach cramped. They'd already had a disagreement about this the mornin, her insisting he stay and care for the bairns while she worked. Why couldn't she understand his reluctance to allow the polis to handle what they were calling an "accident"?

"About what really happened." He pulled her up the steps and onto the flagged entry. "Inside with you. 'Tis too cold oot here."

Blessed warmth and quiet surrounded them the moment they stepped inside the large door.

Maggie pulled her hand from his. "I still don't see why you—"

"If what Breannan said aboard the *Maggie* was true, this was no accident." Ignoring her raised chin and obstinate stare, he turned on his heel and walked to the admissions desk. He pawed through a stack of folders, took note of the room number he wanted, and continued down the corridor.

Who put a bur under Maggie's saddle? Aye, he should be home helping the Townsends with the bairns—that's where he wanted to be—but as commander of the *Maggie*, he had an obligation to those he rescued.

He paused at a door and rapped lightly.

A cough and hoarse, "Fáilte," propelled him inside.

A fair-haired lad lay propped up in a hospital bed, a saline drip connected to one arm, his face turned to the wall.

The window was closed and curtains pulled tight, blocking daylight from the room.

Rob did not turn the lamp on. Perhaps the lad preferred a safe, dim cocoon where he could try to forget the death of his friend—the end of his dreams.

Rob laid a hand on Breannan's shoulder. "I'm Rob Savage, commander of the rescue boat that pulled you from the sea. Are you strong enough to answer a few questions?"

The lad turned his head but did not open his eyes. "Not polis?" His English sounded hesitant, forced.

Rob pulled up a chair. "I speak the Gaelic, as you can hear, and I'm not with the polis. I just need you to tell me what happened to you out there on the sea."

Eyelids fluttered and opened.

Even in the half-light, Rob could see clearly what lurked deep within the lad's eyes: pain, deep and dark enough to drown the fittest man; despair; the loss of hope. He'd seen those same eyes staring back at him from the mirror at the orphanage. *Help me reach him, Faither. Give me the words.*

"Why do you care? Can you bring Rory back? Can you raise the boat from the sea? Can you give us back a future?" Breannan coughed again, spasms shaking his bony shoulders.

After grabbing a cup from the bedside table, Rob inserted a glass straw. He held it to the lad's lips.

He sipped eagerly, then muttered a hoarse, "Thank you."

Rob leaned closer, deliberately invading the lad's space. "I canna do owt for you till I ken what happened. Tell me."

Closing his eyes again, Breannan clutched the sheet and ground it between his fingers. "The wind changed, so Brighde and Marsaili and I were reefing the sails, while Rory held the helm steady." He jerked, dropping the sheet. "One of the girls screamed, and I looked to starboard and saw a boat heading straight at us. We all shouted and waved our arms, but it kept coming, closer, closer, until we could see the peeling paint, ropes dangling like … like the tentacles of some sea monster." He took a shallow breath, then another.

"Did you see anyone on the trawler's deck?"

"Not until we caught on that she wasn't going to stop. Just before Rory shouted for us to jump, two young men came out of the wheelhouse, waving bottles and laughing. I … I carried that sound into the sea with me, the laughing." Breannan grasped Rob's sleeve. "I'm so tired."

"I ken. Just twa more questions. You can handle that." Rob

rubbed the lad's hand. "Only twa."

A weak nod.

"Did the trawler leave after you went into the water, or did it wait till your boat sank?"

"It waited, circling around and around, like a shark stalking its prey after smelling blood in the water. After … after we all surfaced and found one another, it finally left, those two still standing on deck, laughing. That sound will stay in my head until the day I die."

Those words were true. Rob still heard the screams of crewmen hit by flak or machine guns, the cries of the wounded and dying. He steeled himself to ask his final question. "Why wasn't Rory wearing a life jacket when we found you?"

A tear escaped Breannan's eye and rolled down his cheek. "He gave it to Marsaili. Hers tore loose in the collision. If she hadn't found that door and held on …"

"But she did. And Rory's a hero." Rob squeezed the lad's shoulder. "It won't bring him back, but he'll live forever in many hearts—always a hero."

⚓

Waves slapped against the *Maggie*'s hull, retreated, and slapped again, as she rocked in her berth. Perhaps a monotonous sound to many, but Rob found the repetition soothing. He leaned against the starboard railing, face turned toward Innis Fell and home.

Logic, his system for finding the answer to any problem, was failing him. After talking to Breannan that mornin, he'd come away with a stabbing pain in his belly. The lad had given up hope. Though strong of body, his spirit was crushed—not only by Rory's drowning, but also by the death of the dream that had kept him going through unimaginable hardships.

Aye, sending the three back to Lewis was the logical solution, but no' one Rob could live with. There had to be another answer.

Guilt, like sand stirred up from the seabed, clouded Rob's mind, allowing compassion to interfere with clarity of thought. He should be spending time with the Townsends and his bairns.

I'm in a rare fankle, Lord. Maggie's needed at the infirmary, and instead of helping with the bairns and entertaining the Townsends, I'm spending every spare tick of time looking for a way to help those three survivors. He clenched the railing, fingers stiff from the cold wind. *Why can't I allow other folk to find an answer to their needs?*

The answer flashed through his mind like a tracer fired from a machine gun.

237

"Because you spent a childhood so filled with needs nobody met, you retreated into yourself to escape the hurt." He jerked, his mumbled words startling him. Talking to himself, he was. What next? But he couldn't do nothing, couldn't allow three young lives to be ruined by a disaster no' of their own making.

He hurried into the cabin and closed the door. Paper and pencil, that's what he needed. The sooner he solved the problem of how to help the three from Lewis, the quicker his guilt about duties ignored could be put to rest. Pulling a blank piece of paper from the back of the duty roster pad, he licked the lead of a pencil and started two lists, *Needs of Survivors* on one side, *How to Meet Them* on the other.

An hour later, he skirted a stone dyke at Colin Stewart's sheep croft and hailed the crofter, who looked to be training a young Australian shepherd to work a small flock of sheep. "Hoy, Colin, got time for a blether?"

Whistling the shepherd to his side, Colin walked across the girse, smile creasing his weathered cheeks. "Always. What brings you by on a workday?"

"Need some help." Rob shook Colin's hand. "New dog?"

"Bought him from Angus. Quick on the uptake, he is. How're Maggie and the bairns?"

"Never better. And Ruth?"

Colin pulled up his collar and blew on his hands. "Busy tending Betty's bairns while the lass sows her garden with oats for a winter cover. She learned all sorts of new ideas working in the Women's Land Army." He signaled the shepherd to lie down, and leaned against the dyke. "What kind of help?"

That was one thing Rob liked about Colin. Always zeroed in on the right word. "You've heard about the three from Lewis we pulled oot of the sea by Mingulay?"

"Been praying for them. Any word on the skellums that rammed their boat?"

"No' yet, though the Coast Guard's learned of an auld trawler stolen from Oban." Rob buried his icy hands in his pockets. "You came here from Mull, right?"

"Aye, in nineteen and thirty-seven."

"What's the weather like there?"

"Weather?" Colin scratched his head. "Och, wet and windy all winter—it's in the Inner Hebrides, after all—but no' as many gales as here, and no snow like on northern Lewis." The crofter squinted, or was he hiding a grin? "Why, you planning on moving?"

"Never." Rob pulled a piece of paper from his back pocket. "I've been trying to come up with a place to send those three survivors. They lost everything they owned trying to escape their miserable lives on Lewis." He handed the paper to Colin and traced a fingertip down the column headed *Needs of Survivors*. "As you can see, they need a warmer place than their village, which is snowed-in all winter. All three need work of some kind—boatbuilding, crofting, working with sheep, handiwork, or most owt else—a place to stay until they can build or buy a place of their own, and to be around folk who speak the Gaelic."

Colin's calloused finger ran down the opposite list. "Looks to me like you've crossed off most of this list—Innisbraw, Barra, Sanderay, Eriskay, Skye, Oban, Inverness. That leaves only Mull."

"All the others are too small to find work, their economies no' recovered enough to offer support, or too large, with too many people having similar needs, or me not knowing any folk there who could help." Rob rubbed the shepherd's belly with the toe of his boot, hoping Colin was sharp enough to catch his emphasis on the last requirement. He wasn't disappointed.

"Let me do some calling around. We still stay in touch with friends on Mull." Colin folded the paper. "Can I keep this?"

"That's why I brought it."

⁂

The afternoon did much to assuage Rob's guilt. He loaned the Townsends warm sweaters, jackets, and gloves, and sent them off into the snell wind to do more exploring. His lasses, delighted to have their faither home, clamoured for his attention, forcing him to come up with a new Selkie tale to keep them quiet.

That brief respite from noise was shattered when Robbie burst in the door and tackled Rob's leg, eager to relate everything he had learned at school the day.

All the bairns acted pleased to have him home. Even Beth, who eschewed anything she considered "women's work," offered to help make supper. Unwilling to trust his bairns with a knife, Rob diced onions and potatoes for a large pot of bree, while Annie set the table, Beth arranged cheese slices atop bread, and Robbie nattered nonstop about what a better turn he could do with table-setting and making cheesy bread.

"Wheesht," Rob hissed. "If you can't say owt guid, say nowt."

"But Faither …"

The door opened and Maggie stepped inside, saving Robbie from being banished to his bedroom.

⚜

Delighted with the warm welcome, Maggie kissed Rob's cheek, handed him Will, and sniffed the air. "Is that tattie bree I smell?"

Rob peeled off Will's hap and sweaters. "'Tis all I could think of to fix." He set the lad on his feet and pulled Maggie into his arms. "You look spent, luve. Have a lie-down while I finish supper." His gaze pinned her, eyes pleading to hear that their argument was over.

She shivered beneath her coat. "I need a guid, warm hug and a kiss. Where are the Townsends?"

"Oot for a walk, then supper with Alec and Morag."

Her heart skipped a beat. What could be more wonderful? "You mean we're alone?"

His tense shoulders relaxed, and he laughed, hugging her. "If you call Will's hanging on your skirt, Annie's waiting for a compliment on her table-setting, Beth's sulking because you didn't notice her cheesy breads, and Robbie's making faces at Annie behind your back, I suppose you could say we're alone."

She pinched his cheek. "You mean just another een at the Savage house?" Dropping her coat to the floor, she raised her face for a proper kiss.

Mmm, her man smelled guid, of salty air and onions, of heather soap and peat reek, of that special male aroma that made her knees weak and stopped the breath in her throat.

He tasted even better.

⚜

Rob glanced at his watch. Gone 2200, it was.

Maggie dozed in her rocker at his side, head back, a pile of mending in her lap.

He couldn't imagine luving her any more than he did at that moment, yet that luve never stopped growing. Being biggen, she should be abed after the long day she'd spent at the infirmary. And what was keeping the Townsends?

A whimper from the lads' bedroom sent Rob to his feet.

He opened the door and peeked in.

Will whimpered again, then turned over, grabbed a corner of his sheet, and pushed it into his mouth, sooking. Och, that laddie still missed suckling at Maggie's breast.

He turned to find Maggie behind him, and drew her into his arms. "'Tis all right, luve. Will must have had a bad dream."

She yawned and rested her cheek against his chest. "Mebbe I should rock him."

"He's asleep again. And speaking of sleep—" He picked Maggie up and headed for their bedroom.

So exhausted she hadn't even resisted when he insisted on undressing her, Maggie snuggled down in bed, yawning again. "Shouldn't we wait up for our guests?"

He stepped out of his denims and pulled off his shirt and socks. "They're all grownups, luve. And even if they can't find their way here in the dark, you ken Alec will bring them in his cairt."

Rob climbed in beside her, spooning his chest against her back. "Off to see the sandman, lass." His fingers grasped a fragrant lock of her hair. He inhaled the warm-honey scent and tucked it beneath his cheek. "I luve you."

"Mmm, I luve you."

Her breathing settled into a steady rhythm. Asleep already, she was. He resisted the impulse to stroke her silken shoulder, and closed his eyes. With the new description of the trawler he'd radioed to the Coast Guard—no rusting hull, but peeling paint and rusted superstructure, with at least three lads involved—and his willingness to testify at a hearing about the intentional ramming of the sailboat, he could leave it in the hands of the authorities. Now, if Colin's friends came through, perhaps those three victims could regain their faith and strive for a new future. The grief, the trauma they had suffered, would never go away, but he knew from experience it would fade in time, eventually replaced by the joy of being alive and in charge of their own futures.

Snippets of conversations and sights of the day interrupted his thoughts, until they faded into the night and he succumbed to sleep.

241

Chapter Forty-Four

"We enjoy watching your kids." Trish hugged Beth's shoulder, laughing when the lass jerked away with cheeks flushing. "With the weather warmer again, Beth's been showing me the beach below the fell."

Maggie chewed her lower lip. "But you're here on holiday. You shouldn't be having—"

"You don't understand how much fun this is," Paula said. "It's like having grandchildren without the wait." She turned to Trish and Mel, hazel-green eyes flashing a message.

"We have a full day planned, so be on your way." Bill bounced Will on his hip. "Alec's driving us around the island in his cart. We're going to do some real exploring, aren't we, little guy?"

The bairn squealed and hugged Bill's neck.

"If you're certain ..." Maggie buttoned her sweater, still worrying her lip.

"We're certain." Mel pushed Annie toward her bedroom. "Bring your doll, Annie, and a warm blanket, so she doesn't get cold."

Frowning, Maggie paused at the door. "Rob's scheduled a telephone call with the polis in Oban, and another with the Coast Guard. He should be home before dinner."

"Then he'll come home to an empty house." Paula opened the door and gave Maggie a gentle push. "Paddy's packing us a lunch, and I've fixed a thermos of coffee and another of milk. Now go."

Maggie smiled as the door closed behind her. Such dear, dear friends. She turned her face to the lemon-yellow sun rising higher into the sky. No' as warm as last month, but at least the snell north wind only lasted one day, blowing its first icy warning of the winter to come.

Mind a welter of thoughts, she hurried down the path. She had no right to question Rob's decision to talk to Breannan. Rob's first visit had sparked the patient's appetite enough for him to eat most of a bowl of bree. Hopefully, Rob would spend more time with Breannan. And her husband's decision to ask help from Colin was surely inspired by the Lord Himself. Pray God something guid came from it. Those poor souls could not return to Lewis and their fruitless, impoverished lives.

No peat smoke wafting from her faither's chimney. Already at the infirmary, he was, doubtlessly updating the progress of his patients. And Rob? Off to the shed before the sun rose over the horizon. She sighed. Why did their family go months with only arguments between the bairns causing a fankle, then within twa days, face serious problems requiring Rob's and her attention? They needed time to relax and enjoy life.

Late that afternoon, Maggie returned home from the infirmary just in time to hear Robbie beg Rob to take them to the ceilidh that een.

"Uncle Bill and Aunt Paula and Trish and Mel said they're going." Robbie pulled on Rob's sleeve. "Please, can't we go? We'll be guid, we promise."

All the bairns nodded, even wee Will, who must have thought this was a new game. He nodded so vigorously, he lost his balance and landed on his hippen-padded behoochie.

Maggie's heart leaped into her throat. This was exactly what they needed. She sidled up to Rob and smiled, willing him to say *aye*.

He pulled her close for a kiss. "If the Townsends are going, I'll telephone Den and ask him to translate Auntie's story, so I can spend more time with them." He bent and nibbled on her ear. "We could dance a slow one. What say you, luve?"

"Only one?" Maggie wrinkled her nose. "My feet feel the need for at least a reel and a jig—make that twa reels—and a strathspey." Och, she couldn't wait—an een of visiting, laughter, and music.

Den approached Rob as the folk living on the fell gathered to walk to the ceilidh. "Sorry, but I'm going to have to back oot of translating for Auntie. Fern's so spent she's near asleep in her rocker, so we're no' going." He toed the sandy path. "I promised her a guid backrub."

Och, why couldn't anything ever go the way Rob planned? But after the hours Fern had spent on duty, the poor lass deserved some rest. He squeezed Den's shoulder. "Want us to take Katie?"

"She's making supper—a receipt Fern taught her last winter—something involving neeps, tatties, and onions." Den scowled. "And me a meat-luver."

Rob wagged a finger in Den's face. "And you'll enjoy every bite, or I'll take you behind John's cooling shed and teach you some manners." He grinned, spun, and called over his shoulder, "Take care of your lasses. I'll do the translating."

Price

A sharp pain knifed Rob's belly as they passed Elspeth's darkened cottage. She had always left a lamp lit in the front window all night to guide anyone coming up the fell. Tears misted his eyes. How he missed her.

Maggie slipped her hand into his and rested her head against his upper arm, sharing his loss.

The kirk hall teemed with tourists, and the same auld Innisbraw widows sat in chairs lining the back wall. Only Elspeth's chair remained vacant—a testimony to the respect she would long be afforded.

Rob sought out Auntie Mairet. "Den can't be here, so I'll be doing the translating, after all."

The ceilidh got off to a rollicking start. Many of the young bucks took extra care to show the tourists how to dance the reels, pulling them into line when they went the wrong way during a figure eight and pressing their hands into the proper partner's hands when they floundered.

Rob stood on the sidelines, watching the dancers, especially Trish and Mel, attempting the reels.

Trish, seldom hesitating and laughing at herself when she made a rare misstep, outshone her sister.

His mind drifted to the problem ragging his thoughts. Though the polis had changed their focus from "accident" to "an act of deliberate malice," the trawler had no' been found.

Hugh made his way across the hall toward Rob.

"What brings you oot the een?" Rob asked with a grin. "Found a sudden luve for dancing?"

"I'm no' certain." Hugh pushed his eyeglasses up on his nose. "I heard the music and the thought suddenly came that a little diversion from the research might freshen my thoughts."

"Well, 'tis guid to see you here."

"And you, though you're looking a wee bit whummeled. Any problems you're free to share?"

Too perceptive by half, was Hugh. "Och, the Coast Guard still hasn't found the trawler that sank the sailboat. I'm wondering if they ever will."

"With all the inlets and coves around the Western Isles, 'twill take time." Hugh squeezed Rob's arm. "Have faith. Our Lord won't allow those criminals to go unpunished. Sometime, they'll pay the piper. And we're all praying verra hard that Colin will find a home for those three souls."

"Thank ye. 'Tis a fankle only the Lord can solve."

The overhead lights illuminated Hugh's elfin smile, the sparkle in his eyes. "Exactly the kind He likes the most. I'm going for coffee. Can I bring you a mug?"

"No' now. Trish is heading my way, and she's got that gleam in her eye. I'm thinking she's about to claim the next dance."

Seconds into the bob, Trish poked Rob's chest. "I'm about to tell you a secret, and if you tell anyone other than Maggie, I'll do more than haunt you."

Rob smiled and winked. "You're sounding like an Innisbraw lass. Go on, you've got me on hecklepins."

She pulled a gold chain from beneath her sweater and flashed a diamond ring. "I'm engaged."

"Why no' on your finger?" He settled for a broad grin. Young as she was, she might misinterpret a laugh of delight as his making fun of her.

"Because if you think these tourists are nosey, you should teach at a small college. The students act like they own you. It's impossible to find any privacy."

"He'd better be a verra special man."

Trish tapped his shoulder. "You'll like him. He's a professor at the same college, which is another reason for 'the ring on a string.'"

"What does he teach?"

"It's a special class, sort of a combination of Psychology and Sociology, called 'Child Development.' That's why Walt—that's his name—couldn't come on this trip. I have an assistant who's covering for me, but he's writing a paper on child abandonment and couldn't abandon the studies he's conducting."

Child abandonment. Rob quelled a shiver. He could write his own paper on that subject.

Trish looked puzzled when he didn't advance the conversation. "Hello up there. Did I lose you?"

"I was just thinking that must be a verra unnerving subject to study."

"Unnerving? I suppose it could be, though Walt has an entirely different take on the subject than the norm."

"And the norm is …?"

"They say that a child who's abandoned young can never develop into a productive, functioning adult. Walt says that theory is wrong."

"Does he … Walt have a reason why 'tis wrong?"

"He has data that shows there are too many variables, and too many differing circumstances." They danced for a minute and then she looked at him, expression serious. "I'm getting a feeling I hit a nerve."

Though Rob's first impulse was to lie, and his second to run, he considered Trish too close a friend to do either. "You might say that. I was orphaned as a bairnie and abandoned before I turned six."

Trish squeezed his hand. "I'm sorry that happened to you, but you just proved Walt's theory. You're a happy, successful, highly motivated man. End of conversation."

Moments later, Rob returned Trish to her family and meandered through the crowd, looking for Maggie. He needed an anchor for his runaway emotions.

Hugh appeared at his side. "'Tis almost time for the story."

Chapter Forty-Five

Hugh found the kirk service the following mornin a curious mixture of joy and sorrow. He rejoiced to share the news that the victims from Lewis were out of danger and said to be on the road to a slow, but full recovery. A few arms were raised in rejoicing, yet sorrow tempered joy still at Elspeth's empty seat.

He selected the most joyous, uplifting hymns, preparing his congregation for a lesson on the aspect of God's essence he would be teaching the mornin—His unconditional luve. Too bad the patients were no' well enough to attend. Doubtless their kirk on Lewis allowed only the men to chant the Psalms with no musical instruments to accompany them. What a shame most ministers in Scotland focused their sermons on the stifling laws of the kirk, no' on the liberating Word of God. They concentrated on sin, no' redemption, on fear of punishment—both now and in the hereafter— no' the joy of walking daily with their Lord.

A sudden thought brought warmth to his cheeks. Could this be why those young folk had wanted to escape their lives on Lewis? Did the stern messages thundered from lecterns across the northern Hebrides islands defeat lives burdened by bitter poverty? Did they take away all hope for the future?

As the organ wheezed its final notes, he stepped to the edge of the dais and lowered his arms, signaling the folk to take their seats. Waiting for bairnies to be settled for sleep, bairns cradled on laps, Bibles to be readied, and throats to be cleared, he concentrated upon a mind-picture of prayers floating heavenward, like an offering of the sweetest fragrance.

"We will now spend a few silent moments in prayer, cleansing our souls of unconfessed sins and our minds of distraction. Let us pray."

He lost himself in his own prayer. *Forgive me, Heavenly Faither, for no' realizing those three precious souls suffered far more than physical pain and loss. Help me when I visit them later the day, so I can speak Your words of comfort and Truth. And open their minds and hearts to Your unconditional luve—a luve no' bound by church law or man's feeble endeavors to understand what it means to*

247

follow You.

~△~

Early the following mornin, Rob cornered Den on the path outside the boatshed. "I'm taking Bill, Trish, and Robbie up in the floatplane for a look at some of the islands. We'll be off in about twenty minutes."

Den smirked, blue eyes narrowing. "You rubbing it in, or is there another reason you're telling me your plans?"

Rob backed up, hands raised. "What makes you think I'd do that? I'm giving you a heads-up, so you can radio me if you have news from the polis or Coast Guard."

Smirk turned to grin as Den snapped a salute. "Aye, sir, Commander, sir. Message received and confirmed."

Rob turned and walked onto the pier, shaking his head. Guid thing he'd allowed time for a thorough pre-flight check, or absent-minded as he had become, he would miss something important or ignore a warning sign—like not having enough fuel.

He slid down the ladder to the lower dock, reached for the propeller, and pulled it through several blades, making certain there was no hydraulic lock. After stepping onto a pontoon, he climbed into the cockpit. Rob automatically performed each step before firing up the engine. Finally, he switched on the mags, and the engine started with a burst of black smoke and settled into the throaty roar that always gave him hens-flesh. A quick glance at the gauges showed almost-full tanks. He checked his watch and relaxed. Plenty of time to finish the check before his passengers arrived. After opening the door, he slid to a pontoon and got to work.

Despite resolving to keep his mind on what he was doing, his thoughts returned to his visit with Breannan the mornin. Hugh's time with the lad the day before appeared to have worked a minor miracle. Instead of the unkempt, morose, defeated lad Rob expected, he'd found Breannan sitting on the couch in the infirmary entry, clean-shaven, comb marks streaking damp hair, tea mug nearby.

The lad struggled to his feet and held out his hand. "Rob."

Rob clasped his hand, sat, and pulled the lad down beside him. "You're up and about." He grinned. "Getting tired of staring at four white walls?"

Breannan's lips turned up in the semblance of a smile, and the welcoming light in his brown eyes was encouraging. "John said I could do some exploring. I even made myself some tea."

"Sounds like—"

"Faither! Can we come down?" Robbie's shout shattered Rob's

memory into a million sand-like fragments.

Och, they were here for their ride already?

Maggie buttoned her sweater and rubbed her palms together. "Sweaters all on? The shops should be open. On we go."

Beth dragged reluctant feet across the floor. "Do I have to? Why canna I stay home with Shep?"

"But you promised to help me pick out one of Sandy's carvings to take home," Paula said, sending Maggie a discreet wink. "I've never seen a live dolphin or eagle, so how will I know it's a good likeness?"

"And I want a sweater like your mother made you for Christmas." Mel blew a strand of hair away from her cheek. "Don't want me making a mistake, do you?"

Having heard Rob warn the lass to behave or face delaying her first flight in the floatplane, Maggie picked up Will and reached for Beth's hand. "On you come. Let's spend somebody else's silver."

Eyes narrowed, Beth jerked her hand away.

Patience grows with testing. Patience grows with testing, Maggie repeated to herself all the way to the gate.

The sheet cool against her shoulder and Rob's spooned body warm against her back, Maggie smiled into the dark. What a glorious day it had been, filled with laughter and conversation, building memories to be taken out and savoured once the Townsends returned to America and a capricious fall tumbled into a rainy, windy winter.

Rob brushed a hand along her cheek. "Sleeperie, luve?"

"No' yet." She ran a fingertip across his palm, wondering again how such a large, calloused hand could have a touch light as the flutter of butterflies' wings. "I've been remembering what fun it was to shop with women who recognize all the work that goes into knitting a sweater or carving a bird or dolphin from wood. It's grand having our folk's talents appreciated."

"Mmm." He pulled her over, and helped her settle, facing him. "That's better. Since our nights are getting too dark to see your eyes withoot the lamp lit, I need to feel your soft breath on my face when we blether." He cupped her face between his palms and kissed her with great tenderness. "Even better, your breath tasting sweet on my tongue." A rumble grew in his chest, a chuckle being born. Low and soft, it was, tickling her bare flesh and bringing a smile.

"What are you thinking about?" she asked.

"Trying to picture Beth's face when she had to choose between taking her first flight when she's six or making your life miserable."

"She pouted a bit at first, but Paula and Mel asked her opinion about everything they bought. The humoursome thing was Beth screwing up her face and scrunching her eyes closed, like her answer was the most important thing she'd ever speak."

Another chuckle. "I'm certain she thought it was. How often have you asked her help in choosing something at the general store?"

She tweaked his chest hair. "As often as you've asked mine before ordering supplies for the boatshed."

The ringing of the telephone interrupted his laugh.

Rob groaned and sat up, groping for the phone on the bedside table.

Maggie cringed when he answered with a gruff "Savage." Pray God the caller wasn't Hugh or another dear friend.

She wrapped the sheet around her shoulders and sat beside Rob, leaning into his embrace.

He listened for a moment, muscles tensed. "The trawler, Inspector?"

Her body mimicked his tension. Finding the trawler would help put the entire tragedy to rest. Och, if only she could hear what Rob was listening to so intently. *Please, Faither, let it be guid news.*

"Thank ye for calling. I'll contact the polis later for an update." Rob hung up the receiver. "They found the trawler, lass. Or, I should say, it found them."

"Whatsomever do you mean?"

His fingers tangled in her hair. "Maritime Emergency took a Mayday call. When they heard it was a trawler taking on water from a damaged prow, they radioed the Coast Guard with the coordinates."

"And ...?"

"The Coast Guard pumped oot the water, jerry-rigged repairs, and towed the trawler into Castlebay Harbour on Barra. Three lads in their early twenties—them suffering from what the doctor at their cottage hospital called 'a close call with alcohol poisoning'—are under polis guard."

Tears clogged Maggie's throat. "Thank Ye, Heavenly Faither. Justice, at last."

"*If* those criminals admit ramming the sailboat. But if they say they were blootered and didn't see the boat, or even that it was an accident, and they're so verra sorry, they might get off with a slap on the wrist."

"But how? They killed Rory."

"'Tis their word against the survivors', luve. We can only pray the Procurator Fiscal thinks the case worthy to be heard and tried."

She buried her face in the hollow of his neck. "Why is the law so complicated?"

"Our hands are tied, luve. But we can pray that God opens everybody's eyes to what is going on, and that they vote with their minds, no' their emotions." His grip tightened. "I'm thinking I should tell you something I've been considering since I made that trip to the Pentagon." His throat convulsed against her lips.

She pulled away, instant tears springing to her eyes. Surely he hadn't changed his mind about going to war.

His fingers tightened in her hair. "I'll always be an American by birth, but my heart belongs to Scotland. I want to have a hand in shaping her future."

Maggie waited, afraid to breathe, hoping he would speak the words she had waited over seven years to hear.

"I don't want to be separated from those I luve by the colour of my passport book and no' being able to vote."

Aye! Say it, Rob. Say it, please.

"I'm applying for UK citizenship."

251

Chapter Forty-Six

As Rob circled the room, Ellie was the first to snag his sleeve. "I'm glad Robbie told me everybody was gathering here after school. Calum's oot fishing. He wants you to know how pleased he is."

He raised an eyebrow. "And no' you?"

"I think it's—as your Maggie says—glorious." She smiled, grey eyes dancing. "With Calum and Julia born on Innisbraw, I plan to apply for Richie and me. 'Tis only fitting."

"They'll no longer call Innis Fell 'Yank Hill.'" Rob's grin belied his mournful tone.

"Guid. I luve the name Innis Fell. 'Tis so ... so Scots."

Stu was the only partner who appeared uncomfortable. "I hope you understand, but with Brenna being born in America and Chris an American citizen born in Scotland, Jill and I—well, we can't see relinquishing our citizenship."

"Och, 'tis a personal decision." Rob grasped Stu's shoulder. "If I was in your position, I'd never take a step like this. But Maggie and all my bairns are—and will be—UK citizens."

Smiling, Jill pulled Rob down and planted a kiss on his cheek. "See?" she said to her husband. "I told you he'd understand."

Pete shoved out a hand for Rob to shake. "Caroline and I'll be taking the same step. Don't want Malcolm the only Brit in our family."

As Stu and Jill moved off, Pete motioned Rob to join him in the kitchen, where Maggie and Fern busied themselves pouring tea and coffee and placing scones and shortbread on a tray. "Think you'll have any problems?"

Rob grabbed a shortbread and finished it in one bite. "I shouldn't. In late forty-three, John helped me apply for an 'Indefinite Leave to Remain in the UK,' so I'd be allowed a ration book." He grabbed a mug of coffee, tried for another shortbread, and laughed when Maggie slapped his hand. "I've been a legal resident of Innisbraw since July of that year."

A grin revealed Pete's relief. "I applied for an Indefinite Leave the day after I decided to stay on Innisbraw, and Caroline did the same the week after she got back from the States. Mebbe we'll get

252

our citizenships without a hassle too."

"You should, and Den too."

Needing to escape the noise for a moment, Rob stepped out onto the entry.

Hugh leaned against the railing, face turned to the Minch.

"Looks like I'm no' the only one craving a wee bit of quiet," Rob said, joining him.

"Just thinking about the letter I'll be putting forward at the next Council meeting." Hugh jostled Rob's elbow. "'Twill list all the improvements you've made to our island, and be signed by every member of the Council. That should help your application, I'm thinking. We'll do the like for the others." He poked Rob's shoulder. "And no' a word about all the help you say you've had. As far as the folk on this island are concerned, you've been a Scotsman since the day you first arrived on Innisbraw. 'Twill be grand having it official."

⁂

Maggie stood at the side of the path as Rob piled the Townsends' baggage into the back of Angus's cairt. Och, their visit had gone so quickly. And no wonder, as busy as she and Rob had been since the day of their arrival. With all the work the entire Townsend family had done, the hours they'd spent entertaining the bairns, the meals they'd prepared, the arguments they'd refereed, it could be a long time before they scheduled another holiday on Innisbraw. And them such fine friends.

She brushed at tears wetting her lashes. Annie had been near tears all mornin. No reason to encourage a bout of rouping.

Rob caressed her shoulder and kissed her cheek. "I'll help you into the cairt, luve."

"Thank ye." She scooted forward to make room on the blanket for the others.

Mel and Annie, then Trish and Beth joined her. Robbie leaped in by himself, shooting his faither an impertinent grin as he plonked down at the rear, bare legs swinging free. Full of himself, he was. Mebbe they'd made a mistake, allowing him to miss a mornin of school.

Paula climbed onto the bench, Will hugging her neck. Bill took a seat beside her.

Rob jumped onto the bench and turned. "Everybody ready?"

If he was waiting for a hearty *aye*, he was surely disappointed. Annie clung to Mel's arm, tears making wet tracks down her cheeks, and Beth held Trish's hand, head lowered.

"We're ready," Maggie said solemnly.

"Then off we go. The ferry's about to enter the harbour."

A slim snout appeared between the slats on the gate. Shep saying his guidbyes.

Maggie swallowed more tears.

Only Will appeared to enjoy the short trip down the fell. He chortled, waved his arms, and jabbered, bouncing up and down in Paula's lap.

Maggie rubbed her fingertips over the tiny bulge low on her belly. *Better her than me, wee one.*

⁂

Rob pulled Feona up behind a row of cairts and waited until all the B and B hosts' departing guests and their bags were unloaded and on their way up the pier before helping everybody down. At least the activity and confusion kept sadness at bay for a few minutes.

He and Bill gathered up the baggage, both grimacing at the weight.

"Follow us up the pier to the dock," Rob called over his shoulder.

Bill shook his head. "Sorry we bought so much. I warned the girls and Paula about loading down the bags. Know what they told me?" He answered without a pause. "'You get to fly off to all those exotic places, while we're stuck here at home. Those are precious memories you'll be carrying.'"

Rob grunted.

"They don't have any idea how boring my job is. Take off, switch to autopilot, spend hours staring out at the sky, land at another airport, take the shuttle to another hotel, shovel in a tasteless dinner at another restaurant, spend another lonely night on a hard bed, then get up in the morning and do it all over again." Bill barked a laugh. "Exotic! The closest I get to exotic is pulling one of the new Hawaiian routes. Sometimes I get in a run on the beach before it's time to catch the shuttle."

"Why do it, then?"

"At least I'm in the air, not stuck behind a desk in an office with no windows." Again, the laugh. "And the pay's good."

Rob cleared a way through the crowd thronging the dock. "Just stack the bags here. I'll have Colin let his crew know who they belong to."

Bill dropped the bags and flexed his hands. "I want to thank you again for that flight over the islands, Rob. I had no idea the Western

Isles were so rugged and scenic. All of us agree, this has been one of our best vacations ever."

Rob's eyebrow rose. "How can you say that after spending most of your time taking care of our bairns—especially with all the arguing, and Will who hasn't mastered using the watterie?"

"Listen up, Rob. If I'd been paid every time Trish and Mel got into it, I could think about retiring now. And they still argue, though it's snide little digs, not hair-pulling. As for Will, he's started the grandparent juices running. Paula's so tickled Trish is engaged, she's marking off the calendar a year out from the wedding, putting question marks at the end of each month."

A loud, throaty blast announced the ferry's arrival.

Maggie appeared at Rob's side and hugged his waist. "You'd best take Will from Paula, luve. She's about to drop."

"She carried him all this way?"

"She can speak for herself, Rob Savage." Paula smiled and handed him Will, her arms trembling. "I know he can walk—and run—but that's why I couldn't put him down. What if he fell off the pier?"

"Thank ye. You're a guid friend."

Paula hugged Rob and kissed Will's rosy cheek. "Bye-bye, precious boy. Try to remember me, just a little."

Rob held Maggie close as Mel wiped Annie's cheeks and pulled her into a hug. "Whenever you miss me, just remember all the fun we've had." She wiped her own cheeks. "I promise I'll do the same." She stood and smiled. "Don't forget our secret."

Annie clung to her hand for a moment. "I'll remember." She dropped Mel's hand and darted to hide her face in Maggie's skirt.

"I want you to know I'll be keeping a close eye on you," Trish said to Rob. "You have a daughter who wants to be a pilot. Make it happen."

Rob grinned. "And I'll be keeping a close eye on you. I want to see that ring on your finger. Make it happen."

She saluted. "Aye, Commander." Tears misted her eyes. "I will, that." She rested her cheek against Rob's arm, then hugged and kissed Maggie.

Robbie waited until the Townsends were starting up the boarding ramp before dashing forward. He pulled on Bill's leg. "Thank ye for playing ball with me."

Bill ruffled the lad's hair. "Remember what I said, practice makes perfect."

Captain Colin MacNamara stood at the railing, eyebrows raised.

Rob transferred Will to his left arm, preparing to salute.

Bill appeared at Colin's side. Perfect.

They both snapped a brisk salute. "Commander!"

Rob returned a salute. "Captains!" he shouted.

⁂

Rob went for an early run the next mornin, ending at Elspeth's cottage. He sat in a rocker on her entry, reliving the hours they had spent together. He wasn't sure it was a healthy thing to do, but it comforted him.

Shep sniffed at the bottom crack of the front door before settling with a sigh at his master's feet.

Rob's chest still ached with his loss. Elspeth's wit and innate kindness had seen him through many a difficult time. How he wished she could speak her wisdom now, when he needed it.

Sighing, he stood. "Come you on, Shep."

He trudged up the fell, afraid of what he'd learn at the meeting in John's office but knowing he had to attend. Had Colin found a family willing to take on Breannan and the lasses, or were they back to square one? If he had to come up with another solution to keep the three survivors from going back to their empty lives on Lewis, he didn't know where to start. Whistling Shep to the infirmary door, he told him to stay. *I ken 'tis too late to change the outcome, Lord, but please give me a clear mind and fresh ideas.*

The foyer was empty, only a glowing peat fire offering a welcome. Where was Fern? He turned down the hall to John's office, nearly colliding with Mary, who rushed by, arms piled high with sheets.

"They're all waiting in the office," she called over her shoulder.

The door to the office stood open. Rob started to enter, realized there was no room, and backed out.

"Come in, Rob, and please close the door," John said in the Gaelic. "'Tis too tight for another chair, but you can sit beside me on my desk."

Lace curtains pulled tight over the window blurred the view of Ben Innis. Did John fear a view of the Ben would be distracting? Rob squeezed between two of the five chairs crammed into the space, then perched beside John, his gaze raking those gathered.

Fern sat holding the hand of the lass he had pulled from the sea—Marsaili. Breannan and his sister, Brighde, bookended the two. Hugh had the chair next to Breannan, and Colin Stewart leaned against the side wall, bunnet clasped beneath his arm.

Marsaili and Brighde caught Rob's attention. He'd only glimpsed the lasses through half-closed doors on his way to Breannan's room over the past two weeks. Propped against pillows, hair in tangles, dark circles 'neath their eyes, they'd reminded him of the bombed-oot victims he'd seen in London, sitting mids the rubble of their flats, staring off into space with vacant eyes, waiting for someone in authority to tell them what to do.

Now the lasses evidenced the same change he'd seen in Breannan several days before. Hair washed and brushed to a sheen— one blonde and the other auburn—eyes bright with interest, wearing skirts and sweaters donated by the island's young women.

John introduced Rob to Marsaili and Brighde, then called Colin forward.

The crofter moved closer and settled against the wall where he could be seen by all.

"This is Colin—Cailean—our largest sheep crofter and a fine friend," John said in the Gaelic with a wide grin. "He has something he'd like to share with us. Cailean?"

Rob recognized Colin's discomfort. The spasmodic swallowing, the jerk of his fingers when he stabbed them through his hair. He leaned forward and winked at the crofter.

A nervous twitch turned into a smile. "As you probably all know, my wife, Ruth, and I have been talking by radio to Peadar and Sorcha Ros, friends on the Isle of Mull, where we lived before coming to Innisbraw." He averted his gaze from the victims and spoke to Rob. "We're almost certain we've found these three a home, and—"

"Almost certain?" John asked.

Colin's gaze sought John's. "I'll explain, if you let me."

"Excuse me," John grumbled, pulling on his beard. "Please continue."

"Our closest neighbours on Mull, the Roses, are also sheep crofters. Since we left, they've bought more grazing land and added to their flocks." He rocked back on his heels. "They need help with the sheep and in their home, since their family of three has grown to six, and will soon be seven."

Rob glanced at the Lewis three. Tentative smiles, eyes alive with hope.

Colin ducked his head. "Which led me to say 'almost certain.' Their cottage is small, though they've added rooms, and until they can make an outbuilding fit for living, their help will have to sleep on pallets in the cottage's kitchen."

"How long will it take?" Rob asked. "A week, a month, several months?"

"With these three to help, they say it can be ready in a month. It needs a peat-burning stove, new thatching, and beds." He spoke directly to Breannan. "If you're concerned, the outbuilding has never been used for animals, only to store neeps, tatties, oat grain, and such."

Hugh raised a hand. "Do the Roses speak the Gaelic, and even more important, is there a nearby kirk where it is spoken?"

"Yes to the first question, and most certainly to the second. There is a large community of the Gaelic speakers in that area of Mull. Though the kirk is small, the minister holds two services each Sabbath—one in the Gaelic and one in English." Colin, more at ease with absolutes, smiled at Hugh. "You would like the minister. He teaches far more than he preaches, and he has a fine singing voice— even plays the fiddle at the ceilidhs."

Rob noticed Breannan leaning forward, fingers twitching. "Perhaps our three new friends would like to ask questions. It is their life we are talking about."

All eyes turned to Breannan.

A flash of panic appeared in his eyes but disappeared when Hugh clasped his knee.

"What kind of help does this man need? Someone to herd, dip, and shear his sheep, to harvest his crops, make repairs to fences?" Hugh asked.

Colin smiled again. "Everything you have mentioned and more. He operates his croft with the help of his oldest son, who is being schooled at home by Sorcha, and Sorcha herself, when she is not heavy with child." He laughed, a bright flash of teeth against weathered skin. "Sorcha can shear a sheep faster than any man on the island, including Peadar."

Brennan finally spoke. "And the lasses? What will they be expected to—"

Marsaili reached across Fern and poked him with a finger. "How many times do I have to remind you women have tongues and minds? You're as bad as Rory." Darkness bloomed in her green eyes, replaced instantly with resolve. "Brighde, you go first."

Rob laced his fingers around a knee and leaned back. Could this be the same lass too timid to meet him, too frightened to answer the questions put forth by the polis, too traumatized to leave her infirmary room? What had brought about such a profound change? The resilience of youth? A growing trust in Hugh? Or a resurgence of the

258

same desire to improve their lives that had driven them to build the sailboat?

Brighde's brow furled. "What help are they expecting around the house? I am a good cook when I have the food for it, and I can card wool, spin, and weave, but I am helpless with a needle. I do love children, but my schooling ended years ago." She sat back, kneading her hands.

Marsaili's eyes flashed like early spring girse 'neath the sun. "Then you'll cook, I'll do the sewing, we'll share the spinning and weaving, we can both bathe, dress, and feed the children, and Sorcha can do the schooling and shear the sheep—in between birthing babies, of course."

Rob swallowed a laugh. Marsaili was soft and tender, with feminine ways all covering a backbone of steel—like his Maggie.

259

Chapter Forty-Seven

Rob glanced around the boatshed office. Anything else he could do to delay a task he hated? No such luck.

Door closed, desktop cleaner than usual, calendar up to date, file drawers closed. After massaging taut neck muscles, he grabbed a sheet of paper from a desk drawer, reached for a pencil, and licked the lead.

He listed three items, then sat back with a sigh. Not that he *needed* a reminder to get busy. What he wanted was the ability to cross off all three tasks and move on with his life.

First, he filled out the citizenship application forms, attached the letter from the Island Council and a glowing testimony from the Royal National Lifeboat Institution, placed his green American passport book into the envelope, and addressed it to the Home Office in London. Pray God he had no need to travel outside the UK until he received his British passport.

Sighing with relief, he crossed off the first item on his list, leaped up, palmed the envelope, and left the office for a quick jog to the post office.

The second reminder, a late-afternoon call to the polis in Oban, made his blood boil.

The polis sergeant's voice shook, as though he regretted the message he was passing on.

Rob slammed down the telephone receiver and pounded a fist on his desk. How could they release those three lads to their families? They belonged in jile, where steel bars separated killers from the innocent.

Rich or no', those lads had stolen a trawler, destroyed a sailboat, come close to drowning three, and caused a death. What if they took a runner?

He paced his office, hands fisted. *I don't understand any of this, Lord.*

The polis sergeant's parting words sent Rob's pulse throbbing. *"If proper compensation isn't agreed upon, there will be a trial before the Sheriff's Court."*

Proper compensation? How did one repay victims for years of

futile, backbreaking labour? For a lost friend once considered family? A destroyed dream?

This smelled of interference by the Crown Office.

He threw himself onto his chair with a grunt.

The list of tasks to be accomplished lay beside the telephone. He grabbed a pencil and started to line through *Call Oban polis*, then stopped and added a large question mark, circled several times.

A verse from Romans leaped into his mind. "'Avenge not yourselves, beloved, but give peace unto wrath: for it is written, 'Vengeance belongeth unto me; I will recompense,' saith the Lord.'"

Aye, it rested in God's hands. Rob had done all he could.

When good weather allowed, Rob dedicated Saturday mornins to Robbie's and Richie's flying lessons. Both lads were attentive, well-behaved, and so solemn that Rob often shared a few pilot jokes to lighten the mood after the floatplane was tied down.

Robbie, so like Rob himself, should have enjoyed the laughs, but it was Richie who raced home to tell his mither his favourite, repeating over and over, "Pilot to ground crew—mouse found in cockpit. Ground crew to pilot—cat installed."

"Richie should make a fine pilot someday," Rob told Maggie.

"You're going to break Calum's heart," she said, knitting needles flying. "All he talks about is having Richie on his crew, then skippering his own trawler someday."

"The lad can do both." He stared into the peat fire. He waited until she finished a row, took the knitting from her hands, and pulled her onto his lap. "After talking to Pete, I'd venture both Malcolm and Richie will enjoy flying when they can work it in, but it isn't their passion, like it is with Robbie." He buried his face in her hair. "Talk to Calum about going a wee bit easier on Richie, though. If he does, he might be surprised by the ootcome."

"Humph. You aren't the only stubborn man in the family. He always listened to Elspeth. If only ..."

"Then share our concern with Ellie. If anyone can make him change his ways, 'tis that lass. There's nowt he wouldn't do for her." *Thank the Lord for that.*

All the islanders rejoiced when Hugh let it be known that their visitors from Lewis would be leaving for the Isle of Mull in a week to take up their new lives. Unwilling to embarrass the young folk, he passed the word by telephone, appealing to the Innisbraw folk for additional clothing and toilet articles for the three survivors.

Most of his folk had so little, yet they always shared with the more unfortunate, whether a jar of precious heather honey, a sliver of soap, or a tiny packet of seeds for a kailyard garden. Those who lived on Innis Fell and made more silver than most donated bedquilts, eiderdown pillows, warm winter coats, knitting needles, scissors, and heather lotion for the lasses, and a peat tusker, waxed-cotton jacket, two gansey sweaters, and wellies for Breannan—and fifty one-pound notes to give them all a start. How blessed he was to minister to such a flock.

Moved to tears by their generousity, he spent time on his knees before the altar, thanking God.

Though everybody prayed for clear, warm weather, the mornin they said guidbye to the Lewis lad and lasses, a dreich sky held the sun prisoner behind sombre clouds. Maggie looked around the crowd filling the path and pier. Almost everybody on the island had turned out to see them off to their new home on Mull. A brisk wind iced the harbour waves with white foam and blasted weathered faces, bringing salt to tongues and tears to squinting eyes. She pulled up the hap covering Will's head and tucked in his churning feet. Thank the Lord Rob was holding him. As much as he'd grown, she could no longer bear his weight for long.

Annie shivered and opened Maggie's long woolen coat, ducking inside of it for shelter.

Rob leaned closer. "Here comes Alec's cairt, luve. He'll take you and the bairns home after the *Anna* sails." He frowned, most likely at the insistent, loud tap-tap of Beth's heels on the planks. "Beth, if you're too cold to stand still, join Annie 'neath Mither's coat."

"I'm no' cold." She rubbed a sleeve across her red nose. "Are we going to stand here all day doing nowt?"

"As long as it takes, lass. Now, haud yer wheesht and look out at yon floatplane."

Beth turned her back and sidled to the left for a better view of the boatshed dock—and the floatplane rocking in the waves.

Maggie took a deep breath. Didn't Rob realize he was feeding her dreams, making flying even more important?

Huh. Thinking like a daftie, she was. Of course he did. Wasn't that what he wanted?

Sighing, she returned her attention to Alec's approaching cairt—

and bumped her hip against Rob's. "Och, how excited Marsaili and Brighde look—and all the baskets and boxes in the back of the cairt." She slipped her gloved hands deeper into her coat pockets, embarrassed that she'd almost pointed. Unmannerly, aye, but she was that excited.

The cairt pulled up at the end of the pier. Breannan and Hugh pushed aside some of the boxes and climbed down from the back of the cairt, meeting the lasses and John on the path.

Rob's building crew left the protection of the shed wall and picked up baskets and boxes, carrying them toward the dock and the waiting trawler, trotting with the wind at their backs.

One of the baskets fell and rolled over and over, closer and closer to the edge of the pier.

A collective groan went up from the crowd.

Sim dropped the boxes he was carrying and raced after the basket, throwing himself on it just as it teetered on the edge.

Relieved shouts filled the air.

Maggie gripped Rob's arm. "Breannan and the lasses are coming this way."

"I hoped they'd say guidbye."

Breannan pushed through the crowd and offered Rob his hand. "We could not leave without thanking you for your support." A quick nod to Maggie. "And you, missus."

She smiled at the recognition. "You are verra welcome. Our prayers go with you."

Rob gripped the lad's hand. "From what Colin has said, you will find those on Mull as welcoming and helpful as our Innisbraw people. Go with God. He will never forsake you."

A long look passed between the two, as if they communicated a truth without words.

Ducking his head, Breannan pulled the two lasses to his side.

Marsaili smiled at Rob, green eyes bright as spring-born blades of girse. "I remember hearing your voice when I first woke up on your boat. It made me feel safe, for my faither's voice was often compared to the foghorn at the Rudhe Tiompan lighthouse near our village." She looked at Maggie, smile widening, before planting a kiss on Rob's cheek. "Moran taing—thank you so verra much," she whispered before stepping back.

His eyebrow rose. "You're most welcome."

Brighde took Marsaili's place, blushing and avoiding Maggie's gaze. She patted Rob's arm, withdrew her hand as though burned, and shoved it into her coat pocket. "Moran taing."

"You're most welcome."

Hugh joined the three and hustled them up the pier.

John clapped Rob's shoulder. "You're getting better at accepting gratitude, lad. No' perfect, but better." He grinned at Maggie and hurried to catch up.

Rob's smile vanished. "Och, there's no pleasing that man."

Annie's head popped out of Maggie's coat. "Are we going home now? I canna feel my toes."

Maggie smoothed Annie's wind-tangled hair. "As soon as the *Anna* sails, lass. Get back 'neath my coat and hug my legs."

Beth pulled on Maggie's sleeve. "Why did that woman kiss Daddy? She's no' our kin."

Testing brings patience. "Because your faither saved her life. 'Twas her way of saying 'thank ye.'"

Angry brown eyes pinned Maggie. "I'm glad she's leaving. And she'd better no' come back." Beth spun away, arms crossed, nose in the air.

Maggie fell against Rob with a moan. "Don't ever pray for patience, luve. I'm no' certain you'd live through it."

"I'm already living with the consequences, lass. That's been my prayer for years, and every time I voice it, I'm hammered with testing." He pulled her close. "There's the *Anna* leaving the dock. Let's get you home."

The weather remained colder than usual with a few scattered storms, but nothing to approach the wild, unpredictable rains of last year. There was a turkey on each of the three tables at the Innis Fell Thanksgiving dinner. The Townsends had sent three fourteen-pound turkey hens and a note.

> *When we saw how your family on Innis Fell has grown, we realized one turkey would never be enough. Also, we've found the hens to be tastier, with more breast meat. Bon appétit!*

A deep freeze gripped the island the first day of 1951. Crofters worked tirelessly to keep their coos fed in their byres and the sheep cropping the nearest possible girse, and their women prepared large pots of bree, gallons of mashed tea, and piled more covers on beds. Gardens turned black overnight as the last of tender vegetation froze and died. Peat smoke drifted high above each cottage, the folk gathering around fireplaces to keep warm. Grateful such cold didn't happen often on an island surrounded by salty ocean water, the islanders hunkered down to await a warming spell, nattering amongst themselves.

Maggie and Jill held a joint birthday celebration for Beth and Amy, who both turned three on the fourth of January. Jill insisted upon doing most of the work, for Maggie was six months pregnant and had enough to do taking care of her four bairns.

Rob worked late at the shed and built Beth the large wooden airplane she'd been hinting for. Maggie's hand-knit fisherman's sweater with matching cap and mittens were scarcely acknowledged by the lass, who dreamed only of piloting a plane.

Chapter Forty-Eight

Maggie woke with a squeal and pulled the pillow over her head. What a dreadful dream—something ice-cold stroking her cheek, like fingers from a grave.

"Wake up, sleeperie one. Time to get oot of bed."

Rob's voice? In her dream?

The pillow disappeared, revealing the grey pall of early mornin. She rolled onto her back and sat up, clutching the bed covers.

Rob leaned over her, a denim-clad knee pressing into the mattress, his bare arm descending.

"Don't touch me!" She scooted to the far side of the bed, picked up the pillow he'd removed to torture her with his chilly hands, and threw it. "Go away. You're cold as a frozen loch."

He caught the pillow, laughed—and pounced. Strong hands wrapped the comforter around her and pulled her close to his bare chest. "I've added peats to the fire, your tea is steeping, and I've something verra special to show you. Up you come, luve. Look oot the window."

"Oot the—och, no' till you put on a sark and sweater. You'll catch your death."

"You're worse than any mither hen ever hoped to be." He grumbled, pulling on a Jacobite shirt and his gansey sweater. He bundled her into her dressing gown, slid her feet into her baffies, led her across to the window, and opened the curtains wide.

Her breath caught.

Large, lacy flakes drifted down from a pale, luminescent sky, falling onto a white blanket that covered her garden plot, the tops of the dyke capstones, and the fell. The hushed landscape soothed her senses. "It's snawing," she whispered. She pressed her back against his chest, hens-flesh pebbling her arms when he chuckled.

"Aye. There's at least twenty-five centimetres oot there. You should have seen it earlier, luve. It was coming down so hard I couldn't see a thing beyond my nose."

Rob had stood ootside in that? No wonder he was so cold. "How long have you been away from our bed?"

"I don't ken. Too many memories of making snawmen, having

266

snowball fights, feet and nose freezing, but having too much fun to miss a minute of it."

He must be remembering life at the orphanage. "It snowed in New Hampshire?"

No chuckle this time, but a full-blown laugh. "Och, lass, we often had twa to three feet—that's over half a metre to a metre—of snow in one storm, and the storms came one after the other." He nuzzled her hair. "What about you? This is the first snow I've seen on Innisbraw, but you've surely had some since you were a wee lass."

"Never this much, only a light dusting, like the sugar I sprinkle over shortbread." She sighed and smiled. "'Tis magical oot there, like a gift from God, covering all the auld scars our mistakes have caused, showing us what our world would look like if we could begin anew."

Rob tamped down an urge to yell and thrust twa thumbs in the air. He'd take the mornin off and gift his bairns with an experience they might never enjoy again. "Start the brose, luve, while I rouse the bairns. After they eat, I'll take them ootside and teach them how to make snowballs—and memories."

"But Robbie has school, and Annie isn't one to play outside like a lad."

"Robbie can be late one mornin, and I'll show Annie how to make a snaw angel." He hugged Maggie so tight she complained she could scarcely breathe. "'Tis snawing!"

Once Rob showed the bairns the snow, breakfast was a rowdy affair. Maggie, caught up in the excitement, ate only because she knew she must, and Rob eschewed brose in favour of scones, overlooking poor table manners—just this once, he said. The bairns wolfed down their brose, Robbie nattering about Annie and Beth needing to wear his auld breeks, Annie reminding everyone how cold it looked, Beth gloating about being allowed to wear lads' clothes, and Will insisting on feeding himself, resulting in more brose on his face and nightclothes than in his belly.

Maggie improvised when she had to. Both lasses were dressed in twa pair of woolen tights, Robbie's woolen breeks, heavy woolen socks, twa sweaters, their warmest coats, and wellies.

Robbie argued but was soon garbed as warmly as the lasses.

Will put up the most vocal protest. Every time Maggie added another layer of clothing, he pulled away and dashed to the door, screaming when he was pulled back for another garment. Maggie fashioned boots by tying pieces of waxed cotton around his feet. He took one step and slipped, landing on his behoochie.

No tears. Just a scream when she tried to pick him up.

He crawled toward the front door and pulled himself to his feet on a kitchen chair. Beth was the only one with woolen mittens, so Maggie dug out all the small socks she could find and put them on the other bairns' hands.

Rob rummaged around in a box and found an old pair of leather flight gloves before donning his warmest socks, waxed-cotton jacket, and his wellies. He lined the bairns up in front of the door and burst into laughter. "Maggie, these are warm-blooded lads and lasses, no' auld folk tottering aboot on their last legs. Hard as they'll be playing, they'll be wetter with sweat than snaw."

Too tired to argue, she plonked onto her rocker, fighting tears. She'd worked so hard to give him time to play in the snaw with their bairns. Did he thank her? Did he even acknowledge her clever solution to keep Will's feet and legs dry?

He pulled her to her feet and nuzzled her ear. "I'm sorry, lass, but it isn't really that cold ootside. 'Tis snaw, no' ice."

She buried her face against his chest. "But Annie runs so cold, and Will's so short he'll get soaked to the skin."

A nibble on her ear brought hen's flesh. "I agree. Just let Robbie and Beth shed their coats. All the sweaters they're wearing will keep them warm."

Robbie and Beth sent enthusiastic thumbs-up and, coatless, bounded outside with shrieks.

"What about you, luve?" Rob asked Maggie. "You're coming oot, aren't you?"

She swallowed a laugh at how comical Annie looked, like one of those tip-over, rocking dolls she'd seen in a window in London during the war. "I'll be oot soon. On you go."

<hr/>

The other bairns who lived on the fell soon joined them in the side yard, away from Maggie's garden, where tender roots and bulbs slept beneath snow. Rob wasn't the only man playing hooky that morning, nor Robbie the only bairn who would be late for school. All the men romped with the bairns, showing them how to make snowballs and pulling them around on a piece of plywood Pete fashioned into a sled.

That was Will's favourite activity. He climbed aboard every time a different bairn took a ride, cheeks red, mouth wide open, shrieking with joy.

The women gathered on Maggie's entry, a motley group huddled together, clad in multiple sweaters, long coats, scarves, and mittens. Only Jill appeared in what looked like proper snow attire.

"Where did those clothes come from?" Maggie asked.

Jill, hand on hip, struck a pose and laughed. "Stu and I used to ski at Big Bear in California. These are snow bibs and a warm waterproof jacket with a hood. Oh, and gloves."

"They don't look verra warm."

"But they are," Jill said with a teasing laugh. "Somehow, they learned how to cut the bulk without cutting the warmth."

Fern grimaced, hugging herself. "I don't ken who's having more fun—the faithers or the bairns."

"Och, 'tis the faithers, of course," Caroline said, giggling as Pete took a snowball between the shoulder blades.

Rob showed Annie how to make a snow angel, and all the lasses but Beth, who was making snowballs, plodded to the back of the croft where there was undisturbed snow. Their delighted giggles drifted through the windless air, competing with screams and shouts from the lads and Beth, who decided their faithers made better targets than one another.

Rob brought Will to the entry an hour later, soaked to the skin, nose red, protesting every step.

"Let me get you into dry claes. Then you can go back oot," Maggie soothed as he squirmed on the bed.

He slid off and bolted to the door.

"William Wallace Savage, come back here!" She swept him up, tied fresh waxed cotton around his feet, and sent him outside again.

Fern gripped Maggie's arm when Den suggested trying the makeshift sled on the hill. Her hand relaxed when the other men quickly vetoed the idea. "There isn't enough snaw," Stu said. "You'll do a header and come up muddy and mebbe bloody."

⁓⚓⁓

In another hour, the snowfall stopped and the heavy, low clouds broke up, revealing a light-grey sky. Time to take the bairns home, pop them into hot baths, dress the older ones for school and the younger ones for another day of inside play.

Maggie started a large pot of hot chocolate and toweled Will and the lasses dry while Rob filled the tub for the lasses and showered with Robbie. Hours late for school, he was, and still blethering nonstop.

What was that pounding? And why was Will rouping? Maggie

put down the wooden skirdle she used to stir the chocolate and kneaded the small of her back. What had happened to her usually sunny Will? After rounding the kitchen bunker, she stopped.

Will had stripped off the towel and his undergarments and stood pounding on the bathroom door, crying as though his heart was breaking.

Beth tightened the towel around her body. "Tell Daddy to hurry. I want to bathe."

"Will wants a shower too," Annie said, voice soft.

Maggie scooped Will up and patted his bare bottom. "Enough of that rouping." She opened the bathroom door.

Rob and Robbie were toweling dry.

"Don't bother," she told Rob. "You have another lad who's outgrown the tub. He wants a shower."

Will smiled and kicked his legs as Rob reached for him.

"Easy, lad, you'll hurt your mither."

Will squealed and pounded his faither's back.

"It'll have to be a short one." Rob wrapped Robbie in a towel, pushed him out the door, and turned on the shower water. "The girls need in the bath, and the hot water's almost gone."

The cold snap ended and the snow quickly melted as the rain began anew. Maggie's pregnancy advanced without any problems. So much smaller than she'd been with Robbie and Will, she was certain she'd have another lass.

"Don't count on it, luve," Rob cautioned. "One of these days we're going to have a lad when your belly's no' so big."

"I suppose so. But I feel just like I did before I had Beth. Annie was different. She was so wee I barely showed in my eighth month."

It was a big help that Robbie luved school. He practiced writing his letters and numbers every night, tongue sticking out of his mouth as he worked to make each movement of the pencil perfect.

"I used to do that," Rob said one night after he'd tucked in the lad and heard prayers. "I remember my teachers telling me that I would bite my own tongue off if I wasn't careful."

"I canna believe how much he resembles you," Maggie said as she knitted beside him. "Other than the colour of his hair and eyes, he could be your twin."

"Och, heaven help him," Rob said. "I'd wish more for him than that."

She put her knitting down. "Don't start that, Rob. If he turns out just half the man you are, he will be a true asset to the world."

"You're prejudiced, Maggie lass, or blind."

"I said don't start that, and I mean it. I'll not listen to another word if you're going to put yourself down."

"I didn't mean to fash you, luve."

"Well, you did."

"How badly?"

"Verra badly."

"Then I'm ahead of the game if it isn't verra, verra badly."

"I'm serious, Rob."

He leaned over and nibbled on her ear lobe. "So am I."

She picked up her knitting again. "I'll never finish this sweater if you keep doing that."

"Keep doing what?" He kissed the side of her throat.

"That!" she exclaimed.

"This?" He unclasped her barrette and fanned her hair out, burying his face in its fragrance. Then he kissed her. With his lips still on hers, he put her knitting on the floor and scooped her up in his arms. The bedroom door whispered closed behind them.

Maggie's due date was fast approaching. The rains warmed and eased as spring flirted between a dying winter and an eager-to-be-born summer. The early lambs arrived, and bushes and trees set buds, forming pale-green brushes of colour behind slender branches. The harbour seals appeared on the rocks at the base of Innis Fell, the females heavy and ponderous as they sought a place to suckle and protect their newborn pups.

Rob insisted Maggie visit her faither at the infirmary every week. "We don't want to take any chances with this bairn," he told her when she balked. "If it looks like 'tis going to be a difficult labour, I want an obstetrician here."

"But Faither's already told you the bairn's head is down, and I feel fine."

"You were moaning last night."

"That's because I get so tired having to get up on my hands and knees to turn over."

"John said the bairn could still turn again."

"Och, Rob, quit your blethering. What happened with Will isn't going to happen again."

Though he didn't argue further, Rob hoped Maggie wouldn't

experience the suffering she had when Will was born.

They went through the usual precautions, laying in a supply of towels and a rubber sheet in the bedroom closet. Rob placed the scissors and string where they could be reached, and Maggie prepared a hippen, gown, and blanket in one bundle.

Even with their preparation complete, Rob was convinced John would have to deliver this bairn. Will's birthing had shown him how quickly things could go wrong.

⚜

His lack of confidence was put to the test when Maggie woke him in the middle of the night on the first of April. "Och, luve, I've made a midden. My water just broke."

"Are you certain?"

"I'm biddy certain." She grabbed his hand.

"I'll call your faither." He leaped out of bed.

"Don't leave me!" She grunted, strained, and her face turned red. Beads of perspiration popped out on her forehead.

Rob had no choice. It was time to act. He rushed to the closet, got out the rubber sheet and a pile of towels, shoved them beneath her, then took her hands. "Tell me when 'tis time."

She nodded, unable to talk. She gripped his hands harder than he could remember her ever doing before. *Och, Lord, is something wrong?*

Ten minutes passed. Pants turned to grunts as she strained. "'Tis almost … time," she gasped.

He pulled back the blankets and positioned himself between her raised knees. "I see the head."

She pressed harder, grunted louder, and let out a loud cry as the head was born.

He cradled the tiny head in his hands and extracted each shoulder as it came.

One more hard push and the bairnie slipped into his waiting hands.

He held it up. "'Tis a lass," he choked. "Och, luve, 'tis a bonnie, bonnie lass." His hands moved automatically through the rest of the birth. *Thank Ye, Faither. Thank Ye for another precious lassie.*

After everything had been done, he looked down at his new, wee lass. She was about the same weight as Beth had been, but shorter. Her hair was light brown. Long pale lashes swept her round cheeks. He touched her wee fingers with their almost translucent pink nails. This was his lass. He leaned over and brushed his lips over her forehead.

Maggie cuddled the bairnie close to her breast. "Our Heather is here at last."

"Aye. Heather Elspeth." Rob kissed Maggie's cheek, breathing in her sweet scent. "'Tis only fitting."

They both smiled through their tears.

"I hope, somewhere in heaven, Elspeth knows," Maggie said. "Both names are really for her, no' just the one."

"I'm sure she does. 'Twas the smell of the heather soap she sent you that helped bring us together. I'd never smelled anything like it."

Tears slipped down Maggie's cheeks. "Och, Rob, I miss her so."

He sat on the bed and gathered them both into his arms. "So do I, luve, more than words can ever express."

Chapter Forty-Nine

Heather was her faither's lass from the day she was birthed. If she was hungry, she soon learned it was Maggie who filled that vital need, but if she just wanted comforting, Rob was the one she responded to the most quickly. When she was a newborn, he carried her like a football, on his forearm with his hand supporting her head. As her neck muscles strengthened, he put her over his shoulder, so he could nuzzle her cheek or kiss the sweet spot at the centre of her neck.

Annie didn't appear jealous. If anything, she encouraged the growing bond between her faither and sister.

"I don't ken the way my wee Annie's acting," Rob confided to Maggie. "Even Beth is more jealous."

"Beth only gets in a fankle when somebody interferes with the time you spend talking about flying."

"I ken that. But Annie's always sat in my lap before bedtime, but now, 'tis Heather being rocked, no' her. Annie has such a tender heart, I don't want her hurt or thinking I don't luve her anymore."

Maggie smoothed his forelock back. "Then find some time to spend with her, perhaps when you say nighttime prayers."

"Like the time I spent with Robbie when he was acting a skellum?" Rob pulled her onto his lap. "I couldn't believe how quickly his behavior improved, but Annie isn't acting up—just the opposite. Unless she's throwing a tantrum when I'm no' home, they must be one angel short in heaven."

"Tantrums are no' her nature, luve. But if you're worried about hurting her feelings, spend a wee bit of time alone with her. Ask her to sing for you."

⚓

A late afternoon telephone call from the Oban polis sent Rob running up the path to home. Instead of punishing the young sots by sending the lads to jile, the Procurator Fiscal had arranged for their parents to pay a very large settlement. It wasn't the news Rob had been hoping for, but considering how poor the three young folk who'd moved to Mull were, the court-ordered settlement would go to good use.

274

We'll Meet Again

Breannan and Marsaili decided to buy an old boat-making yard and start their own business. Brighde took her third of the settlement and stayed with the family on Mull, not quite ready to start out on her own. There was a rumour that she and a certain young sheepherder— a cousin of the Ros's family—were stepping oot after Sabbath services.

꧁ꙮ꧂

As spring turned to summer, the tourists thronging the path in front of the harbour often voiced surprise to see a very tall Scotsman being saluted by the ferry captain, all while carrying a baby wrapped in a soft plaid blanket over his left shoulder.

Maggie's DREAM

Originally intended to be the final book of the series, the following chapters were written by Dianne as she struggled through the last stage of the cancer which quickly took her life. Though she wasn't able to complete the entire book as she wished, please enjoy the finale of the Thistle series.

Chapter Fifty

Isle of Innisbraw, Scotland, August 1951

Maggie and Rob Savage continue life on the small island of Innisbraw, Scotland, building boats and raising their five children. The academy is going well and the children are receiving a good education without having to leave the island. After Rob presents the idea of providing University scholarships for those students who show promise, the Island Council votes aye.

Maggie plans to wait a few days to tell Rob that she's pregnant with their sixth child, but when Rob comes home from work, she is nowhere in sight. Jill meets him there and breaks the news that Maggie has had a miscarriage. However, Maggie quickly becomes pregnant again …

She was six months pregnant now, and so large even Rob was amazed. This bairnie was the biggest and the most active Maggie had ever carried.

The morning after the Sabbath, Maggie had a checkup, and John used the fluoroscopy machine. "'Tis as I suspected," he told Rob and Maggie. "There are twa bairns. You're going to have twins, Maggie, lass."

Twins! How would they ever manage?

John patted Maggie's shoulder. "They're a guid size right now, but you're going to have to be verra careful. As you know, multiple births are often early, and we're not as prepared to care for preemies as well as a muckle infirmary."

Rob's knees weakened and he sat down. "Should we plan on flying her to the Royal Infirmary a month early, then?"

John shook his head. "Don't even think about that right

277

now. I'll keep a close eye on this. If it looks like she could go into labour early, we'll consider it, but not afore."

Rob took Maggie's hand. "Should I stay home? I mean, shouldn't she be in bed or something?"

"Of course no'!" John exclaimed. "Twins are no' that unusual. Just no heavy lifting or stooping over, lass. Home you go now. I've sick patients to see."

Rob would have carried Maggie home had she allowed it. He was still in shock. Twins! Twa wee bairnies at the same time! How on earth would she ever manage? It would have been bad enough for her first pregnancy, but she already had five bairns to care for.

He'd go to Oban and look into hiring someone to help her. The mother's helper could stay in one of the guest bedrooms upstairs.

⚜

When the ferries filled with tourists begin arriving on the island, a mysterious man and woman, named the Walkers, appear. They start asking verra personal questions about Rob. The islanders suspect the woman is ill. Everyone gives the runaround—and some false information—to the couple. The Walkers, believing the falsehoods they've been told, look for Rob, wanting to explain their behaviour.

Rob had almost reached the door to leave the kirk hall when he felt a hand clutch his arm. He whirled around.

The snoopy American tourist stood before him, his wife at his side. Her face was ashen and tears were running down her cheeks. "Please," the man said. "Can we have a word with you?"

Rob ran an arm over his sweaty forehead. "Why?"

"We want to apologize." His grey eyes behind his glasses were so filled with pleading that Rob could not refuse.

Maybe now he would be finished with them forever. He motioned with his head. "Over there." He led them toward a clear spot along the front wall.

The woman's movements were painfully slow. She took a handkerchief out of her sleeve and dabbed at her eyes.

Rob waited for them. Were they finally going to reveal why they had probed into his verra private life?

"We want to explain," the man said when they once again stood in front of Rob. "Explain about why we've … we've been asking questions about you." The man ran his hand through his thinning hair. "It was a case of mistaken identity," he added in a broken voice. "We thought you were … were someone else." Tears welled in his eyes and he looked down.

The woman gripped his arm. "Let me, Wade. Let me tell him. He deserves to know." The skin was drawn tightly across her emaciated cheeks. Her gaze was dull and lifeless, watery. "You see," she said softly, "we thought you were another Rob Savage."

"Who was this Rob Savage to you?" he asked, his voice softer.

"He was … he was a boy we tried to adopt over thirty years ago."

Rob felt like someone had punched him in the stomach. He couldn't get his breath and his vision blurred. Wade. She had called him Wade. A sudden picture of a slim, brown-haired man in silver-rimmed glasses, wearing flannel slacks, a green plaid flannel shirt, and pulling a red wagon flashed before his eyes.

"Wade, you and Robbie stay close. Supper's almost ready." She was standing on the front porch of a small white house with green shutters. She wore a flowered apron over her dress, and the evening breeze lifted a curl of auburn hair from her forehead before scattering a few yellow sycamore leaves across the gravel driveway.

"We're just going around the block once, Babs," Wade called. "We'll be right back, won't we, son?"

Son. Rob fought back the tears. It couldn't be! This pale-faced man with the sloping shoulders and greying hair couldn't be the energetic, youthful Wade. This wraith-like woman with the ill-fitting blonde wig couldn't be the pretty, plump Babs.

Wade's mouth was moving.

Rob tried to concentrate.

"… So I know you're very angry with us for invading your privacy. Can you ever forgive us?"

"There's nothing to forgive," Rob mumbled. His eyes couldn't seem to focus. He shook his head. "Excuse me," he said as he stumbled for the door.

Several times on the way home from the ceilidh, Maggie felt Rob shudder, but he was soon walking normally, and he squeezed her hand every once in a while as though to reassure her.

Shep stayed close to his master's side instead of racing off ahead with the aulder bairns.

When they passed the infirmary, Den looked at Maggie and raised his eyebrows, but she shook her head. Whatever had happened to Rob the night wasn't physical. Something had upset him terribly, and she intended to find out what it was as soon as possible.

At the gate to the Savage croft, Den lifted Matt out of the cairtie and nodded his head at Fern.

"Do you want me to go in with you and help get the bairns to bed?" she asked Maggie.

"Nae, thank ye. Heather's already asleep in Annie's arms, and it'll only take a tick to get them all tucked in. We'll see ye on the morra's morn."

"Then call if you need owt. Guidnight."

When they climbed into bed, Rob reached to turn out the lamp.

"Leave it on, Rob. I'm no' sleeperie. You need to talk."

He rolled over onto his back and put his hands 'neath his head. "I hardly ken where to start."

"At the beginning, of course."

"That's just the problem. I'm no' sure I can withoot ... withoot ..." He fought to control his anger and grief. Within seconds, the anger came to the forefront and the threatening tears dried up, but he couldn't still his trembling limbs.

Maggie leaned over and put her arms around him.

"Why, Maggie?" he suddenly cried. "Wade and Barbara Walker gave me away. I thought I'd left that all behind me. Why did they have to come now and bring it all back with them?"

"Shh, 'tis all right." She held him until his chest stopped heaving, then caressed his cheek. "I'm thinking 'tis our mystery couple you're talking aboot. Am I right?"

"Aye, only 'tis nae longer a mystery." He opened his eyes

and looked at her. "I didna ken them, they'd changed that much. I didna recognize them at all."

"They're the couple who were going to adopt you."

"Afore they changed their minds. What are they doing here? Why would they want to find me now after all these years?"

"I don't ken. Perhaps it has something to do with her sickness."

Bitterness tinged his laugh. "Well, they're miles off the track if they think I'll just greet them with open arms. They sent me back withoot a single explanation. I was at that orphanage for anither eleven years. They never wrote, never called, never came to see me. What kind of cruel, twisted people could do that to a five-year-auld bairn? I luved them. I called them Mither and Faither and they threw me away. Why?"

She kissed his cheek. "I'm thinking that's something you're going to have to ask them."

"It's been over thirty years. It's too late to hear their excuses."

She rose up on one elbow and turned his face toward hers. "Aye, it's been over thirty years you've lived with the pain, over thirty years you've agonized over the 'why.' 'Tis time to find oot. From your reaction to what happened the night, this is something that needs to be resolved, no' for them, but for you."

"What, and listen to a bunch of excuses? There's nae excuse for what they did!"

"Of course there's nae excuse, but there could be a reason."

"Reason, excuse; what's the difference?"

"There's a big difference. There could have been something going on in their lives you ken nowt about."

"Like what?"

"Ach, Rob, I don't ken. But I do ken you have to ask them. If you don't, you're going to regret it for the rest of your life."

He sighed. "I'll have to think aboot it. I'm going to get some APCs. My head's pounding." When he came back to bed, he turned out the lamp and spooned his body against hers.

"Pray about it, luve," she whispered.

"I already am."

⚜

During kirk, Hugh taught from the Psalms. He talked aboot how

281

much of King David's life had been filled with ups and downs, of times in fellowship with the Lord and others out of fellowship, yet still others where something in David's life blocked his closeness to God. Rob didna want that for himself. He didna want to hold on to the anger, the grief, for it could destroy him spiritually. Until last night, he had thought himself the most fortunate man alive. It was strange how a painful memory could cause such upheaval so many years later.

Perhaps Maggie was right. Mebbe it was time to put this to rest once and for all.

He saw the Walkers as he was walking out of the sanctuary.

They stood by the door, waiting for an opportunity to exit.

He pressed Maggie's hand and leaned down. "How would you feel aboot having twa guests for supper?"

She smiled. "'Tis a splendid idea. We'll wait here while you ask them."

He made his way up to the Walkers, his hand extended. "Guid morn. 'Tis guid to see you here."

Wade looked startled as he shook Rob's hand. "Thank you."

"I have an apology to make for the way I left you last. But with the apology, I also need to offer an explanation, and this is no' the time nor the place."

"Oh, that's not necessary," Wade said. "We were very rude to question anyone about you, we know that now."

"I wonder if you'd care to have supper with us this een." He motioned toward Maggie and the bairns. "It can get a bit noisy with so many, but we'd be honored if you would come."

The Walkers looked at one another.

Then Barbara nodded slightly.

"We'd be happy to," Wade said.

"Guid. I'll bring a cairt to pick you up at the manse about eighteen hun … six o'clock."

Rob prayed for guidance all the way to the manse. The Walkers were on the front entry, dressed in their kirk clothes, waiting. Rob set the brake, jumped down, and tied Feona to the hitching post. He glanced down at his own clothes in dismay. He was wearing a fairly new pair of denims Maggie had ordered him from America and a pale-green lace-up shirt she had made him;

hardly dressy, but it was too late to do anything aboot it. He took the stairs twa at a time. "I hope you haven't been waiting long. I always forget how long it takes to hitch the cuddy to the cairt."

"No, no, you're right on time." Wade helped Barbara to the stairs.

Rob took her other arm and supported her as she descended the stairs and walked to where the cairt stood. It was obvious she was exhausted by the time they got her onto the cairt seat, but she smiled gamely as she dusted off her light coat.

Rob clucked to Feona and they moved off at a smart yet sedate pace.

"This is really a very beautiful island," Wade said.

"It is that. I cannot imagine living anywhere else."

"But don't you miss automobiles here?" Barbara asked. "I mean, it seems everyone here must do a great deal of walking."

"You can't miss what you've never had. And walking's guid for the body ... and the soul."

She didna look convinced. "I suppose so."

Several people along the path waved and called greetings to Rob, most in Scots and a few in the Gaelic.

"You really have to be a linguist to live here," Wade said. "The brochure we got on the ferry said islanders speak Gaelic and Scots, and a few people speak English."

"'Tis nae hardship to speak the Gaelic and Scots, for bairns are raised speaking both languages. English is another story. 'Tis a difficult language to learn."

"Your little boy speaks it beautifully," Barbara said. "And he has excellent manners."

Rob smiled. "I'm happy to hear that. We work on the manners and have English lessons almost every een."

"They don't teach it in the schools?"

"Not until the academy—that's the equivalent of what you call high school—and even then, 'tis only a wee bit."

They were silent until they approached Elspeth's cottage.

"Your house is precious but it's so small," Barbara said. "However do you fit all of those children into that little home?" She turned in her seat as they passed the cottage, her hand going to her throat. "Oh, I thought you said supper was at your house."

Feona spotted one of Angus's sheep dogs running loose and

didn't like it one bit.

Rob sawed on the reins until she was under control again. "Sorry aboot that. The filly can be a wee spirited. Now, what were you asking aboot my house?"

"Didn't we just pass it?" Wade asked.

"'Tis up ahead, beyond that large stane building, which is our infirmary."

"But I thought we saw you and your wife …"

Ah, they had walked by when Maggie and he were at Elspeth's. "We were visiting a friend's cottage. She's been in … in heaven for over a year. Maggie stops by every other day or so to keep the garden neat. This is our home right here." Rob pulled the cairt up to the gate and set the brake.

The Walkers stared at the house, eyes wide. "My, it's so big." Barbara said. "And look at that garden. It never occurred to me to plant my flowers and vegetables in the same plots. How beautiful it is."

Rob handed her down to Wade. "Maggie's a wonder in the garden. I don't think there's a thing she can't grow."

"Well, I imagine that's going to stop any day now when your new baby comes."

Rob tied Feona to the hook, unlatched the gate, and led the Walkers through. "That's no' for three more months, though she will miss out on some of the canning in late August." He had to laugh at their astonished faces. "'Tis twins." He held up twa fingers.

"Oh, my gracious," Barbara said. "Twins! Aren't you fortunate."

Maggie greeted them on the entry, the house behind her unnaturally quiet.

"Where are the bairns?" Rob asked after the introductions had been made.

Maggie took Barbara's light duster coat. "They're in the lads' bedroom. Brenna's reading them a new book she got yesterday from her auldmither in America."

"Heather, too?"

"Aye. She gets to turn the pages."

Shep rose from the hearth rug and came to greet Rob.

"An Australian shepherd," Wade said. "We had one once.

Fine dogs."

Rob couldn't speak. Words caught in his throat.

Maggie seemed to catch his distressed look. "Aye, they are fine dogs. I don't know how I could have raised our bairns withoot him. He keeps them oot of danger."

Rob gave her a quick kiss on the cheek. Saved again. He cleared his throat. "Would you like to sit oot on the entry— porch—for a bit? Supper won't be ready for almost an hour."

"That would be nice," Wade said. "You have a beautiful view from up here."

Barbara tipped her head toward the china cabinet. "What an unusual and lovely piece of furniture. Is it an heirloom?"

"Rob made it," Maggie said. "He made all of our furniture, even the rockers."

The Walkers exclaimed over the workmanship, and, as usual, Rob squirmed. "What are those words carved around the top?" Barbara asked. "Are they Gaelic?"

"They *are* in the Gaelic," Maggie said. "Though there is no exact translation from the Gaelic into English, it says something like, 'Our Love is Eternal.'"

Soon Wade and Barbara settled into twa of the rockers on the entry, while Rob sat on the railing.

"So you build furniture, Rob," Wade said. "That must be an interesting occupation, though somehow I had the idea you built boats."

"The furniture is just something I do oot of necessity and, I have to admit, because I enjoy it a lot. You're right, I do build boats."

"Is that your place down by the dock?"

"It is that."

"Well, I'll be. It looks big."

"I have four partners. We also do all the wood construction on the houses being built on Innisbraw."

"Wood construction?"

"The outer walls are built of stane—stone—as is the custom here. We do the interiors."

"You built this house?"

"Years ago."

There was a long silence. Wade tapped his fingers on his

knees, while Barbara knotted her handkerchief into a ball and fidgeted with her wig.

Rob leaned forward. "I'd like to get that explanation of mine out of the way if you don't mind. 'Twill be hard to do with all the bairns around."

"May we go first?" Barbara asked. "It shames me the way we acted, but we were getting desperate. You were our last hope, you see."

"Last hope for what?"

She looked beseechingly at Wade.

He stopped rocking. "Our last hope to find the right Rob."

Rob's stomach tightened. He had to be so careful now. "You said something last night about a lad you 'tried' to adopt. What does that even mean?"

Wade pulled a handkerchief out of his pocket and blew his nose. "Thirty or so years ago, we brought a bright, handsome little boy into our home. He was an orphan and we thought he would be ours forever, but"—he took Barbara's hand—"we lost him."

"Lost him!" Rob's exclamation startled Barbara so much she jumped. "I'm sorry, I didn't mean to interrupt. On you go, please." He took several deep breaths.

"Anyway, ever since, we've been trying to find him with no luck."

Rob's eyes narrowed. "Perhaps he was adopted by someone else."

"That's what the orphanage told us, though at the time we didn't want to believe it."

"They told you he'd been adopted?"

"Yes. You see, about six months after … after we returned him to the orphanage, we realized we'd made a terrible mistake. We tried to get him back. We telephoned, wrote letters, camped on their doorstep … We even contacted our senator, but we were told there was nothing we could do, that our Robbie was no longer there. It wasn't until he would have been nineteen or twenty that we found out he was never adopted, that he was at the orphanage until he went off to college. They had told us he was adopted because they were afraid Babs's health would fail again, and felt the boy would be too damaged from the loss."

Had they really tried to get him back? But why had they returned him in the first place? That was the one piece of the puzzle he needed above all others. Had Barbara been sick and he didn't know it? Was that why had they taken him back to the orphanage? He got up and began to pace, then turned to Barbara. "I guess I'm a little confused about why you would give him up and want him back again just six months later."

Barbara met his gaze with candor. "I found out I had breast cancer. The doctors gave me only months to live. Our poor Robbie had already lost one mother, and he was such a tender, loving, serious little boy; it took us months to get him to laugh. We couldn't expose him to the pain."

Rob was losing the battle with his tears. "And six months later?" he asked, voice breaking.

"I had a radical mastectomy and they changed their prognosis. I've been cancer-free all these years." Her smile was fleeting. "But the cancer came back in the other breast last year, and since it's so far advanced, I've not allowed another mastectomy. I know I wouldn't survive it. So I take their terrible medicines and do the best I can, though there's no doubt about the outcome this time."

The tears won. Rob felt them spill out of his eyes and down his cheeks. Maggie had been right. There had been a reason. He bowed his head. *Thank ye, Faither.* He took a rocker and pulled it around to face the Walkers. He sat and took Barbara's and then Wade's hand in his. "I'm sorry for your pain."

Conflict played on Wade's face as if he didn't understand why someone he considered a complete stranger would be weeping.

It was time to tell them both the truth. Rob took a deep breath. "You gave me a pup, and I named him Shep. You bought a blue bicycle and you were going to teach me to ride it, Wade. Barbara—Babs—you used to bake oatmeal cookies with raisin faces on them." He ducked his head to wipe the sides of his face on his shoulders. "Your search is over. I'm your Robbie."

"But ... but your middle name, and your age, and you were born here," Wade stammered.

"I'm sorry for that. I didn't know who you were. One of my partners lied to you to stop what we thought was your prying."

Barbara and Wade both began to sob.

Rob kicked his chair back and knelt before them, gathering them into his arms. He wept as hard as they did. All those years of wondering, of asking why, were over. They had wanted him.

After a few minutes, Barbara pulled her hand from Rob's and ran her fingers over his face. "This scar on your forehead ..."

"The scar's from an airplane crash during the war."

Wade took off his glasses and blew his nose again. "But the languages you speak and your accent. You don't sound American."

Rob wiped his hands across his eyes. "I spent over six months here in forty-twa—two—and have lived here on Innisbraw since the summer of forty-three. 'Tis my home now. I learned Scots and the Gaelic so I could communicate with the ones I love."

"Like your Maggie." Barbara smiled through her tears.

"Like my Maggie."

Wade took Rob's hand. "All these years we thought we'd know you if we ever saw you. We were so sure when we saw you on the dock talking to the captain. But there was something about you that bothered us both. There was a hardness there. Not your body; after all, you're a grown man. I can't even explain it. Babs, help me."

"I think Robbie ... Rob knows what we mean. But now we know he was in the war. Perhaps that explains it."

"I was a career Army Air Forces officer," Rob said. "I flew fighters and B-17 bombers."

"Which university did you attend?" Wade asked.

"West Point Military Academy."

Barbara smiled. "I knew it! Remember, Wade, there was a Robert James Savage who graduated from West Point in nineteen thirty-six."

"You traced me that far? What stopped you?"

"Red tape," Wade said. "They weren't very cooperative, and then the war started and we were forced to start all over again."

Rob got to his feet. "We have some major catching up to do. I'll take the cairt over to the manse in the morning to pick up your bags. You'll be staying here with us, of course."

"Are you sure, dear?" Barbara asked. "I mean with Maggie expecting twins and all, and I'm afraid my … my illness doesn't make me very good company."

"You're family, and family belongs together during bad times as well as guid. You can have our bedroom—'tis more convenient. We'll sleep upstairs."

Maggie opened the door and looked out, then smiled as she searched his face. "Ye told them."

He pulled her into his arms, burying his face in her hair. "Aye, and they told me the why."

***

Only the bairns ate much supper. For Wade and Barbara Walker, tears appeared to still be very near the surface, while Rob was concerned about the adverse effect so much emotional upheaval could have on Barbara's health. Maggie whispered that she was busy thanking the Lord that such a painful part of Rob's past had finally been put to rest.

Of course the bairns were curious about the American visitors. For their view, the woman had funny hair, plus she kept staring at their faither with tears in her eyes.

After dinner, Wade gathered the bairns around and performed a simple magic trick with a coin. "Sometime I'll show you how to do it," he told them. "It's very easy to learn."

"When?" Will asked. "I want to do it now."

"There'll be lots of time later," Rob said, tone firm. He glanced at Barbara.

Her face was ashen, and she had eaten very little.

"I'm thinking I should take you back to the manse right after supper. You both look verra tired."

Barbara attempted to smile. "Perhaps you're right, dear. It has been a long day."

Rob reached for her hand and squeezed it. "But a guid one," he said softly.

"Oh, the … very best," she said, voice catching.

They didn't talk on the way back to the manse. Barbara rested her head on Wade's shoulder, her eyes closed.

Rob devoted his attention to keeping Feona under control. When they reached the door, he insisted on helping Barbara to their room.

Wade was pale with fatigue as his feet shuffled down the hall.

They embraced just outside the door.

When Barbara caressed Rob's cheek, her hand was ice cold. "You've given me the greatest gift I've ever received," she said, "my Robbie."

They all had tears in their eyes when Rob took his leave after assuring them he would pick them up the following mid-morn.

⁂

Thank ye, Lord. All the way back to Angus's croft, Rob's heart overflowed with gratitude. Even he hadn't realized the depth of his grief and anger and how they had shaped his life. For the first time in over thirty years, he could let the past go.

He and Maggie redded up the kitchen, then sat on the entry while the bairns played. He put his arm around her shoulder. "I hope you don't mind me asking them to stay here. It just seemed the right thing to do."

"Of course I don't mind."

He nodded, staring out at the sea. "They had a guid reason to send me back, though an agonizing one." He told Maggie all about the conversation he and the Walkers had shared earlier the een.

When he finished, Maggie sat silently for a moment, obviously trying to control her emotions. "Their hearts must have been breaking." Her eyes shimmered. "I can't imagine ever having to make a decision like that. It would tear me to pieces."

Rob sighed and leaned his head back. "I'm thinking it ruined their lives. No wonder they look so auld."

"I was sure she had cancer. That's why she's lost her hair; the estrogen they give her to try to battle the disease will sometimes do that."

When Rob spoke, his voice was little more than a ragged whisper. "She's dying, Maggie. I just found her and I'm going to lose her again, this time forever."

She reached for his hand. "No' forever, luve, just for a while on this earth."

꧁ꕥ꧂

When it was time for their story, Rob told his bairns about his childhood and the role the Walkers had played in it, softening the grief which would have been too great a burden for their tender, young hearts. But he couldn't fool his bairns.

They all crowded around him on the hearth rug, hugging and kissing him while Heather climbed into his lap.

"Then she was almost our auldmither," Robbie said.

"She was," Rob replied with a soft smile. "And I think it would bring her great pleasure if you called her that."

Annie stroked his hand. "She's verra, verra seeck, isn't she?"

"She smells like the infirmary," Beth said.

"And her hair's funny," Will added.

"She is verra sick." Rob pressed his lips together for a moment. "Soon, she'll join Elspeth in heaven."

Annie hugged him again. "Don't be sad, Faither. Jesus will make her all well when she gets to heaven."

His eldest lass had captured the most important thing left unsaid. He pulled her close, kissing her cheek. "Aye, my Wee Annie, He will that."

꧁ꕥ꧂

Rob continues getting to know his parents. They explain how they found his picture in a boating magazine with an article about his new rescue boat designs, and resumed their search for him. Rob takes Barbara to see John and discuss any possible treatments for her cancer. John breaks the news that Barbara has less than a week to live. Rob flies to Oban to arrange for a woman to help Maggie in the future with the household chores and the children, then comes home.

The siren on Innis Fell wailed just as they were sitting down for supper the een. Barbara flinched and turned toward a wide-eyed Wade. Maggie smiled as Beth pressed her hands over her ears. The rest of the bairns looked at their faither.

Rob kissed each of his bairns and Maggie, and then leaned over Barbara. "I'd appreciate your prayers, Mither." He kissed her cheek. "Though 'tis most likely a tow in such calm seas." He pressed Wade's shoulder. "See me off, luve," he said to Maggie.

She followed him quickly.

"Don't turn on the radio," he cautioned as he paused on the entry. "The fright could kill Babs." He kissed her again, then ran to the gate where Den was waiting.

The twa sprinted down the hill.

Maggie returned inside and took her seat at the table. "What Rob said is true," she said as she began dishing up the bairns' plates. "The sea is verra calm. Even if 'tis a rescue, there's no danger from the waves."

Barbara's face paled. "When will we know?"

Maggie mashed some vegetables for Heather. "No' for a while. It depends on where the shout originated. Some are assist calls from Barra's or Tiree's rescue services. They take the longest."

"We won't know until they get back?" Wade asked.

"Aye. Please eat. It could be hours."

Once again, only the bairns ate much. Maggie forced herself to have something, though her stomach was knotting. How she longed to turn on the radio. It would make the waiting so much easier to know if it was only a tow or a medical rescue.

Fern knocked on the door an hour later. "I hope you don't mind a little company. It makes the waiting easier."

Maggie hugged her. "Of course I don't mind. Come in. I'd like you to meet Rob's mither and faither."

Fern, Katie, and Matt filed in. After the introductions had been taken care of, Fern suggested that Katie organize some games on the front entry. "But nowt too noisy."

Heather wouldn't leave Maggie's side. She buried her face in her mither's lap.

There was a lot of small talk, followed by long silences when Wade kept looking at his watch and Barbara sat very still, her hands clenched in her lap.

Heather finally begged to be held, so Wade lifted her up for Maggie.

"I don't see how you take the suspense," Barbara said suddenly. "I know I couldn't."

"'Tis always hard," Fern said, "though in the summer, the waiting's no' so bad. 'Tis the winter storms that are the worst."

"How many times does this happen?" Wade asked.

"We never know." Maggie shrugged. "Sometimes they get shouted out several times a week, sometimes only twa or three times a month. The summers are the slowest."

There was another long silence broken only by the sounds of the bairns playing outside.

Shep paced the floor from Rob's chair to the door and back again, so Fern got up and let him out.

"This isn't what Rob would want us to do," Maggie said suddenly. "Faither, why don't you go ootside and see what the bairns are up to? Mither, let's go into the bedroom and show Fern the new scarves I made for you. Mebbe she can teach us a special way to tie them."

Wade glanced at Barbara before getting to his feet and going outside, and Fern took Heather from Maggie's lap and set her on her feet. "Come on, wee lass, let's go look at the pretty scarves."

Barbara rose very slowly, and the three women walked into the bedroom, Heather clinging to Maggie's skirt.

"Fern is also a nurse," Maggie said as Barbara took the scarves out of the clothes-press drawer. "Perhaps she's seen these tied a special way."

"Indeed I have," Fern said. "Take off that wig and I'll show you."

Barbara removed the wig, revealing her greying auburn hair half an inch long all over her head.

"Which color?" Fern asked.

"I never could wear pink with my red hair. I'd like to try that."

"Pink it is." Fern placed the scarf over Barbara's hair, crossed the ends at the nape of her neck, and brought them around to the front again, tying a neat knot. "There. Now you can wear pink."

Barbara looked into the mirror over the clothes-press and relaxed, smiling. "My, what a difference."

Heather tried to put a scarf over her own head.

Maggie laughed and tied it on, but the lass pulled it off immediately, holding it out to Barbara.

"Oh, you like this green better than the pink?" Barbara

asked. "Well, perhaps it would look nicer." She took the scarf from Heather, removed the pink one, and tied on the green. "I do believe you're right, pretty girl," she said, looking in the mirror. "The green does look better."

Heather held out her arms. "Oop," she said.

Maggie started to pull her away, but Barbara stopped her. "I'll just sit on the bed. Fern, could you lift my granddaughter into my lap, please?"

Maggie held her breath.

Heather settled into Barbara's lap, looking up at her with an impish smile.

"I do believe you like me in green."

The lass put her head against Barbara and nestled closer.

Tears glistened in Barbara's eyes. "Oh, you precious little girl. You're the sweetest, most adorable little granddaughter in the world."

Maggie hadn't guessed how much the ill-fitting wig had affected the youngsters, keeping them a distance away. Now that Barbara was back in the main room and wearing a scarf, they all gathered around Barbara in her rocker. "Tell us a story, Auldmither," Annie said, "about when our faither was a bairn."

Katie quickly organized the bairns on the hearth rug.

"Well, let me see." Barbara squinted as if looking back in time.

Maggie sat quietly at the living room table, praying silently for Rob's safety while Barbara told the bairns about the first time she and Wade had seen their faither, how handsome and tall he was, but serious. She told them how Wade had finally gotten him to laugh aloud, and all about his puppy, Shep. Every time Shep—who was lying next to the bairns—heard his name, his tail thumped, causing them all to laugh. She related the story of the new red wagon they had given their Robbie for Christmas, and how he had wanted to take it outside to play even though there was three feet of snow on the ground.

The bairns listened raptly. They had heard many tales about their mither when she was growing up, but none about their faither.

When Barbara finally ran out of remembrances, their

questions began.

"Did my faither like to fly when he was a bairn?" Robbie asked.

Beth made a face at him, for that had likely been her question.

"Did Faither really eat all those cookies?" Annie questioned. "Didna he get a belly-thraw?"

"What, pray tell, is a belly-thraw?" Barbara asked.

"'Tis a bellyache," Beth said quickly with a smirk at Robbie, proud to show off her command of English.

Not to be outdone, Heather once again asked to be held.

Wade lifted her up into Barbara's lap and wiped at his eyes.

"Mebbe Auldmither will show me how she makes the raisin faces on her cookies," Maggie said.

"I'd love to. And if you have some whole cloves and an orange, I'll show you how to make a pomander like your father, little Rob, made me for Christmas."

"Now, 'tis your turn, Auldfaither," Robbie said. "Did you play baseball too, or just football?"

Wade laughed. "I'm not as good a storyteller as your grandmother is, but I'll try." He launched into a long monologue of all the games the family had played, of the walks around the neighborhood, of training Shep to play fetch. He told of the evenings spent cuddled on the couch reading stories. He even related the story of the bi-plane and how fascinated their faither had been with the idea of flying through the sky like a bird.

Then Robbie told Barbara and Wade about the time he got to fly the floatplane, and Beth took them step-by-step through the construction of a floatplane she'd made from twigs and wood scraps. Annie declared that her faither luved to hear her sing, and Will told how his faither had built his cairtie from wood left over from a rescue boat.

It was getting late and Heather had fallen asleep on Barbara's lap. Fern gathered up her bairns and left to put them to bed. Wade helped Maggie get the younger bairns into their nightclothes and even supervised them while they brushed their teeth, and both Barbara and Wade listened to their prayers.

After the "Now I lay me" prayer, each child asked God's blessing on every member of the family, remembering even their auldfaither and auldmither. They ended with a special prayer to bring their faither home safely.

When all the bairns were tucked into bed, Maggie made a pot of coffee and steeped some tea. She looked at the clock, heart racing. Rob had been gone for hours.

She, Wade, and Barbara moved to the entry to wait. Maggie had brought out some scones, but they remained uneaten. They sat and rocked in silence.

When they finally heard the *Maggie*'s siren, it blew three times.

Extreme emergency! Maggie put her teacup on the table, hands shaking. "They're coming in," she said as calmly as she could. "Perhaps you could stay with the bairns while I go to the infirmary. They just sounded the emergency siren, which means they have medical emergencies onboard, most likely some of the rescued victims, and they may need me."

Barbara wrung her hands.

Wade got up. "Of course we'll watch the children. Do you want me to walk you over? It's still light but there are some shadows."

"No, I'll be fine. Here comes Fern. We'll walk over together." Though she hated to leave the Walkers, Maggie had to know that Rob had not been injured.

The Walkers waited on the entry. Wade sat down and took Barbara's hand in his. "I know you've been praying all evening, just as I have," he said. "But now is the time to put more power in our prayers by petitioning our Lord together."

⚓

Maggie and Fern worked alongside nurse Mary MacGruder, preparing for the victims. Since John was already at the dock, all Mary could tell them was that one crew member had been critically injured and twa of those rescued were near-drowning victims.

The nurses checked the saline and blood supplies and made sure the examining rooms and the operating room were ready to receive patients. Mary thanked Fern and Maggie many times over for the help; she already had several very ill patients under her care.

Whenever Maggie's imagination tried to run wild, she

resorted to counting sterile dressings to keep from thinking about
Rob. The moment the count was over, she lost her battle.

Critically injured.

"Och, heavenly Faither," she prayed, "no' Rob, no' my
Rob."

Chapter Fifty-One

Maggie was out in the hall when the front door burst open and the first stretcher-bearers rushed in. Whoever was on the stretcher already had a plasma IV attached to his forearm. She looked down as he passed, her heart thudding painfully. Black hair! He had black hair! She almost went to her knees, her relief was so great.

"Maggie! Maggie, lass, what are you doing here?" She didn't realize that one of the stretcher-bearers was Rob until he called her name.

She followed the stretcher into the operating room.

They transferred the patient to the table, then Rob came to her, arms outstretched.

She fell against him, crying.

"Hush, lass, 'tis all right," he said, holding her tightly. "'Tis all right." He guided her out into the hall.

John pushed his way past them. "Get that lass home now!" he barked at Rob.

Maggie fumbled for her handkerchief and wiped her eyes as Rob led her ootside. "Who … who was it?"

"Christopher. 'Twas those blasted skerries again. He was slammed against the rocks and chewed up pretty badly. He's lost a lot of blood."

"Och, Rob, we only knew it was a member of the crew. Hold me."

He held her, rubbing her back until her tremors stopped. "I'm going to take you home, luve."

She nodded.

"How's Mither?"

"Scared to death, like all of us. It's been hours!"

He took her arm and helped her down the steps. "It was a

298

nasty one. Another yacht rented out of Oban. What will it take for those eejits to warn people aboot those rocks?"

"I'm fine now. Run ahead and let your mither and faither ken you're all right."

"I'm no' leaving you on the path. You could trip, and another minute or twa won't make that much difference." He fondled her cheek as they walked. "I'm glad you didn't have the radio on. The skerries always make you so fearful."

"With guid cause."

⚓

Rob didn't have the strength to argue. He was going on pure adrenaline. He had spent a total of almost three hours in the water, and it was all he could do to put one foot in front of the other. "I'll change and then I'll have to go back." He unlatched the gate. "I have to be there for Christopher."

"Of course you do."

"You're sure you're all right? You shouldn't have gone to the infirmary."

"I'm sure."

He helped her up the steps and seated her in a rocker, then turned to Barbara. She was sobbing, her handkerchief up to her face, as he gently hugged her. "I'm all right, Mither. There's nowt—nothing—wrong. I'm all right."

As she leaned against him, her fragile shoulder bones moved beneath his fingers.

He held her closely until she stopped weeping. It was only then he addressed Wade, who held onto Rob's shoulder. "I'm no' hurt. It was one of my crew, no' me."

"Oh, Robbie, when I saw you coming up the path, I thought you were all covered with blood," Barbara gasped.

"'Tis just my red wet suit, Mither. I didn't have time to change. I don't even have a scratch."

She smiled up at him, running her fingers over his face. "I see that now. But you were gone such a long time."

"It was a difficult rescue. There were a lot of victims in the water, and it took a long time to pull them all oot."

"You mean you went into the water, son?" Wade's voice thickened.

"We all had to, Faither. The victims had to jump into the sea

299

when their boat sank, so we had no choice."

Barbara looked up at him. "You're exhausted. You need to go to bed."

"No' just yet. I have to change and get back to the infirmary and check on my crew member who was injured."

"But can't someone else do it?"

"I'm the commander, Mither. 'Tis my duty, and besides, Christopher's a dear friend. I'd go regardless." He helped Barbara inside, then went out to Maggie and pulled her up into his arms. "I luve ye, lass."

They walked inside and she turned to him. "Your mither's right. You're exhausted."

"I am, but I have to go. I'll check on the bairns first. I want them to ken I'm all right. Are you sure this hasn't thrown you into labour?"

"Of course it hasn't. I wouldn't be standing here if it had."

He smiled at the truth in her remark as he tiptoed into Robbie's room. Both of the lads were sitting up in Robbie's bed, eyes wide. They leaped to their feet and hugged his neck.

"You should be asleep." He kissed them both and tucked Will into his bed, then went to Robbie. "We'll play football on the morra, so get to sleep now." When he checked on the lasses, he found them all in Annie's bed.

Heather was asleep on her stomach, as usual, with her bottom up in the air. Beth had her head under the pillow, and Annie was watching the door.

He put his finger to his lips. He picked Heather up and she didn't even stir as he put her into her own bed. He went to Annie's bed and pulled both lasses into his arms. He wiped the tears from Beth's cheeks and kissed her forehead, then Annie's. "Faither's fine," he said. "You need to go to sleep now." He carried Beth to her bed and tucked her in with a kiss before he returned to Annie.

"It was bad, wasna it, Faither?" she whispered.

"It was, but 'tis all over now. Pray for Christopher, lass. He was injured verra badly. Guidnight, my Wee Annie."

When he returned to the living room, Maggie handed him a mug of coffee. "'Tis warmed up, but you need the caffeine or you'll fall asleep on your feet."

He nuzzled her, breathing in her sweet scent. "I'll drink it while I change." He smiled at Barbara and Wade in their rockers. "You'd better get to bed. 'Tis late."

Wade got to his feet. "You're right, son. We only stayed up to make sure you made it home safely." He helped Barbara up.

Rob kissed her cheek. "Guid dreams. You don't have to worry aboot me. My work for the Lord isn't over yet. That's been proven to me more times than I can count."

"I believe you're right." Barbara followed Wade into the bedroom.

Rob spent several hours at the infirmary, until he was certain Christopher and the twa victims were out of danger.

Maggie had left the light on beside the front door, even though it never got totally dark outside at this time of the year.

He turned the light off and tiptoed inside. He was so exhausted he had trouble thinking. As he was crossing the living room to the stairs, Barbara came out of the bedroom. He went to her quickly. "Shall I turn the watterie clo—bathroom—light on for you, then?"

She tightened the belt on her robe. "I woke up and couldn't go back to sleep. Could we talk for just a few moments? I know you're very tired, but this won't take long."

"Of course. Do you want to go oot on the entry? 'Tis a warm night."

"That sounds lovely."

He led her outside.

"Don't turn on the porch light. The garden looks so beautiful in the soft shadows."

He seated her in a rocker and sat beside her.

"I just have to let you know how very proud we are of you," she said softly. "If I'd ordered a perfect son, he would have been exactly like you."

Tears stung his eyes as he took her hand in his.

"There are some things you should know about your real parents' relatives. I don't think you know that your paternal grandfather was very interested in those newfangled things he called aeroplanes, and your mother's father was a professor of English literature at a small college in Upstate New York. You'll be most happy to hear that he was very tall, and both he and your grandmother were from Edinburgh, Scotland. Their last name was Galbraith."

Not only was his luve of flying genetic, but he really did have Scots blood in his veins!

She went on for just a bit more, telling him aboot relatives of his real parents, all long dead. "I wanted you to know the people you came from. We researched all this when we were looking for you. We went through the archives in town halls and even churches, hoping to find a clue to your whereabouts. You have a lot to be proud of, son. You come from fine, upstanding people."

Rob was so touched he didn't ken what to say. "I can't thank you enough," he finally whispered. "'Tis a gift to be treasured."

"Every man should know his beginnings." She struggled to her feet. "Look at that lovely white bloom out there, how it captures the ambient light." She pointed to a rose bush with a single white bud on it. "They're my favorite flower, you know. We never could get them to grow in New Hampshire. The winters are too cold." She shivered suddenly.

He put an arm around her and drew her close. "You're like that white bloom oot there. Pure and lovely and full of promise."

She rested his cheek against his chest. "I love you, Rob. I've called you Robbie long enough. From now on, I'll call you Rob—a strong name for a beautiful man."

"Let me take you in, you're shivering."

"Thank you, dear; I am a little chilly."

Rob helped her into the croft and carefully opened the bedroom door. "Guidnight, Mither," he whispered. "I luve you."

She smiled and hugged him tightly. "And I love you."

The sun was shining when Rob woke up. He put on his robe, went downstairs, and turned the shower heater on.

Maggie was in the kitchen, frying sausage.

"Guid morn," he said, lifting the hair off the nape of her neck so he could kiss her.

"Guid morn to you. Are you hurting anywhere?"

He rummaged in the cupboard and pulled out a glass. "Nae. Why do you ask?" He drank twa glasses of water in several hasty gulps.

"You moaned a few times the night."

He poured a mug of coffee. "Probably just dreams, though I don't remember them." He rolled his shoulders. "I'm a wee bit sore, but I don't hurt."

"How's Christopher?"

"He was resting when I left. It took a muckle number of stitches to close the cuts on his legs. He'll be oot of commission for several weeks but he'll recover." Rob grabbed a scone and ate it in three bites. "I'm starving."

"'Tis no wonder. You didn't get to eat your supper."

"I'm thinking I'd rather enjoy a certain lass this morn. You look bonnie, luve."

She swatted at him. "Get your shower and dress. I'm fixing you a grand breakfast."

A half hour later, he came down the stairs, clean, freshly shaven, and dressed. As he was crossing the living room, the bedroom door opened and Wade came oot. Rob's greeting died in his throat.

Wade's face was even paler than usual, and he was shaking his head from side to side as though confused.

Rob went to him. "What is it?"

"She's gone," Wade whispered. "I don't know when it happened, but she's gone."

Chapter Fifty-Two

Maggie moved into the room as Rob grabbed Wade's shoulders. "Gone where?"

"She's gone," Wade wailed. "I tried to wake her up, but I couldn't!" He collapsed against Rob.

Rob walked him over to a rocker and sat him down, then ran into the bedroom.

Barbara lay on her side, one hand beneath her cheek. Her eyes were half open, and her lips were turned up in a slight smile. She still wore the green scarf on her head.

Rob clutched her arms. "Mither!" he cried, shaking her.

Maggie took his hands. "Don't, luve, don't. She's gone away."

He stared at Maggie, eyes wild. "She can't be! I didn't get to say guidbye." He held the still, frail body in his arms, rocking it back and forth.

Maggie sat on the bed and put her arms around him.

Rob stopped rocking and just sat, looking down at his mither's face. "She was telling me guidbye last night, but I didn't know it," he said raggedly. "We sat oot on the entry talking when I got home, and she was telling me guidbye the whole time."

Maggie hugged him tighter. "She's no' hurting anymore."

"I only just told her I luved her."

"Those are the words she wanted to hear from you, Rob. 'Guidbye' doesn't mean owt, but to a mither, 'I luve you' means the world." She stood. "Now you need to go to your faither. Your mither's in heaven but he's still here. He needs you."

Rob closed his eyes for a moment, then laid his mither down verra gently and got up from the bed. He left the bedroom and went to where Wade slumped, his head in his hands. Rob knelt beside the rocker. "Faither?"

Wade looked up, startled. "What am I going to do, son? Where am I going to go?"

"You'll stay right here, with your family, where you belong."

Wade stumbled to his feet. "I know there are things that need to be done, people to call. Help me. I don't know what to do!"

"Come with me." Rob led Wade outside onto the entry.

The sun accentuated the pallor and lines in Wade's face. He blinked and held on to Rob's arm tightly.

"Maggie!" Rob called. "Can you bring me Faither's glasses?"

She appeared moments later and handed Wade his glasses.

He polished them carefully on the hem of his pyjama top before putting them on.

"I've called Fern," Maggie told Rob. "The bairns are just getting up. She'll take them home with her for a while."

He nodded.

Wade looked over at him, eyes beseeching. "What am I going to do, son?"

Rob held Wade's hands tightly. "You don't have to do anything right now. I'll call Hugh and have him come over."

"Hugh? Oh, he's a good man."

"Aye, he is. He'll help you know what to do." Rob's heart was aching so dreadfully it was difficult to take a deep breath, but his faither needed him to be strong.

The two men stood there for several minutes until the side door slammed.

The bairns were gone.

Rob took Wade's elbow and guided him out into the garden. "There's something I want to show you. See this rosebud?"

Wade nodded.

"'Tis one of the last things Mither talked about. She said it was her favourite flower."

Wade grasped Rob's arm again as if to keep from falling. "I tried to grow them for her, but the winters were too cold. They always … always …" He went to his knees, tears streaming down his cheeks.

Rob knelt beside him. Tears spilled down Rob's face, dripping off his chin. He put his arm around Wade's shoulders, and the two knelt there in the garden for a long time, their tears helping cleanse the unspeakable grief from their hearts.

Barbara Payton Walker was laid to rest only a few yards from Elspeth. All the folk on the island had quickly learned she was someone dear to Rob's heart, and all who could attended the funeral service in the kirk. Only Wade, Rob, Maggie, and the bairns were at the graveside.

Hugh quoted Revelation 21:4. "'He shall wipe every tear from their eyes; and death shall be no more; neither shall there be mourning, nor crying, nor pain any more: the first things are passed away.'"

Rob stepped forward to place a single white rose on the casket. "Your favourite, Mither. As pure and perfect as you are now."

That night Rob finally shared the results of Barbara and Wade's research with Maggie. Her smile was radiant. "You're half Scots, then," she said. "Galbraith. There are a lot of Galbraiths on Bharraigh. They could be kin." She kissed his cheek. "You realize you have your own plaid now. I'll have to get busy and research it so I can weave you a new kilt."

"But I like the McGrath plaid."

"You can't wear it now," she said firmly. "'Tis tradition to wear your own family's tartan."

"Och, I'm always making work for you."

She smiled. "This is a task that'll make me most happy. I knew you had to have Scots blood. I just knew it!"

Chapter Fifty-Three

Rob buried himself in his work. He oversaw the launching of four rescue boats and took each one out for its sea trial. Maggie ignored the fact that he was often distracted. He needed time to adjust to losing the only mither he could remember. Wade went home to New Hampshire to sell the house and his car before he could come back to Innisbraw to live close to the only family he had left in this world. Rob received permission from the Island Council for a small home on Innis Fell, next to Fern and Den's and just across the dyke from his and Maggie's. He hoped to have Wade's house built before he returned in the late fall.

The twenty-fifth of June was fast approaching, and Rob still had not told Maggie he had hired a housekeeper/mother's helper. On the way home from the shed on the twenty-fourth, he resolved to get it over with the een. But he had a pretty guid idea what Maggie's reaction would be, and he wasn't looking forward to it. When they disagreed, his stomach always knotted up.

The bairns were playing in the yard. Shep and Heather both came to greet him, the dog's hindquarters switching from side to side, the lass's arms raised.

He picked up Heather and kissed the tip of her nose and both cheeks, then reached down to pat Shep's head.

"Doon," Heather said, wriggling. "Doon."

"All right, lass." He laughed.

She swiped at his pants leg and ran off giggling.

Annie ran up to him. "Faither, I think Mither needs you."

He kissed her cheek. "Where is she, lass?"

"In the bathroom. It sounds like she's rouping."

Rob tore up the path and into the house. The bathroom door was closed. He opened it to find Maggie sitting on the side of the bathtub, her face in her hands, her shoulders shaking. He went to her and knelt down, pulling her hands away. "What's wrong, luve? You're no' in labour are ye?"

307

She shook her head and turned away.

"Maggie! Talk to me. What's wrong?"

She started to roup again, great racking sobs.

He picked her up and carried her into the living room. "Should I call your faither?" He sat down in his rocker with her in his lap.

"Nae!" she wailed. She put her arms around his neck and rouped into his shoulder.

What was the matter with his lass? He felt her forehead.

She wasn't feverish.

He smoothed the hair back from her face. "You have to talk to me," he said gently, "or I can't help you."

She hiccoughed, then looked up at him, her eyes dark with misery. "I … I can't do it. It's just too much."

He caressed her cheek. "What's too much? What can't you do?"

She closed her eyes. "The gardening, the cooking, the cleaning, and the washing." Fresh tears slipped down her cheeks.

"Is that all!" he exclaimed. "Och, Maggie, I thought something terrible had happened."

"It has." She laid her cheek against his chest. "I started to fix supper, but I'm too tired. I can't do it."

"Then you won't. I'm no' a cook, but I can fix sandwiches." He nuzzled her hair. "Don't cry, lass. After the day, you won't have to worry about cleaning the house or doing the washing."

She raised her head. "And just who's going to do it? No' you. I'll no' have it!".

He kissed her tenderly. "No' me. I should have told you this sooner, but I was afeart you'd be fashed. I've hired a housekeeper. I pick her up in Oban on the morra's morn."

Her eyes grew wide. "A housekeeper! Och, Rob!" She started to roup again.

"You'll get used to it," he soothed. "There's too much around here for you to do. It'll give you more time for the things you luve, like the bairns and your garden."

"I luve you so much," she said. "'Tis exactly what I need. A housekeeper!"

The knot in his stomach untied entirely. "You're no' fashed?"

She hiccoughed again and laughed. "How could I be fashed? A housekeeper!" She hugged him tightly.

※

Sarah MacTavish was waiting at the airstrip the next morn when Rob arrived by floatplane promptly at oh nine hundred. She had two bags, which he loaded into the floatplane. On the flight to Innisbraw, he told her how he used to be in the American Army Air Forces, but the fact that he was an American didn't seem to faze her. He also told her how exhausted Maggie was, relating a little of what had transpired the een before.

"It's no wonder, carrying twins and all," she said. "Not to worry. She'll soon be her old self again."

⚜

Over the next few weeks, life finds a new normal with Rob enjoying translating stories at the ceilidhs, the bairns returning to school, Sarah taking care of the housework and meal preparations, and Maggie and Rob preparing for the twins' arrival.

In the wee hours one morn, Rob was awakened by a strange sound coming from Maggie's side of the bed. He lay there, listening for several moments before he finally identified it. She was panting! He leaped up and turned on the light.

She sat up, hands over her belly, eyes wide.

"What is it?" he asked. "You're no' in labour!"

"I am!" Maggie gasped. "It woke me." She strained.

"Don't push. I'm calling John!"

"Nae!" she cried. "The towels, get the …" She strained again.

Rob pulled on his pants and got the towels. This couldn't be happening, not again! He pressed the towels beneath her, feeling the wet sheet against his hands. Why hadn't she awakened him when her water broke? "I don't ken what to do with twa," he muttered. "One is bad enough."

She moaned and panted, her face red with exertion.

"Raise your knees," he said.

She pulled them up as another contraction came.

This is a bad dream, his mind screamed, *a horrible dream!*

"Rob!" she cried.

He threw back the blanket and could already see one bairnie's head. He took a deep breath.

There was a knock at their bedroom door. "Rob, Maggie, is something wrong?"

"Get in here!" he shouted as the bairnie's head was born. He was waiting for another contraction when Sarah burst into the room. "Get a blanket," he ordered as he slipped the shoulders out. "Bottom drawer."

The bairnie fell into his hands. Its roup was loud and lusty as Rob lifted it up.

"'Tis a lass!" he cried, "and she has black hair!" He grabbed the blanket from Sarah's outstretched hands. He wrapped the blanket around the wailing bairnie and handed her to Sarah, who stayed close by. "Hold her, there's another coming. No time to cut the cord."

The second bairnie came almost immediately.

"'Tis a lad, Maggie, a lad with … a lad with brown hair!" Rob laid the rouping lad over Maggie's belly. "I need to cut the cords." He nodded at Sarah. "Make sure he stays put." He raced for the closet and returned with the scissors and string. "Let's take care of the lad first."

His son was still rouping loudly when Rob deftly tied the cord and snipped it off. "Och, I need another blanket."

"Give him to me," Maggie said. "I'll cuddle him while you take care of our lass."

He laid the lad next to Maggie, pulled the cover over him, and took the lass from Sarah, laying her down on his side of the bed.

The lass squirmed and rouped as loudly as the lad while Rob took care of her.

Shep barked.

"Someone's knocking on the front door," Sarah said.

"Then answer it," Rob ordered as he rewrapped the lass.

A moment later, John came into the room. "I saw the light in your bedroom window. Rob, why didna ye call me?"

Rob shook his head. "As usual, there wasn't time."

John pulled back the blanket and picked up the lass. "Cord's already cut," he said, "and 'tis a lass. Listen to that guid, strong voice!"

"The lad's with Maggie," Rob said.

"A lad! Well, my dear daughter, you've had a busy night."

"I need water," Rob said. "They have to be washed."

"I'll get it," Sarah said.

It was only then that Rob realized he had no shirt on and Sarah was wearing only a nightgown and a light robe—a very messy light robe. "Oh, what a muddle." He groaned.

John had laid the lass on the bed and was looking at the lad. "They both look guid. Guid color, guid size. In fact, we now have the answer to why you were so muckle, Maggie. These are both braw bairnies. Rob, you can bathe your lass first. This wee lad is fine right where he is. But we should probably see about getting you certified as a midwife."

Rob guffawed, put on a shirt, then carried the lass into the kitchen.

Sarah was pulling pots and pans from the cupboard.

"I meant the basin on the shelf in the washroom," Rob said. "Here, you hold her while I get everything ready." After preparing everything himself, he bathed the bairnie, then wrapped her tightly in a dry towel.

Her roups had quieted, but she still squirmed. "One down, one to go," he said, smiling at last.

"You're awfully chipper," Sarah said.

"I'm daft, that's what I am." Rob carried the lass back into the bedroom.

John was rolling the soiled towels up into a bundle. "Everything's perfectly normal."

"There's nowt normal about the night." Rob took a hippen, gown, and blanket from the wardrobe.

"You did a fine job, just as you've done with your other bairnies."

"It wasn't supposed to happen like this, John," Rob said, laying the lass at the foot of the bed. "I had it all planned."

John laughed. "There's no such thing as planning in childbirth. Just luck."

Rob dressed the bairnie. She was bonnie, with black hair, white skin, and delicate, dark eyebrows. He finally had a lass who looked just like his Maggie. He got a fresh blanket and went to Maggie's side. "Do you want to hold the lass while I bathe our lad? I'll clean you up right after."

She nodded, looking exhausted.

"They're both bonnie bairnies." Tears pricked his eyelids. "Thank you, luve." He kissed her cheek.

Maggie smiled as tears pooled in her eyes. "At last a lad with brown hair."

"And a lass with black," he reminded her.

❧❀❧

The rest of the night was much calmer. John went home after again pronouncing both mither and bairnies in good health. Sarah dressed and helped Rob clean up Maggie, then disappeared upstairs. The bairnies were in their cradles, asleep at last, recovering from the ordeal of being born.

Rob ran a hand over his face. He needed a shower and a shave, but first he needed to tell his lass how much he luved her. He sat on the bed as Maggie reached for his hand.

"I'm so proud of you," she said, "and so sorra I put you through this. I usually have some warning, but I woke up when the first hard contraction hit."

He kissed her. "They're so perfect, Maggie," he said when he could speak.

"Aye, our Jamie and our Shona."

"Are you sure we should name her that, luve? Only Gaelic speakers will know 'tis pronounced 'Hannah.'"

"'Tis a guid Gaelic name, Rob. 'Twas my auldmither's name."

"Then Shona 'tis."

In the morn, the new bell in the kirk rings out the news of Maggie and Rob's twins, and two weeks later, they take them to their first church service.

⚶

Wade returned to Innisbraw on the thirty-first of October, aboard the last ferry of the year. The tourists lining up to depart the island were entertained by the five auldest Savage bairns' reaction to seeing their auldfaither. They jumped up and down and waved, calling, "Auldfaither!" when they spotted him at the railing. Once Wade came down the gangplank, they crowded around, hugging him and clamouring to be noticed.

He spent time with each bairn, exclaiming over how they had grown and how handsome they looked in their Sunday clothes. He hugged Maggie, kissed her cheek, and remarked on how slim she was, then shed a few tears when he got his first glimpse of Shona, who was in her arms.

Rob waited patiently, his heart filled with gratitude that his bairns were showing so much affection for the man he called "Faither." When Rob's turn came, he embraced Wade, holding him close but making certain not to squish the bairnie in his arms, then he pulled the blanket aside and showed Wade his newest grandson.

"Isn't he the spitting image of you!"

Rob embraced him again. "Welcome home, Faither."

"It is home." Wade suddenly took off his glasses and polished them on a corner of Jamie's blanket.

Rob had Wade's boxes taken to the shed until they could be cairted up to his new house later the day, and then they all walked with him up the hill to their home so he could sit with a cup of coffee and rest after the long, exhausting trip from New Hampshire. He met

312

Sarah and complimented her and Maggie both on the clean, neat house.

After a dinner of toasted cheese and chicken bree, the entire family took him to his new home.

He stood back, appearing to admire the dried, stacked stane wall and the heather and asters Maggie had shown Rob how to plant along the path linking their property to his. "I like the way it beckons me in," Wade said. "That broad porch and the big windows give it the look Babs always loved. It's what she called the 'Welcome Home' look."

When Rob opened the door, Wade stared, then covered his mouth with his hand. The house was a duplicate of Rob and Maggie's, but much smaller. They had furnished it with rockers, kitchen and dining room tables and chairs, a soft, comfortable sofa, a bookcase ready to be filled, and a bright hearth rug. The bairns' drawings decorated the refrigerator, and a shiny new toaster and breadbox sat on the kitchen bunker.

"You've got your own coffeepot," Robbie announced proudly, "so you can have coffee all the day like Faither does."

"And you've got a shower." Annie pulled him toward the bathroom.

Not to be outdone, Beth threw open the bedroom door. "There's a grand closet in there for all your clothes."

Will took Wade's hand. "There's a bedroom upstairs too, so you can have visitors."

Heather seemed flummoxed. She looked all around, shaking her head, her curly hair bouncing about her shoulders. Finally, she raised her arms. "Oop," she demanded.

Wade smiled and picked her up.

She studied his face for a moment before planting a kiss on his cheek.

This appeared to be too much for him as tears spilled down his cheeks. Rob took Heather down and led Wade to one of his rockers, where Wade sat and fought for control over his emotions. "Now I know ... what it means ... to have a family. I'm just sorry it came so ... late."

Rob clasped his shoulder, tears in his own eyes. "So am I, Faither, more than you'll ever know."

After supper the een, each of the bairns scooped up an ember from their fireplace and, offering a prayer, placed it in a bucket. Even

Heather participated, helped by Rob. Then the family, Wade in their mids, took the embers to his new home, where Rob placed some embers first in Wade's new stove and then his fireplace. After the family added several pieces of peat, the house was filled with the pungent, sweet scent all of the locals associated with the word "home." The bairns all looked in wonder at the smoke drifting upward toward the chimney, certain that each wisp was carrying one of their prayers heavenward.

"That's a fine tradition." Wade warmed his hands before the fireplace. "And nothing could bless this house more than embers from your home."

Rob pulled him aside before they departed. "We'll go see Mither on the morra. I know you're anxious to visit her."

"I am. I have so much to tell her."

The next morn the two men visited Barbara's grave. Wade broke down when he saw the rose bush planted by the headstone.

"It doesn't look like much now," Rob said, "but 'tis a white rose. Next spring the fragrance will fill the air all around it—her favourite fragrance."

"Oh, Rob, I only hope you know how much she loved you." Wade clasped Rob's hand. "All those years, there wasn't a day that went by that she didn't talk about you. During the war, we prayed morning and night for your safety, knowing you were surely in some branch of the military. The hardest part was poring over the names of those killed that they published in the newspapers."

"Then your prayers helped me survive." Rob embraced Wade, hugging him tightly. "The only thing giving me peace is knowing we found each other afore it was too late."

An hour later, they left the cemetery arm in arm.

Chapter Fifty-Four

Winter comes to the island. Rob spends the indoor time by pulling out his old Air Tactics manual for Beth to read. He also helps Robbie build a little garage for his trucks. They celebrate Christmas, and Rinait and Graham have their second baby, a lass they name Susan Flora, on Christmas day.

⚔

Sarah approached Rob a few days after the start of the New Year. "I was just wondering how long you thought you'd need me. I don't want to stay a moment longer than that."

What? She had seemed so happy with her job. "You want to leave, then?"

Her hand flew to her throat. "No! I mean, I didna mean I wanted to leave, I only meant I … och blethers, Rob, you ken what I mean."

He stared at her. Two bright spots of red coloured her cheeks and she had used several Scots words. He had never seen her so flummoxed. "Let's start all over again. Aren't you happy here?"

"Of course I'm happy. I've never enjoyed a position more."

"Then we're expecting too much of you. You need more time to yourself."

"I do not. You give me every evening and every Sunday off, and any other time I need a few hours."

"We're no' paying you enough, but you wouldna take the last raise I offered you."

"You're already paying me twice what I would get in Oban. There's nothing around here to spend money on, anyway. I've squirreled almost all of it away."

He snapped his fingers. "That's it! We're too isolated here!"

"Rob, I'm very happy here, do you understand? I just thought Maggie might no longer need a full-time housekeeper. You hired me to help when she was pregnant."

"Och, is that what you've been saying?" He began to pace. "We hoped you'd stay on here, Sarah. Maggie could probably muddle through, but I don't want that. She's happy now. You being here gives her time for gardening in the summer, weaving in the winter, and more time to spend with the bairns year-round. Seven bairns is a load, and we haven't finished yet. Our dream is to have eight. We'd like you to stay long-term. I'm sorra I didna make that clear."

"Nothing would make me happier, but there's something you should know."

He stopped pacing. "You're no' sick are you?"

She laughed. "I'm healthy as a horse."

"Then …?"

She studied her hands. "There's this man I know, or I should say, whom I've known for years. We've been corresponding, and he's asked me to marry him."

Rob's mouth opened and closed. "You mean we're keeping you from the man you luve?"

"No. I mean, yes, I love him, but no, you aren't keeping me from him. I needed time to think. I'm sure you know by now I'm not an impetuous person. I like to think things through before I make a commitment."

"And you've had your time."

"Yes, I have. But the time I've spent here has also shown me what it's like to live in a place where everyone is more than just your neighbor or an acquaintance, where you belong to a huge family of 'folk.' Even if you'd said you don't need me anymore, I don't want to leave Innisbraw."

"I don't understand what you're saying."

"I wrote Luke and told him I'd marry him only if he was willing to live here."

"That's a powerful thing to ask of any man."

"I know that, but I also know Luke. He has no ties, no family to root him to one spot. He's lived all the way from Ayr to Inverness. He says he'll be happy to come here if that's what I want."

"But he'll need to make a living."

"He's a carpenter. With all the building going on here, surely he'll find work."

"A carpenter! What does he build?"

"Houses, businesses, though he's really what he calls a 'finish carpenter,' whatever that means."

"It means he can do fine woodwork is what it means, a skill we desperately need here on Innisbraw."

Her face brightened. "Really?"

"Really. Hardly a day goes by that Pete isn't moaning that he doesn't have a man to do kitchen and bathroom cabinets and window and door sills the proper way."

She straightened her shoulders. "Then that settles it. Luke will have his job, and I mine. It means I'll no longer live in, but that shouldn't be a problem unless your eighth child decides to put in an appearance in the middle of the night."

He grinned. "Och, one bairnie I can handle, it was twa that sent me over the edge."

Hugh performs a small wedding ceremony for Sarah and Luke. Rob goes out on a shout in late February, and the call comes in to the radio operator in the shed that there's "one critical, one dead." Maggie, having heard on her radio at home, rushes to the dock.

⚜

John trembled as he waited alone.

Angus's cairt was just pulling into position when Fern and Maggie arrived on the path by the dock, and several of the rescue crew who were not on duty came running up to join them. The rain gusted in their faces as they ran up the pier to the dock, where John was.

He pulled Maggie and Fern into his arms. "Courage, lasses," he said. "We must have courage."

The bell in the kirk steeple began to toll. On and on the rhythm went, summoning the folk of Innisbraw to prayer.

Maggie shivered in John's arms.

A crowd ran along the shore, some wearing only sweaters against the bitterly cold rain. Cairt after cairt pulled up on the path, their drivers hunched on their seats.

One critical. One dead. No matter who it was, they had lost one of their lads and another could be dying.

Graham joined them on the dock, his face betraying his anguish. He pressed his way into the huddle, doing his best to shield Maggie and Fern from the driving rain. They heard three loud wails of the siren as the *Maggie* entered the harbour.

John, Graham, and three other off-duty crewmen jumped aboard the moment the boat pulled up to the dock. John rushed into the cabin, his eyes darting about. His gaze was instantly drawn to two blanket-shrouded bodies lying on stretchers. His heart pounded in his chest. *Please, Lord*, he pleaded, *no' Rob, please! Nor Den!*

Then he saw Den bending over a stretcher, holding a plasma bottle.

John hurried to his side.

Den was praying the same words over and over, "Help him, Lord, help him, Lord, help him, Lord."

Rob lay on the stretcher, his legs and feet propped up. His eyes were closed, breaths shallow, and his face unnaturally pale. There was a livid swelling on his left temple.

John took his pulse. Very slow and thready.

"'Tis his left arm and shoulder," Den said. "Rogue wave caught him, threw him into the *Maggie*."

John lifted the blanket, eyeing the bloody gauze over Rob's upper left arm. He pulled it away.

A splinter of bone protruded from the skin.

"Any water in his lungs?"

"Can't be much. They pulled him in the minute it happened."

Maggie and Fern pushed their way near. Fern went into Den's arms with a cry of relief, while Maggie leaned over Rob.

"How bad?" Maggie whispered.

"Bad," John said, "I just don't know how bad. This stretcher goes first. On you go, lads, right now!"

Two lads from the boat-building crew picked up the stretcher.

"First cairt in line!" John ordered. "Go with him, Maggie. Put him in surgery. I need a quick look at these others."

She pressed the bloody gauze back over the wound, pulled up the blanket, and took the plasma bottle from Den. "Now!" she cried.

They eased the stretcher through the doorway and across the deck, then down the gangplank. When they reached the pier, they lengthened their strides.

Maggie trotted to keep up. She barely saw the bowed heads and concerned faces of the folk lining the path. The moment they had him in the cairt, she removed her coat and shielded Rob's face and head from the driving rain.

Though it only took a minute or twa, the ride up the hill seemed like it would never end.

The purple-red swelling on Rob's temple worried her the most. "Don't go away from me, luve," she said softly, remembering his long coma after his last B-17 crash. "We need you. Don't go away again."

When they reached the infirmary, she directed the men toward the operating room, motioning Wade, who was pacing the foyer, to follow.

They transferred Rob onto the table very carefully.

Maggie pulled the sodden blankets away and replaced them with warm, dry ones. She put a blood pressure cuff on his right arm and inflated it.

Fifty-five over thirty-five.

Low, very low, but it had been that low before and he had survived.

"How bad is it?" Wade asked.

She carefully toweled Rob's face dry. "I don't ken. I'm worried about his head."

Wade reached across the table and took Rob's right hand. "Where's John? Why isn't he here?"

"He had to check the other victims before they could be transported." She wanted to look at Rob's arm but was afraid to allow Wade to see the wound since he was already shaking so badly. Finally, she could not wait any longer. She had to know how much Rob was bleeding. She moved to the supply cabinet, took what she needed, and returned. "Faither, close your eyes."

"Why?"

"Don't ask, just do it. Please, for me."

Wade closed his eyes.

She raised the blanket and gauze. The sight of that protruding bone fragment made her breath catch, but the wound was only oozing blood. She was just preparing to place fresh gauze over it when John came in, followed by Mary.

"Let me see that first," John said. He studied Rob's left arm and shoulder carefully, then nodded. "Wade, you're going to have to step outside. Take a seat in the foyer. Mary, here, will help you."

Wade shuffled out.

"Put his head down," he told the nurse softly. "Make sure he's all right, then take Fern's place with the rescue victims and send her in here. In the meantime," he told Maggie, "I want you to start a saline. That plasma's almost finished. Add penicillin to the IV, then we'll get Rob into X-ray. I want a skull series and a left arm and shoulder series."

Maggie nodded. "The blow to his head worries you too."

"With his history of a skull fracture, we need to know what we're dealing with." He took her hand and squeezed it. "How are you doing, lass?"

"I'm all right. This is so much better than no' knowing if he was one of the ... dead."

He squeezed her hand again. "I'm thinking if the shoulder X-rays show what I'm sure it will, I'll have to fly in a surgical team from the Royal Infirmary. His left shoulder's going to have to be rebuilt, just like I've been warning him it would. I'm verra concerned about his humerus, though. A compound fracture of that bone can be difficult to get to heal properly, especially one so high up."

"What can I do, John?" Fern asked as she came into the operating room.

"Get the X-ray room ready while Maggie finds four strong lads to lift Rob. I don't want to disturb him any more than we have to."

Twenty minutes later, John finished reading the last of the X-rays and called Maggie and Fern over. "You can see there's no fracture." He pointed to the picture of Rob's skull. "Most likely 'tis a bad concussion." He clipped a new set of films into the viewer. "Now look at his shoulder and humerus. Even a layman would call it a real muddle. His humerus snapped on impact, then splintered. And that's just the beginning. His shoulder must have hit the boat with tremendous force to displace and shatter so much bone. I can just imagine what the muscles and soft tissue look like."

"Can you save Rob's arm, Faither?" Maggie asked brokenly.

"If you mean do I think he'll lose it, the answer is definitely no. How useful it will be when this is all over is any man's guess right now."

Shona's and Jamie's roups echoed in the building. Sarah must have needed to bring them to Maggie. "When will you request the team?" she asked.

"I'll call right now. I'd like them here first thing in the morn."

Maggie nursed her twins in the foyer, sitting close to Wade.

"Do you have updates?" he asked.

She told him all she knew, and he took the news better than she expected. She hoped he was so relieved Rob was alive he would be able to bear up under the stress of seeing his son's pain when he awakened.

When he awakened. When would that be?

She didn't want Rob to remain unconscious, yet a small part of her preferred that over what he would endure when he woke up. When the bairnies were both fed, she called Sarah to take them back and added that she would be home as soon as she could to talk to the aulder bairns.

"Caroline and Ellie are still watching the bairns," Sarah said, "and Caroline called to say they'll all be staying the night with the families on the fell, but they need to know about their faither as soon as possible. Can you tell me any more about Rob? I just know he was the one critically injured."

Maggie told her about the concussion and the impending surgery.

Rob was still unconscious when Maggie returned to his side. They had moved him into the same large room at the end of the hall he had occupied for so long twice before. And some thoughtful soul had seen to it that an extra bed was already waiting for her.

She pulled over a chair and sat beside him, holding his hand. She studied the strong, capable hand with its long, tapering fingers, the hand that had cradled six of his seven bairnies at birth, the hand that had worked such magic with wood yet caressed her with such tenderness. She laid her cheek down on the bed and sobbed. "Hold him up, Faither," she prayed. "Help him bear the pain."

"Don't cry, lass."

So many times he had said those same words. She wiped her face on the sheet and raised her head.

He was trying to focus his eyes on her.

She clasped his hand tightly. "I'm all right, luve," she said brokenly.

He closed his eyes, then opened them again. "'Tis hard to see you," he whispered.

"Don't try. You had a bump on the head. It will be hard to focus for a while."

"My crew. How's my crew?"

Maggie panicked. She had forgotten all about it. One crew fatality. She had promised him she would never lie to him, but she really didn't know enough to tell him anything. "I don't ken," she said. "All I've thought about is you."

"The victims?"

"Rob, I really don't ken. I haven't wanted to leave your side."

He closed his eyes again and moaned.

"I ken 'tis bad," she said. "Hold onto my hand."

"Can't move my left arm." His voice was thick with pain.

"You broke it, luve. Don't try to move it."

"Hurts, Maggie."

She brushed her lips against his cheek. "I ken, luve, I ken."

John came in and leaned over Rob. He was carrying a syringe. "I ken you're in pain, lad. I've brought you a little something."

"Need more than a little." Rob groaned.

"I know you do, but you have a concussion. I don't want you to go to sleep just yet." He shot the syringe contents into the IV portal. "This will take the edge off."

"My crew," Rob said. "How's my crew?"

Maggie looked at John.

He shook his head. "There'll be time for that later. Right now, we need to talk about your shoulder."

"Shoulder!" Rob jerked, and rolled his head from side to side, sweat popping out on his forehead.

"Easy, lad. You've made a real muddle of that shoulder, plus you've broken your arm. I have a team from the Royal Infirmary coming in early tomorrow morn. We're going to have to reconstruct your shoulder, Rob, and I have to tell you, 'twill test all of our skills."

"Don't take my arm," Rob muttered. "Please."

"That won't be necessary. We'll no' take your arm, Rob, do you understand?"

Rob nodded.

John straightened up.

"The victims?" Rob asked.

"All doing well," John said.

Rob closed his eyes and his face relaxed.

John clasped Maggie's shoulder. "I'm sending Fern in to sit with him while you go talk to the bairns. After a few more hours, we'll let him sleep as much as he can, but no' now." He kissed her forehead. "Take care of yourself, lass. This is going to be a long, long ordeal."

She watched him walk away, his shoulders slumped. Then she went into the pantry and made Wade some coffee. When she took it out to him, he was still sitting on the couch, his head in his hands. "I'm going home to talk to the bairns. Will you be all right for a while?"

When he looked up, he appeared to have aged ten years. "I'll be fine. I'll pray you say the right thing."

❧

The rains had stopped but the snell wind made her shiver. Sarah was playing with Shona and Jamie on the hearth rug. The twins brightened and clamoured for attention as Maggie scooped them up and sat with them in her rocker.

"How is he?" Sarah asked.

"He's awake," Maggie said, "and he's in agony."

Sarah bit her lip. "I know it's wrong but I can't help but question why God allows bad things to happen to such good people."

"'Tis human to think that, I suppose. They'll operate on the morra's morn, and after that, I may join you in that question. I've seen what such surgery does to Rob—how he suffers."

"You need to eat, Maggie. I've fixed some soup. Let me heat up a bowl, then after you eat, I'll go get the bairns so you can tell them."

Maggie choked down a bowl of bree and drank two cups of tea, heavily laced with honey. When she was finished, she sent Sarah for the bairns.

They filed in very quietly, all of their faces streaked with tears.

Heather buried her head in her mither's lap.

Robbie stood tall in front of her, his entire body trembling. "Is … is Faither … is Faither … in heaven?" he asked at last.

She reached for him, held him tightly. "Och no, lad, Faither's no' in heaven. He hurt his shoulder again."

Tears slid down his cheeks, and all the other bairns began to sob.

Maggie gathered them all close. "Shh," she said. "Faither's going to be all right. Shh, don't roup. He's going to be all right."

Heather wriggled closer. "Oop." She didn't ask for a kiss. Instead, she cuddled close and patted her mither's shoulder with her chubby little hand.

"They're having a prayer service at the kirk the een," Annie said. "I want to go."

"So do I," Beth said.

"And me," Will echoed.

"We all do," Robbie said, "don't we?"

All the children nodded their heads, even Heather.

"Then you shall go," Sarah said, "with Uncle Luke and me."

"Are you sure?" Maggie asked. "'Tis a lot to ask of you."

"Of course I'm sure. Now, come on, bairns, your mother needs to feed Shona and Jamie so she can get back to your faither. You know how good it feels to have someone you love holding your hand when you've hurt yourself. Kiss your mother and then it's back to Caroline's until time for kirk."

They all kissed their mither.

Heather didn't want to go, so Sarah had to pick her up and carry her out the door.

Maggie could hear the lass rouping as they all trooped across the yard.

Maggie nursed Shona first, handed her to Sarah when she returned, then fed Jamie. It felt like she had been up for days, yet it wasn't even supper time. When Jamie was finished, she made a sandwich and filled a thermos with coffee for Wade. She knew he'd sleep on the couch in the infirmary foyer tonight.

The steeple bell was tolling slowly as Maggie stepped out onto the entry. One of Rob's crew was dead—one of his brave lads had made the ultimate sacrifice, and she didn't even ken which one—but 'twas better this way. If she didn't ken, she couldn't answer Rob's questions. And he would keep asking until he got an answer. His loyalty to his crew had always been one of the things that had endeared him to his men—and her.

Wade was still sitting on the couch in the foyer when she got back.

She sat with him while he ate part of his sandwich and drank two cups of coffee. "We both have to be strong through this," she said. "'Tis going to be long and painful, but Rob needs us to help him. We don't know how God's going to use this, but He will."

"I'm so glad Babs isn't here to go through this. Even when she wasn't so sick, she couldn't have borne this."

Maggie took his empty coffee cup. "I'm thinking she would have surprised you with her strength. Mithers have a way of doing that."

He nodded. "I suppose you're right. Go to him, Maggie. If you get a chance, tell him I love him."

"I will. I'm sure you'll be able to see him before he goes into surgery tomorrow. I'll come oot later and tell you how he's doing."

When Maggie tiptoed into Rob's room, she found both Hugh and Den at his side.

Tears streamed down Rob's face as he looked up at Den, his eyes pleading. "No' Christopher," he said in a hoarse whisper. "Och please, God, no' Christopher."

Den was holding Rob's good hand tightly, his own face streaked with tears. "He didna suffer, Rob. He was caught by the same rogue wave that hit you. He was killed instantly."

Rob shook his head back and forth. "He was just a lad, Den, a lad. Why? Why do they all have to die so young?"

"They don't all die, Rob. We're no' at war anymore. Christopher's the only one in all these years."

Hugh leaned over Rob. "You have to be strong. The other lads are looking to you to set an example. Be strong for them."

"I'm ... I'm so tired," Rob whispered.

Hugh rested his hand on Rob's right shoulder. "Give it all to the

Lord—the pain, the fatigue, the sorrow. We can't bear these burdens ourselves, for 'tis too much. Let Him take them, lad. He promises He will if we but ask."

"Can't think, so tired."

"Then I'll do it for you." Hugh and Den bowed their heads. "Heavenly Faither, we ask Ye to take these burdens from our Rob. Where there is pain, give him the strength to bear it. Where there is fatigue, bring him rest. Where there is sorrow, comfort. In Jesus's name we pray, amen."

Den leaned closer and whispered something Maggie couldn't hear, but Rob nodded.

Hugh squeezed Rob's hand. "There's a prayer service the een for everyone."

"Tell the MacLeans and Christopher's Patricia I'm so ... so sorra," Rob whispered.

"I will. Rest, Rob, we all luve you." Hugh wept as Den led him out of the room.

Maggie could not stem her own tears as she took up her vigil at Rob's side. "I'm back, luve."

"Why, Maggie?"

"Why what, luve?"

"Why didna ye tell me?" 'Twas not just a question; it was a roup from his soul.

"I didna ken it was Christopher, Rob." She buried her face in her hands. "I didna ken."

He moved his right arm awkwardly, trying to hug her. "I'm sorra," he whispered. "I'm so sorra."

He fell into a deep sleep and she let him drift away, knowing he had been awake long enough.

The sleep would do more guid than all the painkillers.

She bowed her head and prayed for Christopher's family. She wept when she thought about his young wife, Patricia, and the grief she was suffering at this very moment. Patricia and Christopher had been talking about starting a family, and it broke Maggie's heart that the young lass would never hold Christopher's son or daughter in her arms so a part of him could live on. "Hold her up, Faither," she begged. "Be at her side every minute, whispering Your words of comfort."

Fern relieved Maggie several hours later so she could give Shona and Jamie their final feedings for the day. Once again she nursed them in the foyer so she could be close to Wade.

She handed him Jamie to hold, and Wade cradled the bairnie close, gazing into his face, eyes dimmed with tears. "There's so much pain in this life," Wade said to Maggie, "pain at birth and pain at death and pain in between."

"And joy, Faither, don't forget the joy. We have much to be grateful for. Our Rob's alive, Faither—alive. We're no' grieving like Christopher's parents and his young wife. We're no' standing vigil like the relatives of the dead victim. Don't forget that, Faither. Our Rob's alive."

That seemed to snap him out of his melancholy. "You're right," he said raggedly. "My Robbie's alive."

326

Chapter Fifty-Five

Maggie spent the night in Rob's room, though the bed they'd brought in remained unused. She sat up all night, holding his hand, whispering words of comfort when he moaned, restraining him when he thrashed in pain. She couldn't even imagine how he was suffering since she had never had to endure such agony. She bathed his face with cold flannels and sang to him when he was restless. Toward dawn, he once again fell into a deep sleep, and she dozed next to him, her hand holding his, her head on the bed at his side.

✳

The new day dawned cold and clear. Pete took off in the floatplane to pick up the medical team in Edinburgh.

Sarah tiptoed into the room twa hours later and touched Maggie's shoulder. She awoke with a start. "It's only me," Sarah whispered. "Luke and I stayed at your home with the twins last night. I want to tell you about the prayer service before they get Rob ready for surgery." She poured Maggie some tea from the thermos she had brought.

Maggie sipped it gratefully. "'Twas a guid service, then?"

"It was, and moving beyond measure. Your Annie had everyone in tears."

"Annie?"

"Yes, Annie. That lass has the most beautiful voice I've ever heard, and her only seven."

"She sang?"

"She did, and without any accompaniment. Hugh and several others had just offered prayers—wonderful prayers, I might add, especially from Hugh and Auntie Mairet—when the most remarkable, sweet voice could be heard. It was Annie, standing right next to me. She was singing 'The Lord's Prayer.' There was such a hush in the sanctuary, it was almost unnatural. No one stirred, no one coughed. There was just utter silence while that blessed child sang her heart out."

"Annie sang at kirk?" Rob's pleased voice strengthened as he spoke.

"Yes, she did. That child can sing like an angel."

"I ken," Rob said. "My Wee Annie."

Maggie wiped the tears from her eyes and leaned over to kiss his cheek.

It was hot.

She felt his forehead.

There was no mistaking it—he had a fever.

She got a cold flannel and bathed his face and right arm.

"Feels guid."

"Sarah, go get my faither," Maggie said.

Sarah left immediately.

Maggie got a thermometer from the clothes-press and placed it under Rob's right armpit. John came hurrying in just as she was reading it. She handed the thermometer to him.

He read it and shook his head. "We can't postpone the surgery, lass. I'll have Mary bring in the maximum dose of penicillin we can give him. Keep bathing his face and arm, and his chest too. The team should be here and set up in twa hours at most. Pray his fever doesn't go any higher."

⁂

The surgery took a grueling six hours. John was exhausted when he came into the foyer to talk to Maggie and Wade. "He came through it, but I'll be honest and tell you there was a time about halfway through when we almost lost him to excessive bleeding. We faced the same old problem we always have with Rob. We had no AB positive whole blood on hand, but we were able to get it under control, and he rallied with twa pints of O negative blood. 'Tis a guid thing he was in such fine physical shape going into the surgery."

"His shoulder, Faither, could you repair it?"

He ran his hand across his face. "If all the plates and screws we put in were bone, I'd say he has a whole new shoulder and humerus, but of course, that's wishful thinking. However, the neurologist and the other ortho both agree with me. With a regimen of extensive therapy, he should be able to function fairly normally in a year to fifteen months."

"What about in the meantime?"

"His arm will stay strapped to his side for a while. I couldn't cast his upper arm because of the angle of the shoulder, so we're going to have to rely on a tight wrapping and the restraining sling until the arm mends, then we'll put him into a metal brace that will hold his

328

shoulder at the correct angle."

The restraining sling was bad enough, but the brace would make Rob miserable. "Will he need more surgery?"

"Time will tell. Not unless he builds up too much scar tissue like the last time. But even if he does, 'tis a simple surgery, as you ken."

"What about his fever?"

"'Tis still high, but not climbing. We'll keep him on maximum penicillin until his temperature's back to normal." He massaged the back of his neck. "Why don't you go in now, lass? And after he wakes up, you can see him, Wade."

Maggie went into Rob's room.

Mary was checking his vitals, while Fern, who had acted as head surgical nurse, sat in the corner, sipping tea. Fern rose and embraced Maggie. "He's a fighter, our Rob is. I've never seen a patient fight any harder to survive than he did."

"Thank you." Maggie kissed her friend's cheek. "I only wish Faither had allowed me to assist, but I suppose I can understand why he couldn't."

"It was hard enough for John … and me. He'd not put you through that for owt. I'm so glad the surgical team could help us keep level heads."

"Go back to your tea. In fact, go home. I just fed the twins, so I don't have to leave Rob's side for hours."

"I think I will go home for a while. Den took the bairns to kirk, and knowing him, they're still wearing their Sabbath clothes." They smiled tiredly at one another, then embraced again. "Just sit by his side, Maggie. He'll be unconscious for a while yet."

Rob continues his recovery and soon returns home.

Because Rob could not remember the accident which had almost cost him his life, and was so bereft at Christopher's death, no one ever told him that one of the rescue victims had also died; he found out when the results of a formal inquiry were mailed to him.

An Act of Nature resulting in the deaths of one Christopher J. MacLean, twenty-six, of the Isle of Innisbraw, and one Michael N. MacEwan, thirty-seven, of Oban.

Rob's hand shook as he called Den at the shed. "I need to see you now," he told him. "Come up right away."

⊱⧽⊰

Den couldn't imagine what the problem was, but he recognized the tone. Rob was very upset about something. Den walked quickly up the hill to find Rob pacing the entry, his A-2 jacket thrown over his shoulders.

Rob thrust the inquiry results at him. "Why wasn't I told?"

Den skimmed the report. "Because you were in no shape to hear it."

"A man died and I'm the commander of the *Maggie*. As a rescue victim, he was my responsibility, and I had to read about it in a formal inquiry report? Did he drown?"

There was no holding back now. Rob would have to hear the whole truth, and it would devastate him. "No, he didn't drown."

Rob held his left arm. "Then how did he die?"

"He was caught by that same awful rogue wave."

Rob sat down on the railing, still clutching his arm. "Tell me," he said quietly. "All of it."

"He's the man you were towing in. He hit the *Maggie* head-on."

Rob's face blanched. "The man I was ... Why didn't I shield him?"

"You tried. He was behind you, over your right shoulder. You put oot your free hand, your left, which pivoted your body, otherwise you'd have hit head-on like he did. He was going too fast, and the impact broke his neck."

"I don't remember him." Rob's voice was ragged. "I went oot to save him and he died."

"And you almost died yourself."

"But I didna." His eyes were dark with grief when he looked up. "Why didn't you tell me when they notified you there'd be a formal inquiry?"

"Because you were fighting for your own life. You wouldn't have understood what I was saying." He put his hand on Rob's arm. "'Tis over, Rob. It was a nasty, nasty rescue, one the likes of which none of us ever want to see again. You saved twa men's lives that day. Let it go at that. Even if we tried to do it all over, we couldn't change the force of that wave."

⊱⧽⊰

The fact he was still so weak did not deter Rob from walking down to the kirk after his talk with Den. Maggie, Sarah, and the bairns were at Jill's, talking about a reading program for the pre-school bairns, but he didn't stop by to tell Maggie where he was going. He went directly to the family pew and knelt. He was trembling all over. First Christopher and now … another man dead. He bowed his head and wept.

So many gone, so many dead.

He cried for all the crew members he had lost, for each plane in one of his squadrons which had gone down, taking ten good lads with it. He cried for Rich, for Malcolm, for Elspeth, for the wee bairnie they had lost, for Barbara, for Christopher, and for Michael MacEwan, whose face he couldn't even remember.

Hugh slipped into the pew and put his arm around Rob's shoulders.

"So many gone." Rob moaned. "So many dead. I couldn't save any of them, Hugh."

"No, you couldn't. Nor could I." He handed Rob his handkerchief.

Rob wiped his face. The tears had ended but the trembling hadn't.

"How did you get here?"

"I walked, I think."

"Can you walk to the manse? I've a fresh pot of coffee on the stove."

Rob nodded.

Hugh helped him to his feet. "I'm thinking 'twas a bit too far for you to walk so soon, and 'tis cold oot."

Rob tested his shaking legs. "I'm thinking you're right."

Once they made it over to the manse, they sat at Hugh's kitchen table, and he clasped Rob's hand. "You'd like to save them all, but you can't. You have to remember, lad, God has His own perfect plan. All our days are numbered, Rob, even yours and mine."

Rob sipped his coffee. "I don't ken what happened. I just knew I had to come to the kirk. I'm sorry I interrupted your day, Hugh."

"Enough of that! Does Maggie ken you're here?"

"She wasn't home when I left."

"Then I'm thinking we'd better get you home before she starts worrying."

"I can't make it. I'm spent."

"I'll call Alec."

Rob was so tired he could hardly hold his head up, but for some reason, his heart felt lighter than it had in a long time. *All our days are numbered.* Somehow, he'd forgotten that.

Maggie still wasn't home when they arrived. Rob was too tired to even undress. He collapsed onto the bed and was asleep within moments.

⚜

Rob returns to work. In May, he has a metal plate put into his arm and must wear a metal brace, but his arm pains him so much because of built-up scar tissue, they have to surgically remove the tissue. Within a week, he returns to work. Caroline and Pete adopt another child, Catherine. When she was three years old, she was thrown down the stairs by her mither's boyfriend, which left her with an injured leg. She has a leg brace, and she and Rob bond over their hurts. He encourages her, through sharing his own journey, to have surgery for her leg, and after the operation, she recovers.

Maggie's life became much easier when the twins both began walking the week after their first birthday. Lifting them had been a real chore. Now, Rob knew, she began craving naps and there were some days she had a hard time keeping her eyes open. She was so sleeperie one Sabbath afternoon she went to sleep in her rocker on the entry while Rob was playing with the bairns.

"Am I keeping you awake at night, lass?" he asked when she awakened at his touch with a start.

"Och, no' at all." She got up and hugged him. "Don't you remember? 'Tis perfectly natural to be sleeperie when you're biggen."

His arm tightened around her. "You're biggen?"

"Aye. We'll have our eighth bairn in March."

"Lass, lass, I can't believe it. Are you sure you're all right?" He held her close and kissed both of her cheeks.

"I'm sure. Are you really happy, Rob?"

"So happy I'd like to shout it from the rooftops."

"Don't you dare."

He laughed. "No' to worry, luve. I can't climb that high with this brace on." He kissed her again, his heart swelling with luve. Eight bairns.

In seven short months, the dream that was their family would be complete.

Chapter Fifty-Six

At the beginning of November, Rob began to get concerned. His and Maggie's tenth anniversary was the seventeenth, and he still had no idea what to get her. He finally decided on a gift and called all over Scotland to locate it. This gift, though practical and something she would luve to use, was about as unromantic as it could possibly be. He'd always planned to fly her to Edinburgh for a night at the opera or a play on their tenth anniversary.

The brace took out those possibilities.

He finally decided on the next best thing. He contacted a Shakespearean theatrical company in Edinburgh and hired them to put on a play on Innisbraw. "We'll have to get you here by trawler, but I trust the sum I've offered will help make up for any discomfort your cast has to put up with," he told the booking agent.

Hugh delightedly turned the kirk hall over for a night of Shakespeare. "'Tis about time our young people were exposed to some culture. 'Twill be a grand night."

Pete's crew enlarged the stage in the hall, and extra beds were brought into the manse for the actors. Flyers were printed by the academy students and posted on every business on the island.

The elders, however, were concerned that the play would be presented in Elizabethan English. "How will we ever understand it?" they asked one another in the Gaelic.

Alistaire MacIver, who had seen several of Shakespeare's plays as an aulder lad, assured them that the actions of the actors would be explanation enough, for he had enjoyed them greatly and he spoke little English.

꙰

When the big day arrived, the debarking acting troupe attracted a large crowd of folk, who eyed the actors in their outlandishly modern clothes, so skimpy on such a cold, blustery day. The troupe was made up of young lads and lasses who were in seemingly high spirits despite the miserable trip across the Minch in a smelly fishing boat, and they pranced down the pier, bowing and blowing kisses to everyone.

Rob directed the producer to the manse, while cairts carried their costumes and props. The producer kept staring at Rob and finally tapped him on the shoulder. "You'd make an excellent Henry or even Macbeth. You have the stature and carriage for it."

"But no' the desire," Rob said with a smile.

After the actors were off the pier, Rob brought a heavy dolly from the shed and had his men load Maggie's gift onto Angus's cairt. "Take care. Don't drop it," he warned as he climbed up on the seat with Angus.

"Another of your new-fangled betterments?" Angus asked. "There's hardly a cottage on the island without a refrigerator, including ours, thanks to Sim."

"It is. Stay while we unpack it and you'll see."

When Rob opened the side door and stuck his head in, Maggie and Sarah were preparing pumpkin pies to freeze for the Thanksgiving celebration coming up in a week and a half. "Maggie, go in the living room," he called.

She wiped the flour off her hands. "What have you been up to this time? Surely you haven't been able to build something."

"No' with one arm. Now get on with you, 'tis cold oot here."

"Does that mean me too?" Sarah asked.

"You can stay."

When they uncrated the gift, Angus's brow furled. "What is it?" he asked. "I never saw the likes of such a thing."

"You'll ken in a minute. Come on, lads, twa of you should be able to carry it. It isna verra heavy without the crating."

They carried it into the laundry room.

"Where to now, Commander?" Norman MacDougal asked.

"Right over here, next to the washing machine."

They got the gift into place, and Rob plugged it in. "I'll be right back."

Maggie was standing in front of the fireplace, warming herself.

"Close your eyes, lass. I'll lead you."

"Och, Rob, what have you done?"

"You'll see." He took her shoulder and guided her through the kitchen to the washroom. "All right. Open your eyes."

She stared at the large, white metal box with dials. "What … what is it?"

"'Tis something just on the market, something that will save you

334

a lot of work and frustration.

"And that is …?"

"'Tis a clothes dryer, lass. An electric clothes dryer."

Her eyes widened. "I don't understand."

He opened the dryer door. "You put the wet clothes in here, turn it on, and an hour or so later, take them oot, all dry and ready to fauld."

"You mean I don't have to hang them all over the house when 'tis raining?"

"Nae. We're done with hippens flapping in our faces all winter from the racks on the ceiling."

She clasped her hands together. "Och, Rob, surely it can't work. Somebody's played you for a daftie."

He ran into the living room, lowered a drying rack, and returned with an armload of damp hippens. "It'll work. You'll see." He put the hippens into the dryer, closed the door, and pushed a knob.

The load made a thumping sound.

"'Tis a bit noisy. I'm thinking mebbe it should have more in it." He grabbed the instruction booklet and leafed through it, then fooled with a dial. "It does need more and it says when the clothes are dry, 'twill buzz, signaling you to take them oot."

She still looked skeptical. "But I like to hang things oot in the summer, especially the sheets. It makes them smooth and smell guid."

He had an instant mind-picture of the dance she still did when she finished hanging the clothes on the line. She would whirl from item to item, touching each first with her forefinger and then her pinkie, eyes sparkling, smile wide. He had to restrain himself from grabbing her up and covering her face with kisses. "You can hang whatever you want, luve, for I ken how you enjoy it, but now you don't have to when the rain's pishing doon."

She began to smile, but quickly moved on to a delighted laugh. "Och, Rob, what will you think of next?" She hugged him. "Thank ye, thank ye, luve. I've always hated the damp in the house all winter."

The lads and Angus were all shaking their heads as if wondering who'd ever heard of such a thing.

Sarah smiled broadly. "This will save the hours we spend just trying to find a new place to hang something." She touched the top of the dryer. "It's warm. It's really warm!"

They all gathered around closer, touching the dryer, their eyes wide with wonder.

Maggie hugged Rob again.

He bent down and kissed her. "Happy anniversary, luve," he whispered.

Sure enough, less than an hour later, the hippens were dry and ready to fauld.

"I still can't believe it," Maggie said, tears in her eyes.

⚓

The een, Rob dressed with care. John had given him permission to put his brace on the outside of his clothing, so he wore his dress kilt and jacket, grateful that the vest and coat had good, trim fits, though they were still a little loose around the waist from the weight he had lost.

Maggie helped him tie his tie, pull up his socks and flashes, and fasten his sporan before she buttoned his shirt and vest. "There."

"It's still hard getting used to this Galbraith plaid."

"I ken, but 'tis who you are, luve. You look verra braw."

"Not as guid as you look." He caressed her neck.

"Och, I'm already using the rubber band on my waistband," she lamented.

"You're bonnie, Maggie, and I luve you just exactly the way you are."

She raised her head for his kiss. "We'd better hurry or we'll be late."

⚓

The hall was filling rapidly when they arrived. Chairs had been borrowed from many homes on the island to augment what the kirk had. John carried Shona, and Wade held Jamie, so they wouldn't be trampled in the crush of people as everyone took their seats.

Rob had never seen Maggie so excited at the prospect of an een's entertainment. How had he not realized how starved she was for the culture she had enjoyed while receiving her education in Edinburgh?

Her cheeks were flushed and her violet-blue eyes danced with happiness.

Even the bairns were excited, though they had no idea what a play really was.

Rob told Annie it was all right if she sat on her knees so she could see the stage, and Will, Beth, and Heather soon followed suit.

⚓

When the overhead lights were extinguished, the buzz of voices died instantly. The makeshift curtain was drawn aside, and the audience gasped.

The stage had been transformed into a street lined with houses and crowded with people in bright costumes. And off they went into the first act of William Shakespeare's *Romeo and Juliet*.

The balcony scene might have drawn laughter from a more cosmopolitan audience, as Juliet sat on the top of a ladder, which had been decorated with artificial leaves and garlands of flowers, but it seemed that to the folk of Innisbraw, it was magical. The audience booed Tybalt and smiled at one another when Romeo and Juliet declared their luve.

The intermission before the final act was boisterous as those who had some English attempted to explain the intricacies of the plot to the Gaelic speakers. Rob was grateful he had taught his bairns as much English as he had. They might not understand all the nuances of the Elizabethan language, but they certainly got some of it. Sweets were devoured and lemon skoosh, Irn Bru, hot tea, and coffee consumed before Hugh turned the lights off and on again to signal that the intermission was over, and they all hurried back to their seats.

There was a total hush when Juliet drank the potion which put her to sleep, and sniffles when Romeo kissed her, hoping to join her in death. A few loud groans were heard when Romeo took his own life, but when Juliet awakened and fell on Romeo's dagger, there were audible sobs. The magic was over. The lovers were dead.

Maggie looked up at Rob with tear-filled eyes. "At least they died together," she whispered just before the audience began clapping.

There were numerous curtain calls. The cast may have performed before more prosperous audiences, but never before a more appreciative one.

When Maggie checked on the lasses the night, she found them all in Annie's bed, cuddled together.

"I don't ken why I built them all their own beds," Rob said, "when they sleep together so much of the time. Mebbe I should make them one muckle bed."

"'Tis an idea. If our Shona ever decides to join them, there won't be much room for her." She and Rob changed into their robes and sat in the living room, holding hands. "It was a magical een. I can't thank you enough."

"Can ye believe we've been merrit ten years?"

"I don't ken. Sometimes it seems as though I've always known you, and other times it's as though we just met."

He kissed her hand. "I feel exactly the same way."

"Are you ready for bed?"

"No' before I give you your present, though 'tis not as grand as what you gave me." She got up and went into the bedroom. When she returned, she held out a large box.

"Now, what have we got here?" he asked, grinning.

"Aboot three hours of long distance calls made in the mids of the night is what."

He opened the box. Inside was a brand-new Eisenhower jacket, twa pairs of dark-green uniform pants, and twa pairs of "pinks," plus matching shirts. "Where did you find these?" he asked, pulling them oot. "And in my size?"

She laughed. "Would you believe they have military surplus stores in the United States? I had a hard time fitting you, but I finally found what I wanted in a store in Los Angeles, California."

"I luve the way you say that, lass. Say it again."

"What?"

"Califor-r-rn-ia."

"Och, you're making fun of my burr."

"Never." He put the box on the table and pulled her to her feet. "That was one of the first things I luved aboot you," he whispered as he buried his face in her fragrant hair.

They celebrate Thanksgiving and talk about the tourists and a possible increase in ferry activity to the island during the next tourist season.

Rob was grateful when John finally told him he only had to wear the restraining sling during the day. At last he could shower again, and hug his Maggie as they spooned in bed. His therapy was going well but, to his mind, too slowly. Though he could raise his arm out to the side to shoulder level and back several inches, he longed for the time when he had full movement. He did start running regularly again, choosing flatter ground where he didn't have to fight for his balance.

As his activity level increased, so did his appetite. Maggie was finally satisfied when she started moving the buttons on his pants out again. Her own belly was huge, making sleep difficult. For the first time in any of her pregnancies, her ankles and feet swelled a lot, and Rob insisted she see her faither.

"'Tis normal to have a little swelling," John said. "Drink more water, lass. That should help." After he examined Maggie, John drew Rob out into the infirmary foyer while Maggie dressed.

"Is it serious, then?" Rob held his breath.

"No, I meant what I said. I just wanted to ken if you finally realize you'll most likely be the one to deliver the last of your bairns."

Rob shook his head and sighed. "I'm getting there. I just don't want to put her in danger should anything go wrong."

"You ken she'll not agree to staying here the twa weeks before her due date. Less than twa would be useless. Look at what happened last time."

"She won't do it. I've already pleaded with her, but she only sets her lips in a straight line and shakes her head."

John smiled. "Then go with it, lad. Just take it easy on that shoulder. I'm right next door if there's any difficulty."

"If I do decide to go with it, I'm going to have a telephone extension put in our bedroom. I can't leave her side to run into the office for the phone."

"'Tis a guid idea."

Though Rob did not *want* to deliver this bairnie, he did have another phone installed in their bedroom. He also made the usual preparations, stocking their closet with the rubber sheet, towels, string, and scissors.

The second and third week of March passed without incident. The swelling in Maggie's ankles and feet got a little better when she forced herself to drink more water, but Rob was still concerned. She was every bit as large as she had been with both Robbie and Will. Rob prayed this bairnie would not be a breech birth, and he watched Maggie's every movement.

She finally rebelled. "I'm no' sick!" she exclaimed. "Rob, we've been through this so many times afore. Stop treating me like I'm an invalid."

"I wouldn't have to if you'd just go to the infirmary where you belong."

"If you'd had your way, I'd have already wasted a perfectly guid week flat on my back instead of doing what I want to do at home."

That deflated his argument. She was right. "So you'll no' change your mind, then?"

"I'll no' change my mind."

He kissed the tip of her nose. "Then I guess I'm going to deliver our last bairnie."

That brought a smile. "'Tis only fitting."

By the end of the fourth week in March, Rob was a nervous wreck. He jumped every time the phone in the shed rang and ran home every een lest he miss her call and arrive too late. "We're not going to kirk on the morra," he told her Saturday een as they were preparing for bed. "It would be foolish."

For once she agreed with him. "We'll stay home. The others on the fell can take the bairns."

He stood behind her and put his arms around her.

She leaned back and sighed when he buried his face in her hair. "I luve you, Rob."

His arms tightened. "And I luve you, my Maggie, more than I can ever express."

Her water broke before they had even gone to sleep. "'Tis time, Rob."

He pulled on his denims. "'Tis a guid thing we put the rubber sheet on. No soaked mattress this time." He leaned over her. "Have the contractions started?"

"No' yet."

"Then there's time to call your faither."

"Please don't, luve. This is our last time. I want … Och, they're starting!"

He retrieved the towels and placed them beneath her, eyeing the phone on the bedside table. His eyes narrowed. He could do this.

She began to strain in earnest.

He took a corner of the sheet and wiped her forehead with it. "Talk to me, lass," he implored. "Tell me you're all right."

She panted and grabbed for his hand. "I'm … fine." She groaned. Twenty minutes later, she clutched at the bedding.

He pushed up the covers to find the bairnie's head was crowning. "One more push, lass," he said.

She arched her back and cried out.

He released the breath he had been holding as the bairnie's head was born. He slipped out each small shoulder, and suddenly he was holding their eighth child in his hands. His chest heaved with sobs as he lifted the bairnie up. "'Tis a lad, Maggie." Tears slipping down his cheeks. "A braw, braw lad."

The bairnie began to roup loudly.

Rob suddenly laughed. "Things are still muddled. It looks like he's got brown hair." Rob wrapped the bairnie in a towel and placed him on Maggie's belly. Then he tied and cut the umbilical cord and got a basin of warm water. He couldn't seem to stop his tears. This was their last bairnie, according to their plan. Over and over he thanked the Lord for a normal birth.

He bathed the lad, then dressed him and handed him to Maggie.

She cradled him close, studying his perfect, tiny face and light-brown hair. "Welcome to our family," she whispered. "Rob, don't call anyone until the morra."

Rob got Maggie cleaned up, changed the sheets, and fixed her a cup of tea with milk and three teaspoons of honey. He resented every moment he had to leave her side. He finally lay down on the bed so their lad was between them. "We're so blessed," he said, choking up again. "He's perfect."

"I'm thinking he's going to be verra tall. He has such long legs and arms, and look at his hands."

He reached over and kissed her. "Thank ye, luve."

She beamed. "We have our Drew. Now our family is complete."

He brushed his lips over his lad's forehead. "Aye, complete."

Maggie caressed Rob's face. "I can't thank you enough for giving me my dream."

"It was my dream too." He kissed her hand. "I never imagined eleven years ago how richly God was going to bless me. My life with you has been filled with such luve and happiness there are times I can scarcely believe it."

"You've paid a high price, Rob." She fingered the scars on his left shoulder and upper arm.

"Och, it was nothing when you think of all we have, lass. A comfortable home, a thriving business, a family that includes all the folk on Innisbraw, but most of all, eight perfect, healthy bairns. Plus each other forever and ever and ever."

"Aye, forever and ever and ever." She blinked away her tears.

He reached over and took her face between his palms. "Do you ken how fine you are to me, Maggie?"

She nodded as she placed her hands over his. "Aye, as fine as you are to me." They stared into one another's eyes for a long time, then Maggie smiled. "'Twill be exciting to watch our bairns grow into adults and see what kind of careers they choose, what kind of people they become."

He chuckled. "As for careers, we can plan on having at least twa pilots in the family. I'm thinking Robbie and Beth aren't aboot to lose interest. And Annie? With her voice, she could become a singer." He thought for a moment. "I don't ken about Will. If his interest in boats continues, he could take over the boatworks from me some day.

341

Heather, Shona, Jamie, and wee Andrew here are too young to even imagine what they'll become, but with the Lord guiding their steps, they'll be guid people, luve, I ken it in my heart." He smoothed a tendril of hair back from her forehead. "Just like I ken we'll grow auld together in this home, surrounded by our bairns and grandbairns." He leaned over and kissed her, savouring her sweet taste and the scent of heather in her hair. This was his lass. This was his Maggie, who brought such joy into his life and he couldn't be any more grateful.

He climbed out of bed, scooped the sleeping bairnie up, and laid him in the cradle. Rob pulled a warm blanket over him, tucking it in firmly. Then he stepped out of his denims and got back in on the other side of the bed, spooning his body closely against hers. "Coorie doon with me, Maggie, lass," he whispered. "And tell me the tale of the Selkie."

"Aye, my Rob," she replied, pressing her back against his belly.

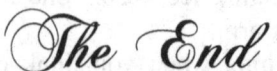

The kirk bell rang out four times the next morn, heralding the birth of Andrew McGrath Savage, and all the folk on Innisbraw rejoiced at the news. Another new lad and, at last, eight Savage bairns. Maggie's dream come true.

The End

Acknowledgments

From the Publisher

In past books in the Thistle series, we used Dianne's own acknowledgments, which she had penned before her death. However, she was not able to work far enough ahead to have that material ready for this final book.

Accordingly, we have to assume that she would be thanking the same people:

Paddy MacKinnon, for her hospitality.

All Dianne's children, for their love and support.

The Ashberry Lane Editors—Christina Tarabochia, Sherrie Ashcraft, Kristen Johnson, Tami Engle, Andrea Cox, Rachel Lulich, and Amy Smith—who are blessed to continue their work in bringing Dianne's legacy to print.

And to her readers. We know she loves you all!

Bio

Dianne fell in love with writing at the age of five. Because her father was a barnstorming pilot, she was bitten early by the "flying bug" as well. She attended the University of California, Santa Barbara, and met and married the man God had prepared for her—an aeronautical engineer. After their five children were in school, she burned the midnight oil and wrote three novels, all published by Zebra Press. When her husband died, only three years after he retired, she felt drawn to visit the Outer Hebrides Isles of Scotland, where her husband's clan (MacDonalds) and her own clan (Galbraiths) originated. Many yearly trips, gallons of tea, too little sleep, and a burst of insight birthed her Thistle series.

PUBLISHER'S NOTE: Dianne, born August 1933, lived joyfully despite dealing with terminal cancer and died in August 2013, a mere week before the release date for the first book of this series, *Broken Wings*. Everyone involved with the production of the five books in the series has been blessed beyond measure to be part of giving readers a chance to meet Rob and Maggie and visit the beautiful, fictional isle of Innisbraw.

Leave a message for her family and sign up to hear the latest at
www.ashberrylane.com/dianneprice or
www.facebook.com/authordianneprice.

Glossary

All words are Scots, unless otherwise noted.

APC: headache medicine.
auld: old.

baffies: bedroom slippers.
bairn: child.
bairnie: baby.
bannock: oat griddle bread, similar to English muffins.
ben: mountain.
biddy certain: very sure.
biggen: pregnant.
blether: talk, visit. (In the plural, nonsense.)
blootered: very drunk.
bodhrán: Gaelic (pronounced *bo-rahn*), one-sided drum.
bonnie: beautiful.
braw: handsome, a pleasing sight.
bree: soup or broth.
breeks: pants or trousers.
brose: creamy oat porridge, soaked overnight.
bunker: counter, like in a kitchen.
bunnet: a flat cap.
burn: small stream.

cairt: cart pulled by a horse.
cannie: shrewd, expert, skillful, or lucky.
ceilidh: Gaelic (pronounced *kay-lee*), party with music, dancing, sharing of news.
chaumer: parlour or gathering room.
clootie: steamed, sweet dumpling pudding dessert served with clotted cream.
clothes-press: dresser for clothing or bedding.
coo: cow.
croft: piece of land.
crofter: farmer, or one who owns a croft used for agriculture.
cuddy: small, shaggy horse, usually used to pull a cart

daft: insane.
disremember: forget.
dreich: dreary, dull, grey, usually describing weather.
dumfoondert: confused.

eejit: idiot, fool.
een: evening, can be written e'en.
entry: porch, passage into house.

faither: father.
fauld yer fit: rest, sit down.
fankle: disorder, entanglement.
fash: worry, vex.
fell: mountain or hill.
flag: piece of stone used as the floor of a cottage.

girse: grass.
gleg as a gled: starving, keen as an eagle.
gloaming: twilight.
grandbairn: grandchild.
grandfaither: grandfather.
grandmither: grandmother.
guid: (pronounced *gid*) good.

halflin: adolescent, teenager.
handsel: gift, usually handmade for a special occasion, like marriage.
hap: knitted blanket, afghan.
haud yer wheesht: hold your tongue.
hippen: diaper.
howff: pub.
hoy: greeting.

infirmary: UK, hospital.
Irn Bru: soda with a taste of tangerine, very sweet, national soft drink.

jawbox: kitchen sink.
joint: UK, roast.

keek: look at, peek.
ken: know, understand.
kirk: church.
kittled up: excited, enlivened.

lemon skoosh: sparkling lemonade.
louring: dark, black, heavy clouds or sky.

machair: Gaelic (pronounced *ma-K-er*), alluvial plain, unique to
    Outer Hebrides.

mebbe: maybe.
medicaments: UK, medicine.
merrit: married.
midden: dirty, messy, untidy place.
Minch: arm of the Atlantic Ocean between Outer Hebrides and Scotland.
mither: mother.

natter: chat, talk, often nag.
neeps: turnips.
no': not.
nowt: nothing.

owt: anything.

polis: police.
press: cabinet.

redd: clean, organize, tidy (up).
rouping: Scots, crying, usually a baby or small child.

skellum: little imp or misbehaving child.
skite one's lug: box on the ears.
sleeperie: sleepy.
slubber: slobber.
sma': small.
smoorich: cuddle.
snell: cold, if wind, usually from the north.
strathspey: regal, gliding dance.
swither: bemused, perplexed.

tatties: potatoes.
the day: today.
The Lift: Outer Hebrides, bearers carry casket from kirk to grave after service.
the morra: tomorrow.
tick: a second in time.
turns: jobs, chores.
twa: two.

verra: very.

wedder lambs: lambs born prematurely.

BROKEN

THE *Thistle* SERIES

BOOK ONE

Wings

DIANNE PRICE

He lives to fly—until a piece of flak changes his life forever.

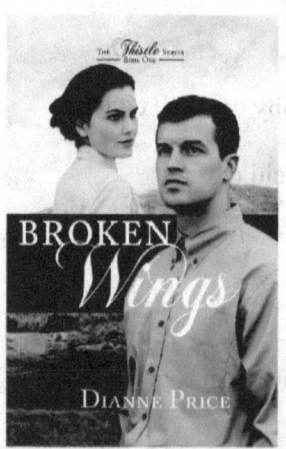

A tragic childhood has turned American Air Forces Colonel Rob Savage into an outwardly indifferent loner who is afraid to give his heart to anyone. RAF nurse Maggie McGrath has always dreamed of falling in love and settling down in a thatched cottage to raise a croftful of bairns, but the war has taken her far from Innisbraw, her tiny Scots island home.

Hitler's bloody quest to conquer Europe seems far away when Rob and Maggie are sent to an infirmary on Innisbraw to begin his rehabilitation from disabling injuries. Yet they find themselves caught in a battle between Rob's past, God's plan, and the evil some islanders harbor in their souls.

Which will triumph?

ASHBERRY LANE

ASHBERRYLANE.COM

Wing AND A Prayer

Dianne Price

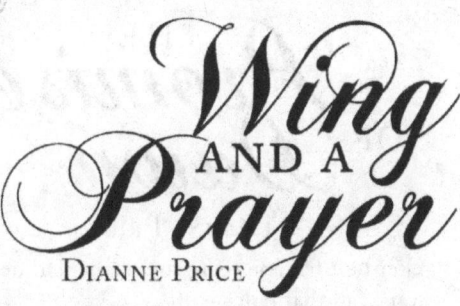

Confronting death isn't the
most difficult challenge he will face.

When Colonel Rob Savage
recovers enough from a near-
death accident to resume
command of the demoralized
Heavy Bomber Group at
Edenoaks Air Base in England,
he faces many challenges. As
Rob labors to make his group
best in Wing again, his bride,
Maggie, works long, exhausting
hours as an RAF nurse, all the
while fearing for Rob's safety
during bombing missions.

The unthinkable happens. Rob and Maggie return to their
Scots island of Innisbraw, battling to keep alive their dreams
for the future. Rationing, blackouts, and the threat of
German U-boat invasions conspire against the newlyweds.

Can Rob and Maggie cleave to their faith in God through
such hardships and trials as the devastating war goes on
and on and on?

ASHBERRY
LANE
ASHBERRYLANE.COM

THE Promise OF Dawn

DIANNE PRICE

Constant fear, piercing sirens, the darkness of war ... all that fades with

World War II is over, but there's much rebuilding to be done on the wee Scottish isle of Innisbraw. Now a wife and mother, Maggie Savage longs for other lasses to return to their island home, but how can they when there is no way to provide for themselves and their families? Her husband, Rob, driven by his unrelenting dream to build a rescue boat for the local fishermen, continues to be plagued by nightmares of impending disaster.

Will their simple faith in God and love for each other help them find a new dawn for their beloved community?

ASHBERRY LANE

Never Say Goodbye

Dianne Price

True friendship lasts a lifetime, no matter the distance between …

Rob and Maggie Savage, busy with their growing family and never-ending sea rescues, welcome the return of Rob's former Air Forces mate, Den Anderson. However, the person Den missed the most on storm-tossed Innisbraw—the very reason for his move to the Scots isle from America—is sweet Fern. She's determined to close her heart to any man who doesn't share her beliefs, while Den has no use for a distant, overbearing God.

ASHBERRY LANE

ASHBERRYLANE.COM

Daughter
OF THE
Cimarron

SAMUEL HALL

Divorcing a cheating husband means disgracing her family, but Claire Devoe can't take it anymore. Forced to provide for herself, she travels the Midwest with a sales crew. Can she trust the God who didn't save her first marriage to lead her through the maze of new love and overwhelming expectations? The long twilight of the Great Depression—with its debt, disgrace, drought, and despair—becomes the crucible that remakes her life.

ASHBERRY
LANE
ASHBERRYLANE.COM

The Memoir *of* JOHNNY DEVINE

CAMILLE EIDE

In 1953, desperation forces young war widow Eliza Saunderson to take a job writing the memoir of ex-Hollywood heartthrob Johnny Devine. Rumor has it Johnny can seduce anything in a skirt quicker than he can hail a cab. But now the notorious womanizer claims he's been born again. Eliza soon finds herself falling for the humble, grace-filled man John has become—a man who shows no sign of returning her feelings. No sign, that is, until she discovers something John never meant for her to see.

When Eliza's articles on minority oppression land her on McCarthy's Communist hit list, John and Eliza become entangled in an investigation that threatens both his book and her future. To clear her name, Eliza must solve a family mystery. Plus, she needs to convince John that real love—not the Hollywood illusion—can forgive a sordid past. Just when the hope of love becomes reality, a troubling discovery confirms Eliza's worst fears. Like the happy façade many Americans cling to, had it all been empty lies? Is there a love she can truly believe in?

ASHBERRYLANE.COM

ASHBERRY LANE

The
Journey
of Eleven
Moons

Bonnie Leon

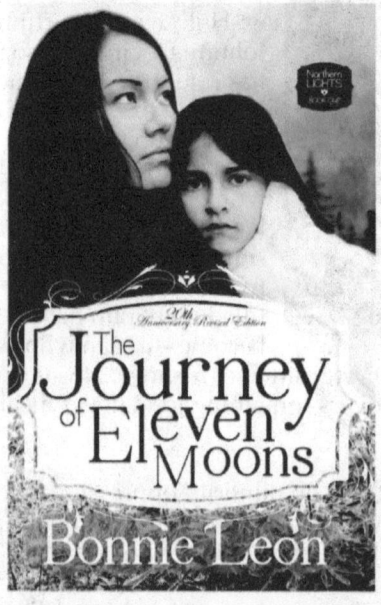

A successful walrus hunt means Anna and her beloved Kinauquak will soon be joined in marriage. But before they can seal their promise to one another, a tsunami wipes their village from the rugged shore … everyone except Anna and her little sister, Iya, who are left alone to face the Alaskan wilderness.

A stranger, a Civil War veteran with golden hair and blue eyes, wanders the untamed Aleutian Islands. He offers help, but can Anna trust him or his God? And if she doesn't, how will she and Iya survive?

ASHBERRY
LANE
ASHBERRYLANE.COM